Whispering Whale

a novel by
Edward J. Zivica

Dear reader:

The only way to purchase this book is through the Internet. If you enjoy the book, please direct another reader to the following web site.

www.ravensintheskypub.com

Thank you.

Published by:
Ravens in the Sky Publishing
Post Office Box 71113
Eugene, Oregon 97401

ISBN 0-9744328-0-6

Library of Congress Control Number: 2003095759

Acknowledgments

First acknowledgment goes to the whale species. Always marvelous, always an inspiration and some how close, all my life.

Second acknowledgment goes to Dr. Jeff Connie. A teacher of graduate fiction writing and screen writing at Northeastern State University in OK.

After completing *Whispering Whale*, I was referred to Jeff for his editorial direction. Jeff took me by the hand and showed me what a novel is. His first comment being, "Ed, to start with. Get some damn dialogue into this story."

After years of work, following his pointing finger and drill sergeant instructions, I have reached a point of satisfaction. Jeff has not only been my educator, he is my good friend.

The next acknowledgment goes to Ms.Nancy Gillim, a friend of many years and the financial provider for the publication of *Whispering Whale*, she has my deep gratitude for her unfailing belief in the project and allowing the use of her hard earned money.

And lastly, I thank myself.

Credits:

Ken Mann, K M Graphics. Cover art, Eugene, Oregon

Christine Beneda, Beneda Design. Book design, Eugene, Oregon

Aria Seligmann, final edit, Eugene, Oregon

Edward J. Zivica

Born and raised in New York city, Edward left the metropolis to join the U.S. Navy in 1960. After seven years of service in the submarine force, functioning as a nuclear reactor operator, Edward left the service a married man and the father of one child.

He was discharged in Charleston S. C. and moved to Los Alamos New Mexico and took a job as a reactor technician. It was here, in the land of enchainment, that Edward found his interest in sculpture.

I was many years later that Edward, when living in Oregon, envisioned the story Whispering Whale. It took twenty years of on and off effort before its complection was achieved.

Voyage
to New Atlantis

The all that "Is." A tiny word encompassing everything. When partitioned, the "Is" yields the spiritual and the physical. This story is concerned with both and I start with the physical.

On the outer edge of a rotating pool of stars, a sphere of nuclear fire spun. And around that heat spun other spheres. One cool, and blue, the blue a reflection of seas that dominated its surface. Daily, half the planet bathed in its own shadow, although, periodically, a moon intruded and paled the darkness with reflected light.

In a shadow-cast sea, deep and beyond the penetration of the moon's rays, swam a leviathan. In body and brain it is the largest creature on the blue planet. Oddly, its ancestors once walked the dry earth, though the species found that situation unsuitable. This aged male, earth's last whale, suffered the ill health of time.

The whale rose toward the surface through a blackened sea. Tiny phosphorescent creatures flashed with the intrusion, illuminating the whale as if a comet in a starless sky. Above, in limpid air, a bright moon gleamed, and the sea's surface loomed as black marble. Nothing indicated the approaching comet.

The whale shattered the tranquility with surging water and expelling breath. Shimmering black waves moved toward sea and shore, while the whale maneuvered to observe a nearby land of low hills that in the light of the day were green with jungle growth.

Near the shore, the sailing craft *Cristine,* illuminated white by the moon, tugged smoothly at her anchor line. The whale had accompanied the *Cristine,* unknown to its inhabitants, since the start of its voyage, a long voyage that originated far to the north in a colder sea.

Motionless, the whale pondered the human's thoughts. His intrusion, nearly imperceptible, swirled in soft colors, charming the leviathan. Satisfied with the situation, the whale submerged.

A small wave nudged the craft, and its anchor line groaned. The vessel, fifty feet in length, had a broad beam. Although this girth slowed her speed, it compensated with stability. Within her heavy fiberglass skin, large cabins fore and aft and a cockpit amidship comprised her basic accommodations. Once a pleasure craft, once a pretty lady, time and circumstance had dulled her brilliance. A shortened main mast made her squatty. Patchwork sails, when hoisted, gave her a tattered appearance. Large aluminum chests, lashed to her forward deck, comprised the primary burden under which she labored. Below, more aluminum containers consumed the forward cabin space. Aft of that cabin, a small galley contained a table, two sitting benches and a few storage cabinets, all constructed of rough-cut wood. A small, homemade wood-burning stove sat to port, and a supply of firewood to starboard. Two steps from the stove, a small ladder led topside to the cockpit. Here a bench, again of rough-cut wood, spanned the width of the command space. A stainless steel helm glittered in the moonlight.

At the stern a large cabin served as a stateroom, its interior was broad and had a high overhead. A large, crudely constructed berth, centered beneath an open hatch, allowed moonlight to illuminate the reclining forms of two humans. One, a man, his name Justin, strong of body and nearly fifty years of age, slept on his stomach. In deep sleep his breathing was barely perceptible. Next to him lay a woman, Nicole. Awake, her mind murmured with the soothing energy of recent lovemaking, while the moon appeared blue through her half-closed eyes.

Nicole mused on the moments before sundown when she and her lover swam in the warm sea as the sun hovered, huge and red on the blue-gray horizon.

Nicole and Justin stood naked at the stern of the *Cristine* and scanned the calm sea. With spontaneous synchronicity, they dove into the sumptuous waters and were enveloped with tender pressure and absolute smoothness. Nicole swept her arms backward and arched toward the surface leaving a trail of tiny bubbles escaping from her long, black hair. She saw Justin dive beneath her, roll to his side and then to his back. She watched him watching her.

When Nicole surfaced, she ignored Justin, finding interest below. She swam toward land in a series of dives with the relaxed motions of someone having fun. Justin followed, floating on his back when she dove, and spinning onto his chest when she surfaced.

Soon Nicole and Justin were close enough to shore to touch the sandy bottom with their feet. Their swim became a walk while the steep slope of the beach produced ebbing waves that tugged vigorously at their legs. Both grinned with inner contentment.

Nicole took Justin's hand as they turned to walk the path of wet sand at the sea's edge toward the half circle of the setting sun.

"I love this part of the day." She turned to face Justin, and walked a few steps backwards looking past him into the eastern sky. "The count log indicates the moon will be at its fullest." She wheeled back to his side.

Justin pulled her close. "When we get back to New Atlantis, what say we organize a moon festival." He squeezed her hand. "Moon-time parties. There's a need for more celebration times."

Nicole smiled. "I like that." She paused in thought. "We could do it on every blue moon." She yanked the back of his hand to her lips and sucked a kiss.

Justin glanced at the *Cristine* before turning to Nicole. "Dancing to the blue moon."

Nicole's eyes squinted. "We'll give it a female name, of course." She looked down as a tiny wave washed across her feet. "The moon's female and so is the night." She turned to Justin. "Diana's Moon."

Justin tugged her hand. "You're not going to exclude men, are you?"

Nicole's eyes twinkled. "Of course not. We'll need a sacrificial something."

Justin chuckled. "Eons from now, a new civilization will celebrate the blue moon ceremony." He raised their clasped hands and pointed his thumb in her direction. "And all because of you."

Justin abruptly stopped. "Damn. We'll carve the story on a stone and bury it at the cavern."

Nicole continued. "And thousands of years from now, they'll dig it up." She mockingly lowered her voice into a deep tone. "We have found conclusive evidence to the origin of The Blue Moon Celebrations in a place once known as New Atlantis."

Justin smiled. "The ancient moon ceremony." He bowed toward Nicole. "Brought to you by Nicole, high priestess and Justin, the sacrificial something."

Nicole elbowed Justin in the ribs. "It'll be quite the honor to be the first sacrificial something." She paused. "And you'll be listed at the top of the credits, of course." She smiled. "To make it more civilized, we'll just mess you up a little."

Justin squeezed her hand. "A bunch of naked women knocking me about."

She squeezed his hand. "The old, rejected women will be doing the knocking about."

Justin looked up into the sky. "Perhaps we should rethink this whole thing?"

When the sun dipped below the horizon, the couple returned to the blue-black sea and swam to their floating home. They hauled themselves aboard near the stern where buckets of fresh water waited. They scooped handfuls and basted their skin free of the sea salt.

Nicole brushed drops of liquid from Justin's back, pushed his hair aside and wrapped her arms around him as she planted a kiss on his shoulder. "Time for bed." She kissed him again. "But not for sleep."

Justin turned to face her, his dark blue eyes flashed and he spoke with mock romance. "The night has fallen; the moon is on the rise." He kissed Nicole's smiling lips and spoke through the kiss.

"And I give myself willingly as the sacrificial something."

These were special moments. In the past their love, of necessity, was more spiritual than physical. With death perpetually present, few opportunities arose, and the simple act of holding on to one another had to suffice.

Now, Nicole and Justin no longer moved in fear. The earth spun with regained stability. Life and death were once again in balance.

Nicole blinked, clearing the blue tinge of moon rays. She rolled to her side, kissed Justin's back and joined him in a comfortable slumber.

Hours later the cabin aft was illuminated with the dim light of a rising sun. Justin awoke and looked through the hatch at the early morning sky. Mornings were his favorite time of the day; mornings were new beginnings and Justin loved new beginnings. He rose to a sitting position, swung his legs off the bunk, and his toes touched the cabin deck. Sinewy muscles rippled in reflection of a strenuous life style. He rubbed his clean-shaven face with a calloused hand. The last time he had a beard was during the wilderness days, before they found their way to New Atlantis. But that was years ago. He fetched his trousers that hung from a peg near the ladder and slipped them on. Next, he sat on the ladder, grabbed his shoes and fitted them onto his feet. They were homemade shoes, moccasin-like, the only kind now existing. As Justin tied the laces, he gazed at Nicole's sleeping form. He knew every part of her body. In early life she pursued the sport of swimming and the art of dance. These activities produced a body that women admired and men noticed.

Nicole lay on her stomach, her lengthy hair, the color of onyx, feathered across her back. The hair covered long scars that ran from her shoulders to her buttocks. There were also puncture and tear marks on the left side of her face and at the back of her neck, all reminders of a moment of horror, a moment Justin had witnessed. With a blink of his eyes, Justin vanquished the hideous thoughts. He rose to his feet.

Six foot two, his lean face made him appear even taller. He glanced at his lover and thought of waking her; instead he turned and moved topside.

On deck he looked to the east. The sun, half above the horizon, flamed in quivering red, and the sea before it shimmered in deep blue-pink. The sky faded from yellow near the sun to blue directly above. Justin turned to the western horizon where the last of the night was studded with a few lingering stars. He scanned the sea surface. Near shore a whale spouted.

He searched the shoreline for the location of a small stream. The *Cristine's* fresh water tanks needed replenishing. A task he could do alone. He strode to the stern where a small dinghy laden with water cans bobbed at the end of a tether line. Justin pulled the tiny craft alongside, climbed aboard, and pushed it free of the larger vessel.

Sitting in the middle seat, his back to the bow, Justin locked the oars in place and made a few strokes toward land. Eyeing the larger vessel as he rowed, he whispered the craft's name. "*Cristine.* Who gave you that name? And why?" He would never know the answers to these questions.

Justin had some difficulty when it came to rowing. The ring finger and the little finger of his left hand were missing. A wild dog had bitten them off. However, having a thumb, he maintained his gripping power.

Pulling twice on the left oar and once on the right, Justin swiveled the little craft toward land. He watched the *Cristine* as he rowed. It was now more then a year since he had first seen her, long after the time of fire and ice. Then, he, Nicole, and nine others from New Atlantis were on an expedition to the Northwest Coast to retrieve Justin's buried supplies. The long trek required six months to complete. Their destination was the mouth of a river, a river once known as the Umpqua. Prior to the bad years, Justin's home sat near the river's mouth. The location was central to the buried chests, now secured aboard the *Cristine*. The twenty-four chests contained food, tools, clothing, medical equipment, seeds and books, and other things. Because Justin was once a man of cozy wealth, the hidden items were of high quality, well protected, and intended to aid his family in their struggle to survive in a time when death moved faster than life. Justin recalled the re-encounter with the coastal forest.

Then, only a few mature trees stood tall, but mostly the land was thick with the bright green of a new forest. The soil, soft with mulch, had a musky smell. Ferns seemed to grow everywhere, and clusters of mushrooms dotted the cool, damp terrain. But the river was the true delight. It would lead to yet another love, the ocean.

Justin, scouting ahead of the main party, moved with anxious energy. It was early summer, the weather hot, and the river level low. Small stones covered the bank. Justin felt their shape and the sun's embedded heat through his thin-soled moccasins as he watched seals hunt and play in the slow-moving waters. The seals barked at his intrusion and swam away. But Justin smiled. The animals indicated the nearness of the river's mouth.

He turned to ascend a small jetty of large stones. With his eyes cast down to find footing, he made his way to the top of the structure. When he looked up, he nearly lost his balance. No more than thirty yards from the tip of his nose, the huge whale-like hull of a boat rested. Justin found his balance with arms extended. The craft lay on a gravel bar on the down-stream side of the jetty. With its starboard side up, the bow pointed into the river. Overcoming his astonishment, Justin descended to the beach and ambled over to the derelict. For a few moments he stood before her, quietly thinking.

Eventually he touched the hull. Taking long strides, he slid his hand over the vessel's skin. The rubbing act tingled his palm and bristled the hairs on his arm. It was the beginning of a seduction, and the man was reluctant to release his touch.

The hull, constructed of heavy fiberglass, had no obvious soft spots; at least in the places Justin could reach. He smiled at the intact rudder and massaged his chin as he studied the broken main mast, its upper quarter missing. Justin's eyes surveyed the top deck, his mind conceiving a plan, a plan in which sails were essential. A small hatch at the bow gave Justin hope. Two large, brass thumbscrews, secured the hatch.

Standing on the boat's railing and using a heavy stone, Justin hammered the corroded screws loose. When he tugged on the hatch, its hinges resisted. But Justin persisted and with a groan the hatch opened. He placed a hand on either side of the opening and poked his head into the compartment. Slowly his eyes dilated and, like magic, sail bags materialized. "Beautiful," he whispered.

With a loud whoop he jumped from the bow railing and ran to the stern. "What's your name? Where're you from?"

Nothing indicated her origin, but when he stepped farther away the tattered remains of her name took shape. Justin spoke it loudly. "*Cristine.*" A smoldering excitement took flame. He clasped his hands in front of his chest. "Destiny. An arrow pointing into the future."

When the remainder of the traveling party caught up, they found Justin with his back to the hull and a broad grin on his face.

Justin's thoughts returned to the present moment when the dinghy broached in low surf. He gave the left oar a few tugs, and the craft straightened. Moments later its bow dug into the beach with a grinding hiss. Justin jumped out and pulled the craft halfway onto the sand. Returning to the water's edge, he scooped a handful of seawater and drank it down. He took a deep breath, turned and trudged through the sand toward the vegetation line.

He sat at the base of a large palm and wiggled, making the sand conform to his bottom. He pondered the sandy whites of the tropical beach and smiled at a whale spouting on the green sea.

"Hi, big fella. You spending the day with us?" His chest swelled with a deep breath and he closed his eyes. "I'm sure glad you guys made it."

Moments later with his eyes still closed he whispered. "We're survivors, too." A smile crossed his face. "We survived...we survived." He opened his eyes to see the whale spout again. "Now the land is different and even the seas flow a different way."

His chest rose with another deep breath and he held it for a long moment before driving it out with a huff. He did this three times and relaxed into stillness.

———————————

Later a breeze ruffled his hair, and his eyes opened to see the flukes of the whale as it slid into the deep. He got to his feet, took a few long strides and began to jog down to the dinghy.

Once there, he pushed the boat back into the sea, quickly found the oars, and commenced rowing parallel to the shore searching for the fresh water stream. In less than a quarter of a mile, Justin beached the little craft again, and the refilling chore commenced.

———————————

An hour later, after two trips to the *Cristine*, Justin stood on the last container, watching the escaping bubbles. Suddenly, a bird screeched from the jungle. Justin winced at the cutting noise. He looked inland. "Time for a little distraction," he thought. He stepped off the water can and sloshed upstream.

At its mouth, the stream broadened and was only inches deep, but in the jungle it narrowed and deepened. The waters curled around Justin's knees.

Large trees lined the stream, their bases hidden by bundles of brilliant green foliage. Orchid-like flowers studded the greenery and perfumed the air. From a massive tree, a wide cascade of vines, thickly covered with tiny violet flowers, hung to the water's edge and ceaselessly shed petals that drifted and swirled in a warm breeze. Small, multi-color butterflies fluttered in the flowers, while large, iridescent blue butterflies gathered on stony patches at the water's edge.

Large birds, bright blue and trailing long black feathers, swooped from high trees tops. They screeched a protest at Justin and soared over the canopy. Flying close to the water, small yellow birds darted upstream only to reappear moments later. The air reverberated with a constant cicada-like buzz.

Tiny fish populated the stream. They darted with lightning speed and when motionless, found invisibility with skin that matched the stream's bottom. Farther on the stream widened, and Justin swam across a small, circular pool.

A half-mile from the beach, Justin considered turning back. Then from his left, a pulse of light burst through the foliage. He backed up a step, and the flash glowed steadily. "Glass or metal?" He thought, "Something man-made."

He bit his lip. "Worth a look."

He often found things of use in such places. The onboard cooking stove, for instance, and the water containers. He left the stream and pushed his way into the vegetation. At first he struggled, but once under the canopy the plant life thinned, and he walked easily on sandy soil.

Shortly, Justin found a small building of corrugated metal. Rusted red with many holes it was a dreary sight in the vibrant jungle. The reflecting object, a solar cell, set on the roof. Justin walked around the building with an inspecting eye. The door lay in the sand, a shadow of rust. A black rectangle in the building indicated its former place. Justin peered into the semi-darkness. At the center of the sandy floor, the ramshackle remains of a bed lay scattered. In a far corner, a pile of pots and pans and a broken chair was discernable. He looked to his left at a metal table. A radio receiver, a transmitter, and a telephone gave a hint as to the shack's purpose.

Justin squinted at the shadow-clocked phone. "Military," he thought. His eyes traced the path of wires from the phone that lead outside. "Probably to another building…but, most likely far off."

Another set of wires snaked through the sand to a half-buried battery and then climbed the wall. "Those go to the solar cell." He paused and bit his lip, thinking the equipment could be of use at New Atlantis. He walked over to the battery and nonchalantly toed one of the terminal connectors.

When the phone rang, Justin leaped backward, stumbled, and fell as the piercing sound echoed in the metal building. An unheard sound from long ago. His heart pounded, and his mind struggled with the implications. Shaking, he confronted the phone.

"Holy shit. Son of a bitch." He took a deep breath. "That scared the crap out of me."

He took another deep breath and smiled. A moment later he laughed. He leaned over the battery and studied it, hands on hips. Once more he nudged the terminal with his toe, and again the phone rang, and again he jumped, though this time under better control.

Justin stood quietly and thought of Nicole. Slowly a smile came to his face and he slapped his right thigh and dropped to his knees. With both hands he dug a hole deep enough to contain the battery. He concealed its top with a thin layer of sand and positioned a small stick above the loose terminal. He stood up and applied foot pressure to the stick. Inwardly braced, he pressed until the phone clamored. Justin still flinched.

Laughing, he clapped his hands and ran to the stream. He swam almost all the way to the beach and the waiting water cans. Energetically, he loaded the cans and rowed back to the *Cristine*.

As he came alongside, he thumped the larger craft with an oar to notify Nicole of his return. Nicole, in the galley eating a piece of fruit, climbed topside and spoke a welcome.

"Hi, what've you been up to?" She smiled.

Justin delighted at the sound of her voice. "I'm topping off the water tanks." He suppressed a smile, but his eyes twinkled. "I found an old shack. There's some stuff inside that I am sure we can use. Let's take a look later." He smiled. "After the fruit is gathered…it's a short walk upstream."

Nicole lifted her eyebrows. "OK. Sounds good. But first, a bath."

She tossed her fruit overboard, stepped to the side of the *Cristine* and paused before diving into the crystal-like blue water. Justin watched her flight and then studied her distorted image beneath the surface. Nicole went deep, pulled a few hard strokes, rose to the surface and swam toward the shore.

Once there, she stepped from the sea and headed for the jungle stream. She looked back at the *Cristine*. Justin poured water into the starboard tank.

Her eyes diverted to the plume of a spouting whale. "Did you find something to eat?" She had watched the whale earlier. Nicole thought of the many whales seen during the voyage. She frowned. "I've seen a lot of you guys, but why only one at a time?"

When Nicole arrived at the stream, she followed its bank to the vegetation line. There she removed her clothing and strode into the sweet water, its feel exceedingly soft as compared to the harsh salinity of the ocean. After washing she left the stream and allowed a warm breeze to dry her skin. Nicole slipped on her leather breeches and then laced her leather vest as she retraced her steps back to the beach.

She looked toward the *Cristine*, but there was no sign of Justin. She turned inland and headed for the jungle, her mind occupied with the task of picking fruit for the morning meal. When circumstances were right, she often got quite elaborate with the shore meals, a pleasant break from the makeshift situations at sea. Today however, with other chores to accomplish, time was a factor.

Nicole didn't have to venture deep into the brush to find a stomach-filling quantity of fruit, and a few large leaves to separate fruit from sand. She arranged the meal beneath a palm tree.

She again looked toward the *Cristine*. This time Justin sat in the dinghy. He pushed off and rowed for shore, and she walked down to met him.

When the dinghy hit the sand, she held onto it as Justin climbed out. Together they pulled the craft ashore.

Nicole grabbed Justin's hand and squeezed it. "Breakfast is prepared. The usual ham and eggs, blueberry pancakes, fresh squeezed orange juice, et cetera, et cetera."

Justin smiled. "I'm hungry enough to eat a monkey." He paused. "Did you see any monkeys, by chance?"

"I think we're the only monkeys here."

Justin stared into the jungle. "There has to be a primate out there. Somewhere."

Nicole sighed. "I didn't see much animal life, other than birds. There's lots of fruit about. It'll be easy to get what we need."

Together they unloaded the storage baskets and proceeded to where Nicole arranged the simple meal.

Justin dropped the baskets. "Some of that fruit looks familiar." He scanned the leaf and pointed. "I really like those plum looking things." He bent down and picked one up. "They need a name. Something with blue."

Nicole sat in the sand and looked seaward. "They're not blue." She turned back to Justin. "I guess we can make another three to four-day trip before coming ashore again." She looked to Justin for agreement.

"Yeah. As long as the weather stays good and we catch a few fish on the way." He presented the plum-like fruit to her. "Are you sure these aren't blue?" And then he took a bite of it, and the escaping juice ran down his chin as he talked. "We've been lucky with the weather. A few squalls, some choppy seas." He spat out the tough skin of the fruit. "I wonder if there'll be hurricanes again."

Minutes passed as they silently ate their meal. Justin tossed a pit in the direction of the ocean. "We have plenty of firewood and the water tanks are topped off. We're ready for sea, mate. Time to cast off!" And in a louder voice. "It's time to head for home!"

Nicole jumped to her feet when the word 'home' registered in her head. Previously, the references were to 'getting back ' or something like that. The word 'home' charged her with sudden delight, and she smiled broadly. "First the fruit and then we go. Homeward bound."

"Wait a minute. I almost forgot about the shack. We should do that. We have the time."

"The hell with it. Let's go."

"No, no. There could be treasure me hardy."

Justin's light-hearted approach added the aspect of fun to the little adventure.

"OK, Black Beard, but I get all the jewels. You can have the bullion."

After gathering the fruit, they pushed the basket-laden dinghy back into the sea. Justin swam while Nicole rowed. On board the *Cristine*, they left the fruit in the galley, proper stowage waiting until they returned from the little expedition.

The couple moved upstream at a leisurely pace, looking at the flowers and watching the colorful butterflies. At the deep pool they lingered, enjoying the warm clear water and the singing birds. Justin lazed half submerged, his back resting on the shore, his eyes closed, his torso basking in the sun. Nicole, more energetic, repeatedly swam to the upstream side of the pool and buoyantly reclined on the surface allowing the slow current to carry her back.

When a bird screeched, Justin opened his eyes just as Nicole floated by. Immediately his prank came to mind. From a sitting position he rolled forward and dove below the surface of the pool and reappeared at the upstream side.

"Come on, let's get the treasure."

"Aha captain."

Together they sloshed along, Justin in the lead, looking for the disturbed vegetation where he previously entered the jungle. In short time he found the spot and directed Nicole into the tangle. "You go first, it's only a short way." Nicole headed in and Justin's hand went to his mouth.

Nicole inquired. "How far do we have to go?"

Justin mumbled.

"What did you say?"

No sooner said, the pair arrived at the shack. Nicole walked to the entrance, stepped inside and looked about. Justin followed her silently.

Nicole took note of everything, including the telephone and radio. However, her attention focused on the pile of things in the far corner. Hands on her hips, she walked to the heap.

"Looks like a pile of crap to me."

Nonchalantly, Justin moved over to the stick lying in the sand. He looked down at his footprint from the previous visit, hesitated, then smiled. He placed a foot on the stick. His eyes squinted, he bared his teeth and shifted his weight. Instantly the phone rang, loud and clear.

Justin flinched. On the other side of the room it was sheer pandemonium. Nicole screamed and danced a little jig before stumbling into the pile of rubbish.

Again the phone rang. Nicole lost her balance, lurched, and fell into the trash. Justin unmercifully rang the phone a third time. Nicole screeched in pain from the poking of numerous pot handles and the sight of spiders and bugs scurrying in the commotion.

Justin rushed to the phone as Nicole regained her feet. "I'll get it!"

She stared wide-eyed as he passed by. Justin reached for the phone, stopped and turned to Nicole. "Perhaps I shouldn't?" He shrugged his shoulders, turned away, and reached for the phone.

Nicole, stunned, stood as she was, her mouth open, a pot in hand.

Justin picked up the receiver. "Hello!"

He waited as if listening and then mumbled something. He turned his back to Nicole and mumbled again.

Justin sat the phone down and turned to Nicole. His face expressionless. "I think we won a trip to Las Vegas. They'll call back later."

With squinting eyes Nicole followed Justin as he turned and headed out of the shack.

A moment later her jaw clinched and she raised the pot. "Crap head!" The pot flew through the door way and hit Justin on the head.

Justin started laughing as he rubbed his head. "I'm glad you didn't find an iron skillet."

Nicole's shoulders suddenly slumped and she leaned her head back. A puff of breath escaped her mouth and she ambled into the light of day, her eyes bulging with tears.

Justin's face sagged. He stepped toward her. "You OK? It was a joke. I was hoping for a smile."

Nicole raised a hand to stroke her forehead. "Oh, it's been a long time." She whispered. Her eyes drifted from Justin to the high tree canopy. "The world we lost." She paused. "It all came back to me in a rush."

She blinked. "That fear you get...I was afraid." She paused. "Why should I be afraid? I don't think I was afraid when I lost it." She shivered.

Justin led her to a fallen tree. Nicole sat, her elbows on her knees, her head bowed. Justin leaned to see into her face. "I'm sorry. I thought it would make you laugh."

Nicole's raised her head and took a deep breath. "I'm OK." She gave him a peck on the lips. "I'm OK." She took another deep breath, straightened her back, braced herself with her hands on her knees and stared into the brush. "A time warp." She paused. "The old world." She bowed her head. "I felt it. I felt it the same as I felt it then."

She looked at Justin. "I loved it, I lost it and then I was afraid. All in that short moment." She smiled. "How did you do that? Make the phone ring."

Justin explained in a few short sentences and finished with a sigh. "It was meant to be fun."

"It was really quite clever." She smiled and gave him another kiss. "I'm sure I'll laugh about it later."

Nicole rose to her feet. "Let's get back." She shoved him toward the stream. "Justin. Do you miss it?...all that technology...all the people...and now being almost alone on the planet."

Justin didn't look at her. "Yeah, I think I do." He turned to face her. "We're an endangered species, you know."

They headed back to the beach.

"I think you aged me a good ten years. Crap head." She shoved him again.

Later that day, Justin, alone, towed the dinghy upstream and retrieved the phone equipment, the solar cell and the aluminum pot.

Troubling Seas and Thoughts to Flee (Justin)

In the Northwest corner of America, in the state of Oregon, where the land meets the sea, rugged cliffs rose to ridges where twisted pine crouched to the pressure of onshore winds. At the base of the stony walls, cold, blue-green waters alternated between pounding and caressing.

To the north and south of the walls, stretches of white sand heaped into huge granular waves assail and abate in slow movement, harassing legions of tall pines.

Midpoint on the coast, where the Umpqua River flowed into the Pacific sea, the tiny harbor of Winchester Bay huddled. Protected on three sides by low-forested hills, it faced the western sea. Here, fishing people made their home, alongside a few loggers and those who catered to seasonal visitors.

One of those fishermen, Justin, lived with his daughter, Michelle, and his two sons, Paul and David. The wife and mother of the family died years earlier in Virginia, a victim of cancer. Soon after her death Justin moved with his children to California, briefly staying with his sister and her family. He made an exploratory trip to Oregon and found the small hamlet of Winchester Bay. Falling in love with the town, he moved his family there and built a new life. With determined effort, the group achieved a substantial livelihood through commercial fishing and the wise investment of surplus money.

After Justin's retirement, Paul, the oldest son, captained Justin's fishing vessel, *Orca*. The fifty-two-foot stern trawler functioned primarily for shrimping and occasionally for crabbing. Justin seldom went to sea anymore, but when he did, it was usually during the migration of the gray whales.

In early spring, with the whales headed north for a summer of gorging, the *Orca* rode the steep and choppy waves at the mouth of the river. Justin stood at the helm with Paul to his right. Paul, in his early twenties, with a strong body, stood nearly the same height as his father. His blue eyes studied the weather on the western horizon. Like his father, he had a prominent nose, but a softer jaw line. His shoulder length hair protruded from a watch cap.

The *Orca's* helm required a strong hand and near constant movement as the craft struggled in the channel chop. The sky, light blue, waited for the sun to peek over the eastern hills. The men planned a short day, pulling a few crab pots and watching for whales.

A confusion of waves at the river mouth gripped the *Orca* and jerked her about, only to release her a moment later. Justin held the boat's heading firmly to west and seaward toward deeper ocean water, where the seas rolled large and smooth, and would soothe the *Orca's* motion.

Paul looked north. "There was a pod or two up north yesterday." He turned to his father. "That's where the pots are that I didn't get."

Justin nudged the engine throttles to increase speed. "What made you turn back with just a few pots to pull?"

"It was getting sloppy." Paul braced himself as the *Orca* lurched to starboard. "There wasn't much crab in the other pots, and I knew we would be coming out today."

Justin handled the helm with obvious pleasure. His first trip of the year, his blue eyes sparkled under bushy eyebrows. "As soon as we're out of this chop, I'll swing her north." He looked at his son and pushed his watch cap to the back of his head. "How far north and how deep?"

"A couple of miles, thirty fathoms."

A few minutes later, Justin shifted the helm to starboard, beginning a slow swing to the north. Justin looked at Paul as the boat's motion calmed. "Time for a cup of coffee."

Without a word, Paul went aft to the galley. He hollered, "Want an egg sandwich?"

"Just coffee."

Having coffee after crossing the bar was almost a ritual for the father and son. The first time, a salmon trip, Paul was twelve and on his first trip as a deck hand. Justin again controlled the helm, but had turned it over to Paul after crossing the bar. They spent three days and two nights at sea in a venture special to both.

On this trip, Justin would not transfer the helm. Paul, who had given his two-man crew the day off, functioned as the deck hand.

Paul returned to the wheelhouse and handed a cup to his father.

Justin put it to his lips and watched the ponderous swells roll out of the west. "If you need some time off later, let me know. It'll be my pleasure." He smiled, put his coffee cup in a holder, and with the same hand, switched the sonar machine from reading feet to reading fathoms. Justin turned toward his son. "I was looking at the books the other day. It's shaping up to be a good season."

"Yeah! With the good weather, I got an extra twenty days of fishing in."

Justin took another sip of coffee. "It's a lot different from when I first started fishing here." He leaned over the helm for a close study of the compass. "The storms are fewer." He turned to Paul and squinted. "But more intense." The compass reached due north and Justin swung the rudder to port to check the starboard swing. He held it there for a moment and then positioned it amidship. "I think we're getting the weather they used to get in southern Oregon."

Paul took another bite of his sandwich and mumbled his words. "The patterns have shifted north. I talked to Steve in Alaska. He says that things are kind of that way up there, too."

Justin looked at Paul. "How's he doing?"

"Not too good. He's coming back. Asked me for a job."

Paul slid the side window open and tossed the remainder of his egg sandwich over the side. "Things are messed up. The water's warm and then the water's cold. When it rains, it pours."

Justin let out a slow breath. "The rhythm's gone."

Paul pulled his hat off and scratched his head. "I try to push all that shit out of my head." He sighed. "But I can't. It's in front of my face all the time." He slid the side window shut with a loud thump and turned to his father. "We've pulled a lot of deformed crabs out of the pots this year. Hell, the deckies don't even bother mentioning them anymore."

The *Orca* crested a huge swell and Justin turned to the next one coming. "Shit."

The carcass of a gray whale crested the top of the oncoming wave as it drifted toward shore. Justin instantly pushed the boat's throttle forward. Both men watched as the whale disappeared over the top of the swell, its flipper rising into the air as the body rolled with the motion of the wave. Macabre, it seemed a farewell gesture. Paul lowered his head and looked the other way. "Yeah, that to. I haven't said anything to you about it, but it's not so uncommon."

Justin spoke softly and slowly. "What...a...mess. What...to...do?"

Paul's expression shadowed. "There's nothing *to* do. There's just too many people, Dad. Too many *damn* people." Paul turned toward his father, his face twisted with disgust. "Everybody wants...but who volunteers to do with less."

Justin bit his lip at his son's sudden show of anger and studied the approach of another swell. Of late, climate change and the degeneration of the environment were common subjects wherever you went. Apprehension undercut even the daily small talk. A warm day in winter was suspect. An earthquake or a volcanic eruption echoed as an omen. A little war here and a little war there projected an overall attitude. Quiet, sullen moments passed. Justin's anticipated joyous day at sea clouded with Paul's demeanor and the harbinger of the dead whale. He turned and spoke sternly to his son. "We don't have to surrender to it." His eyes drifted to the horizon above the bow of the *Orca*. "But, we can't fight it. We can only keep our eyes open. Go with the flow of the surge." More quiet moments passed.

Abruptly, Paul hoisted his cup. "Well, here's to open eyes and going with the surge."

The men sipped their coffee in silence as ponderous seas rolled beneath the *Orca* and the hefty diesel engine throbbed.

Later, after the men pulled up the last crab pot, the *Orca* dashed back to port just before the winds of noon.

Justin sat in a soft recliner on the back deck of his home, his eyes squinted at a glittering sea under the late afternoon sun of a midsummer day. His home, built from Douglas fir logs, sat high on a hill, presenting a view of the Pacific Ocean, the Umpqua River, and Winchester Bay.

The view did not relieve his agitation. Moments before he silenced the TV after learning of a new form of antibiotic resistant tuberculosis. He spoke with anger. "Keeping that depressing stuff away is like shoveling shit against the tide."

The doorbell rang, and he heard a familiar voice. "Justin."

He smiled. "On my way Zoe."

Zoe was a New York City transplant from almost four years ago. She was close to Justin in age, but never specified in exactness. A dark haired, dark-eyed beauty, her Mediterranean genes were obvious.

Justin met her at a Blessing of The Fleet festival. In the late hours of the beer garden dance and at the prodding of his friends, he asked her to dance. An unknown entity at the time, she projected mystery with her beauty and big city style. That night a hot relationship ignited between Justin and Zoe, but it cooled quickly to a comfortable warm.

Her perfume swirled in the folds of a cool breeze that meandered through Justin's rustic living room, into the adjoining dining room, and out the French doors to the covered deck where Justin stood in its flow. Its clean, yet exotic bouquet provoked waves of eagerness in Justin.

Zoe stood in the light of the open house door. A full-bodied woman, she wore jeans that were not tight, just tight enough.

A light yellow windbreaker protected her from the ever cool and windy Oregon coast. She wore primitive looking sandals, her toenails painted a crisp red.

Justin watched her ample lips spread in a pleasant smile. "I came to town to get a few things and thought you might have time to take a lonely gal to dinner."

Justin, joyed by her surprise visit, walked quickly to her and gripped her by the waist with both hands. He planted a sumptuous kiss on her neck.

She stomped her right foot on the floor. "I love that." Her brow knitted, "But I hate it as well." She stepped back from him. "I'll take that as a 'yes' to dinner."

"It's a yes all right and please stay the night."

She smiled. "Let's go to my place. I've prepared potions of chocolate."

Justin only had a general idea of her background. Her first career was as an actress in the New York Theater and she did well, but not great. In her early thirties she changed careers with the help of a friend to some sort of Wall Street situation and made a lot of money. She never married, had no children and as she put it, "Oregon keeps the family at bay."

Justin moaned. "Chocolate." He took another breath of her perfume and spoke softly. "Yes, yes, yes." He stepped backward to contain his urges. "Is the hot tub hot?"

"With my intuitive anticipation, yes." She pouted a kiss.

Justin took her by the hand. "It's a bit early for lunch. Let's have a glass of wine."

With familiarity they moved toward the table in the dining room. The table consisted of large heavy, unfinished planks retrieved from the beach after a winter storm. It now functioned as the gathering place for all who came to Justin's home.

Unmatched chairs surrounded the table. Stuffed, with high backs, very comfortable, and not at all formal. Zoe sat in her favorite, an old Mediterranean type with carved mystical animals and soft leather upholstery. Justin went to the kitchen for the wine, a cream sherry. He found an ashtray and joined Zoe. He sat across from her, in David's chair. Its wood was simple oak and the upholstery overstuffed blue denim. It leaned backward like an office chair.

Justin poured the wine, sat back in his chair, and took a deep drink. "You've lightened my day. I've been brooding."

Zoe rummaged through her bag and pulled out a small wooden pipe. "A little of this will be nice before dinner." She laid it on the table. Her hand went back into the purse, but she suddenly stopped and looked up. "Brooding...don't tell me." She stilled, leaned forward and looked deep into his eyes. "I see fear." She paused. "Also...indecision." She leaned back, her attention returned to the purse. "Ah, here it is." She pulled out a silver and gold pillbox.

Justin raised his eyebrows. "You can read eyes?" He smiled. "And you're right. What's the source of that talent?"

Zoe filled the pipe with a pinch of pot and handed it to Justin. "It relates to dramatics. Drama school. It can be learned, to some degree." She paused. "A must, if you're going to teach acting."

"I didn't know that you taught."

Zoe relaxed back into her chair. "Now and then...between theater engagements...at Columbia and a few times at Julliard."

Justin's eyes lit up. "That picture at your house, the group shot."

"Yes. My last and best class." She looked beyond Justin at the view of the ocean. "There were two special talents in that group." She paused and her eyes drifted back to Justin. "They both died...and let's not talk about that."

Justin instantly granted her the wish.

Zoe lived in a cozy house overlooking the same river that flowed passed Justin's place. Her only companions were a couple of dogs and a cat. Zoe came to Oregon seeking isolation to pen a book. To her surprise, the isolation became comfortable.

Justin took the pipe and struck a wooden match. Zoe watched. "What's causing you to brood, Justin?"

Justin positioned the match carefully and drew in a breath. A moment later he blew out the breath and the match. "The world, the mess, and the seemingly no way out scenario."

She took the pipe. "And, of course, there are your children."

Justin sat back. "What of you?...Do you worry?...Are you making plans?"

"I'm cognizant as to what is going on." She struck a match and lit the pipe. A moment later the smoke streamed in a thin line between her pouted lips. "The book is near finished...I will be taking it back to New York." Her eyes shifted back to Justin. "I'm going to keep the house...I love the place." She paused and rearranged herself in the chair. "In short Justin...Life as usual." She picked up her glass of wine and took a sip. "Nice."

Justin loved her self-assuredness. Unlike some women it was inoffensive and authentic, not some sort of proclamation or ultimatum. "World stability has a skin about as thick as a soap bubble."

Zoe's face shadowed. "I prefer it *pop*...while I'm in New York."

Justin drank more of the wine. "It's going to be ugly."

Zoe took a deep breath. "Listen to your gut, Justin. It's what I do. We have our destinies and our guts show the way." She paused. "Relax. Allow the thoughts to come."

Justin flopped back in his chair. "You're right! Let the revelations come. I will think with my gut." He smiled. "And right now it tells me eating time is near."

Zoe smiled back. "I'm really in the mood for seafood. Crab, salmon and oysters...where should we go?"

"The Crabby Wench. Of course."

They stood and headed for the door.

One winter day, Justin walked the beach just south of Winchester Bay. The sun brightened the cold air as it moved from sea to shore. Huge chunks of trees, some simple in shape, most true sculpture, decorated the beach. Washed ashore by winter storms their visit lasted only to mid-spring. Justin never understood how most found their way back to sea.

He looked to the southwest. A dark wall of clouds pushed shoreward beneath a lid of thin gray clouds. Another storm on its way. Large drops of wind driven rain would soon be pelting his form. He always found that acceptable and even welcoming.

Justin walked the wet sand behind a still receding tide, his interest on a large root wad less than a quarter of a mile away. It arrived on the beach only hours ago. Justin pressed his weight into the southerly wind and headed for the carcass of wood.

When he arrived, he paused in the lee of the stump and for a moment studied its shape. Eventually he raised a hand and rubbed a smooth segment. The thrashing sea scrubbed the wad clean of all small roots and most of its bark. At its base, a shallow pool shimmered in the gusty wind. Justin reached into the sea puddle and grasped a cockleshell. Being careful not to spill its contents, he raised it to his mouth and poured the liquid in. One of Justin's shore walk rituals. As he put it, "A bit of the sea within."

As the seawater ran down his throat, Zoe came to mind. He was close to loving her, but knew better. Instinctively he knew that if he made a step in that direction, she would instantly cut him loose, like the swipe of a Samurai blade. Zoe had a hidden agenda.

Justin smiled. He knew that some said he was being used. "Perhaps, and perhaps not. In any case, she did it in a nice way." He looked at the huge storm-driven waves, icy green with a frothy white across their chaotic tops. Zoe had disappeared into another life. "It's been months since I've heard from her."

An exceptionally strong gust of wind rushed passed the huge root wad. Justin stepped into the open and turned south. The thoughts of Zoe fluttered away and his conversation with Paul fluttered in.

"Flow with the surge," he thought.

Justin came to a sudden stop. His body froze as if poised before a precipice. He shouted into the wind. "Take control of your life. What crap."

He stepped forward resuming his walk. "Think with your gut."

Justin mused. "Birth. One step leads to another. Cause and effect. You must have control at the beginning, or you never have control. Given genes. Subjected to environment. Now here."

He closed his eyes and walked blindly. "Six billion people doing what they want."

He stopped again and opened his eyes. "I don't think so."

Again he walked. "The control is somewhere else. And the effort is not for me or for us."

A seagull, troubled with the man's approach, took two gawky steps with spread wings and rose into the air. Gracefully it veered west and then north, but quickly grounded after establishing satisfactory distance.

"Well, excuse me!" Justin followed the flight of the bird and walked backwards as he waved a good-by and turned south once more.

His mind resumed its philosophical flow. "Separateness is an illusion created by the Powers That Be." He lowered his head to the contemplation of being one with the seagull. "Neither of us is perfect and if we are one with the One, then the One is not perfect." He spun his back to the wind and stopped. "I'm being used!" He looked at the seagull. "We're all being used!"

"My life and yours." He pointed at the seagull. "Are being used. Used to achieve Their perfection."

Justin turned back to face the wind. He spread his arms out and looked down.

The remnants of a wave washed close to his feet and ebbed back to sea. Struck by the sudden urge to be near the action, he lowered his arms and followed the wave, at a trot. The flat subsiding water slid under the next incoming wave causing it to break and join its rush back to sea. Cold water seeped into Justin's walking shoes as he ambled through the slouchy sand. Abruptly, a burly wave swelled in front of him, green and strong. Justin took another step, halted, and took a step backward. The wave paused and then rushed at him. He turned and ran. Peripherally he saw the wave catching up, forcing him to sprint.

He reached dry sand and spun around, watching his challenger retreat. He smiled. "Sorry, my drowning wasn't meant to be. I'm not finished being used."

Justin stood quietly and surveyed the turbulent sea far beyond the breaking waves. He sucked in a deep breath and savored the moist, salt air. His mind cleared and rested. He stood that way for close to twenty minutes.

A single large drop of rain struck Justin on the left side of his neck and ran beneath his clothing. Instantly he turned north, back to the truck. As he walked, he pulled the hood of his jacket over his head. An instantaneous hush occurred when the heavy fabric covered his ears. Justin anticipated the effect and the now silent wind pushed at his back and levitated his steps.

"I'm not responsible." He smiled. "And I haven't anything better to do anyway."

Justin, light of heart, followed his past footprints back to where they climbed the small beach dune leading to the parking lot. The large globules of rain pelted his back with increased intensity, though they felt more like pats.

"It would be foolish not to prepare."

Justin drove up the small private road he shared with two other neighbors. His house was large, four bedrooms, two baths. Old cedar trees screened its eastern side. A comfortable home, warm and secure for his family. It would be difficult to leave; a trepidation Justin already wrestled with.

He parked the truck and walked into the house. "Is anybody here?"

A response came from one of the back rooms." Yeah! I'm here. In my room." It was David.

David was eighteen and just out of high school, a bright boy and a sure candidate for college. These days he made periodic fishing trips with Paul earning pocket money. He planned to take a year or two off for what he called 'fooling around' before going to college. A computer wiz, he did a lot of reading and sometimes talked about writing. Justin didn't mind the schooling delay. He was mature beyond his age and Justin trusted his decisions.

Justin spoke loudly. "Did you check with Paul? I think he had some work for you." Justin heard the boy's footsteps coming down the hall.

"No, but I will. Can I use the truck Dad?" He stopped at the end of the hallway and faced his father.

Justin looked at his son's long hair. Wavy, brown, and shoulder length, it enhanced his angular face, giving him an intellectual look. "Sure, the keys are in it." Justin watched him turn and head for the door. His somewhat frail body moved with grace, but not strength. Running around in the wild could be difficult for him. "Be home for dinner and if you see Michelle, tell her the same."

David spun around, his brown eyes squinting. "Something up. What?" David possessed a special insight that always caught Justin off guard.

Justin hesitated. "I've made a decision and I want to tell all of you at the same time."

David studied his father for a long moment before turning for the door again.

"I always have faith in what you do, Dad." He twisted the door handle and spoke over his shoulder. "Michelle's working at the café. I'll stop by and tell her." He opened the door, stepped through and closed it.

Justin stared at the closed door and mused. "David would be good at the navigational skills needed in the woods; gather maps, find places to hide supplies, and how to get back to them."

Michelle, the middle child, close to twenty years old, worked part time for Paul as well, taking care of the books and sometimes waiting on tables at the Crabby Wench. She was saving money for college and planned to attend the University of Oregon when, as she put it, "I am absolutely sure what I want to be." Michelle, like Paul, a former high school athlete, possessed a strong body.

Justin mused again. "Putting the foodstuff together. Information on edible wild plants. I'll give her some help. There's also the medical supplies. And how to use them."

His thoughts switched to Paul. "Weapons, shelter, hunting techniques."

Justin pushed his plate away and took a sip of wine. "There's a serious subject I want to talk about." He rubbed his chin. "It's about the mess the world's in. And how to deal with it."

His children were quick to voice opinions. Michelle spoke with anger about the struggling environment and overpopulation. Paul cited examples of society's decreasing ability to maintain order and scoffed at the police state rules that only increased the chaos. David's contribution related to the terror tactics popping up everywhere and he saw no meaningful leadership from any quarter.

Justin stopped the conversation. "OK, OK. We know all that shit." He bit his lip. "What counts is how we deal with it."

A few moments of quiet ensued. Justin leaned toward the table. "I have a plan. I'll state it to the point, without details."

The children waited. Justin bit his lip and took a breath. "Well...most likely we'll end up living...in the woods...moving from place to place." He looked at his children. Paul wore a slight smile. Michelle's eyes widened. David sat expressionless, almost relaxed.

Justin continued. "Living off the land and hidden supplies." He took another sip of wine.

The smile on Paul's face grew to a grin. "So you really want to do this." He slapped the table. "We're going to live in the woods!"

Justin held up one hand. "This is preparation. We're not heading out the door in a few weeks. The preparations will take months. And hopefully it won't be needed. "Michelle looked directly at her father with a serious expression. "Dad, tell me this is a joke." Justin made no comment, he just stared back at her. Michelle's face calmed and she leaned back in her chair. "Count me out. I'm not living in the woods." She ran her fingers through her long light brown hair.

David toyed with the scraps of food on his plate.

Michelle spoke again. "We can't just run off and start living in the woods. That's crazy." She had her father's blue eyes and they darkened with each passing moment. "We can pile things up here."

David responded. "He said that we should prepare and that we *might* wind up in the woods."

Michelle smirked. "My little brother, our father has done peculiar things before."

Paul leaned forward. "OK. The world's a mess. We can all see that." He sat up straight. "Preparation. No big deal. Money in the bank." He relaxed back into his chair.

Michelle slapped the table with both hands. "Wait a minute, wait a minute." She looked at her father. "This talk is scary. Are things getting that bad?"

Justin frowned. "Scary is a good description."

Paul smirked. "Fucked up is another."

Michelle placed her elbows on the table, her face resting in her hands. Justin knew her plans for the future, love, marriage, career, et cetera. But what could he do? Paul's eyes were bright. Justin mused to himself silently. "Paul will do just fine. The action, the adventure. It'll stimulate his blood."

Justin turned to David. "What do you think son?"

David bit his lip and studied the table before him. "Living in the woods will be hard and dangerous."

Justin swallowed and cleared his throat. "We'll do some training. Build up our endurance."

Paul spoke up. "Are we going to put up some kind of house or shelter?"

Justin sat back in his chair. "The plan is to be independent. We move a lot. We stay for only short periods of time at any given spot. We don't want to be put in a position of defending a place. There's no way of telling which place will be safe and for how long. We'll have buried supplies. We'll live off the land as much as possible." He paused. "Eventually things will calm down and order will return. It's the in-between time that we need to worry about."

All three of his children fell silent; they did not look at one another. After a few moments Michelle pushed her chair away from the table, picked up her plate and tableware, and walked slowly into the kitchen. David still toyed with food scraps on his plate. Paul leaned back in his chair, his hands behind his head. He stared into space.

Justin broke the silence. "Let's clean up the dishes. The plan needs to cook awhile."

As the boys rose to a standing position, Justin added a closing statement. "One important thing to remember. Our plans are to remain a closed family matter. No one else is to know. It'll be difficult enough to save ourselves." He drank down the last sip of his wine. "We'll talk again Tuesday."

Tuesday arrived and the family was again at the dinner table. Justin finished the last of his second plate of spaghetti. Michelle questioned Paul about some invoices for the last load of crab he sold. David rocked in his chair, knotting his hair at the base of his skull.

Justin pushed his plate away and reached for his glass of wine. "We have been chit chatting about the plan all week. Now is the time for a yes or no." He settled back in his chair and took a deep breath. "We have to be together on this thing. A divided decision is unthinkable." He paused, looking at each of his children in turn. "If the vote is a tie, I'll give myself a double vote."

David looked at Michelle. "I see no reason not to prepare. In fact, it would be a mistake if we didn't. I also think it's important to keep it all quiet."

Paul nodded his head in agreement. "I agree with it all."

Michelle's eyes shifted from one brother to the other. "What about our friends? What about our relatives? Don't we tell them? Don't we say something?" She turned to Justin. Her eyes widened. "What about Zoe?"

Justin's shoulders slumped noticeably. "Zoe's in New York. I haven't heard anything from her." He turned to Michelle. "No, we don't tell anyone. The world situation is obvious, preparation is a choice." All went suddenly quiet.

Justin rubbed his chin. "There are a lot of people preparing, but not all." He took a deep breath, shook his head, and let his words spill across the table. "I don't want us to be in the situation where those who didn't prepare attempt..." He left his sentence hanging. "Well you know what I mean."

Michelle put her hands to her cheeks. "I hate this. I really hate it. But, yes I agree." She spun her head toward Justin. "When will we have to leave?"

All eyes shifted to Justin. "We'll know when the time comes."

For the next half hour Justin added a few details to the plan and then gave them their assignments. The children listened to their father without interruption. When he finished, they rose silently, cleared the table, and departed to different parts of the house. Justin remained at the table, sipping wine in quiet repose.

In this unfamiliar situation, they proceeded slowly. Each task started as a group effort, but ended with an individual. They spent hours with maps that led to expeditions to affirm choices.

Simultaneously, they prepared their bodies with medical examinations, dental care, and physical training that emphasized endurance, such as running in the sand dunes. They expected the wilderness lifestyle of itself to give them the strength they needed. They experimented with shoes and clothing, read books, watched videos, and talked to people, seeking survival skills.

Supply choices demanded extensive scrutiny. With added consideration for needs after the calamity, a mammoth list resulted. However, time ironed out the problems.

They stored the supplies in aluminum chests and buried three at eight different locations, one on top of the other. The top chest, buried two feet down, measured 4' x 3' x 3'. Fifty percent of its space consisted of food, ten percent for medical supplies and forty percent for clothing. Below that chest lay a shovel, an axe, a rope and a light cable, all wrapped in oiled canvas. The second chest, two feet further down, measured 8' x 4' x 4'. Thirty percent of its space consisted of food, mostly dried, including vitamins, minerals, and seed for a garden. Another ten percent went to medical supplies, including surgical equipment and information on its use. The remaining space was for clothing. An inventory of tools and weapons, also wrapped in oilskin, lay beneath this second chest.

The last chest, allocated to the recovery time, measured 6' x 2' x 4'. It contained material related to the arts and sciences. It was a noble effort, but the collection, though far from complete, instilled hope for the future.

Into the unused nooks and crannies of every chest, they stuffed all sorts of items, mostly personal and impulsively chosen.

The weapons of choice consisted of compound bows, blowguns and knives. Firearms and ammunition, heavy in most cases, required constant care. Any repair work seemed difficult and procurement of additional ammunition, unlikely. Their noisy quality was counter to the plan of avoiding detection.

They situated all the supply sites away from the coast as a precaution against tidal waves. Establishing them on hilltops deterred visits and reduced their loss from landslides or covering debris. They placed multiple markers, large and durable, at the burial sites and others in a circle five miles from the area. Pointing them in random directions made them meaningless to all except the family. The project was exhausting, expensive, time consuming, and vital.

All members of the family memorized the location of each cache, and every chest contained a coded map of all the chests. Pencils, pens, and paper were added with the thought that if the family got separated, a message could be left.

They trained with their weapons, practiced hunting techniques, built shelters, and learned different ways to make fire. They studied emergency first aid, minor surgery, and combat medicine. They acquired knowledge of edible plants, fungi, animals, and insects. They learned where to look for water and how to purify it.

At their home in Winchester Bay, departure supplies and equipment sat ready. A four-wheel drive vehicle stood by to deliver them to a predetermined place for entry into the wilderness. The family never strayed more than twenty miles from one another and all members knew the location of the others at all times.

Keeping their plans to themselves required intensive effort, not only because of the practical problems involved, but the emotional ones as well. The family lived in this area for close to twenty years and the children had friendships going back to grammar school, pals, confidants, and partners in mischief. People from the joyous times of growing up, people they would leave without a word.

Justin's worldly notions came to pass. The world situation deteriorated. The family's departure into the wilderness was imminent. With plans perceived as both justifiable and plausible, they retreated into isolation.

Dwindling Serenity (Nicole)

The Cessna 150 swooped in a low pass over the Circle 11 Ranch. The pilot, Teddy Stanic, sat next to his wife, Maya. Nicole and her husband, Adam, sat behind them. The plane's maneuver informed Adam's and Nicole's daughters, Julia and Chimene, of their parents return from Seattle.

The ranch sat in the northeast corner of Washington state. It was a sprawling, prosperous ranch that Adam's ancestors pioneered over one hundred and fifty years ago. With succeeding generations, acreage was added, and improvements made to both equipment and stock. The well organized ranch, part green rolling hills dotted white with grazing sheep and part flat land roamed by huge red cattle, was profitable and a model to similar establishments in the area. Forested hills greened the northeastern corner of the ranch. Pristine in tone and appearance, the area supplied timber to the ranch's modest sawmill.

The plane banked to the left, two hundred feet above the ranch house. Nicole elbowed Adam. "Look, the girls." Two waving figures ran from the house as the plane completed a half circle and leveled off. The girls dashed to a truck parked near an old apple tree.

Adam tapped Nicole's knee. "Ten bucks, Julia gets to the drivers seat first."

Nicole smirked. "She's already at the door."

Nicole studied the land passing beneath the aircraft. Her first sky-view at springtime. An enchanting site of pink blooming fruit trees and yellow spotted pastures.

Nicole touched Adam's knee. "Everything is so lush." She pointed. "The sheep are little balls of cotton in high grass."

Adam squeezed her hand. "I'm happy you're happy living here."

Nicole started life as a city girl in Seattle and later lived in San Francisco. For her, the ranch had a fascination tinged with adventure.

Nicole turned, her eyes narrowed with a smile. "I loved San Francisco and teaching. And, of course, the opportunity to dance. But here," she turned back to the window, "I found something special." She spun toward Adam. "A home."

Adam squeezed her hand.

Nicole sat back and closed her eyes. The airy sensation of dance swirled through her mind. She missed the bodily movement. However, her dance play with her daughter Chimene softened the loss.

Nicole took a deep breath. "I love flying."

The plane, now level, flew to the south. Teddy turned to Adam. "Same spot, Adam?"

"Yeah, it's been mowed and the wind sock's up."

Adam and Nicole had taken the train to Seattle to see Nicole's parents and spend a few days with the Stanics. An impulsive decision, it broke the routine of ranch life.

Once again the plane banked to the left as it descended behind a low hill to a newly mowed pasture. Teddy pushed in the throttle and nosed the plane into a sharper descent.

The aircraft made a comfortable touch down, came to a stop, and Teddy silenced the engine with the flip of a switch. "Sorry we can't stay, but Maya doesn't like flying at night."

Nicole undid her seat belt. "The kids will be disappointed. I'm sure they were expecting a flight."

Maya opened the passenger's door, climbed out, and turned to Nicole. "Tell them I'll give them an extra special ride next time."

After unloading the luggage, they exchanged good-by hugs. The Stanics climbed back into the plane, Maya the pilot.

The engine started after a quick spin of the propeller, and the aircraft rolled a short way, turned a sharp 180-degrees, and headed back to the sky.

Nicole and Adam watched the plane lift into the air. Nicole squeezed Adam's hand. "That was fun, and I got to see my parents." They turned to the clamor of a speeding truck billowing a cloud of dust.

Adam chuckled. "They're going to be pissed."

The truck slid to a stop. Chimene jumped from the passenger side. She slammed the door. "Julia drives like a jerk." Her eyes squinted. "Sixty on a dirt road." Adam and Nicole walked to the road.

Chimene, seventeen, the oldest of the two daughters, pointed to her sister. "Her driving is a hazard. She won't listen no matter what I say." Like Julia, she had her mother's black hair, which they both wore long. Chimene's whipped through the air as she spun toward her sister, still sitting in the truck. "You're not driving back!"

Julia was fifteen, smaller than her sister, but a good athlete with surprising strength. She loved horses and played the flute. "You're my sister, not my mother." A sarcastic smile came to her face. Julia scooted across the seat, opened the door, and dropped down in front of her sister. "You're such an old lady. There's no traffic around here."

Adam hoisted the luggage into the back of the truck. "Sixty miles per hour on this road is too fast. If nothing else, it's very hard on the truck."

Julia hugged her mother. "Why did they leave so fast? I thought we were going to get a ride."

Nicole pushed her back to arm's length. "Oh, did you want a ride? I didn't think of it." She turned to Adam. "Did you know they wanted a ride in the airplane?"

"No, I didn't." He looked at Julia with a puzzled look on his face. "Did you want a ride in the airplane?"

Julia stepped to her father, planting a kiss on his check. "Very funny."

Chimene, still sulking, quietly kissed her parents and immediately climbed into the driver's side of the truck. The truck was the ranch worker with a crew cab. Nicole and Adam got into the back seats and the family headed for the house. Nicole put a hand on Adam's knee as she studied her daughters. They would soon be going to college and after that seeking a life of their own.

Nicole remembered her parents' sadness when she told them of her plans to move to San Francisco. "Mom, Dad. It's what I want. I'll be teaching at Brentwood Academy and I'll have a chance to audition."

Teaching proved rewarding beyond her expectations. With an active social life, her situation became most comfortable. She even spent an entire summer touring the nation with a small dance troupe. However, her stay in San Francisco lasted only a few years.

Chimene shouted. "Look who's coming." A large, liver and white Appaloosa stallion pranced a fast trot toward the truck. He was Adam's horse, and at over twenty years of age, was seldom ridden. Adam showed his face and the horse whinnied, nodded and snorted with obvious glee.

The truck slowed, and Adam rolled down his window. "Hi big fella. I'll get you some apples later."

Nicole leaned forward to see the horse. Named "Prepared," Nicole had seen the animal for the first time in a San Francisco horse show. Shortly after that, she had her first sight of Adam.

The horse show occurred in the winter following her summer dance tour. Nicole attended at the invitation of her friend Heather, a fellow teacher. After the show's conclusion, the ladies proceeded to the stables seeking a closer look at the animals.

Nicole wore cream-colored slacks, loose about her legs, but clinging to her hips. Her blouse, white with an opened collar, showed a "v" of powder-white skin between her very ample breasts. Being sleeveless, it exposed arms of real strength. Her hair, long and black, framed her cool-blue eyes. Definitely overdressed for the stables, she had watched the show from the table section, sipping wine coolers. The visit to the stable was unexpected.

They paused to pat the head of a huge Persian draft horse. Nicole spun to her right with a sudden sensation of someone standing next to her. With no one there, she followed the feeling to a man fifty feet away. He stood by a horse Nicole recognized from the show. His back to her, he tinkered with horse equipment. Nicole liked what she saw and liked what she felt.

Nicole maneuvered herself and Heather to within fifteen feet of Adam. Adam looked over his shoulder at the sound of their voices. Nicole pondered his shiny black eyes as he smiled and spoke into his horse's ear. "Now there's a pretty lady." He continued to look at Nicole with a grin that flashed above a strong chin and under a thick blonde mustache.

Their subsequent romance flowed like skiing in powder. Fast, soft and lots of fun. Quick to be lovers, they married after a short ten months and headed north.

Prepared whinnied and halted. Adam shut his window and the truck drove on.

He spoke to the girls. "We've got presents for you guys, but most of the things are being shipped." He squeezed Nicole's knee. "Your mother's ferocious when she shops and she knows Seattle like the back of her hand."

Julia spun around to face her mother. "Tell us what you got."

Nicole smiled. "Later. After dinner."

Chimene spoke over her shoulder. "*At* dinner, please."

Adam inquired. "Were there any calls from the Cattlemen's Association?"

Adam spent a great deal of time with ranch business, a diligence that related more to a sense of duty than desire. It reflected a peculiar side to his personality, a type of paranoia. To be more exact, a fear of unpreparedness. The notion was strong, although not debilitating. Nicole and the children considered it more amusing than serious. They thought it a result of his parents' early death, caused by a sudden storm on Mt. Hood, where they were caught and died of exposure. They were unprepared.

On the premises of the ranch, Adam did his best to prevent that type of scenario from occurring again. He stored extra food, medical supplies, and ammunition. He even built a bomb shelter, installed an auxiliary power generator, acquired two four-wheel drive vehicles, and cut four different departure routes through the brush, one to the north, one to the south, and two others leading east and west.

Adam instructed Nicole and his daughters in the use of all the equipment and its location. He had only a bit of success in getting them to read the survival books that he put about the ranch house. The man's insistence with these precautions was at times difficult, however the women indulged him. They couldn't resist his sincerity and open concern for their well-being.

Chimene answered his question. "All the messages are written down."

The truck arrived at the ranch house and the entire family went in to enjoy the meal the girls had prepared. Life at the ranch remained agreeable and very comfortable, even in a world of troublesome happenings.

On a bright, sunny summer day, Adam called Nicole from the nearby town of Kettle Falls.

"Hi sugar. I just bought a new pickup. A big sucker, four wheel-drive, diesel powered, extra fuel tanks. You'll love it."

Nicole grinned and nodded. "Another truck. I'm sure I'll love it. I already love the other two."

Adam chuckled. "Well...you know. Keep the kids close. I want to show it to them. Let' m drive it."

"Will do love."

"OK. Later."

Nicole folded the phone and put it in her pocket. In a loud voice she called. "Julia!"

Julia was saddling her horse "Buttons" at the far end of the barn. Buttons was a big, fast, and agile animal. Nicole worried when Adam suggested giving it to her, knowing her daughter's aggressive nature. However, Adam's wisdom held the day. "It's better she have a horse with the ability to match her nerve than one she might push too far."

Julia hollered, "Almost finished. What's up?"

"Your father's bringing home a new truck. He wants you and your sister to stick around until he gets here."

Julia rode out of the stall and walked the horse up to Nicole. She looked down at her mother. "Mom, please. I know how to drive a truck, shift gears, four wheel-drive, all that stuff. No need to go through it again."

"Yes, again. Go find your sister and tell her to stay near."

"I don't know what to do with all the keys I have now." She kneed her horse slightly. "Come on, Buttons. The horse carried her out of the barn at a slow walk as the girl continued talking. "Keys for the trucks, keys for the house, keys for the shelter, keys for the generator. My friends come over and ask me, 'What's with all the keys?' And I..." She turned left as she exited the barn and the sound of her chatter ceased.

An hour and a half later, Adam drove up with the new truck, got out, and walked to the women standing at the barn door.

Chimene slapped her thighs with both hands. "Dad. It's another truck. We know about trucks."

Adam waved his right hand. "This won't take long." He bent slightly toward Chimene. "I do this because I love you and care about you."

He took them to the truck and showed them this and that then gave them all keys. Next, the girls were each obliged to drive the truck into the corral, put it in four wheel-drive, and run it back.

Julia, without an invitation, climbed into the truck, drove into the corral, shifted into four-wheel drive, cut the wheel hard and stomped on the accelerator. The truck did a donut and sped back to the barn. Julia jumped out, a big smile on her face.

Chimene walked over to Julia and snatched the keys out of her hands. "Ass. When will you grow up?"

Chimene drove with deliberate calm. Back at the barn, the girls disappeared in an instant.

Nicole ambled over to Adam and gave him a hug. "Maybe we should have a tank on hand." She paused. "I know what we need, a balloon. We could just float off. Just in case all the trucks don't run."

Adam hugged her back. "I'd love to float off with you." He kissed her on the top of the head as they walked into the barn. "I know I am over-reacting, but I read the paper and get scared silly. I feel helpless. So I buy a truck."

"You need a distraction." Nicole stood on her toes and kissed him. "You scared the kids off. They won't be back for hours. And…" she pointed her thumb toward the barn's hay loft, "there's fresh hay up there."

Adam's foresight would prove lifesaving for the family, but naïve in development. Adam's preparations were known by all the locals, including the unprepared and the unscrupulous. The times pulsed with strangeness and trepidation.

The Crumbling

The prophets of old predicted the end of this age would be preceded by the appearance of many fiery objects in the sky. And so it came to be. From the cosmos, streaking comets and meteors adorned the night sky, beautiful and jewel-like. But for many this was a terrifying beauty. Within religious groups, people hung their heads in submissive dread. Others, more optimistic and convinced of their purity, looked skyward anticipating deliverance through ascension.

Public penance became commonplace, and many of the rich surrendered their wealth. Spiritual fanaticism flared, stimulated by prophecy, spectacle, and proclamations of heavenly visitations. At the other end of the spectrum, inner fear of impending doom fostered the extremes of murder and suicide.

Among the flamboyant and frivolous, skywatching became the vogue. Commercial aircraft, refitted with special viewing ports, ferried the rich to high-altitude viewing of the cosmic extravaganza. Books and songs dramatized the events. Clothing and fashion designers, makers of movies, and toys, all found inspiration in the celestial show.

The scientific world, entirely enraptured, fired rockets to sample the wakes of the interstellar objects. Data fed computers hummed and produced information faster than it could be read.

On earth, the long occurring and gradual phenomena of global warming suddenly surged. The band of heat normal to equatorial earth expanded north and south into the major food producing temperate zones. The sterilizing effect of the winter freeze was compromised. Crops endured assaults of insect blooms and disease infestations. Food became the major issue when humanity experienced its first worldwide crop failure.

The majority of cultivated food plants, of similar hybrid types, lacked diversity, which amplified worldwide vulnerability. Starvation touched every continent.

The earth's hot places blistered and cracked in the increasing heat. From within, it rumbled and groaned with terrifying frequency. In California, a long series of closely spaced moderate quakes reduced most major cities to a pile of rubble.

The state's manmade dams crumbled and released rivers that rampaged through towns and cities. Unchallenged fires raged, fed by broken fuel lines and spewing oil wells. The wild lands of brush and forest burned. Of the heroic and desperate who ventured into the smoke and rubble, few returned.

California was not alone in the devastation. Similar disasters occurred worldwide. Large cities suffered the most. Panic and confusion raged. Hospitals ceased functioning, and the sick had to fend for themselves. Law enforcement dissipated into self-defense. Collapse, collapse, collapse.

Where the rains did fall, they were ponderous. Rivers broadened, lakes expanded to seas, and the polar ice shrunk. In Antarctica, a large portion of the western ice slope slid into the sea. Ocean levels rose dramatically evoking coastal flooding. Collapse, collapse, collapse.

Shadow Places
(Justin)

As California rumbled, its population scattered, many people arriving in Oregon. At first Oregonians took the refugees to heart, providing them with what they could. However, as in the town of Winchester Bay, most places soon posted signs indicating the town could hold no more. Charitable efforts vanished. Those with supplies became defensive and those without, aggressive.

Federal officials conducted self-indulgent preparations, and all agencies discontinued contact with the populace. Politicians disappeared into military compounds, which they sealed with zealous security.

Departure time for Justin and his family arrived. Hostilities erupted throughout the area and the periodic sound of shots crackled in the air.

In early fall, the northwest anguished under a persistent drought and the forest dried to kindling. Justin apprehensively studied the sky for signs of rain. However, a greater danger loomed in the eyes of neighboring people. He knew they would fight to live and he wanted no part of that struggle.

The family sat at home waiting for the night and the rising of the moon. They dealt with their fears and sadness, and many silent tears fell in the gloom of their awareness.

At midnight, Justin rose to his feet.
"Let's go."

They walked out the door to their waiting vehicle. They got in and Justin started the engine. "I'm going to make a quick stop at the sea view."

He stared through the windshield. "One more look at the sea and a good-by. It'll only take a moment."

He took their silence as an affirmative answer.

A short, five minutes drive brought them to an overlook, one hundred feet above a sandy beach. Justin and Paul got out of the car. The moon glittered the sea with silver sparks. The air was still, cool and moist with the breath of the sea. Justin's chest expanded and contracted in three deep breaths. "Perfumed femininity."

He turned to Paul. "It'll be a long time before we see her again."

Paul shuffled his feet on sand dusted stone and reached down to pinch a small measure of white granules between his forefinger and thumb. Part of the sand he placed in his trouser pocket. The rest he handed to his father. "I think of the *Orca*, sitting and waiting for an ugly end. That hurts." He strolled back to the car.

Justin gazed across the sea and whispered. "Forget me not." He then turned in the direction of the moored *Orca*. "Sorry gal."

He looked to the east. "Take care, Zoe." Looking at the sand in his hand, he let it drop to the ground.

Not so very far at sea a whale's head rose above the shimmering waves and looked toward land. The creature held the position for a very long moment and then slid slowly beneath the surface.

Justin returned to the car, started the engine, and the family headed inland. They left their home, they left the sea, and focused on the future. A future sure to have pain and struggle, and sure to not leave them unmarked.

They drove through Winchester Bay watching shadowy figures move among the unlit buildings. The four-wheeler never stopped. David stared through the back window until a turn in the road blotted out the view of the little town. Michelle never looked back. She leaned her head against the side window in quiet repose.

They came to and turned down a gravel road that headed east into the dense Oregon coastal forest. When they reached their pre-selected spot, they parked the truck and covered it with brush. Justin turned to the direction from which they came.

He toyed with the keys. "Perhaps a miracle." He put the keys into his pocket.

With packs loaded, the foursome disappeared into the thick dark forest.

Fearful, Bedeviled (Nicole)

Adam's diagnosed paranoia transformed into insight. The locals now praised him and a few apologized for past criticisms. "You did the right thing Adam. Should've done the same thing myself."

However, the congratulations dwindled with the dwindling of supplies accessible to the populace. The local attitude toward Adam and his family changed to an inquiring nature.

"Tell me Adam, just how much food and stuff do you have on hand?"

"Adam, are you willing to share your supplies?"

Adam sat in his favorite living room chair. Nicole lay across from him on a plush, deep red couch. Her eyes studied the heavy beams of the high arched ceiling. The room was large and old and little changed from generations back. Nicole's left arm cushioned the back of her head. Her right arm caressed a hollow and nervous stomach.

Adam rubbed his chin as he stared down at the plush Asiatic rug. "Everybody around here knows I've got piles of supplies." He looked at Nicole. "I've been talking about it for years." He shook his head. "I've even tried to get the others to do the same."

Nicole swung her feet to the floor and leaned forward, her hands went to the sides of her head and her long black hair draped over the rug. "So, you think there's going to be trouble?"

Adam slumped down in his chair, his head eased back and he closed his eyes. "The stuff we have...social order is breaking down." His head moved like a ponderous weight. He rubbed his eyes. "Trouble is on the way."

After a long silence Adam spoke again. "Envision a mass of people...our neighbors? In desperate need...marching on our home?" He took a deep breath. "It's a matter of time...they will soon need things. We can't stop them." He looked deeply into Nicole's eyes. "We wouldn't want to."

Nicole sat back into the couch, her body weak from continued stress. "Perhaps we can give it away now, before anything happens."

Adam stood up and strode to the large stone fireplace. There was no fire; it was late spring. He extended his palms to the mantel and leaned his weight against the stones. "Who gets what? And how much? In the end they'll take it all. How can we survive with nothing?"

Nicole spoke to his back. "Are you saying that we have to leave?"

Adam's head dropped between his arms. "No other way."

Two days later, a very demoralized family gathered in the living room, the girls on the couch, Nicole in Adam's chair, and Adam standing in front of the fireplace. They sat before him, quiet and solemnly attentive. Adam proceeded. "I made a mistake...I don't know why I didn't anticipate it." He looked up and shook his head. "Most of the people around here are totally unprepared. They're running out of everything. And they know we have a lot of what they need."

Nicole sat quietly, her chin resting on entwined fingers. Chimene watched her father with puffy eyes as she wrung a wad of tissues in her hands. Julia curled up at the other end of the couch and pulled an afghan across her body. The girls now spent these days at home avoiding the neighbors and the town's people.

Adam continued. "I was in town yesterday. There isn't much left in any of the stores."

Chimene spoke in a shaky voice. "Why don't we give some of our stuff away?"

Nicole turned solemn eyes to her daughter. "They'll keep coming until everything is gone." She paused. "We don't want to get involved in any sort of confrontation."

Adam took a deep breath. "No, no, we can't fight. We have to take what we can and go somewhere."

Julia's eyes brightened. "Perhaps we can go to grandma's and grandpa's in Seattle."

Adam shook his head. "No. No...perhaps later when things simmer down." He looked at Nicole and turned back to the children. "Things in the city are probably worse."

Nicole's voice cracked as she spoke. "We spoke to grandma and grandpa. They told us to stay away." She couldn't say anymore. She couldn't tell the girls that her parent's phone only beeped a busy signal for the past week. She closed her eyes with a silent sigh.

Chimene spoke in a whisper, her words quivered. "I guess we can go somewhere for awhile? Wait things out? Come back later?"

Adam straightened and spoke with firm words. "Right. We'll take the two big trucks, load'em up with supplies and find a spot to hunker down for awhile. Camp somewhere."

Chimene forced a smile. "When do we go? What do we bring?"

Adam moved to his daughters and stood before them. "We'll take it one step at a time. First step, I'll turn all the livestock loose." He looked at Nicole. "Your mother will start gathering the camping stuff and food...You two," he looked at Julia, "Go upstairs and get your camping clothes together." Julia uncurled and stood. Chimene rose, walked past her father and stood at her sister's side.

Adam sighed. "Do it now."

The girls turned with heads down and walked out of the room and up the stairs.

Adam turned to Nicole. "We'll set up a camp site down the south road, near Chippy Creek. I can make a few runs back to get more stuff." He exhaled a deep breath. "Then we'll decide on step two."

Nicole's eyes welled with tears, she blinked and the tears rolled down her checks. She took a deep breath and looked at Adam. "The good times are over…aren't they?"

Adam didn't answer. In the silence they could hear the girls moving about and talking through their tears.

Adam whispered. "I'm going out to the barn."

They established the campsite at Chippy Creek. Nicole and the girls stayed at the site and Adam made trips back to the ranch for additional supplies. The trucks' AM-FM radios kept them up to date on world events, which continued to deteriorate, panic spreading, cities in riot, and the roads filled with fleeing. Their cellular phones still worked and provided communications. Calls to their neighbors gave the impression that the situation at the ranch remained unchanged. To add to the deception, Adam drove through town several times.

Adam finished unloading the truck after his fifth trip to the ranch. Nicole wrung her hands. "That should be enough." She looked at the pile. "It's more then we can take with us, even with two trucks." She waited for Adam to answer. Then she pleaded. "Let's cover our trail. Onto step two."

Adam kicked a few stones in the dusty soil. "I want to make one more trip. A few more medical supplies." He looked at her. "We can hide some of this stuff and get it later."

"Adam, we have enough!" Nicole's hands started to shake and she clasped them together.

"It'll be OK …I'll call you on the phone before I go in." Adam's eyes shifted away. "We need a reserve." He shrugged his shoulders. "Just in case." Adam walked to the truck and climbed in. "I'll look the place over with the field glasses. If anything is amiss, I'm outta there."

"I don't like this Adam, please stay. Please!"

"It's OK. One more trip." His hand reached for the ignition key and the truck's engine roared into life. Nicole stepped back. She unclasped her hands and whispered as the truck rumble away.

"It'll be OK." The truck went over a little rise and was gone. Nicole continued to watch for several long moments. She took a deep breath, turned, and took long strides to the other truck to await his call.

About forty minutes later the phone rang. Nicole picked it up and pushed the appropriate buttons.

"Hi."

"It's quiet. I'm going in. This won't take long."

"Leave the phone on."

"OK."

The engine rumbled as Adam drove to a storage building. She heard the truck door open and close. Later she heard sounds of things dropping into the back of the truck.

"That's enough Adam, that's enough!"

Minutes later the cab door opened and she heard sounds of Adam climbing in. The truck door shut, but almost instantly, reopened and a powerful blast sounded..

Nicole flinched and sucked in a breath. Terror rose from her bottom, passed through her heart and filled her mind.

"What the fuck?...You asshole. You killed the sucker." A husky voice, a voice Nicole knew. A matching facial image flashed in her mind. Rufus Dawn, the owner of a dilapidated ranch close to town. Nicole's legs trembled. The phone spoke with a younger voice. "What' d you wan' a do?...Take prisoners?" Nicole's quivering hand rose to her mouth.

Rufus spoke again. "He was taking that shit somewhere... he came from down that road."

Again the younger voice. "Hey, is that cell phone on...Shit." The phone went silent.

Nicole's swallowed. The phone fell from her grip and her vision blurred. On trembling legs she exited the truck, her hands groping across the truck's front fender. She blinked to clear the blurring in her eyes and scanned the campsite. A large pile of equipment, two tents and a smoldering fire sat near the shallow stream. Chimene sat with her back toward Nicole, her legs drawn up tight to her chest, held by her arms. Her chin rested on her knees as she gazed at the stream. Julia stood at her sister's side, facing her mother. The young girl's hand reached out and shook Chimene's shoulder.

Nicole squinted at a strange droning sound that blocked all other sound. Her hands shook and her stomach hollowed. Her gaze turned to the stack of supplies. Her mind whispered. *The killers will follow the road to this place. You have to do something. The children, the children.* She looked at them.

Chimene rose and turned to face her. Her mouth moved, but the words were inaudible to Nicole. The girls started walking toward her, grimacing, their strides queerly labored.

Nicole ran to the supplies and shouted hysterically. "Load the truck! As much as we can. *Hurry.*"

The girls came to a sudden stop and gawked at their mother. Nicole picked up a box and shouted. "Do what I said."

The girls didn't respond. Nicole dropped the box and rushed to them. She grabbed each by the hand and dragged them to the supplies. "Pick something up and put it in the truck!"

Nicole picked up a box and threw it in the truck. The girls responded with ugly scowls, and barraged Nicole with questions. Questions that fell on deaf ears.

Nicole spun around, her eyes glaring. *"Do it. Do it now."* The girls responded and tried to match their mother's speed.

They filled the truck and covered the contents with a tent. Nicole directed the girls into the cab. She climbed in behind the steering wheel and gave the ignition switch a quick twist. The big engine roared with power that restored Nicole's hearing. The girls were again jabbering for an explanation. Nicole raised her hand to silence them. Tears welled and ran down her checks.

Her voice stammered. "Your father...is dead...someone shot him." Her hands gripped the top of the steering wheel, and she rested her head on her knuckles. "I heard the whole thing on the phone." She took two short breaths. "They know we're here...our supplies. They're coming to get them." She rolled her head toward them. "We have to run." Her hands trembled.

Chimene's eyes widened and she shouted. "What?"

Nicole ignored the question, pushed herself back into the seat, shifted the transmission lever into drive and depressed the accelerator. The truck's back tire sprayed gravel and proceeded down the bumpy, primitive road.

Nicole acted with pure instinct. Step two presented itself as going. Simply going. The world was now a jungle and they were pursued by predatory animals. They could hide in the jungle, but they couldn't get out of it.

Nicole drove with sporadic shivers, the sound of the shot echoing in her mind. *My lover's gone, his strength's gone, we're alone.*

Julia sat next to her, rocking back and forth, her hands covering her face. Chimene's hands moved in a silent one-person conversation. Nicole hung onto the steering wheel, eyeing the darkening shroud of a day's end. *I don't want the night.* She looked in the rear view mirror. *We're alone.*

The primitive back road ended and a paved one began. Intuitively, Nicole turned to the southerly direction. No sleep needed, she drove on and on. Periodically the girls talked to each other in short conversations. At other times, one or the other cried. Questions directed at Nicole where answered by the phrase, "I don't know." Silence enveloped the trio.

Droning hours gave way to a new day. Nicole stared through weighty eyes and slouched behind the wheel. Exhaustion provided a near vacant mind and the sun's light bestowed a touch of warmth. The girls, awake, stared hypnotically, their eyes merely slits.

Nicole slowed and turned left at an intersection. She didn't know why; she just did it. The road separated two fields of knee-high, brown-dry grass. The matching images enveloped her scattered mind with simplicity.

Three miles down the road, to her left, a group of bushy trees stood like a bundle of green umbrellas. Nicole slowed the truck, shifted into four-wheel drive and turned into the surprisingly smooth field.

She drove to the trees, stopped and silenced the truck. Nicole slumped across the steering wheel with her head turned toward the girls. "Get the sleeping bags." She blinked. "Find a place under the trees. I'll sleep in the truck."

Julia and Chimene listlessly climbed out of the truck and when they returned, Nicole lay across the seat, asleep. They covered her and withdrew to the trees.

Hours later Nicole, startled by a dream, sat up. Still dreamy, she fumbled to open the door. Slowly she stepped to the ground and walked to the rear of the truck. With her bladder in urgent pain, she dropped her trousers and squatted with a relaxed sigh. Wheel tracks led back to the road. Nicole mused. *A trail. The killers. They'll find us.*

Jerking up her jeans, she rushed to the spot where the truck left the road. Sure of emanate danger, she panicked and attempted to make the trodden grass stand. Again and again she tried, only to yield to exhaustion and frustration. Teary eyed, she crumbled to the ground. "Adam's gone. Adam's gone. Adam's gone."

She lay there for close to an hour. Without the imposing thought of her children she would have stayed there. Instead, she struggled to her feet. Her fingers brushed sweat from her eyes, and her lungs sucked in a weak breath. On languid legs, she followed the twin trails back to the truck.

Halfway there Nicole knelt, gasping with stomach pain and a pulsing pressure in her skull that fluttered her eyes. The golden grass turned a shiny red. She slumped to the ground and rolled to her back. The new position calmed her.

Moments later she opened her eyes to the thump of feet. The concerned faces of Chimene and Julia stared down at her. Julia held her interlaced fingers beneath her chin, as if in prayer. "Are you OK?"

Nicole extended a hand to Chimene, who pulled her to her feet. "I'll be OK." She looked around trying to remember where she was. "We should eat something. Keep our strength up." All three ambled back to the truck.

The next few days dribbled by slowly. With little enthusiasm, the family set up their tent and arranged their food and water. The shock of their situation surged in waves of panic, provoking bouts of crying. Their sleep was intermittent, and always restless.

Days passed, the panic eased into lethargic depression and long periods of empty sleep. Conversations were short; food was consumed in tiny bits.

A week passed. In the early light of a new day, Nicole strolled to the back of the truck, nibbling on a dry cracker. She stopped and turned in the direction of the road. A vision of its firm blackness extending afar stimulated a curious desire and she made slow steps toward it. The flattened grass had regained some of its height and she tore at the tops.

For the first time since the shooting, she functioned without pain. A comfortable sensation, but empty.

Near the road a bird whistled and a breeze rustled the grass. Nicole's eyes shifted to a drone-like sound that came from her left. "A bee, perhaps a fly?"

She looked for the insect, but only tiny white butterflies fluttered above the grass. The noise persisted and undeniably grew louder.

Suddenly alerted, Nicole's body stiffened, her dreamy mind cleared and she instinctively crouched, her fingertips touching the ground. People were coming. Nicole dropped flat to the ground. She never saw the vehicle, she just heard the Doppler effect of its coming and going. She closed her eyes with relief. "Still safe."

She lay there, the left side of her face cushioned comfortably on the top of her right hand. Her black shirt absorbed the rays of the sun, relaxing tense muscles. She studied the miniature forest of leafless trees and a black ant that scurried among them. It zigzagged across the top of her left hand and fled back to the grass foliage.

Feeling colossal, she pondered the plight of the insect. So many ways to die. "Might even kill it myself. Perhaps when I walk back to the truck." Nicole rolled to warm her chest. "But that's your life." She exhaled a breath. "And you will live it."

Nicole rose into a cooling breeze that swirled about her torso. The smokey veil of confusion that came with Adam's death evaporated. She blinked an acknowledgment. What are we doing?

Her mind immediately clicked off the factors of their situation. Nicole got to her feet and stood quietly listening for the bee sounds. There were none. With long strides and swinging arms she headed back to the truck and her moping children.

Half-way there, she yelled, "Julia, start unloading the truck."

She cupped her hands over her mouth. "Chimene. You help her. We need to know what we have."

The girls turned to her shouting, but stood quietly, gawking. Nicole went to the cab, found a pen and paper and returned to her daughters. "Call out each item you unload."

The girls didn't move. "Let's go, girls. It's time to get our shit together."

Chimene leaned on the truck's tailgate. "Why?"

Nicole hesitated only a moment. "Because we are alive." She walked past Chimene, stopped, and turned to face her. "Let's go. Start unloading."

Chimene smirked, spun around, and grabbed the tent covering the supplies. With a yank she tore it from the truck. She hefted a box. "Dried food, noodles, and vegetables." Nicole wrote it down.

They had plenty of food, ample medical supplies, including stores of vitamins. They had enough weapons to equip all, including the needed ammunition, four boxes of extra clothing, and most importantly, manuals on survival. They found a few tools, an ax, a small shovel, and some rope. Their complement of items showed a good balance.

Chimene leaned on the truck. "We don't have much water left."

Nicole looked at her. "True."

Chimene spoke in a monotone. "We have to find some."

Nicole's face was deadpan. "You have something to think about."

Nicole estimated their fuel at near a hundred gallons of diesel. Enough to travel many miles and many more if they kept their speed down. Nicole smiled at the girls. "We got lots of fuel and perhaps we can find more."

She walked to the cab. "Put everything back into the truck." She paused and turned. "Put the guns in the cab. With some ammunition."

Julia slumped against the truck. "What are we doing? Are we going somewhere?"

Nicole answered without looking at her. "Yes! We're going somewhere. We're definitely not going to sit here." She turned to Chimene. "No water. Right?"

Chimene looked at her feet. "We need a river, a stream?"

"Right. We'll find one."

Julia picked up a box of trapping devises. "Maybe a well?"

Nicole smiled. "Maybe. We'll go south...and think about things as we go."

Nicole reached into the cab and popped the hood latch. At the front of the truck she raised the hood. Her eyes scanned the engine compartment. "Oil, transmission fluid, water."

She put her hands on her hips. "No law and three women traveling alone with a truck-load of goodies." She pulled the oil dipstick from its tube. "Trusting anybody will be foolish...we have to be careful...even if we meet someone we know."

Everything looked fine and she shut the hood. The girls were talking at the back of the truck.

Julia handed a box to her sister. "Yeah! I think it's time to get out of here."

Chimene put the box in the bed and gave it a shove. "It won't matter what we do."

Nicole stepped forward. "It matters. We have a chance. Things will get better. We'll find a place and stay out of the way. We're strong and we have supplies. We have weapons."

She sat on the tailgate. "Come on guys. The good days are gone, but some day the bad days will be gone." Her eyes brightened, and she shook her head. "We'll go on." She jumped from the tailgate and went to the pile of supplies and opened a box. "Here." She waved a book in the air. "How to Catch Small Game and Cook in the Wild." She picked another. "This one, "Battlefield First-Aid." And this one, "Shelter in the Wilderness." We have what we need, except a place to hide."

Her smile faded. "Remember, whoever doesn't try will be a burden to the rest." Her eyes darted from one girl to the other. "Do you understand?"

Chimene shouted. "No! I don't understand, I don't understand anything!"

Julia repeated the statement. "Mom, I don't really understand either."

Nicole's face clouded. "Then don't understand. Just do as you are told."

Chimene expelled a long breath. "Where are we going?"

Nicole threw the books back into the box. "We'll head south toward northern Nevada. Your father's...cousins live there." She gripped her stomach with one hand. "They came to visit us years ago. You two were very young at the time."

Julia toyed with a length of string. "Are things OK there?"

Nicole expelled a breath and put her hands on her hips. "I don't know what their situation is, but it's a place to go."

Chimene turned to her sister. "It may be worse there."

Nicole made no reply, just walked away and leaned against the front fender. A few moments later Julia headed for the trees dragging her sleeping bag.

Nicole closed her eyes. "We have to be prepared to defend ourselves." She let the words sink in. "Even if it means shooting someone."

Julia froze in mid stride. "Shooting someone?" She started to walk again. "Now I have to shoot someone." She flapped the sleeping bag. "The good days are gone. No shit." She turned and again headed for the trees mumbling all the way.

Chimene put her hands on her hips. "Shoot...someone! Shoot someone! Sure! Why not."

Nicole, satisfied that the thought was planted, opened the door of the truck and climbed in.

———————————

The next day, a bright and sunny day, they got into the truck, drove back to the road and turned, following its southerly path.

———————————

Near noon, from the other direction, a sedan approached. The distance between the two vehicles dwindled quickly. Nicole held her breath, and in a flash the car passed.

She looked at the girls. "Hopefully...nobody will want to make contact."

Here and there, abandoned vehicles, like carcasses of the dying society, littered the roadside. They passed a tent city that dotted a field near a small creek and were not tempted to stop.

As night neared, they sought a place to camp. The road wandered through farmland with an occasional house and barn. There were no signs of life, neither human nor animal.

———————————

After rounding a curve on a downhill grade, Nicole slipped the transmission into neutral to save fuel. Up ahead, built close to the road and surrounded by open fields, a farmhouse stood silently. A large oak tree shaded its southern exposure and a tire swing dangled from one of its limbs. A cozy porch spanned the front of the house.

Nicole conjured an image of a young family. Two small children played near the swing and their mother stood on the porch, waving a towel and calling their names. Behind the house a dust cloud followed her husband's tractor. Nicole sighed a sadness.

Chimene sat up and pointed. "Why don't we stop there?" She paused. "It looks quiet enough. Perhaps there's something we could use."

Nicole depressed the brake softly. "We'll slow down and take a look. Don't get out of the truck if I stop." The truck slowed, its engine rumbling at ideal speed. The girls fidgeted. A gravel driveway extended to the side of the house. Nicole shifted the truck back into gear and eased it up the driveway.

The house was a simple two-story, peaked roof dwelling, painted sunny yellow with white trim. Broken windows on the porch allowed curtains to flutter a welcome in a warm breeze. The front door stood open.

Nicole held the transmission lever tightly, anticipating a quick shift into reverse. They were almost to the side of the house, no more than thirty feet from the porch. Nicole hit the brakes hard, shifted into reverse, looked over her right shoulder and depressed the accelerator sharply. The truck spun a bit of gravel and moved backward.

Julia screamed. "Stop."

Nicole hit the brakes. *"What, what?"*

Julia pointed. "Mom, that's a playpen on the porch."

Nicole stared. "Oh God, oh God."

Her eyes shifted back to the grass near the house where corpses were lying. A man, a woman and one large, yellow dog. All three had dark, circular stains in the area of their chest. There had been madness here.

Nicole wiped the sweat from her brow and ran the same hand down her jeans. "Maybe a baby." She shifted the truck into park. "Chimene, hand me the pistol and when I get out, you get behind the wheel." Wide eyed, Chimene whispered as Nicole carefully stepped out of the truck. "You're going in there?" She handed her mother the pistol and slid behind the wheel.

"The faster I do this the better." The pistol, a 44, hung at Nicole's side. She turned to the girls. "Leave the truck door open." She took a few steps and turned again. "I'll have to look through the entire house."

She turned back to the house and walked hurriedly to the porch steps and up to the playpen. "It's empty."

Nicole looked through the open door and listened. A cricket fiddled from somewhere under the porch. Other than that it was quiet.

Carpeted stairs led up into darkness, and a hallway led to a kitchen. There, an open door showed part of the backyard. Nicole took a breath and stepped into the house.

She looked to her left and flinched at the sight of another body lying on the floor of a small bedroom. Another adult. Nicole moved quickly to the kitchen. A startled chicken escaped out the back door. Nicole pointed the gun in the chicken's direction. Scared silly, she sighed. "Chicken burgers for lunch, almost."

She lowered the gun and went to the back door. The yard area, cloaked in the deep shade of two large oaks, had only a few tufts of grass. Nicole mumbled. "No baby." She turned about sharply.

She made a check of the rooms upstairs and dashed out the front door, running to the truck. Chimene slid over and Nicole slid in. "No baby. We're outta here."

She backed out of the driveway and headed down the road. "We'll drive through the night. We can rest during the day." They took turns behind the wheel, and the night passed slowly.

At dawn, Nicole drove, and the girls unfolded a road map. Nicole stopped, and Chimene sprawled the map out with both hands. "Where the hell are we?"

Julia pointed. "Here, here." She moved her finger to another position. "We passed that bridge last night." The map indicated an unpopulated area to the east with only small, unpaved roads apparently wandering aimlessly.

Nicole's finger traced one of them to its end. "We'll take this road to the end and see if there's a place to camp." She looked at Chimene. "OK?" Then she looked at Julia. "Sound OK?"

Chimene spoke first. "Looks like a long way to go for a one night stay."

Nicole bit her lip. "What we saw yesterday is making me nervous...perhaps we can find a spot to stay longer."

Julia yawned. "A place to hide. I'll go for that." She looked at her mother. "I'm sure Dad's cousins are in as big a mess as we are."

Nicole folded the map. "OK, we have the time. Let's check it out." The girls nodded, and Nicole depressed the accelerator.

They found the road and turned east onto its gravel base. On either side of the road the land was uncultivated. It had a wild appearance, semi-desert with low hills to the east. No buildings and no fences. They drove over one hill and to the top of another. Here the gravel gave way to dirt, and the land spread out into a broad plateau. Nicole shifted the truck into four-wheel drive and cruised slowly for another half hour.

A small grouping of trees to the north came into view. Nicole spoke as she studied them. "I'm going to head for that bunch of trees."

The girls said nothing. Nicole turned toward the trees and drove slowly over bumpy land that rose gradually. The trees, about two miles away, seemed small and lonely on the broad plain. However, the need was isolation and water.

They found what they wanted. Eleven trees surrounded a small pool fed by a slow-moving creek. The creek came from the high hills to the north and made a sweeping turn before wandering to the west.

Nicole jumped out of the truck. "Perfect! We'll camp here."

Chimene ran to the pool. "It looks plenty deep." She smiled at the others. "Plenty deep for a bath."

The cove provided security in its remoteness, and the ample water supply satisfied the last of their survival needs. The family set up a campsite with little enthusiasm.

They stayed a week and then another and yet another. They familiarized themselves with the area and its wildlife, practicing hunting and trapping techniques. More weeks passed.

Life went reasonably well. Julia had not forgotten her beloved flute, and her sweet music added to their leisure time. They seldom used the radio. In fact, an asteroid impacted without their notice. However, periodic earth tremors served as reminders of the unstable situation. On one occasion, after a particularly strong rumble, the creek dried up. They waited a full two days for the water flow to return, and were at the point of packing up when the stream refilled.

Only once did humanity make an appearance. It was on a hot, quiet afternoon. A moving cloud of dust appeared from the east on the dirt road they had traveled. Its speed indicated some sort of motor vehicle.

Julia pointed. "Mom! There's someone on the road. I think it's a motorcycle."

Nicole looked up from her task of skinning a rabbit and watched with mild interest. She glanced at the fire pit, its breath, a tiny spiral of smoke.

"I'm not interested in meeting anyone."

Chimene came running from the stream. "Let's find out who they are! We need help." And she waved her arms.

Nicole shouted. "No, no. We can't take a chance. We don't know who it is."

Chimene fired back. "We need help!...What do you know about things?" She moved a few steps toward the cloud. "We're in the middle of nowhere...we need someone to help us." She ran to the fire pit. "I'm going to start a fire and keep it going." She glared directly at Nicole. "I'm not going to sit here forever."

Nicole lowered her voice. "You're not going to make a fire."

Julia ran to Nicole. "Maybe she's right. We can try."

"No! We can't take the chance." She glanced at the dust cloud and turned to the girls. "We're OK. We're doing fine." She motioned with her hand at Chimene. "Leave the fire be and come over here."

Chimene grimaced and walked to Nicole. Nicole put an arm across her shoulders. "Nobody can be trusted. Have you forgotten that our neighbors shot your father? Have you forgotten the dead people on the side of the road?" Tears welled in Chimene's eyes.

Nicole continued. "We have each other. That will have to do for now...It's a matter of time, just a matter of time." The girls made no reply and simply went back to what they were doing.

In the following days the weather changed. Cooler air carried a scent of moisture, making Nicole nervous. She and her little group would not do well in cold conditions. Their location, much too exposed, had open plains on all sides.

At the next meal Nicole brought the subject up. "I believe the warm weather is nearly over. This place is going to get cold. We're too exposed. I think it best that we move south before winter."

For a few moments they sat in silence, eating and thinking. Julia laid her half-empty plate at her feet, rested her elbows on her knees, and gripped her hair on either side of her head while she talked to the ground.

"This is all so crazy. I wish it would end."

She let go of her hair and jerked her head up. "Maybe it's over? Maybe it's almost over?"

Chimene interrupted. "It's not over. The world doesn't fall apart and come back together in a matter of months."

Chimene stood up. "Maybe we can find a cave up there." She pointed to the northern hills. Nicole didn't bother to look. "We can't get up there and we don't want to be up there."

Chimene pleaded. "But if we leave here, we'll be looking for trouble. Why not stay and let it try and find us?"

Nicole poked at the cooking fire. "The winter will be trouble, and it will find us."

Nicole had always had an enchantment with the south. It was one of the reasons she had gone to San Francisco after college. Strangely, its feel danced in her mind again. With a wrinkle of her brow she brushed the reflections aside.

"The past winters have been mild. Most likely global warming. In any case I don't think we will have to move very far, but we should move farther south, just to be sure." She paused. "Here, we're too exposed."

Chimene took another look at the hills. "No, we can't go up there. You're right. And we can't stay here." She paused. "Perhaps we'll meet others."

Much later, long after the sun had set, Nicole contemplated a star-filled sky. A meteor streaked a quick slash from the north. Nicole whispered. "Somewhere to the south there's warmth and comfort."

Nicole got to her feet and went to the tent. The girls slept and Nicole wiggled into her sleeping bag and closed her eyes. The meteor's flash replayed in her mind and conjured images of whales and dolphins swimming in a starry sky. She slipped into a very restful sleep.

Two days later the family packed up and sat in the truck waiting for the long-idled engine to warm up. Nicole stared through the windshield. "This place has been good to us." She waved her right hand. "Thanks for the rest." She turned to the girls and smiled. Their facial expressions exposed a touch of fear. "We can handle it. We're strong." Julia and Chimene forced a smile.

Nicole shifted the transmission into drive. The engine's throb accelerated. The next two days were uneventful. The land was flat, the road mostly straight, the weather hot. They traveled at a slow speed. To their comfort, the road was void of traffic in either direction. At night they parked off the road, hiding in the darkness. One of them slept in the cab and the other two under the truck.

At the beginning of the third day Chimene drove while Nicole sat on the passenger side of the truck, her eyes lazy with boredom. She blinked at something large and yellow and immediately sat up straight. "Construction equipment up ahead. That could be fuel."

Julia's eyes followed her mother's pointing finger. "Oh yeah. It's a bulldozer and…one of those road things."

Chimene drove to the equipment and stopped. Everybody got out, excited with the break from the tedium of the drive. A quick inspection showed that the dozer had the prize they sought in a tank behind the driver's seat. Julia looked up at the large tank. "How do we get it out?"

All three sat down near the truck and pondered the situation. After fifteen minutes, Nicole stood up. "What we need is a fuel can, which we have, and a rifle, which we have."

Chimene gave her mother an incredulous look. "You're going to shoot a hole in the tank?"

Nicole spun in a half pirouette. "You bet." She stepped to the door of the truck, opened it and pulled the rifle from behind the seat. She explained. "It'll work." She smiled at the unbelieving girls in front of her. "The fumes burn, not the liquid."

Julia eyes widened. "Are you sure?"

Nicole replied. "You bet." She hefted the rifle. "I've never done it, but I remember it from a TV show, or something. I think it was a war movie."

Julia elbowed Chimene. "OK mom, let's do it."

Chimene got up. "I'm not sure about this." Julia gave her another nudge with her foot. Chimene looked at her sister and smiled. "But...what the hell."

Everyone got behind the truck and Nicole took aim. The shot penetrated the tank and diesel fuel poured from the hole. Nicole smiled. "Julia, get that fuel can. Chimene, get a stick and make a plug."

The dozer tank, nearly full, refilled the tanks of the truck easily. They hammered in the plug and set off with Nicole driving.

Hot, still air hovered on the black, broad road that stretched as far as the eye could see. The truck droned at 35 mph. The girls dozed, bored by the slow speed, and the monotonous scenery. Nicole watched for wildlife, her window rolled down, and her head resting against the door.

She glanced at the large side view mirror. A dust devil approached from the left, spiraling smoothly over the rough terrain.

Nicole muttered. "Bad omen." The notion, a soft whisper in her left ear.

The dancing dust slowly dissolved. But Nicole's stomach knotted. She studied the road ahead, then looked to the right and left before returning her attention to the rearview mirror.

A blurry thing sat poised in the shimmering heat. It materialized into something black and narrow and moving at high speed.

Nicole alerted the girls. "I think there's a motorcycle behind us. Take a look."

The girls repositioned themselves. And Julia spoke first. "You're right. It's a motorcycle."

Nicole gave instructions. "Get the guns out and make sure they're loaded."

In short time the motorcycle caught up. It slowed and moved into the left lane. Painted a brilliant green, it carried two people. Both people wore dull green leathers and bubble face helmets, also green. The machine passed slowly, the riders scrutinizing the truck and its occupants. Nicole observed. The girls rubbernecked.

Abruptly the cycle's engine roared and it raced ahead. The mysterious machine rippled and dissolved into the heat patterns.

The girls relaxed. Julia yawned. "Nice bike."

Chimene leaned forward. "I can still see them." A moment passed. "Now they're gone."

Nicole frowned and tapped the steering wheel with rapid beats of her thumb.

Chimene flopped back in her seat. She shrugged and shook her head. "I still think we should talk to people."

Near noon the family stopped to eat and relax. Nicole sat in the shade of the truck, her back to the front wheel, and munched rabbit jerky. Chimene sat next to her. Julia, perched on the truck cab, sat on a sleeping bag and watched for traffic.

Nicole looked skyward at the vapor trail of a high-flying aircraft. "Everybody's headed south."

She loved flying. Whenever she and Adam vacationed, she insisted on flying.

Chimene followed her mother's gaze. "I remember the time I flew to L.A." She blinked. "It's strange to sit here and think of people way up there." She turned to her mother. "Sitting in soft chairs, reading magazines and beautiful women offering them things to eat and drink."

Nicole swallowed her jerky. "It's probably military, but I know what you mean."

She brushed at a few pebbles stuck to her palm. "Perhaps we could find a government station. It could be a place to go." She turned to Chimene. "Your father did have some political weight. Maybe we could get in." The radio warnings to stay clear of government installations contradicted her thought. But the notion sparked Chimene. "Mom! Do you know where one is?"

"No Chimene, I don't." Chimene's face brightened with a smile. "I'll look at the map." She nodded her head. "I'll find something."

Later that day while Nicole was again driving, she glanced into the rearview mirror. Her expectation was an empty road. Instead, there was another blurry image rising in the heat.

"Mirage, I hope. I hope," she thought and took a deep breath.

Long moments passed. Nicole adjusted the mirror. The blur separated into two blurs. She alerted the girls. "Take another look out the back window. We have more company."

Chimene moved lazily and stared briefly, her voice, singsong. "Motorcycles, at least two and I think more."

Nicole sat up in her seat. "Shit!"

Julia yawned. "It's probably OK. They'll pass like the others."

Nicole depressed the accelerator. The truck sped from 35 mph to 70 mph. The objects behind faded.

Chimene questioned. "What's the problem?"

Nicole wiggled on the seat. "Just testing."

Minutes later Chimene reported. "I can see them again." And a moment later. "They're getting closer."

Nicole spoke through clenched teeth. "They're trying to catch up." She glanced at the weapons at Julia's feet. "Julia, hand me the .44."

Julia looked at her. "Mom!"

Nicole extended her hand. "Hand it to me. We'll play it safe." She took the weapon and placed it on her lap.

Nicole slowed the truck to 50 mph. "No need to waste fuel. They have more speed than we do." She paused. "Let's see who they are." Another pause. "Perhaps Julia's right and they'll simply drive past and be gone."

The apparitions took on distinct forms. Julia reported. "Four motorcycles and getting closer."

The motorcycles moved within one hundred feet of the truck and came no closer. The grouping of vehicles continued to travel in unison for about five miles. Nicole waited and the girls watched.

Nicole was about to say something when the inside cycle broke ranks and sped to the driver's side of the truck. Nicole's right hand dropped to the .44.

The truck's large wheels gave it exceptional height. Nicole looked down at the riders. A beautiful machine with a huge engine gleamed with many chromed parts. Two riders wore pale yellow leathers and shiny helmets of the same color. A dark plastic bubble covered their faces. Nicole wondered how they could tolerate such cover in desert heat. The bright blue cycle had fairing in front and storage cases attached to the rear. The riders scanned the truck and then Nicole.

Nicole's fingers drummed the sun-warmed steel of the .44.

She watched the driver twist the handle bar control and the motorcycle decelerated back into formation.

A moment later it accelerated again. This time it drew up on the passenger's side of the truck, a dangerous maneuver for the cycle was no longer on the road. However, they accomplished the feat with ease, and the girls crowded the window. The cycle maintained the position only briefly and decelerated to its previous position in the formation.

Nicole gripped the steering wheel with both hands, her right thumb again tapping its plastic. "Where have these people come from?"

Chimene studied the motorcycle contingent. "The motorcycles are so clean." She looked at her mother. "They want us to stop. Don't they?"

Nicole nodded. *"That's* something we're not going to do."

She looked into the side view mirror. "They must have a campsite somewhere in the desert."

She looked in the rearview mirror. "Aren't the riders in back wearing green?"

Julia answered. *"Yeah!* And the ones on the outside are the ones that passed us before...I'm sure."

Chimene's turned to her mother. "They went and got their friends." She paused. "This is not good."

Nicole bit her lip. "They've come a long way to look at us." She paused. "And I guess they like what they see." Another pause. "They want to see if we'll stop on our own...or...perhaps they are waiting for the truck to run out of fuel."

With that thought Nicole glanced down at the fuel gauge. It registered a little less than a quarter of a tank. Nicole reached down with her left hand to touch the fuel tank selection valve at the base of her seat. "We can cruise for a very long time. Far longer than they can."

Suddenly, the motorcycle next to the riders in yellow came roaring up close to Nicole's side of the truck. The manner of the maneuver indicated annoyance. This machine also carried two riders. They wore red leathers and rode a black bike. The rider on back repeatedly pointed to the side of the road. Nicole ignored the gesture.

She scanned for signs of weapons and saw none. A twinkling light on the side of the cycle's fuel tank caught her eye. The rider, realizing the object of her attention, raised his knee. The effort was late and the image etched itself into Nicole's mind: a five-pointed star inscribed in a circle, the sign of Satan. Alarmed, Nicole sucked in a short breath. She made no mention of the new information to the girls.

Again, the back rider motioned Nicole to pull over. Nicole again ignored the gesture. The cycle reduced speed and drifted back, the rear rider pounding his fist on his knee. Nicole accelerated the truck to 75 mph. "Perhaps they're low on fuel."

Two of the cycles flashed by, their engines screaming with high rpms. These were bikes from the back of the formation, the riders in green leathers. When approximately one quarter of a mile ahead, one of the machines moved into the truck's lane, sealing off its path on the paved road.

Chimene rubbed her knees and unintelligible sounds issued from her mouth. Julia stared ahead, her mouth gaping, her eyes wide. Nicole watched the cycles maneuver, her knuckles blotched white on the squeezed steering wheel. The truck speed was 70 mph. Nicole spoke softly, "Chimene, take hold of the .38. Julia, get the shotgun, load it and hold it with the butt to the floor." The girls fumbled with the chore and kept glancing up at the riders ahead.

Nicole yelled, "Get it done." The girls settled and completed the task.

Ahead the cycles maintained their position while slowing down. Nicole looked at the speedometer. Their speed had dropped to 65 mph. "Shit."

She accelerated the truck back to 70 mph. The cycles were suddenly on top of them. Nicole engaged the auto speed control and drew her feet away from the pedals.

She shouted to the girls, "They're trying to slow us down...stop us. I might have to run them down."

The back rider on the machine in the truck's lane made a complicated move. When finished, he faced the truck. The separation narrowed to thirty feet and continued to close. Nicole locked her arms at the elbows and her face contorted as she jammed her heels against the seat.

The distance closed to ten feet. Julia squirmed nervously and shielded her eyes with her hands. Chimene watched, her hands extended to the dash and continued to mumble incoherently.

Simultaneously the bikes drifted closer. The backward rider on the cycle in front could no longer be seen over the hood of the truck. Nicole grimaced, and beads of sweat pushed through the skin of her forehead and rolled down her cheeks. A vision of broken, mangled bodies beneath the truck made her gag. In fear and courage she persisted. The distance shrank to no more than two feet.

All three women screamed as the back rider's head popped above the hood of the truck. His left hand gripped some part of the grill, and the other pounded the metal of the hood. The drumming, though not loud, was dreadful. The rider's arm rose high like a hammer and slammed into the hood. His green helmeted head gave him the appearance of a gigantic insect, a creature void of feelings. The fist pounded six times in three sets. The women twitched with each blow.

Then abruptly the insect head vanished, and its cycle shot ahead, veered to the left, and rapidly decelerated. The back rider reversed his position to face forward and in short time they were back in formation. The game was over, at least that one.

Nicole, shaken, brought her feet forward and blew a weak whistle. Chimene lowered her head between her arms. "Holy shit!" The cab filled with the stench of Julie's vomit.

Nicole took quick glances at her daughters. "Easy, easy! It's not over."

She looked for the .44. Its use, imminent. The weapon had fallen to the floor in front of Chimene. Nicole reached down and released the seat latch. The seat slid back to the stops with a thud. Nicole grabbed Chimene by the arm. "We have to change places. You have to drive."

Chimene's eyes bulged, and she shook her head emphatically. Nicole pulled her half way onto her lap. "You have no choice. You have to."

Nervously, Chimene took hold of the wheel and Nicole slid under her to complete the transfer. It took several tries in a coordinated effort to get the seat back to the forward position.

Nicole picked up the gun, released the safety, and contemplated its use. Her stomach turned in a surge of fear. She wished from the bottom of her soul that the riders would just turn and leave.

That did not happen. Instead one of the green motorcycles left the formation and sped toward the truck. The green rear rider reached forward to grip the controls while the front rider rose to a crouching position on the gas tank. After a quick swerve at the truck and an acrobatic move, the front rider transferred to the truck bed. It took a moment for him to find his footing among the supplies. His green head looked up as he high stepped toward the cab.

Nicole's mouth dried as she slid the back window open and pointed the weapon to show her intentions, hoping for his departure. She would have allowed it, had he made the effort. However, he did not and took one more step.

The blast of the weapon was horrendous. The .44 caliber projectile hit the rider in the chest and levitated him into the air. For a moment, he looked much like an astronaut in gravity-free space. Then, as the wind caught his body, he flew away and dropped to the road. His blood splattered his companions and they swerved to avoid his body.

Nicole, narrow-eyed, ears in pain, watched the body bounce as its limbs broke and dangled.

His co-rider lifted his face shield revealing little except a red mouth and white teeth. From that cavity he issued a scream as he accelerated his machine toward the back of the truck. Nicole would not permit another intrusion. In a wooden, relaxed manner she aimed the weapon and pulled the trigger.

Another deafening explosion filled the air, the rider's helmet shattered, his head vaporized into a cloud of pink mist dotted with dark fragments of plastic that fluttered in the blasting wind. The headless rider continued to advance. Blood spurted a red, lace-like pattern that disintegrated in the speeding air. Nicole shrieked as the cycle slammed into the back bumper. The handlebars twisted and the front wheel folded, stumbling the beautiful machine. It vaulted into the air and slowly twisted with the headless man still clutching. It flew off the road and in a blast of dust, dirt, and rock, it disappeared

The other riders slowed with the first shot and were at least a fourth of a mile behind. Nicole slammed the rear window shut and faced forward. She paled and gasped for breath. Her ears throbbed in pain. The hideous images of the shootings flashed in her mind. Her lips dripped with saliva as vomit threatened to rise.

Chimene's panic-induced grimace, relaxed. After looking into the rearview mirror, she slowed the truck to 50 mph.

The engine droned, and Nicole retched. Julia reached to comfort her mother, but Nicole, unable to relax, stiffened at her daughter's touch. She took a deep breath and slumped into the seat.

Chimene smiled and spoke without taking her eyes from the road. "We made it! I'm proud of you Mom. You did the right thing."

Unresponsive, Nicole stared at the gray dashboard.

Julia turned to the back window, the shotgun in her hands. It was late afternoon.

Twenty minutes down the road, Julia punctuated the silence with a fear-filled, child-like voice. "There's a cloud coming."

Nicole's trance broke with the words. "What do you mean, a cloud's coming?"

"Over there." Julia slid the back window open and pointed. "A cloud of dust."

To the east, the dust of two speeding motorcycles rose above the desert. They were almost even with the truck and they would soon pass.

Chimene watched the cycles. "They're not going to make it that way." She depressed the accelerator. "It's the ones in yellow and red."

Julia's voice cracked. "The green one's are coming up behind."

Nicole, exhausted from the surge of adrenaline, hung her head back and stared at the top of the cab. "Not again, please, not again."

Chimene shouted. "They're going to try and cut us off." She turned to her mother. "We can go west, cross-country."

Nicole shook her head. "No, no, they can follow us and they're faster in the desert. No, you're doing the right thing. Keep going. We can outrun them. Just don't let them get ahead."

Chimene's eyes brightened. "OK."

Nicole continued. "If the cycles get close, we'll use the guns to keep them back."

Chimene grumbled through clenched teeth. "Bastards. Bastards. They're bastards!" The speed of the truck reached 80 mph.

Nicole tapped Julia on the leg. "What's going on behind?"

Julia, kneeling on the seat, spoke without looking at her mother. "They're a ways back and staying there."

Nicole turned to look. Her energy sapping, revulsion progressed to hatred. She took a deep breath and tightened her grip on the pistol. "Why don't they get closer?"

As the race neared the five-mile mark, Nicole studied the cycles to the east. "They're moving this way." She paused. "They know we're onto them."

She leaned back and took a breath. "They have only one option left." She looked back at the cycles. "And that's to stop us by any means, even if it's a crash."

Nicole thought of the rifle behind the seat. However, before she could act, the truck's big engine coughed, sputtered and died. The vehicle's speed rapidly slowed. Nicole slammed her fist into the seat. "I forgot to switch the fuel tanks. Even the fuel lines will be dry."

She screamed at Chimene. "Switch the tanks."

Chimene reached to the dash with her right hand. "Is it here on the dash?" Her fingers fumbled. "I can't remember."

Nicole's eyes flashed. "No, no! There's a lever on the left side of the seat. Move it one position back. Hurry, hurry."

The truck rolled to a stop. The cycles to the east moved ahead and then back to the road. They made a wide turn reversing their direction.

Chimene groped for the fuel switch. "I can't find it."

Nicole pulled her back and leaned across her lap. She found the switch and repositioned it. "Quick now, start the engine."

Chimene turned the ignition key and the starter motor whirled the fuel vacant engine.

Nicole looked down the hood of the truck and sucked in a deep breath. The two cycles were closing in fast. She turned to the rear. They too were closer. The trap nearly closed.

"Julia, point the shot gun at the green riders...and shoot. It'll keep them back."

Nicole picked up the .44. Chimene kept the starter motor engaged. "Start you son of a bitch, start."

Julia fired the shotgun and Nicole was unprepared and jumped, striking her head on the roof of the cab. "Shit. Shit.

Shit." She rubbed her head vigorously, but her eyes remained focused on the approaching cycles.

She groaned. Her only shot was through the windshield. She twisted to view the bikers to the rear. They had slowed. Julia glanced at her mother and aimed the shotgun once again.

Nicole spun back as a bullet smashed through the windshield exploding it into tiny pieces. Chimene screamed in pain, her left arm dangled, but her right hand kept its grip on the ignition key and the engine roared into life. She slammed the transmission lever into drive and stomped the accelerator. The rear wheels spun blue smoke as the truck charged forward.

Julia hunched when the glass sprayed the cab. But she quickly rose and fired a panicky shot to the rear. Nicole rose off the seat and again banged her head. *"Shit."*

Denying the pain and squinting into the wind, she tried to aim the .44 over the hood of the truck. But the force of acceleration on the heavy weapon made the effort impossible. She saw the flash of more shots being fired by the bikers. They made thudding noises on impact. Nicole turned to Chimene.

The girl stared ahead showing no pain and no fear. In fact, she displayed a slight smile, and when the cycles were almost upon them, Chimene, without indication, yanked the steering wheel hard to the left. The three machines smashed into one another with a combined speed of close to 130 mph that produced an explosion of metal, glass, and flesh.

The blue bike, second to the left, impacted the truck's bumper, amputating the lower left legs of both riders while slamming the bike to the pavement. The spinning machine held the driver's right arm and leg to the road. Chomping like the jaws of a beast, it devoured the man and smeared the road red.

The back rider flew into the air and returned to earth with downward momentum only. He struck the pavement face first and snapped his neck. The stump of his leg hit the ground like the blunt end of a fence post and held his torso grotesquely in a posterior up fashion.

The bike with riders in red struck the center of the bumper and grill of the truck. The helmet-covered head of the driver drove deep into the hood, buckling the metal all the way to the windshield. The man's backbone fragmented, and with that limpness his legs lifted up over his back, and his heels came to rest against the windshield casement.

The back rider and cycle disappeared beneath the truck, the front-end bouncing high. When it came down, the rear axle seized the machine, and the truck twisted from side to side, before breaking free. Within the truck, only Chimene remained in the same position. Nicole, thrown forward, got tucked under the dash panel. Julie, still watching to the rear, flew backwards, her bottom impacting the glove compartment with the shotgun discarding at the same moment.

Chimene absorbed the force with her legs and her right arm which bent the steering wheel, but she maintained her grip and her foot still depressed the accelerator. The truck left the road only briefly after impact and now rumbled on with gaining speed.

Nicole struggled pass Julia's kicking feet and crawled onto the seat. The wind buffeted her face and she tried to fend it off with her right hand as she turned toward Chimene.

The girl stared ahead, her eyes narrow slits in the wind. Nicole shouted, "Slow down. It's over." Chimene turned in Nicole's direction and smiled, but continued to depress the accelerator.

Nicole switched off the ignition. The truck slowed and with Nicole's help stopped. Chimene relaxed and slumped across the steering wheel.

Nicole turned to the rear window. The two remaining cyclists, clad in green, stood near their fallen comrades. She frantically searched for a weapon and found the .44 at her feet. She hoisted the vomit-slippery weapon and studied the last of the riders.

Julia pointed the shotgun and fired. Nicole, again startled, banged her head once more on the cab roof. "Oh shit. Not again."

The .44 slipped from her grip and she wiped her hand on her shirt; she did not take her eyes off the riders. She again heard, but only faintly, the awful animal-like scream, after which the riders remounted their machines and sped away into the pale shadows of a day's ending.

Chimene moaned, and Nicole turned to her injured daughter. She pulled her away from the steering wheel, and Julia jumped out of the truck and ran to the driver's side to assist. Nicole gave Julia immediate instructions. "Get the medical kit."

The bullet struck Chimene just below the elbow and apparently broke a bone. They put a tourniquet on Chimene's arm, removed her limp form from the cab and placed her on a sleeping bag.

The bullet wound was jagged and long. Nicole could see small chips of pink bone. With the military field surgical kit and its manual of instructions, she fumbled through the necessary treatment, which included a plaster cast. It held the arm bent and across her stomach, but left the wound exposed. Mercifully, Chimene remained unconscious through the entire procedure.

Nicole closed the field kit and placed it back in the truck. Julia, exhausted, found another sleeping bag and reclined near her sister. Nicole sat in the dirt, her back against the rear tire and her daughters before her. She looked into the eastern sky at the rise of a full moon. Fatigue pervaded her aching body, but her mind stayed alert.

Agonizingly she rose to her feet and commenced inspecting the truck. As she walked, she rubbed her head and counted the lumps. At the front of the truck she startled. In the emergency of her daughter's plight she had forgotten the contorted corpse embedded in the hood.

She mused. "The windshield gone, but it's not a necessity." She looked under the truck. Oil dripping from the transmission caught her attention and she fetched a container to catch the liquid. "The leak will be worse when the engine's running."

She knew the truck would be useless when the fluid was gone. They had to find a safe place and find it soon. The heavy bumper protected the truck's front end and the all-important radiator. Nicole took a deep breath. "The truck will run. But for how long?"

She stepped back and studied the body crammed into the hood. "I have to get rid of that." Amazed with her composure, she approached the body unruffled. Nicole stepped up on the bumper and pulled the man's legs away from the windshield. She calmly watched them fall to the front of the truck. The crumpled metal of the hood gripped the helmeted head and the man's arms and legs dangled. Nicole climbed down and stepped back to pondered the situation.

A moment later she stepped forward and grabbed a handful of leather from each pant leg. She gave a hard tug, but quickly released her grip. The torso, with its pulverized backbone, hideously and very noticeably lengthened when she pulled. Nicole shuddered and went to the truck cab. She found the jack handle.

Leaning through the windshield she pried the helmet loose and the dead man slid to the ground. She exited the truck and went to the body. Still composed, she tucked the man's feet, one under each arm and stepped backwards. Her eyes widened when the torso lengthened again. She looked into the night sky and continued.

At the side of the road she stopped and looked down at the body. The corpse was even longer. Nicole's sagging face erupted into a smile. She scolded herself for her stupid and gruesome humor. With waning energy she completed the task. She left the body behind a bush, a short way from the road. Giggling in a low tone, she returned to the truck.

However, she could not resist another look. Immediately her hands went to her mouth to block any loud laughter. The man's head protruded from one side of the brush and his feet from the other, indicating a human of ridiculous length. Nicole rushed back to the side of the road and found some lose brush to cover both the head and feet.

With a hand-covered mouth, she walked to the bed of the truck and found a sleeping bag, threw it to the ground, and collapsed upon it still trying to contain herself. She drew her body into a fetal position and used a portion of the sleeping bag to gag her mouth.

She lay there, shaking as the tension of the day drained from her body and mind. She found release, not in a flood of sorrowful tears, but in laughter, uncontrollable, body-trembling laughter. Nicole's red, swollen eyes welled with moisture and her stomach muscles ached. Rolling to her back, she peered up at a twinkling star. Her lungs expelled a large volume of air and she was instantaneously asleep.

Cosmic Punch

As Justin and his family sought shelter and seclusion in the wilderness of the North Pacific, and Nicole and her family ran for survival, the world tumbled at an ever-accelerating rate into chaos. Nature no longer tolerated the indulgences of the planet's human inhabitants, and nature has but one remedy for the over-population of any species.

From space, an object of iron and rock traveled at great speed toward the earth. Through observation, its lethal trajectory was asserted.

The capability to remedy the asteroid problem was eliminated by the worldwide collapse of structured societies. The oblong object, approximately the volume of a sphere one eighth of a mile in diameter, was calculated to impact the earth fifteen hundred miles due west of the cape of Africa at an angle of fifty-six degrees, coming out of the east. Tidal wave action and the disruptions of the weather patterns comprised the predominant forms of destruction. Radio recommendations to evacuate the coastal areas concluded governmental preparations.

Two weeks later the rock from space pushed into the earth's atmosphere. The atmospheric resistance produced a heat that altered its color from dull black to bright orange and ultimately to a whiteness that rivaled the sun's intensity. With a booming voice it announced itself to half the world's population. Its splash produced a water-trench of unimaginable proportions.

The heat of the rock boiled the sea, and no moisture touched its skin. The encroaching water exploded into steam expanding one hundred times the liquid volume, producing an enormous geyser and a powerful shock wave to herald its deadly arrival.

To the north of the impact on a small island, a lone man walked the uninhabited southern beach. It was a bright and clear day and the man concerned himself only with the finding of turtle eggs.

But a sun-bright object shattered his tranquility as it blazed across the sky and disappeared below the horizon. Enchanted, he watched, and soon a ponderous noise rolled upon the island, engulfing the witness. Bellowing clouds rose and spread across the blue tropic horizon. Another thunder hammered, and an invisible force slammed him in the chest. He staggered a few steps backward and grimaced in confusion. He couldn't imagine. He just couldn't imagine. He sat in the sand, and pondered with gluing curiosity.

A short time later, he jumped to his feet and watched the sea drain away as if by suction. It drained a long way out exposing rock and coral that had never felt the rays of the sun, nor felt the dryness of air. Countless sea creatures flopped, crawled, and squirmed, as their ocean suddenly constricted to a series of small puddles.

He remembered a story he heard as a boy, a story of a giant wave, and what preceded it. Now his eyes comprehensively studied the receding sea, and he quivered at the site of a rising mist beyond the coral reef. He coughed with fear when a dark wave, like moving marble, rose above the mist.

The man turned a pale face inland. His legs wobbled. His arms reached with fingers that clawed the soft air. He moved slowly, the sand sucking at his feet, his eyes bulging.

He uttered a female name and tears dripped down his cheek. The ground rumbled with the heavy weight of the wave and its shadow cooled the skin of his back. The enormous force pursuing him bristled every hair on his body. In shaking courage, he turned to meet the inevitable.

Urine warmed his legs as he trembled before the liquid wall. He never saw the top of the wave. He looked into its middle, clenched his fist and bellowed from the fathoms of his soul.

The wave surged across the island effortlessly. It then subsided into the deep ocean to again hide its presence. It moved through the sea toward other lands, dispersing energy with the movement of soil, rock, plant, and animal. It ran over the flat lands and squeezed into river valleys, reaching far inland to grasp with liquid claws. Few shores had the height to deflect its force.

The splash wave struck the Atlantic Coast of South America and ricocheted back across to Africa. From there it found its way into the north Atlantic where its final energy dissipated. Millions died.

The body of the asteroid burrowed deep into the earth's crust and eventually came to rest, though the energy it carried from space proceeded to the earth's molten core. The core quavered and nullified the binding force of gravity that gave the earth's crust its stability. Deep slabs shuffled, closing ancient volcanic vents.

In the southeastern part of the United States, the rumbling land rose at mid-central Alabama. The land ruptured and grew to mountain-size, exposing ancient stone. The rise trailed to the southwest, making its way to the east coast of Texas. In Texas, the land sank and was soon flooded by the waters of the Gulf of Mexico.

South of Mexico, on the thin strip of land that connected the two continents, the countries of Costa Rica, Nicaragua, and Panama underwent violent tremors that lasted nearly two months. These lands then sank beneath the waves of the two great oceans, leaving the span dotted with a string of small islands.

Current changes altered ocean temperatures, and sea life that could not flee perished. The waters reddened with the rotting dead. Mammoth storms formed off the western coast of

Africa and sped across the open sea gathering strength from the heated waters. Most slammed into the coast of the Americas. Others spiraled at mid-ocean, charging and recharging in pockets of heat before bearing down on the lands of Europe.

The Antarctic spawned storms on a daily basis and kept the southern hemisphere in constant chaos. These sea-born tempests spiraled into the north Pacific, assaulting one landmass after another. Their raw, unbridled power made life on most islands impossible. The coastal ranges of even the large landmasses were habitable only on a temporary basis. Life soon learned to retreat inland to avoid the raging weather.

The number of living creatures scrambling about on the planet rapidly declined. The weak died first; the strong followed. In time, most humans struggled alone or in small groups, living like wild animals, darting from hole to hole in search of food and shelter. Existence became a horror of degeneration and death.

Sky Rock and Devil's Deed (Justin)

Justin's family, living in the forest, kept to their plan, and responded to other people by disengagement: avoiding contact and fading away. Seldom did the family stay in one location for more than a few days, and they always put effort into covering up their trail. However, the temptation to linger at a comfortable location was a constant temptation.

On a late summer day the family had just finished their evening meal. Justin took the last sip of his herb tea. "Let's get a good night's sleep. We move in the morning."

Michelle stood up. "Dad, why not stay a bit longer. We haven't seen anybody or heard anything." She pointed to the east. "We have that little stream over there and lots of berries in the meadow and…"

Paul cut her off. "Michelle, don't start that crap again. We move for safety. Somebody may have seen our smoke or something and could be moving this way. When it's time to go, it's time to go."

"Buzz off Paul! I have a right to my say." She threw a twig at him. "You're like a horse. You go tromping off with a load on your back and you could probably eat bark off a tree. I happen to be a little more human then you." She turned to her father. "We have a nice place here. Let's stay awhile."

Justin took a deep breath. All eyes were on him. "Safety first." He was tired. His daughter's pleading gripped his heart, but it was a repeated conversation. He turned away and walked to his sleeping bag.

Michelle sat down, defeated by two words. She put her face in her hands and kicked the dust at her feet.

She looked up to the sound of David's voice. He walked toward her as he pulled a paper from a leather packet. "Sis, I want to show you something." The packet held maps and navigation stuff.

Justin reclined and listened. David sat down next to his sister and unfolded the paper. "See here." He pointed with his finger and tapped the paper. "Here's where we are." His finger zigzagged across the paper. "And this is the way we go tomorrow." His finger moved again. "Then we will most likely go here and then here." He looked at her and smiled. "It's something of a circle. We could be back to this spot in three or four weeks." He stood up and refolded the paper. "What I am trying to do," he hesitated as he carefully returned the paper to the packet, "is to set up a type of circuit. A whole series of special spots." He smiled again. "Then we will move from one good spot to another." He waited a few moments for her response, but none came. He took a short breath, his eyebrows went up. "Summer at the sea shore, winter in Paris. Give it time. It'll be fun."

Michelle smiled. "Yeah! It's going to be fun." They both started to laugh. Michelle stood up and pointed at his packet. "Tomorrow I want to see those again. I'll help you plan."

Justin closed his eyes, a smile on his face.

In times to come, Michelle's pleading did result in extended stays at some comfortable locations. But never did they stay longer than five weeks at any place. Michelle enjoyed the stays, and the men often indulged her whims. Surprisingly, Paul was the one most willing to help with campsite adjustments. He'd start as if he wasn't interested, but then suddenly agree and start working on the task. When finished he'd find her and ask, "Does that look OK?" Michelle always lavished him with praise and found ways to return the favor.

The next day the group broke camp and headed off with David in the lead. They traveled quickly in the fair weather, headed for a new region where the map indicated a number of promising campsites with water and open space where game might frequent.

Justin, after spending most of the day at the rear of the contingent, jogged ahead and caught up to David. "Let's go to that high spot you showed me this morning. The one to the east." He adjusted his backpack with a little bounce and a tug at the straps. "I want to use the radio, catch-up on world news." David thought a moment and replied. "Sure. It won't make much of a difference." He frowned. "You really think they're still broadcasting?"

Justin smirked. "Oh yeah. It's a government station. And I'm sure they want to keep their fingers in the pie, regardless of how messy it is." David stopped and grasped the compass that hung on a string around his neck. He studied the instrument a moment. "OK, we make a forty-five to our right and it should be the next hill over."

About an hour later they reached the top of the hill. They dropped their backpacks, broke out some jerky and relaxed. Justin dug into his pack and found the radio. He turned it on and it crackled with static. A moment later, soft music drifted through the air.

David huffed. "That old crappy music again."

Justin studied the jerky in his hand. "I like it. Nice and easy for these troubled times." A large smile spread across his face. "The big bands, Bing and Bob, Fred and Ginger."

David smirked. "Bing and Bob? That sounds like a dance." His eyes squinted at his father. "Is that what it is? Some sort of dance?"

Justin laughed. "You got it. The old 'Bing and Bob.'" He stood up and shook his left shoulder. "You bing to the left." Then he bobbed up and down moving to his right. "Then you bob to your right. And that's what they call the 'Bing and the Bob.'" He kept dancing to the rhythm of the music, binging and bobbing across the top of the hill.

Paul sat watching to the south and east and turned to observe Justin's antics. He smiled broadly. "No, no. 'Bing and Bob' is something you do in boxing." He fell to his back and laughed into the sky.

Justin did a pirouette. "The dance came from boxing. I think it was Sugar Ray Robinson who made it popular."

Michelle, watching to the north and east, shouted over her head. "I don't get it." And then to herself. "'Bing and Bob.' Everybody is falling out of their tree."

The music stopped and Justin sat down. A deep male voice issued from the radio. "We interrupt the show to recap the ongoing story of the asteroid 'TREX.' Impact will occur in seven days at a location west of South Africa in the mid-southern Pacific. As stated before, if you are in range of this broadcast you are *not*, I repeat, you are *not*, in immediate danger. However, you are advised to move away from the coast. Move at least five miles inland." He then gave the usual warning of government security regulation. "All people are to stay clear of government installations. This is a requirement related to national security needs. This rule is strictly enforced. Violators will be prosecuted with extreme prejudice. There will be no exceptions."

Michelle rose to her feet and spun around to the others. "An asteroid! An asteroid! What the hell next? I'm sick of this. I'm just sick of it." She sat back down, crossed her arms in front of her and rocked back and forth.

David spoke up. "We're at least ten miles inland."

In the days before impact the family paused in their travels. The forest grew progressively quiet and even the breath of the wind appeared too still. From above, whether real or imagined, a nearly inaudible hum announced the asteroid's presence. Birds spent most of the time perched. Even the noisy crows hushed. The sun beat down with hot rays, and living things languished as death spiraled from above. Justin spent hours of the ensuing nights staring into the sky seeking the deadly form. A form he never saw.

The day of the asteroid arrived. Justin and his family, after a restless night, rose early. They cooked venison and heated herb tea over a small fire. Each member of the family found a place to sit at the fire. Conversation was almost nonexistent.

David retrieved the radio and tuned in the government station. The familiar voice of the announcer spoke on the expected subject, the asteroid 'TREX.' Ground zero was pinpointed at two hundred nautical miles, northeast of Tristan de Cunea. The ETA stated to be 2:18 p.m., Pacific Standard Time.

Justin pulled out his watch. "It's 11:11."

He got up and signaled to David to turn off the radio. Again, his senses detected the low hum that pressed from above. He looked at the faces of his children and saw their sadness and fear. Justin took a few steps from the fire and with repeated deep breaths he filled his lungs with fresh air. He forced himself to stop squinting and stood as straight as his back would allow. Compelling a smile he turned and strode back to the fire. After pouring a cup of tea, he hoisted it high into the air and toasted the planet earth.

"Here's to you, you ancient bag of dirt. And the punch in the belly you will soon receive. I know you're going to make it. Therefore, so will we." He drank a mouthful of tea.

David rose and offered another toast. "A punch in the belly. I've had a few of those."

Paul jumped up. "Yeah, it's happened before."

Michelle stood slowly, a tear in her eye. "I love the earth. She's mother earth."

Justin strode over to Michelle and put his left arm around her. "Let's have a special noon meal. A little party for mother earth. *A victory party.*"

The mood of the group, though not festive, moved with acceptance. They had two rabbits to roast and honey for dipping, instant mashed potatoes to boil, and wild mushrooms to fry. With diligence they prepared the meal.

Later, after eating, they engaged in easy conversation. At 2:00 pm, they turned their attention to the radio. A scientist, his voice strained with emotion, presented factual information on expected damage. Most of it related to tidal wave action.

Presently, the transmission switched to an aircraft circling ground zero. This broadcaster, a scientist as well, commenced a precise description of the event. At first he did well. However, when the situation progressed to awesome dimensions, his voice succumbed to sobs, and the transmission ceased.

Michelle, with shaking hands, switched off the radio and went to sit near her father. Sensing her unsteadiness he put an arm around her. The treetops swayed when a strong gust of wind rushed by from the west. Silence and still air followed.

A month passed, and the family continued their movements through the forest. During one of these movements they came upon a deserted town located on the banks of a small river. The town's back pressed against a steep wooded hill. Half way up the hill, Justin and his children crouched. Their backpacks lay in a pile nearby.

Justin studied the empty town with a pair of binoculars looking for signs of movement. Approximately twenty-five buildings of different sizes composed the town, almost all being private homes. An asphalt road led to and passed the little burg following the track of a shallow, tree-lined river. Streets of gravel branched into the town proper. Maple and myrtle trees gave cover from rain and sun.

The town sat quietly. Leaves whispered in the wind and petite birds fluttered about. A few abandoned pickup trucks and passenger cars, most with their doors hanging open, grimly dramatized the peaceful scene. The green grass surrounding the picturesque homes sparkled with broken glass. Most house doors either dangled from one hinge or lay flat nearby. The black skeleton of a large, burned out structure added to the somber appearance of the lifeless town.

Justin spoke without lowering the binoculars. "I wonder what happened here?"

Paul spoke questioningly. "Riot?"

Justin handed Paul the glasses. "No, I don't think so. Too small of a town."

The family, being very cautious, completed their second hour of observation.

David stood up. "Let's go in."

Justin made no comment, but Michelle agreed. "I'm ready. Maybe we can find something worthwhile."

Paul spoke from his stomach. "Ohoo! I'd love to find some canned fruit."

Justin relented. "OK. Me and Paul go in first." He looked at David and Michelle. "You two stay here and both of you," he raised his eyebrows, "keep watching. If anybody or anything starts to move around, you give us a yell."

He handed the glasses to Michelle. "If all is OK, I'll wave."

He turned to Paul. "We stay in sight of one another."

Justin and Paul preceded down the hill and into the back-yard of an old house. After the shade of the forest, the heat of the baking sun penetrated their clothing. Justin followed Paul past a white picket fence and onto a gravel road. The crunch-ing noise of their boot mingled with the buzz of insects and the chirping of small birds. They walked about one hundred yards to the paved road and stopped. Justin turned and waved to David and Michelle. He spoke to Paul. "This place is empty. Let's get back to David and Michelle."

The family gathered in the shade of a large maple near the white picket fence.

Justin spoke to Paul. "You and David team-up. Take the hill-side of the town." The two brothers set off at once. Justin hollered after them. "Be careful!" He moved in the direction of the paved road. "Come on Michelle, we'll go this way."

The two groups moved alertly, occasionally turning to check the area behind them, never going into a house alone.

In every house of the thoroughly sacked town, broken fur-niture littered the rooms. The small amount of food remaining was either contaminated with bugs or partly eaten by animals.

Eventually the two groups united at the other end of the town.

Paul pointed. "Look at that." A five-pointed star inscribed in a circle-blazed red on the side of a white house. The emblem, depicted with precision, indicated dedication. Below and to the right of the emblem, a single word showed in a bold red script, Spade.

Justin contemplated the graffiti. "What happened here was no simple riot."

David changed the subject. "I've seen lots of tools. Perhaps we could bury a bunch and mark the spot on a map."

Justin shrugged his shoulders. "We don't have any way to protect the stuff, and it would be a lot of work for a maybe." He rubbed his chin. "I don't like the feel of this place."

Paul, in a less serious manner grinned. "Lookie here." He slung a small sack from his back and knelt down before it. Reaching in with both hands, he pulled out a large assortment of candy bars. Sweets were rare in the forest with only honey and fruit as a source.

Paul laughed. "Junk food, real live junk food."

He displayed the treasure with pride and after a few moments divided the cache, keeping a few extra bars for himself. The family wasted no time in sampling the stuff. The stale candy quickly rendered their jaw muscles weak. As they chewed their prize, their words were washed with saliva, and sentences abruptly ended when teeth stuck together.

Justin unwrapped a chocolate bar. "Let's make another round. This time we stay together." They strolled through the town, trading candy and making jokes.

Michelle spat a piece of candy out. "Let's find a house, a big one and spend the night."

Justin entertained the temptation. "Wouldn't it be nice to sleep in a bed?"

Paul agreed. "Oh yes. Lay on a bed and eat candy." Walking in front of the others, he suddenly stopped and spun around. "A television, music, a can of beer."

David yelled. "I saw some beer in that big blue house."

Paul's eyes widened. "You saw beer and only now mention it?"

David smiled and held his hands out. "It was only a six-pack."

They altered their course, following David's pointing finger. The route took them past the burned out building. Justin noticed something white in the black ash and when he went to investigate, the others followed. A bone protruded from beneath scorched wood, unusual looking yet, oddly familiar. Justin nudged it gently with his boot. David moved ahead and peered behind a partially standing wall. He pulled back momentarily. "Oh shit."

The others in turn looked behind the wall and then shuffled back through the rubble to the center of the road. Behind the wall a pile of entangled human bones lay on black wood, dusted with gray ashes. Half-burned shoes and clothing intermingled with the bones.

Paul cringed. "Why so many people in one little room?"

Justin knitted his brow. "There must be fifty people in there."

The bones were clustered in one corner, most absurdly the last refuge at the time of fire and death. The skulls varied in size indicating people of all ages. The sacking of the town probably took place in the light of the fire. It took little imagination to comprehend the horror of the evidence.

Justin, Paul, Michelle, and David turned their backs on the little town and headed up the slope to their waiting backpacks. They discarded the prized candy bars as they walked.

The day started out as sunny and warm, but now, clouds moved in rapidly from the west. They were dark and rain, imminent.

The group was unaware of the disrupted ocean currents and weather patterns that brewed colossal storms in the southern oceans. The storms would drive the family from the coastal forest and sadly reduced their number by one.

Wind and Death
(Justin)

In the equatorial south, the Pacific ocean spawned immense cyclones at a constant rate. They spun west, or to the north, whipping spirals with velocities exceeding one hundred and fifty miles per hour. Cloaked in torrents of rain, many pushed inland transforming deserts into swamps and swamps into seas.

The storms assailed the lands of tall timbers in northwest America, reducing the foundations of the giants to a slimy paste. The winds slashed the wobbling woods as scythes in a field of wheat. Soon, many of the gargantuan plants lay prone, and immense craters pocked the forest floor while tentacle roots dangled in the wind. Other storms pin-wheeled to the north, rounded the Aleutian chain, and in a further oddity, dashed westward into Russia or southward into Asia. Most living creatures hastened inland to escape the fury. Among these life forms, Justin's family struggled.

Caught in the open by a fast-moving storm, Justin's family sheltered in a precarious hovel of toppled trees and fallen limbs. They huddled as mice, wet and cold. The air was filled with the high-pitched howling of the wind and the thundering groans of conifers dying a violent death. It took two days for the storm to pass.

In still wind and sunny light the family emerged from the organic ruins. In a small clearing, they built a large fire to dry their clothing, absorb its heat, and cook a hot meal. A deer crushed by a fallen tree supplied the meat. Paul found it while gathering wood and tended to the task of butchering the animal. Michelle gathered wood and Justin and David studied maps.

David pointed at the map as Justin looked over his shoulder. During the days of hiding, the family made the decision to seek sanctuary in the Cascade Range on the far side of the Willamette Valley. David's finger indicated their present location.

"We're here and the supplies are there." David's finger moved to another spot on the map and tapped it repeatedly. "There's a cave here that we can hold up in." He looked up. "And it's not far from the supply dump."

Justin walked a few steps away and turned back to David. "Judging from the past, we'll have about four days before the next storm."

David looked at the map. Justin lowered his head and walked back to David. "I don't think we can make it."

David didn't look up. "We have no choice." His finger touched the map again. "The stash we're headed for is on the top of a hill. It's totally exposed. A bad place to be in a storm."

Paul stuck his knife into the deer carcass, stood up, and walked over to David. With hands dotted with pieces of meat, he took the map and studied it for a moment. "We can get to the supplies OK, three days moving fast. But it's going to be tight getting to the cave." He handed the map back to David. "I remember that cave. It'll be a good place to hunker down."

David, with two flicks of his index finger, dispatched two morsels of meat from the map. He looked at his father. "Then that'll be it. A hard push to the hill and a hard push to the cave?"

Justin nodded. "That's it." David folded the map and Paul returned to the deer.

The fire blazed high that day. Michelle purposely made it so. They all had wet clothes and were without fire for the last two days. Michelle stood with her back to the blaze, the men before her, her tone questioning. "We run for four days and then a nice cozy cave?"

Paul finished washing his hands in a puddle and stood up. "That's it. Run and duck."

Michelle turned to face the fire and whispered. "Life is great."

Justin pointed at the meat hanging in the tree. "We cook all of that. Eat a bunch now. We'll take the rest with us."

Justin scowled and his stomach tightened with an uneasy vague premonition. He walked over to the meat. The carcass, strange to look at with all the broken bones, drooped into something unrecognizable. He looked up into the trees. Moisture clinging to pine needles glittered like crystals in the clear sunrays. He listened to David's optimistic words.

"We can make it. We might get a little wet, but that's no big deal."

A chill swept Justin's heart, and David's frail face grinned with the usual assurance. "Things will go the way they are supposed to, Pop."

Inexplicably, Justin's eyes watered and he turned away.

Three hours later, their clothing dry and their bellies full of warm meat and many cups of hot tea, they shouldered their packs and headed for the supplies at a brisk pace.

They traveled under a blue sky with calm air and ate their meals on the move. Justin, in a rare talkative mood, scurried amongst the marching contingent in conversation with each of his children. His talk had very little to do with the situation at hand. Michelle found it most peculiar. "Why all the chatter Pop? It's not like you."

Justin laughed. "True. I just had a surge of pride. I'm proud of you guys, and it makes me want to talk." Michelle grabbed his hand and squeezed it.

On the third day, the group arrived at the buried supplies. They dropped their packs and located the bogus surveyor's plaque. Paul unfolded his utility shovel and dug to the first chest. Only a few things were taken, which included maps of the Cascade Mountains. They hoisted the chest out of the hole and acquired an axe, a rope, and a light cable. They buried the chest, distributed the items, and returned to the cover of the woods.

With night upon them they built a small fire and cooked a quick meal of rice and dried vegetables. With bellies warm and full, they reclined beneath a large fir tree for a night's rest.

Just before dawn Michelle awoke to the clamor of rustling tree branches. She got up, lit the prepared fire, and heated the tea.

Only a light touch awakened Justin. "The storm's close. We'll have to hurry. I'll wake the others."

After packing, they gulped the tea and headed for the cave. They ate deer meat on the march.

Large drops of rain found a way through the foliage of the trees, giving testimony to the nearness of the storm. The family spoke few words and stepped long strides, knowing they needed at least six hours to get to the cave.

Here and there, fallen trees slowed their progress. To compensate, when the terrain permitted, the family quickened to a moderate trot. By early afternoon the wind howled. Rubbing tree branches groaned and snapped as they lashed at one another. Torrents of rain pummeled the tree canopy and amassed the liquid into large drops that fell on the travelers with annoying weight. The clamor of the storm grew from moment to moment.

David made numerous appraisals of their location with compass and watch. Late in the day he ran to the head of the line and touched Michelle on the shoulder. She turned and he shouted to be heard in the din of the storm. "We should be close." He pointed to his left. "It should be to this side." Michelle nodded. David drifted back toward the rear, stopping to repeat the information to the others.

In less than an hour Michelle stopped and pointed at the slope to her left. The cave, a black orifice, gaped below the trunk of a large fallen cedar. Other fallen trees lay haphazardly from the base of the hill to its top. It would be a precarious climb. The family gathered in a tight circle facing one another.

Paul hollered into the circle. "I'll take the lead. I've got the rope. I'll tie it to something."

Justin nodded and Paul promptly turned and started the climb. The others waited a moment and then followed. First Michelle, then Justin, and David trailed. The ascent was nerve racking. Sudden surges of wind made the fallen timbers shudder. Bits of wood, dirt, and stone clattered past the climbers.

Paul, with the agility of a goat and the strength of a bear, was soon at the cave. He ran inside, dropped his pack, ran back to the ledge and seized the coil of rope. A protruding root at the cave entrance served as an anchor for the rope. He flung the other end down to Michelle. She quickly scrambled to Paul's side and went directly into the cave. Next came Justin. He relieved Paul, who joined Michelle in the semi-darkness of the chamber. The wind intensified and the rain hammered. The body of the storm was present.

Justin looked down at David as he held onto the rope and struggled over some crisscrossed logs. He had only a short distance to go. Suddenly the timbers around him began to shift.

Justin yelled. "Hurry!"

The log David stood on slid away and the boy dangled from the rope. He reached with his feet, stepping at the slippery slope, but swung away in the effort. Justin dropped to his stomach and extended an arm. *"Grab my hand."*

The commotion brought Paul back to his father's side. Instantly he saw his brother's predicament and prepared to heave on the rope. From above the cave a stone and some dirt vibrated loose, slid down, and struck him on the back. As Paul looked up, the large cedar moved.

Justin strained toward David. The boy hoisted himself with two overhand pulls. Now, within arms reach of his father's hand, David looked up, his face surprisingly calm.

Paul, without a word, grabbed his father's collar and yanked him from the ledge, toward the cave. Justin retched from the pressure on his throat, and his arms extended outward to stop the movement, but found no substance. Paul swept him into the darkness of the cave, his eyes bulging. He landed on his bottom and stared in disbelief as a huge dark shadow crossed the mouth of the cave. More debris followed and flashes of dim light illuminated the chamber. The hill trembled, and from the depth of his soul, Justin bellowed.

The trio stood as they were, in the noise, in the shuddering, in the pulsing darkness. They could do nothing as their brother, their son, their friend, died a crushing death nearly at their feet. The stream of debris seemed endless. It finally stopped, abruptly, and the family stood in shock.

The wind howled mournfully. The light from the clouded sky, suddenly annoying with its gray glare, illuminated the cave. Justin ran to the ledge and peered down at the unoccupied rope swinging loosely, uncaring in its failure. Justin gripped the line and lowered himself to the pile of rubble. As he descended, he squeezed the rope with all his strength. He wanted to inflict pain. He wanted it to scream and plead for its life. "I will burn you in fire and send you to hell."

He hated the rope; he hated the wind; he hated the rain; he hated the mud. And he welcomed the hate and gave it freedom. He felt a demon within, and the muscles of his chest quivered. His eyes heated, and his vision colored as if he were looking through blood. His anger gave him strength and he powered through the tangle of debris.

"Where are you? Where are you?" He moaned into the wind. But, he knew. He knew what he would find. His path was straight and guided.

"I don't want it to be! I don't want it to be!" He dropped to his knees and crawled beneath a huge log. His strength surged. He was fearless.

Justin rose to his feet. Before him lay David draped across a log. His back broken, his arms broken. His head, crushed.

Justin bowed and the frenzy within escaped into the screaming wind. It left a hollow beneath his ribs that filled with sour anguish. Strike a man's body, and his mind explodes. Assail his soul, and he doubles in belly pain. The ancients were right; the soul of a person resides in the liver, the kidneys, and the intestines.

Paul and Michelle had followed their father, allowing him his rage. Now they stood at his side, their own eyes burning with pain and despair.

In the driving wind and rain of the fearsome storm, Paul dug a shallow hole in the mud at the base of the hill that partially filled with water. David's body sloshed the liquid when lowered into it. The boy's face, wrapped in a shirt, disappeared into the muddy ooze. They filled the grave with pasty soil, its mounding was difficult. Justin and Michelle watched as Paul struggled and sobbed. The wind muffled their moans, and the rain diluted their tears.

When done, they again climbed the slope, again grasping the dangling rope. At the top, they disappeared into the dark cave.

The next two days were inactive and wearisome. David's pack had to be emptied, and its contents divided. This was a difficult thing to do and Justin couldn't muster up the strength to help. The storm kept them confined and chained to their thoughts.

On the third day, the storm abated. The family, with hearts twisted in despair, ignored the weakened storm and departed. They descended to the floor of the little valley, again using the rope. At David's grave they paused to mound it higher. When done they bowed a short farewell. For them, the mound did not contain David, it contained only his body. David was somewhere else. The family turned and went its way, leaving the hated rope dangling.

To escape, at least in some part, the fury of the endless storms, the group set their course due east and moved into the exposed land of the Willamette Valley. This was fertile land, a farming land, where there were few trees. The openness caused apprehension for the now shy travelers. With anxious steps, the travelers took one long day to cross the valley and move into the foothills of the Cascade Mountain Range.

Unfamiliar with the terrain, the problems of an already difficult life intensified. In the Coastal range they established something of a migratory route. Here, it would take time to explore and delineate new maps.

Time moved on and the needed information on the new territory accumulated. They continued to avoid contact with other humans, but occasionally saw signs in the form of fire at night and wisps of smoke at day. They saw vapor trails of high-flying aircraft, and the dust of speeding vehicles that streaked through the valley. These sightings were a temptation to the lonely group, especially for the two younger ones.

On a warm, quiet day, the family sat on the slope of a hill overlooking the valley. They rested and munched on jerky. Not far from the hill, Paul spotted a pickup truck as it slowly moved down an empty road. He picked up the binoculars and focused on the vehicle: a large pickup with three individuals and a truck bed packed full.

Paul pointed with a piece of jerky. "That truck. That's a small group like us." He turned to his father. "I guess they know of a place to go." He took another look at the truck. "We could talk to a small group like that." He looked at his father again. "What the hell."

Justin's reply was immediate. "No."

Michelle propped herself up on one elbow, turning toward her father. "Let's put it to a vote."

Justin's reply was the same. "No."

He turned to Michelle. No longer the teenager that followed her father into the forest, she now carried a pack equal to his. Tougher of mind, she had seen her brother die and no longer did she hesitate to kill, skin, and eat animals. Paul gave her no special attention, the type of attention one gives to those who are a bit inadequate for the task.

Michelle did not alter her gaze. "Why not?"

Justin, lying on his back, sat up. "Neither one of you is thinking with your head. You're thinking with your heart. You're lonely." He reached to the stack of jerky and flicked an ant off a slice. He grasped the meat and inspected it before putting it to his mouth.

Paul sighed. "Our isolation is our security, I know, but it's been a long time."

Michelle followed Paul's lead. "The people in that truck could help us."

Justin used his tongue to push the jerky in his mouth to his cheek. "And maybe not." He directed a stern gaze at his daughter. "Who says we need help? Do we need a ride somewhere?"

He lay back down and looked into the sky. "Look at it this way. Our situation is temporary. It's like we're looking at a river in flood. You have to sit and wait for all the wreckage to pass, and the level and speed of the waters to drop before you can cross." He sat back up. "One more thing. We aren't a democracy. I have the last word on all things. I have the most knowledge, the most experience, and know how to put it together."

Nobody said a thing for a long minute until Justin spoke again. "I've spent the most time on earth. I have the best chance of making the right decision." He paused before again reclining. "That's not to say I won't listen to your input."

He chewed more of the jerky and swallowed. "This isn't an ego trip. It's simple logic."

Michelle got up and walked to her father. She squatted near him, wrapped her arms around her legs and spoke crisply. "Pure logic will be our guide?"

Justin rose to one elbow and faced her. "That's right. Logic rules."

Michelle's brow wrinkled. "What about emotions? What about one's inner feelings? Intuition, that type of thing. You've mentioned them a lot."

Justin reclined to his back with a sigh. "Yes, I have."

There was a short pause. Michelle's mouth moved to say something, but Justin spoke abruptly. "You have to take everything into consideration." He rolled his head toward Michelle. "You think with your mind. You feel with your heart. Intuition comes from the soul." He watched her eyes. "The wise will pay heed to a hunch."

Michelle stood and bit her lip. "Right. Take heed of it all. Right." She turned and walked toward a shady tree. Paul looked at her and smiled. She flipped him a one-finger salute.

Of particular concern to the family was the appearance of a different type of people. These were people who apparently spent most of their time in the valley. They were crude in appearance, even barbaric. Their clothing was contemporary but rag-tag. They were unkempt and dirty with signs of poor health. Paul swore that he could smell them before he could hear them. For weapons, they carried simple clubs and spears of tied knifes at the end of sticks. Their groups tended to be large and composed of both men and women, but no children. They were a very noisy lot, easy to detect, and even easier to avoid.

Justin considered their regression into a primitive state as a result of their sudden and unprepared plunge into wilderness living. As understandable as this may be, his contempt for them persisted. His effort to empathize only led to anger. Michelle shuddered at their sight and her intuition often informed her of their nearness. "They're evil and obviously stupid."

While engaged in a hunting expedition, the family came upon an encampment of these wretched humans, whom they now referred to as "goons." Rather than chance detection by circling the group, the family positioned themselves on a slope above their camp and waited for the goons to move off.

At the start of the second day, Justin went to an outcropping overlooking the goon's campsite. He carried binoculars with him. Though he detested these beings, he was intrigued by them as well.

Paul had once questioned Justin on the subject. "Why do you find them so interesting? They're just raggedy and dirty wanderers."

Justin hesitated as the words formed in his mind. "Not so long ago they were normal people. Doing their job, families, all of that stuff, but look at them now." Justin frowned. "One would think the ugly animal had always been in them. Just waiting for the right circumstances." He paused and looked sternly into his son's eyes. "I wonder if it dwells in us. Perhaps, for us, the circumstances aren't quite right. Perhaps it could happen to us." He paused again. "Then again, maybe we're different."

Paul broke the eye contact. "No, no, that won't happen to us. We're different. There's nothing inside of us like that."

Justin cautiously crouched behind a bush as he judged these people to be dangerous. He raised the binoculars and scanned the group. "Two, four, six, eight, nine and about ten more."

He tried to categorize them into males and females. This was not as simple as one might think. He counted twelve with beards and the rest without. A few chewed on some sort of food while most hung around the campfire.

Justin lowered the glasses and thought. "It looks like they have food. They may not move for a while. Shit."

Justin raised the glasses again, his attention drawn to the far end of the camp where two males were molesting a female. The struggle was fierce, but totally ignored by the others. Justin scanned the rest of the group and stopped at the center of the camp. A male individual stood pointing directly at him, yelling loud enough for Justin to hear, but not understand.

Justin watched in momentary confusion. Lying on his belly and peering through a bush gave him concealment, and his distance from them was adequate. Justin inched back into the brush. He got to his knees and looked at the sun.

"Shit! The sun." The field glasses were flashing in its brightness. Justin scooted away from the brush and rose to a crouching position. "Shit, shit, *shit*."

Justin took another look at the camp. Some of the goons hoisted weapons and headed up the hill. Justin spun around and made haste back to Paul and Michelle. He found them comfortably reclined and munching jerky.

Justin jumped in between them. "The goons spotted me and are headed this way. Get your stuff together. We're outta here."

Paul gathered up his gear. "No shit."

Michelle jumped to her feet. "Really? Those pigs are headed this way?"

In short order, all three headed across the top of the hill. Never having been chased before, they simply ran through the sparsely treed forest, hoping their speed was adequate

---

After a half-hour run, the fatigued family comprehended that flight was useless. The goons may have been ugly and dirty, but they were also fast afoot, carried no packs, and were capable of tracking. Their noisy progress gave warning of the closing gap.

Justin stopped near a tree halfway up a small hill and shouted to the others. "Get behind a tree." He took his pack off and laid it in the open. "My pack is bait." He paused to catch his breath. "We can't outrun them. We'll defend this spot."

All three dispersed. Keeping the backpack in view, they concealed themselves behind trees. The noise of the goons neared. Michelle called to her father. "Dad, do we shoot to kill?"

Justin took a deep breath and closed his eyes. To wound would surely lead to a slow death and would not remove the danger to his family. Paul hollered. "What do we do Dad?"

Justin shouted. "Protect the pack. Shoot the first one that goes for it. Don't worry about where he's hit."

The approaching goons thrashed through the bush, shouting to one another. "Get the fuck over here. They went this way."

Justin crouched on one knee, only his head exposed. He could see the lead goon running toward them with abandonment. Confrontation seemingly assured, Justin made one last effort.

He stood up. *"Back off or you'll be shot."*

One of the pursuers broke from the bush and without hesitation ran toward the pack. Justin, Paul, and Michelle took a step from behind their trees, aimed and fired. The volley of arrows struck the goon in the chest, and he fell into the brush. Two more goons broke into the clearing, unaware of their arrow-shot comrade. Two arrows hit one, once in the shoulder and another in the neck. He fell to his side. The other, hit in the left side, stumbled into the brush screaming horribly.

Justin shouted, "Watch to the left and right."

Justin saw a man dashing from one tree to another. He took aim and waited. In a moment the man ran straight at him. Justin let loose an arrow that struck him hard in the chest and drove him off his feet. "Damn!" He turned toward the clearing as two arrows flew at two goons running for the pack and both fell. But one, almost instantly, got back up and ran into the brush, his weapon discarded.

A few more shouts were heard, but nothing understandable, and the noise appeared to be drifting away.

The family waited in the silence. Justin scanned the area all around and stepped from behind the tree. He approached the prone figures. One man took his last breaths. His chest heaved several times and blood gushed from his mouth. "They're gone." His children were quickly at his side. "We need to retrieve the arrows."

Justin watched Michelle who, with no show of emotion, pulled the arrow from the man's chest and placed it back in her quiver. She turned and looked at Justin but said nothing. Justin turned to Paul. "Give a hand with the arrows."

Paul stood clear of the human kills. He did not look at them nor had he seen Michelle's action. He stared in the direction of the escaping goons. "We should follow them. They may come back, sneak up on us."

Justin picked up his pack. "You're right, and we'll do that. But we can't leave the arrows. Let's get it done."

Paul bit his lip and sighed. "Right." They quickly accomplished the gruesome task leaving only one arrow that resisted tugging. To their amazement, the first man shot was missing.

Justin looked at the bloody arrows in his quiver. "Damn."

Michelle stood fast. "We did the right thing." Paul said nothing, but his face was shadowed.

Justin took a deep breath. "It's not over." He paused. "We'll follow, but just to see what they're up to."

He turned from the bloody corpses. "I'll take the lead. You two follow, twenty yards to the rear and twenty yards to the side." The reverse pursuit commenced without another word.

Fifteen minutes later, they found the body of a goon, his feet protruding from a bush. The trio approached with weapons at the ready. Paul pushed a berry-laden branch aside. The goon was recognized to be the first shot, but the arrows that killed him were missing. Justin lowered his bow and took a step backward. "I wonder why they put him here?"

Further on two more bodies, half hidden in some brush, lay side-by-side. Justin stepped back. "They're the two that ran off together."

Paul stroked his throat. "Look at their heads! They've been busted with a club."

Justin shook his head. "Why would they do that?"

Michelle scoffed. "Hideous creeps. They obviously want the bodies."

Justin headed on. "Sickening shit."

Paul found two arrows and put them in his quiver. "This is getting creepy." He shook his head. "If I got to that point, I'd kill myself."

Michelle moved to her left. "We did the right thing."

The family continued the pursuit all the way back to the outcropping of Justin's observations. As expected, the goon's camp was in turmoil. Justin studied the situation with the field glasses. Two goons stood at the center of a circle. They talked and the others listened. Shortly, one of the talking goons pointed up the hill.

Justin's shoulders slumped. "I was hoping that they would run off." He took a deep breath. "But, now I think they may head back." He looked at his children. "The bodies." He paused. "Let's avoid another fight."

He rubbed his chin. "They probably don't know that we're up here."

Paul kept his eyes on the goons. "They're getting excited. Perhaps they'll move off."

Justin put the glasses to his eyes. "But if they do head this way, we make our presence known. Hopefully that'll scare them off."

Justin handed the glasses to Paul. "Keep watch."

Paul adjusted the lenses to his setting. "How do we do that, Pop? Make noise, throw rocks, what?"

"All of that." Justin looked at Michelle. "If that doesn't work, we fight again." Michelle nodded in silent agreement.

The family did not have to wait long. The circle broke up and six goons headed up the slope. With fearful screams, the family made their presence known. They threw rocks and shouted threats. The effort worked.

The goons ceased their climb and retreated to the camp. They shouted among themselves while gathering their possessions and made a hurried escape into the valley. Paul kept a close watch and only when they were far off did the family descend the hill. They moved cautiously, but with curiosity as well.

Within the camp, the smell of smoldering wood mixed with the reek of human excrement. Near the fire lay a pile of blackened bones. Paul kicked through them and noticed a scorched hide. He gripped the leather and stepped backward. As he did, a trail of human bones, two skulls, ribs and other parts, tumbled from beneath the hide.

Paul called to his father. "Dad, take a look at this."

Justin and Michelle went to his side. Michelle smirked. "Well that's proof of what they are. And shows why they did what they did up the hill."

Michelle spat. "Pigs, scum."

Justin turned. "True, true."

The months passed and the family's wanderings continued. Their life settled into quiet solitude and even boredom. Only mild adventure came their way. This monotony allowed too much time for thinking. Conversations were often about civilization lost and attempted recovery theories.

To say that none of the family weakened in their resolve would be a falsehood. Their near perpetual movement, lack of social involvement, and the constant visible deterioration of the environment produced periodic depressions that were difficult to shake off.

Ravens in the Sky
(Nicole)

Nicole rolled onto her back and opened her eyes. A full moon glared down, its intensity saturating her eyes. She rolled to her side. The ugly chase with the motorcycles flickered in a series of snapshots, providing exoneration. Her thoughts shifted to Chimene, and she replayed the medical procedure performed. After several minutes, reassured, she expelled a deep breath.

Her body ached, and she struggled with fear for her children. She reached out and touched the road surface. Its raspy feel was annoying. Nicole struggled to a sitting position. "Don't let panic grab you."

Her stomach knotted, and she trembled. Awkwardly, she freed herself of the sleeping bag and rested a moment on hands and knees. Staring at the still forms of her daughters, she crawled to their side and made a quick inspection. She whispered, "It's OK, kids. It's OK."

Nicole got to her feet and nervously wrapped her hands around her stomach. "Oh, God." She stepped quietly to the cab of the truck to check the time. "4-O-7." She turned and surveyed the silent desert. "We have to get out of here." She walked a short way into the desert to relieve herself and when she returned she took a long drink of water.

Remembering the leaky transmission, Nicole dropped to her knees and peered under the truck. A drip formed at the bottom of the transmission and plopped into the collecting can. Carefully she retrieved the can and carried it to the front of the truck. "Oh yeah, the crumpled hood." She placed the can behind the right front tire. "Shit, how am I going to get that open?"

She retrieved the jack handle. First she pried at the middle. That had no effect and she went to the right side. To her relief, the hood rose a few inches. She made a bit more progress on the left side. Nicole pulled the jack handle free. It hung heavily at her side. "Damn it, Adam."

Depression competed with the need to concentrate. Her left hand supported her weight on the truck fender, and she gawked at the large, black tire. "This shit is going to last a long time."

At that moment Julia's hand touched her shoulder. Nicole spun around, her eyes bulging.

"Mom, it's me. I heard noise. I didn't mean to scare you." Julia cupped her hands in front of her chest. "I'm sorry. I'm sorry." Nicole stood glaring, her mouth open. She took a deep breath and pushed past Julia and stomped to the other side of the truck.

Julia followed. "Mom, don't be mad. I want to help."

Nicole clinched her teeth and jammed the jack handle under the hood with force. She yanked down on the handle with a loud grunt. The hood moaned and slowly rose to its full height.

Nicole stepped back and smiled at Julia. "It's OK, I just didn't expect it." She peered into the engine compartment. "Julia, get something to make a funnel with, a piece of cardboard."

Julia, in relief, rushed to the back of the truck and tore a leaf off a cardboard box. She rushed back to her mother. "Why do you need a funnel?"

Nicole didn't answer. She reached into the engine compartment and removed the transmission dipstick and handed it to Julia. "Hold this." She took the cardboard, fashioned it into a funnel, and then stuck it into the dipstick tube. Stepping away from the truck she instructed, "Julia, hold that in place." She retrieved the fluid and poured it into the transmission and handed the empty can to Julia. "Put that back under the transmission." Nicole reinserted the dipstick and tied the hood shut.

Nicole put an arm around Julia and ushered her to Chimene. "It's time to get your sister into the truck and it's time to get out of here." She looked down at Chimene and then at Julia. "The only place for her is in the back of the truck."

Nicole bent down and gently shook Chimene's leg. The girl's eyes opened slowly and her brow knitted. "My arm hurts." She squinted. "Is everybody OK?"

"Yes. Yes, everybody's OK. Do you remember what happened?" Chimene's eyes shifted from Nicole to Julia. "Yes...oh yeah...oh God. It did happen." She trembled and sucked in a short breath.

Nicole grabbed her uninjured arm and squeezed it. "It's OK. You did real good. You're our hero. You saved us." She leaned over and kissed her on the forehead.

"Now we have to get out of here. And the first thing is to get you into the truck." She kissed her again. "Your arm is broken, but we patched you up. Do you think you can lie down in the back of the truck?"

"A broken arm?" She looked at the crude cast.

Nicole smiled. "We'll set things up in the truck. We can make it comfortable." She gave her another kiss. "Is there anything you need?"

Chimene spoke drearily. "I have to pee."

"OK." Nicole and Julia helped her to her feet. She cringed in pain and wobbled unsteadily. All three shuffled to the side of the road, where Chimene relieved herself.

"Mom, I really think I can manage to ride in the cab. I don't want to be alone."

"We'll give it a try. I'd feel better if you were in the cab."

Later, Chimene sat in the truck next to the window, her injured arm supported by rolls of clothing. She assured everyone of her comfort. Nicole and Julia repeated the transmission fluid procedure and retied the hood.

After taking a look at the map, Nicole climbed in behind the steering wheel and prayed that the truck would start. Without hesitation she reached for the ignition key and gave it a quick twist. The starter motor engaged and the engine roared into life. Nicole sat back in the seat feeling more confident. She turned to Julia. "Now it's the transmission's turn."

124

She shifted the lever and waited a few moments. There were no strange noises so she depressed the accelerator and the truck moved down the road.

Nicole smiled. "We're off. We're cooking. We can do this." She looked at all the gauges. "We need a place to hold up, and it would be good if we find it today." All the gauges read normal. "We're going to head east." She smiled again. "Like we did before. Find a place to hunker down, heal up, and make plans."

Julia exhausted a deep breath. "Yeah, that's good. A place to hunker down."

Miles from the crash scene, they turned east on a small paved road that again, after a short time, turned south. A few miles later, they turned east on a dirt road. Nicole stopped the truck and got out.

She motioned to Julia. "Go back to the paved road and use a branch or something to brush out our tracks."

Julia climbed out and headed down the road. "Another trick from the movies."

"Yeah, a western." She watched Julia complete the task.

The little dirt road extended many miles to the east before coming to an abrupt end. Nicole shifted into four-wheel drive and continued at a slow pace, but the truck began to make unusual noises. The area had dusty soil and rolled with gentle hills. There were no houses, no fences, nothing to indicate a population. Their needs for isolation were met.

While trying to navigate through a ravine, the truck's left front wheel rose up on a mound. Nicole gunned the engine and the truck moved off the mound. However, the undercarriage bottomed out on the same mound and held the left wheel off the ground. Using the truck's power again, Nicole depressed the accelerator. For a moment the truck strained, but the effort ended with a loud bang.

Nicole turned to Julia. "Trouble for sure."

She turned off the engine, jumped out of the truck, and looked beneath the chassis. The transmission hung from its forward mounts and was no longer attached to the rear wheel drive shaft.

Nicole hollered. "We'll make camp here."

Julia, already out of the truck, looked around. She walked to her mother's side. "There's no water here."

Nicole climbed a small knoll to the north of the ravine and studied the terrain. She waved to Julia. "Come on up here."

When Julia arrived, Nicole pointed to the north. "Tomorrow you climb to the top of that hill and from up there you'll see water." She smiled.

"Yes, tomorrow I will climb the hill and see the water." Julia laughed and gave her mother a kiss.

They returned to the truck, set up camp and tended to Chimene.

The next day, Julia made the trek to the top of the hill. Nicole watched her leave and waited hours for her return. When she did, the news was good. "I saw a stream about two miles farther on."

It took them close to three days to carry all the supplies to the new location. They hid the truck with brush, making sure to cover all the glass. They took some of the fuel with them.

The days turned to weeks and the weeks to months. Chimene's injured arm became infected, but thanks to Adam, their medical supplies included antibiotics. When combined with Chimene's youth, her wounds healed quickly. Unfortunately, as a result of lost bone parts, the arm bent inward near the elbow and prevented full extension. However, Chimene made no complaint. Nicole apologized once and never spoke of it again.

The campsite sat near a shallow stream in an area of sparse vegetation and dusty soil. Small trees and high brush supplied fuel and shade. For shelter, they built a lean-to. Actually it was a pair of lean-tos built facing one another, or perhaps it could be called an "A" frame. A tarp covered the branch walls, and leaves and grass supplied a rain-shield. The shelter was large enough for a small fire within, and they installed a flap on the roof to vent the smoke. They did well at capturing small game, and there were few times without fresh meat. Vitamin pills, dried fruit and vegetables provided a balanced diet.

Confidence and optimism were Nicole's routine encouragements to her daughters even though she had doubts. Their hiding place seemed adequate. Located far from the paved road there should be no intrusion. If the motorcycle riders were looking for them, it would be a difficult search.

The weather moved through seasonal changes and the little group persevered through a mild winter, a wet spring, and into a summer of continued isolation.

It was a hot summer day. Nicole returned to camp after checking a rabbit trap. She swung the prize in her right hand and grabbed at tall weeds with her left. Close to camp, she heard the girls quarreling, no longer an unusual occurrence. The girls were restless, their minds still consumed with paradise lost. The demons of despair roamed the campsite. Nicole moaned loudly and the girls spun to face her, their eyes intense with anger. Nicole held the rabbit high. "Got one." The girls continued to glare.

Nicole hung the carcass on a limb that projected from the structure of the hut. She turned, took a deep breath and smirked. "Is there a problem?"

Chimene's chest heaved with short breaths. *"She cut three inches off the legs of my jeans."*

Julia held up the jeans in her hand. "They're too small for her. She's gotten bigger."

Chimene glared at Julia. *"They're my jeans. They're my jeans. They're my jeans."*

Nicole eyed Julie. "Wrong thing to do."

Chimene spun back to Nicole. *"You're God damn right it was the wrong thing to do."*

Julia threw the jeans to the ground. *"Don't you yell at my mother."*

Chimene hissed back. "Stuff it, you little shit head."

Julia's face clouded and she stepped toward Chimene.

"Hold it, hold it!" Nicole stepped between them and glanced from one to the other. "This is absurd. We struggle together."

Nicole looked at Chimene. "Clean the rabbit." She turned to Julia. "The water containers need filling."

The girls stood as they were. Nicole's face clouded with intensity. *"Do it now."* The girls moved in opposite directions, Chimene kicking the dust with each step.

Nicole took a deep breath. *"There will be peace in the valley."* Then, in a whisper. "Or we all shall surely die." Her shoulders slumped in her own depression.

Days later Nicole wandered, free of the campsite, free of her daughters, and free of her responsibilities. Walking with head down, she mumbled every few moments.

"It would be nice to talk to an adult." She closed her eyes in a long blink and raised her head to the sky. "It would be nice to talk to anyone other then my two *nitwits.*"

Continuing her walk her right hand reached out and with a harsh snap she tore the top off a strand of struggling grass. Pale green, it would die soon. "I could shoot them both...and myself."

Her eyes seeing, but not noticing, Nicole expelled a breath and forced her children from her thoughts. With the next breath, despair bloomed in her belly, drenched her heart, and the sliver of grass dropped from her hand.

Nicole's head drooped as she pondered each and every step she took. Her left foot rose, glided through the air and dropped to the earth, prompting a puff of dust. Then the right foot lifted to repeat the pattern. She spoke as each foot ascended. "Step...after step...after step." Her arms swung in a matching cadence. Abruptly, unconsciously she twirled beautifully on her left foot, her arms gracefully lifting outward. A rhythm guided her steps.

Time ticked by with stride after stride in Nicole's melancholic dance. Staring ahead, she smiled as her eyes welled with tears. Suddenly her body quaked with panic. Her right foot impacted an unmoving stone.

Nicole's knees struck first and the ground rushed at her face. She turned her head to the left and shut her eyes. Her torso slumped, her left arm extended forward. With her right arm at her side, she hit the ground, billowing the dust.

Nicole's eyes slowly opened to pain in her knees and in the palm of her left hand. Her mouth open, she tasted the soil. The ground was hot and immediately penetrated her body. An ant, half red and half black, having nearly succumbed to the falling colossus, scurried in and out of Nicole's vision. Nicole blinked and remembered another ant.

She rose to her hands and knees, her body sagging at the middle. She used her tongue to push the dirt inside of her mouth to her lips and spat. "All that to remember an ant."

Weakly, she fell to her side and rolled onto her back. The uncomfortable heat again assaulted her body. She closed her eyes to the high sun and covered them with her right arm. "Adam!"

"I pay. The kids pay." Her hands balled into fists. "I'm tired Adam. I'm not both man and woman." The unrelenting heat forced her to sit up. She took deep breaths while slowly rising to her feet. Her shoulders slumped from nothing more than the weight of her arms, and her shuffling feet turned her in the direction of the campsite. She stood there for many minutes.

"Was I...?" She took a step and then another. "Step, after step...after step."

Two miles later Nicole sat resting in the shade of a tall bush, watching small birds fluttering about in another. She studied them, her brow wrinkling. "Fragile creatures, a handful of tiny bones and feathers." A hot breeze rustled brittle leaves in a crescendo of timid clatter.

"The world didn't fall apart for them."

She smiled at their acrobatics. "You bounce through the air and pop through the bushes."

Cooled by the shade, Nicole rose to her feet. She broke a dry twig from the bush and raised the smooth end toward her mouth when a quick moving shadow traversed the ground before her. Looking up she saw a hawk sailing to the south, its wings motionless. "An omen." She put the end of the stick in her mouth. "A message delivered." Nicole visored her eyes with her left hand, watching the bird shrink to a black dot. "Perhaps deliverance."

Near camp, the chatter of her daughters flowed from the area adjacent to the stream. Nicole headed that way, anticipating a cooling bath.

Rounding a high bush, she waved to the girls sitting on the bank. Chimene stood up with hands on hips. "Where the hell were you? You've been gone for hours."

Julia joined in. "I was really scared. Where were you?"

"I lost track of time. Everything's OK." Nicole waved her hand and kicked off her shoes. She entered the stream at its deepest part, ignoring the questions from her daughters. Fully clothed, she submerged below the waters of the stream.

Facing upstream, she dug her toes into the gravel and looked through the surface at the shimmering shapes of her daughters. She rose to the surface, opened her mouth for a drink and rolled to sit on her bottom. As she scooted to the bank, Chimene spoke demandingly. "Why didn't you tell us where you were?"

Nicole propped herself on her elbows, her legs in the stream. "I went to the mall, got a flat, and had to wait for a tow truck."

"Very funny." Chimene kicked the water. "We've been walking all over the place. Yelling and hollering." She paused. "How were we to know...that you were at the mall?" She smiled.

Julia squinted at her sister, turned to her mother, and spoke through clenched teeth. "Next time, leave a note."

Nicole laughed. "Yes, Moms."

Nicole closed her eyes and allowed the last of the emotional happening to drain. She succumbed to a pleasant daydream of blue color with liquid texture as she reclined on the smooth stones of the stream's bank.

Her lips moved without sound. Safe place. Her eyes shifted beneath shut lids. I'm not alone. A voice sang or moaned. "Well...to be well ...to be very well."

The blue moved like visible wind. Nicole gave herself to it and rose into the flow. Nicole's head pushed against the ground and her back arched gently as she swooped through the dream. Large, liquid diamonds shimmered above. The sea. The southern sea. I'm in the beautiful southern sea.

The blue faded. "Mom. Mom. Are you awake?"

Nicole opened her eyes to the unmoving blue of the sky. "Mom, tell Julia to give me the brush."

Nicole sighed. "Julia!...Give your sister the brush."

Julia hesitated. "I'll give her the brush off." But, she smiled and extended the brush to her sister. "Asshole."

Nicole spoke in a singsong manner. "What I seek are the southern seas, the beautiful, blue, southern seas."

Chimene smiled.

Nicole suddenly sat up and turned to Chimene. "When you're finished with the brush, please let me have it."

Chimene's eyes squinted as she stared at her mother. "What do we do when this brush is worn out?"

Julia stood at midstream. Her eyes brightened. "Yeah, Mom, what do we do then?"

Nicole tilted her head. "As soon as the car is fixed, I'll go back to the mall and get another."

She stood up, left the stream, and pushed her feet into her shoes. With long, determined strides she headed for the campsite.

Julia splashed toward the shore. "Talk to us, Mom. This is important."

Nicole snapped a gaze at her. "Don't be so naïve!"

Julia frowned. "Naïve! What are you talking about?"

Nicole moved faster and the girls hastened after her.

Chimene shouted. "Wait!"

Nicole yelled over her shoulder. "What's the matter, did you forget the way back to camp?"

"No, it's my bad arm. I need help getting my shirt on."

"Bullshit."

Julia struggled to move with her pants halfway up and fell to the ground. "Mom, wait. I want to ask you something important."

"I will not answer any more stupid questions." The girls stopped to complete their dressing.

Nicole walked as fast as she could. Although by the time she reached the camp, the girls caught up with her and again pressed her for answers to more unanswerable questions. When they reached the pile of campfire ashes, the girls resorted to physically restraining their mother in desperation.

Nicole sucked in a full breath to shout them down. Instead, it dissipated to the sound of another voice, a voice of deep tone, the voice of a man. "Stay as you are."

All three women froze in the heat of the sun and a chill passed down their spines. Wide-eyed, the girls turned in the direction of the voice. Nicole shifted her eyes, and the voice spoke again.

"We mean you no harm. Stand where you are. We have your weapons."

Nicole cursed under her breath. "Shit." Julia muttered something, and Nicole spoke with forced courage. "If you mean us no harm, show yourself."

Immediately three men strode from the brush, two quite young and another at least middle-aged. All carried rifles and were dressed in buckskin. They had a tired look, and their eyes indicated stress or even pain. The older man moved to confront Nicole. "My name is Matthew, and this is Joey and William. We'll not harm you. We can help."

Nicole, seeing that they didn't wear motorcycle leathers, relaxed a bit. "If you mean no harm, give us back our weapons."

Matthew spoke firmly, but a bit weakly. "In due time."

Nicole eyed his rifle. She had not heard a shot, other than their own, since the encounter with motorcycle riders. The men also carried knives strapped to their legs. *If they're not friendly, all is probably lost.* Nicole stared at the older man's face in a quick study. It showed intelligence and even dignity. His eyes were soft and unthreatening, and he had a rather large nose. Nicole remained guarded.

Matthew waved a hand and the younger men disappeared into the brush. He walked to a large stone and sat down, hesitating a few moments before speaking. "Answer my questions quickly and to the point. We can't waste time in chit chat." He showed no concern for the possibility of additional members in her group. His tired eyes relaxed, and he hunched forward with his forearms resting on his thighs. Nicole decided to tell him the truth.

His questions stepped backward in time. And he sometimes stopped Nicole's answers with the raise of a hand. He seemed to have a habit of kneading his bulbous nose with his right index finger and thumb.

Eventually Nicole's story reached back to the bikers, and here Matthew asked for many details. "Tell me exactly what the emblem on the side of the machine looked like."

"It was the sign of Satan, a circle with an inscribed star. Haven't you seen them before?"

"Yes, I have. Yes, indeed." He took a shallow breath and rotated his head as if stretching stiff neck muscles.

He rose to his feet, his cheeks puffed with a breath, and he rubbed his forehead. "I'm surprised you survived the encounter with the bikers. They're a bad lot. They usually kill everyone and everything."

He closed his eyes and rubbed his nose. "There is…the possibility of revenge."

He went back to the stone and sat down again. He looked directly into Nicole's eyes. "Your victory over the riders is an omen. You must be special people with the protection of The Powers That Be.

Nicole was taken aback. "The Powers That Be? I don't follow."

As strange as his words were, somehow they were reassuring to Nicole. But as much as she wanted this encounter to be a rescue, she could not allow that desire to fog her thoughts.

Matthew stood up and took a deep breath. "Our meeting was pre-ordained, just as all things are." He paused and, for the first time, smiled. "The hollering of those two," he pointed at the girls, "brought us to your campsite." He stared at the girls and spoke in a deep tone. "Ordained guidance." The girls fidgeted under his steady gaze. Nicole sat silently in astonishment.

His gaze turned back to Nicole. "We will be your protectors for as long as we can." His eyes shifted from one female to the other. "We'll lead you to a settlement in the east. There are people there you can trust." He took a sluggish breath. "You'll be a lot safer there."

His face clouded. "You can't stay here. It's just a matter of time before you're discovered. In fact, it's a miracle that you haven't been."

Nicole frowned. "Discovered. By whom?"

"The crazies, and possibly the bikers are looking for you." His voice rose. "There are crazies all over this area! This is a dangerous place."

Nicole's eyes widened. "Crazies?" Her eyes squinted. "What are crazies?"

Matthew looked away and then looked back at her. "You have never encountered them?" He rubbed his chin. "It's hard to believe."

He scratched the back of his neck. "The crazies are the ones that have gone mad. Barbaric, killers, cannibals. There are lots of them. I'll tell you more later."

Matthew gave a low, bird-like whistle, and a few minutes later his two companions reappeared at the campsite. He took them aside and talked to them at length in low tones. The young men periodically nodded their heads or shrugged their shoulders.

The girls watched with bright eyes and big smiles. Nicole mumbled to herself. "No need to ask their opinion." Then more loudly. "Stay alert. When we get our weapons back keep them near."

Nicole puzzled over Matthew's words in reference to The Powers That Be and her family being special. Still, this was an offer of protection and an invitation to some sort of settlement. And that meant people, and hopefully lots of them.

Matthew returned to Nicole. His companions moved back into the brush. "They went to get your weapons." He rubbed his nose. "Then we'll leave. But, we'll be back before dark." He strode to the fire pit. "Could you cook us some grub?" His right hand went to his lower back and he arched backward. "We've been moving fast for days with little rest and almost no food."

Nicole stood up. "Rabbit?"

"Yeah, that would be great." He shifted his backpack until it fell from his shoulders. He dropped to one knee and rummaged through the pack. Shortly, he pulled out a packet of dried vegetables and tossed it to Nicole. "A little something for the pot. Do you have salt?"

"Yes we do, and pepper as well."

"Pepper. That's great." He smiled. "A lot of pepper would be nice."

Nicole smiled. "Well, rabbit stew it'll be."

Matthew hoisted his pack to his back and hefted his rifle across his arm. "We have to check the area before we can rest. Then we'll spend the night close by. In the morning you must be ready for the trip to the settlement."

He turned to the noise of his returning companions. They carried the confiscated weapons. Matthew pointed to the hut. "Put them where you found them."

He turned back to Nicole. "Keep your traveling load light."

He turned, but Nicole stopped him with a question. "I'm grateful for your help, but could you please tell us more about yourselves and where we're going?" Joey and William returned from the hut and stood next to Matthew.

"I apologize, but this place is dangerous. Too many crazies." He huffed a breath and his head hung to the side. "I'll give you a brief description. Questions tomorrow. When we're on the move." He moved to the stone and laboriously sat down. The young men squatted where they stood. Their eyes shifted from the girls to Nicole and back to the girls.

Matthew described himself as a survivor of the bad times and a member of a settlement of people who had made preparations. The place they would travel to was a fortification very similar to the ones built in the pioneer days, log cabins ringed by a wall of timbers. "It's called Ravens in the Sky."

"We have been attacked many times by the crazies, and with each attack some lives were lost. We're out trying to find replacements."

He spent another few minutes telling them of the route they would travel and how to prepare for the journey. After that, all three men rose slowly to their feet. Matthew again arched his back. "We're going to check the area." He waved a hand and headed into the brush.

Nicole and the girls watched them leave. "We're going to go with them. It might be our last chance to get out of here." Her eyes shifted to the girls. "Any disagreement?"

Chimene smiled broadly. "I'm ready and so is Julia. What do we have to do?"

Julia poked her sister with a finger. "I can speak for myself." She turned to her mother. "Yes, we should go. They look safe to me."

Nicole clapped her hands. "OK, we pack everything up and see what we can take when it's time to go." The girls ran anxiously to the shelter.

Just before dark the three men entered camp. Matthew walked quickly to Nicole. "Is the food cooked?"

Nicole smiled. "Yes it is."

Matthew quickly stepped to the smoldering fire and kicked the ashes around. "Put some water on this. You have no idea of the danger. You should have a fire for no longer then you need it."

Nicole apologized and dumped water on the ashes. However, the stew was hot and ready to eat and the men were quick to accept it. They wolfed down their food never stopping to talk. Nicole had assumed a shared meal with conversation, including more information. In fact, the girls were in the process of primping.

One of the young men, Joey, went to the pot, looked into it, and then looked at Nicole. Nicole smiled. "Go ahead, finish it up. You look like you need it."

Within ten minutes of the men's entry into camp the cooking pot sat empty. Just before the girls made their grand entrance, the men rose to their feet. Matthew explained. "We gotta go. We won't be far off. It's better we're out there." He frowned. "Like I said before. The crazies." He wiped his mouth with his sleeve. "Thanks for the meal. We'll be back before first light." That quickly, they were gone.

Nicole looked at the dead fire and the empty pot. Disappointment shadowed her face, and the girls, looking neater than they had for months, strode to her side.

Chimene walked to the fire pit. "Why is the fire out? What happened to the food? Where's everybody? What the hell happened?"

Julia, almost frantic, ran to her mother. "Did you say something wrong?" She slumped onto one of the sitting stones. "Oh my God. They didn't run off, did they?"

Nicole's smile blossomed to a laugh. The girl's expectations of an evening with male company fell to earth like an overripe peach. Laughing, Nicole turned and headed for the hut. "We have a lot of packing to do. Grab what you can to eat."

Julia ran after her. "Where did they go? Are they coming back?"

"They have things to do. They're going to stay somewhere else. They'll be back in the morning."

Chimene yelled after her mother. "There are questions to ask. Things to say. Maybe if we yell, they will hear us."

Nicole spun around. "Don't yell. Remember what they said about the crazies." She turned quickly away to avoid showing her broad smile. "It's no big deal. Men are like that. Things to do, et cetera, et cetera."

Julia looked at Chimene. "Et cetera, et cetera. What the hell is she talking about?"

"You're an ass, Julia."

Nicole, anticipating a night of fun, disappeared into the hut and the girls followed.

The next day the group of six packed what they could carry and buried the rest. They took weapons, ammunition, medical supplies and a portion of the women's personal things. With parts of the "A" frame they constructed a litter. The women were given the burden of hauling the device, two of them pulling while the other rested. It proved to be more cumbersome than fatiguing.

Matthew walked to the women as they stood by the litter. "If trouble comes up during the trip, take cover. We'll be doing the same."

Nicole nodded and turned to the girls. "You got that?" She turned back to Matthew. "We can handle it."

Matthew put a hand on her shoulder. "You're going to make it. No doubt about it. These are hard and ugly times and your survival to this point is not without meaning. Destiny." He smiled. "Let's go."

The group moved in a column with Matthew positioned thirty yards ahead of the women. He sometimes moved to the right or left flank. Joey scouted up to a quarter of a mile ahead. William protected the rear.

Days later they moved into the land once known as Utah. The terrain traveled consisted of low hills, sparse vegetation and eroded rock. To the north, high snow-capped mountains glared under a bright sun.

Within three days they established a routine. Warm meals in the mornings and evenings, a rest and a snack divided the days at noon. They took game when it presented itself and cooked all of the meat when possible. They gathered any nuts or fruit they found and sometimes stopped at abandoned farms to harvest unattended crops.

On one occasion, Joey, while ahead of the others, spotted a pronghorn antelope and downed the animal with a single shot. The kill occurring at mid-day, Joey at once began preparations for cleaning and cooking the animal.

Nicole stood by the dead animal. Chimene trotted to her side, a smile on her face. "I'm going with Joey to get firewood."

Nicole hesitated with her answer. Dangers to the request swirled through her mind. Chimene shifted her weight to her right foot. "Well?"

Nicole replied. "Oh, sure. Of course. We need the wood."

Chimene spun around and ran to Joey, who stood near some brush, waiting. He smiled when Chimene reached him. Nicole shouted, "Stay alert."

Nicole studied them as they walked away. The earmarks of young love were evident. Nicole took a deep breath and bit her lip, knowing that young love was quick and deep. She frowned. But what chance did they have in this frightful world? Nicole turned away thinking that perhaps their destination would provide stability for the relationship. The relationship did not go unnoticed by the others either, but they let the couple be without comment.

Joey toted his rifle and scanned the area for trouble that he knew could be near. Chimene gathered the wood.

She spied him looking to the north. "Joey, could you pull this branch free for me?"

Joey came over, pulled the branch loose and handed it to her. Chimene added it to a small pile. There were a number of piles leading back to the camp. Joey smiled. "I think we have enough. Let's sit awhile."

Chimene nodded and sat down in the dry soil. Joey sat next to her and adjusted his rifle to lay across his knees. "The others have been watching us. Even William smiles at me when I look at you."

"William is so serious and sad. How long have you known him?"

"We met at the settlement during construction, just before the shit hit the fan. He used to be a lot more fun, but he lost all of his family." Joey flung a small stick at a nearby bush. A rabbit jumped from behind it. "It's pulled him down. He's lost hope or something like that." A long moment of silence followed.

Chimene scooped a handful of dust and let it sift through her fingers. "I don't hope for much anymore. I don't see how we can last." She scooped another handful of soil. "What's to look forward to?"

Joey stretched his legs out. "The settlement will be better. Lots of food. People running around. Cabins to live in and beds to sleep on."

Chimene brightened. "A hot bath. I want so much to have a long hot bath."

"You'll have it. And a bunch of guys hanging around, too."

"What's that supposed to mean? You're my guy." She nudged him in the ribs with her elbow. "We made love twice. That puts us together."

Joey looked at her. "I'm not going to hold you to anything. It's a world of sudden changes."

Chimene looked away. "What did you want to be before all the trouble?"

Joey looked skyward. "Let's see." He paused and turned to Chimene. "Not much. Just, some kind of a job. No big deals. You know, just move along in life."

Chimene thought a moment. "I didn't really have anything in mind, but I did want to go to college." She pulled her knees up and rested her chin on them. "For what, I don't know, but one thing is for sure. It would've been something safe and solid. I wasn't looking for adventure."

"Well, it's adventure you got and more to come."

"Are there any books at the settlement?"

Joey stood in a quick move. Quietly he scanned the area with a three-hundred-and-sixty degree turn. "Let's get the wood and head back to camp. Things don't feel right." He looked down at Chimene. "Books? You bet. Lots."

Nicole watched the distant shape of Matthew as he ascended a nearby hilltop. He wanted to determine if the shot that had downed the antelope attracted attention.

Nicole, William, and Julia had the task of cutting and deboning the carcass.

The animal lay on its back. Nicole held the hind legs and Julia, the front. William skinned the hide from its chest. Julia looked at her mother. "I wish we had water to wash this meat."

William pulled hard on the hide. "The fire will clean it."

Julia grunted as William pulled. "I don't mean bugs. Most of the time I get some dirt or a little stone in my mouth. And of course, ash."

Nicole changed the subject. "William."

He didn't look at her. "Yeah."

"Matthew thinks of us as some sort of special people. Do you have any idea of what he is talking about?"

"Matthew knows a lot." He took his knife and made a slash that exposed the animal's internals. He looked up at Nicole, his expression serious. "Some call him wise."

Julia let go of one leg and brushed a fly away. "Is he into some sort of religious thing?"

William huffed. "Oh no! Not at all, not in the least."

Nicole again looked at the figure of Matthew on the hilltop. He crouched, looking to the north. "What did he do before the bad times?"

William pulled the liver out. "I don't know." He stood up and leaned backward to stretch cramped muscles. He held both hands away from his clothing and looked up the hill at Matthew. "He once told me that he finds all of this...interesting." William uttered a short laugh. "Interesting. For sure!" He again crouched before the carcass and draped the liver across the animal's throat. "I think he knows what he is doing." He paused. "I just follow his lead."

Nicole spread the back legs as Joey cut deep into a joint. She tilted her head. "I sense a lot of optimism. And he acts as if he knows something we don't."

William replied sharply. "I see no reason for optimism." He stabbed his knife into the carcass. His face darkened as he rose to his feet. "It's all crap." He spun around and stomped away. Julia let go of both legs and leaned toward her mother. "What was that?"

Nicole shrugged her shoulders. "It's OK." She looked at the carcass. "I'll cut, you hold."

The trek eventually crossed Utah and moved into Colorado, a journey requiring nearly five weeks. For the most part, the men and the women were separated due to long traveling hours. But as the days rolled by, Chimene and Joey continued to find time together. Nicole accepted the situation with its touch of normalcy. Julia kept track of the entire affair and spent a lot of time chit-chatting with her sister. She tried to get near William, but he wanted no part of that type of thing as he brooded over his losses in silent solitude.

Nicole found a comfortable relationship with Matthew. His adult presence was in itself delightful. His conversation with its reassurance that, in the end, all would be well, was contagious to all except William. Little by little the women accumulated information about the settlement and looked forward to the comforts described. The establishment consisted of two hundred individuals or so. When first organized, admittance had more to do with individual skills than anything else. The place was stoutly made and well provisioned. Matthew assured Nicole that a cabin would be available, though, more than likely, they would have a roommate.

Nicole periodically questioned Matthew on the finer points of her anticipated comforts. "Are there potatoes and eggs at Ravens in the Sky?"

Matthew laughed. "We have domestic animals and gardens of vegetables and fruit." He leaned forward and whispered.

"There are even more goodies. Hidden in my cabin is a stash of candy."

"Candy. I wasn't even thinking of candy. Do you have any chocolate?" She clasped her hands to her bosom, her face pleading.

Matthew's mouth twisted to the left. "No. I ate the chocolate a long time ago." His eyebrows raised. "Sorry. What I have is hard candy. Lemon drops, mints, stuff like that."

"But no chocolate." Her eyes squinted and she glared. "I'll forgive you this time, but don't let it happen again." She shook a finger at him and they both chuckled.

Near sundown, Nicole and Matthew sat alone watching the last of the fire die out. Nicole stirred the fire with a stick and remembered a conversation from the past. "Did you like being in the Navy?"

"I was a young man looking for adventure and fun." He paused. "Those things were there, but there was a lot of crap as well. I'm not the military type."

"From what I see, I mean this expedition, you're the leader, and you do it in a very military manner."

"I have to. It's a military situation." Matthew stood up and found a place close to Nicole, very close. "My life hasn't been very special. Kind of typical of the times. High school, Navy, marriage, three kids, and a divorce. No high-paying jobs. A commercial fisherman. A powerhouse worker at a sawmill. And a lot of this and that."

The tip of the stick Nicole held glowed bright orange. She raised it into the air. "And regrets." She was trying to draw him out, searching for the source of his optimism.

"My divorce happened near the collapse of everything. My ex went off with the kids to the East Coast. I should have followed and stayed closer. Now I know nothing."

Nicole poked the stick around in the fire, lost for words. What he said was dreadful. A separation like that from her children was unthinkable. She would have headed east regardless of the odds. She saw no source of optimism here. In embarrassment, Nicole said nothing.

Matthew threw a twig into the fire. "You're wondering why I didn't seek them out. Wondering why I am here."

"Yes…Yes I am."

"Well, I did try to reach them. That's how I got to the settle-ment. Walking east. Hiding, fighting, starving, and thirsting. Hunters found me unconscious and took me to Ravens in the Sky."

He said no more and rubbed his face and nose with his hands. Nicole could feel his distress. She quietly poked at the fire.

Matthew raised his head, looked to the east, and spoke in a sad tone. "I recovered from the ordeal and I was about to head east again." He lowered his head. "The last I heard of them they were in Red Bank, New Jersey."

He looked at Nicole. "Some of the people at the settlement asked me to help in a situation." He sighed. "It wasn't a big deal, and I owed them something. So I helped." He shrugged his shoulders. "Then there was another situation that had to do with saving lives and then another. I went from one thing to another and now I am here, escorting some other guy's wife and kids."

Nicole's heart sank. Guilt and gratitude mixed. His loss, her gain. Nicole leaned toward him and kissed his cheek just above his dark black beard. "Thank you, Matthew, thank you so very much."

They moved into an embrace and laid back upon the ground in the glow of the dying embers.

The land continued on as semi-desert, spotted with clumps of brush and trees. The greatest danger came from the crazies whom they encountered on three different occasions. In the first and second encounter the intruders were driven back with a short volley of gunfire. Some were killed. Nicole noticed that the men put a great deal of effort into the shooting of these crea-tures. Their deep hatred was evident, a hatred that would find its way into the hearts of the women on the third encounter.

It was early morning. The group had just begun the day's march. Joey scouted ahead. He left at a trot to open the distance between himself and the main party. No more then ten minutes went by when the sound of shots shattered the tranquil morning. As preplanned, the main group took cover with the women together. The men were close at hand and slightly ahead to absorb the brunt of any attack.

Soon they heard the incomprehensible shouts of the crazies. Long moments later Joey ran into the clearing. He stopped momentarily and then staggered forward, his face surprisingly calm, yet his mouth hung open. He quivered strangely and tried to say something. He looked up to the sky and his arms reached above his head. He dropped his rifle and fell to his hands and knees, a small thin spear protruded from his back. The boy slowly collapsed into the dust. Matthew signaled William to go to Joey's aid. William stood and so did Chimene. Quickly Nicole pulled her down. Joey struggled back to his feet. Out of balance, he stumbled to his left, and fell into the brush. William ran toward him as a crazy jumped into the clearing, a club in hand. Matthew fired. Although the bullet pierced the man's chest, his momentum carried him into William, and they both fell to the ground. The crazy fell on top, William struggled to get him off.

A commotion erupted near the brush where Joey lay. His legs showed briefly before being dragged from sight. Matthew opened fire. William threw the dead man off and regained his feet. Matthew jumped up and ran to the spot where Joey had fallen, William at his side. They charged into the brush, but were quickly out again.

Matthew shouted. "The fuckers have taken Joey." William nodded. "Shit! Shit! Shit!"

Matthew dropped his pack. "Hide your stuff." He glared at the women, his face full of rage and his speech a snarl. "We're going after the fuckers. We're going to kill them and you'll help."

Nicole and the girls were shaken, but they made no protest. The men eyed the woman for evidence of resistance as they dragged the litter behind a bush. Quickly, the women emerged with their weapons, and all five departed at a trot.

It was easy to follow the drag marks in the soft soil. Nicole stayed close to Chimene and Julia. A quick hand signal from

Matthew and William bolted ahead. Matthew slowed to a walk and the women followed suit.

Nicole whispered to the girls. "Stay quiet. Stay together." In a short time they caught up to William, who waited on one knee. He looked at Matthew. "Joey's dead." He glanced at Chimene. "We have the high ground. It'll be easy. Only twelve or so, about thirty yards ahead. That's where they are. In plain view, in a gully." Chimene paled.

Matthew looked at the women. "Stay in a group and keep to our left. Wait for my shot before you shoot." He patted William on the back. "We're going to execute every last one of them fuckers." He turned a stone face toward the women.

Nicole nodded and stepped to the left, stopped, and turned. The girls stood immobile, watching the men move away. Nicole rushed back and grabbed Julia's arm, pulling her and then pushing her in the proper direction. She did the same with Chimene. In a crouch, all three stepped slowly forward.

Nicole's heart thumped a drumbeat in her head. She had killed before and now she was about to do it again. She glanced at the girls. Julia stumbled and fell, but bounced back up, her eyes wide with fear. Chimene, closest to Nicole, stared straight ahead, tears dripping. Up ahead, the brush thinned out and the muffled noise of the insane grew louder.

Twenty yards farther, at the gully's edge, the auditory horror became visual. A milling group of half naked and dirty humans clustered around Joey's body. Only his legs could be seen. The crazies seemed to be arguing. One man shoved another and then knelt down with a knife in hand.

Nicole heard Julia vomit. The kneeling man's head exploded when Matthew and William opened fire. Nicole swallowed and steadied her rifle. She pulled the trigger and one of the humans fell. Chimene, equipped with the shotgun, blasted haphazardly. Julia continued to vomit. The crazies dropped quickly, and only one made it to the other side of the gully before disappearing into the brush.

All went quiet. Joey's body, nearly naked and extensively lacerated, lay among the other dead. One of the downed crazies made an effort to get up. A volley of bullets shuddered his form and he fell back, his warm blood steaming in the cool morning air.

Nicole ushered the girls away. Chimene's body shook with tremors. Julia, her head down, found support from the thin trunk of a small tree. Nicole pulled Chimene into a tight embrace.

Matthew hollered from the gully. "Go back to the supplies." Only Julia hesitated. Nicole touched her on the shoulder. "Julia, come on, back to the clearing."

The travelers struggled forward in anguish, Joey's absence and Chimene's grief darkening the journey.

A few days later, after a hard day's march, the group sat quietly digesting a meal of boiled rabbit. Matthew stood, went to the fire, and poured a cup of tea. William huddled in his selected place for his night's rest. Chimene rearranged things on the sled as Julia stood nearby, chatting in a low voice. Nicole sat away from the others, toying with a bit of grass. Matthew hoisted the pot of tea toward her. "Want some?"

Nicole shook her head. Matthew put the pot down and walked over to her. He looked beyond her to the western sky bright with pink clouds and a sun hidden behind a low hill. "Sailors' delight."

Nicole said nothing, her mood still somber. She and Matthew had spent little time together since the incident. Matthew sat down close to her. "Perhaps we should talk?"

She gave him a brooding look. "I grow tired of the struggle, Matthew. Only my kids keep me going."

She studied him for a moment. "What keeps you going? You've had great loss and you know that tomorrow will likely bring more of the same."

Matthew took a long drink of his tea. "These are dark days. I have lost my family and most of my friends. This expedition started with seven and now we are two." He paused and again looked at the glowing clouds. "It's simply the way things are." His brow furrowed. "But I refuse to believe there is no reason to it."

Matthew's face reflected some of the red light from the west. Nicole spoke in a whisper. "God's will...is that all you need?"

Matthew's posture straightened as if poked in the back and irritation colored his words. "I put no name on it. None of it, none of the pain." He paused. "And not just the pain of these times." He turned to her, half his face now in shadow. "History is full of pain." His head nodded as if he had just heartfully agreed to something. "It's not for nothing." He turned to the dark east, raised his cup, and almost yelled. "It can't be for nothing."

He spun to face Nicole. "You'll learn the importance of that." He sat down next to her, leaned forward and whispered. "All of this has reason. I know it. I feel it. I even dreamt about it." He leaned away from her. "You've been guided."

Nicole sighed. "Matthew! I've been lucky. Luck is luck."

Matthew shook his head. "Bullshit. Luck's a word that means nothing. Some sort of arbitrary thing that comes and goes. It can be good or bad. Some people have it and others don't. It's a word for people who believe in nothing."

Nicole jumped to her feet. "I believe in something. I believe in a Power." She stared down at him. "There has to be." His words kept sinking in and she angered at the illumination.

He looked at her. "Why are you here?"

"*I don't know!*" She stomped away and then spun around. "The world has fallen apart. I'm dodging crazy people in the middle of nowhere." She flung her arms outward. "Following this bearded guy." Nicole, almost crouching, glared into his eyes.

Matthew absorbed the words. Slowly his expression softened and he smiled. "A bearded guy?" He laughed. "A bearded guy?"

Nicole straightened her back and kicked a little dirt at him. "Yeah! A hairy dude that wandered into camp."

Matthew stood and put his arms around her, and she hugged him back. He spoke past her ear. "Storms are not forever."

William, quietly lying nearby, jumped to his feet. "I've heard you talk that shit before. We're animals and we die. That's it." He bent at the waist and glared at Matthew, pointing into the east. "Storms are not forever?...God or Gods, they want my ass, they want my guts. They eat me like I eat meat and with the same gusto. We're meat for the Gods. When Their bellies are full, the storm will end. Their full bellies are our only light." He stood up straight. "Fuck you and fuck the Gods and I hope They get Their fill soon!" He stomped away into the dark.

Matthew released Nicole. He turned west, the sky now dark, and hung his head. Nicole waited for words, but none came. She turned to the girls who were watching. She walked to them and sat down. A tear rolled down Julia's face. Chimene stared with somber eyes. No other words were spoken that night.

The next morning, after the meal, just before departure, Matthew approached the women. He took a shallow breath and spoke softly. "We're close to Ravens in the Sky." His mouth twisted. "There'll be great disappointment when we get there." He paused. "You three are not what they were hoping for." He cast his eyes down in a moment of thought and then looked up. "Please be tolerant with me." He rubbed his nose. "I'll be talking to the council..." He looked directly at Nicole. "And I will state things as I see them. They'll understand."

Nicole stiffened at the words. "Please Matthew, don't do that. I don't see us as having that type of importance, and it's embarrassing. Plead for us on a humanitarian basis."

Matthew's eyebrows lifted. "The humanitarian part is automatic. They know me and will understand my take on the situation. The statement will go no further than the council." He took a deep breath. "I know you don't understand. Someday you will."

Nicole watched him walk away. Chimene stood up. "He always sings the same tune."

Julia, rankled, spoke facing Chimene. "He believes what he says. And look at all he has done for us. You don't know anything." She looked defiantly at her mother. "I believe him. I stand up with him, or beside him...or is it for him? Whatever." She sat down and buried her face in her hands.

Chimene, angered, moved to hover over her sister. "We're meat, just like William said."

Words sprang from Nicole without thought. "Everyone's special. Everyone's meat."

She slapped her hands on her thighs. Frustration moved to anger and she yelled. "Get the sled ready! We'll be on the move soon."

After two days of the conversation, they arrived at Ravens in the Sky. They departed a wooded area and to the east they viewed the settlement situated in the middle of a large flat field on the top of a low mound. Fort-like in structure, the strategy of the location was obvious. In the light of day an unobserved approach seemed impossible. Perhaps a night assault, but without solid cover, the attackers faced a great risk.

The two men and three women moved into the open plain. Matthew stopped and shaded his eyes. "I'm sure they know we're here."

That proved true. As they watched, massive gates slowly opened, and a contingent of people headed in their direction. The travelers, exhausted from the last two days of hard marching, watched solemnly.

Matthew instructed the women. "Put your loads down and wait for their help."

Nicole studied the fort. Huge twenty-foot logs, perpendicularly stuck into the ground, composed the walls. The west wall extended two hundred feet from corner to corner. Men and women peered over the top.

As the contingent from the settlement arrived, they mulled around the men, seemingly oblivious to Nicole and her daughters. A young girl ran to William and hugged him. Another group surrounded Matthew. Matthew spoke to them with quiet words and a few of them cried.

One woman fell to her knees, and an old man struggled to help her up. Chimene watched without expression. Julia's eyes watered, a tear slid down her cheek. "Joey's parents are probably there." Chimene hung her head. Nicole turned to the west, her heart torn.

She turned back to a loud female voice. "Hi, welcome to Ravens in the Sky. My name's Awa." A young woman with a nice smile, long black hair, sparkling eyes, and a lively voice inspected the supplies on the litter. She wore blue jeans and a buckskin blouse; her native American heritage was obvious.

"Leave these here. The men will carry them."

Nicole extended her hand. "I'm Nicole and these are my daughters, Chimene and Julia." Awa embraced Nicole and spoke over her shoulder. "A short time ago, I too, came to this place as you do now. I was found by a hunting party." She pushed Nicole to arms-length. "You'll like this place. Plenty of food, a roof, a bed, and a bath." Her eyes darkened. "However, grief is everywhere." She nodded toward the weeping woman. "I too came with grief." She fingered a little pouch around her neck.

Some men came over and took the bundles off the sled and gathered the women's packs. The contingent walked slowly toward Ravens in the Sky.

Nicole and her daughters followed Awa through the gates, and a small silent crowd showed them scant interest. Preoccupied with Matthew and William, they followed them in the opposite direction.

Awa spoke with a turn of her head, repeating herself. "You'll like it here. The people are kind." She looked ahead and spoke louder. "When they saw you coming, they sent for me. I'm the last arrival and we'll share a cabin. There's plenty of room." She stopped and faced Nicole. "I also have a baby...It's not such a good thing, I know." Her eyes darkened. "There are the devils about." Her head nodded. "You have seen the devils, I'm sure." Nicole nodded affirmatively. Awa turned and walked on.

Julia tugged at her mother's sleeve. "A baby, holy cow, a baby." Nicole returned Julia's smile. Chimene's seemed indifferent. As they continued walking, the women noticed the fire damage here and there, but made no mention of it.

The house they went to, like all the houses, consisted of adobe walls with a log roof. It was quite large. They stepped into one large room with four beds and a fireplace that glowed with an old fire. To the right of the fireplace, a small kitchen, and to the left a bath, but no toilet. Awa faced the women. "The toilet's outside. Communal type. A five seater." She smiled an immense grin. "It beats the woods."

She showed them the beds and explained that the pillows and mattresses were all stuffed with chicken down. "They're warm and soft." She smiled. "There's also down quilts for the winter time."

Julia walked to a pillow and poked it with a finger.

Their next investigation constituted the huge bathtub, large enough for four, and full of heated water. Beneath the raised tub, a steel box sat with a wide pipe extending up through the tub and on through the ceiling.

Awa pointed. "You take a shovel or two of coals from the fireplace and put them in the steel box. It heats pretty fast." Then she pointed to a pipe and levered valve above the tub. "That's a shower head. You fill the tub with it, too. The drain is near the wall." She bent down and pointed. "Over there."

Awa straightened up. "The beds and the tub are the best two things in the settlement."

She put her hand into the tub water. "The bath's ready." She turned to look at them. "I gotta get my baby now." She smiled. "It's the only baby in the compound. Everybody wants to touch him." She walked to the door and closed it behind her.

Nicole, Julia and Chimene turned from the door and stared at the bath. Chimene spoke first. "A hot bath! A hot bath! I don't believe it." Nicole stuck her hand into the water. "Oh, it's ready. It's nice."

Awa returned within an hour with her baby and another woman who carried a stack of fresh clothing that she dropped on a chair near the tub. "Here. Some clean things." Her words were short and crisp and she quickly left.

Weakened by the hot water, the women simply gawked. Awa sashayed to the tub, her baby cradled in both arms. "They're not all friendly." She turned sideways to display the child. "This is Cheveyo." She kissed him on his forehead. "He's not in a good time. It makes me sad." She looked up at the women. "Many bad things happen." Her eyes blinked slowly. "Devils look for babies."

Nicole broke the mood with a broad smile. "A baby. I love babies. Haven't been near one in a long time."

Awa turned, walked to her bed and laid Cheveyo down. She went to the kitchen area where she picked up a potato and a knife.

Nicole and the girls lingered in the tub and only the smell of food lured them out. They donned the clean clothing and approached the kitchen with high expectations. The smell was wonderfully familiar. Fried potatoes, sausage, sliced tomatoes, toast, and fresh strawberries in goat's milk were waiting. Awa smiled brightly. "How do you want your eggs?"

Nicole swallowed. "We're all scrambled egg eaters."

Awa turned to the stove. "That makes it easy. You'll have them in a jiffy."

She cracked eggs and spoke without turning. "Sorry, no coffee, but it's good herb tea and we do have a bit of honey."

Her tone suddenly saddened, again. "They have lots of food here, but the reason isn't so nice. I'll explain later." Awa stirred the eggs frantically in the hot pan. The women filled their plates.

In the days to come, the women learned of the many battles fought, the great loss of life, and that the abundant food supply was a bequest of the dead. The somber atmosphere at Ravens in the Sky became understandable and infectious.

Although both sexes engaged in the battles, the men bore the brunt of the attacks, staffing the ramparts. The remainder of the personnel fought the fires, ran ammunition, or cared for the wounded. In appearance, the settlement offered security, but in truth it was dying a slow death.

There were only two people below the age of ten. Communal judgment pronounced the times too difficult for pregnancy and child rearing. Contraception was rigidly practiced.

Cheveyo, the only infant in the compound, symbolized the sad and dreadful circumstance of the times. Awa and her husband, after the collapse, were part of a small group living in the wilderness. Eventually over-run by crazies, all the men were killed, and Awa, along with a few other women, were dragged away into a situation of true horror. In time, Awa became pregnant, and soon after, found a way to escape. Alone, she found her way to the settlement. Months later, the child conceived in revulsion became the darling of the community. Whenever Awa needed time, there was always someone eager to care for the child. Now Nicole, Chimene, and Julia could be added to the list.

Two days after their arrival, Matthew came to visit Nicole. In hand, he carried a canvas bag containing the candy he promised her. He presented it to Nicole. "Don't let other people know where you got this." He smiled. "I don't want a mob banging on my door."

Nicole peered into the bag. "Oh yeah, the candy, I had forgotten." She cinched up the bag and kissed him on the cheek.

"I would've been here sooner, but the council took a lot of my time." He cast his eyes to the ground. "I also made visits to the family and friends of the men lost on the expedition."

He bit his lip. "I explained my view of things to the council."

Nicole's eyes squinted. "And, of course, you told them that we were on some sort of divine mission."

"Well I didn't use those words, but they got the idea."

"And what did they say?"

Matthew stroked the side of his nose with his index finger. "The short version," he grinned, "is that they didn't take it as significant information. But, they found it very interesting," He tilted his head.

Nicole's eyes burned into him for a long moment. "I love your sincerity and your honesty." She paused again. "And if it weren't for that." She clinched her teeth.

Matthew smiled. "They didn't say they didn't believe me!"

Nicole took his hand and squeezed it. "Let's drop the subject."

"They do believe your survival is extraordinary, and needless to say you and yours are welcome to the community. You'll be afforded all the protection we're capable of." Matthew squeezed her hand. "You, in turn, will be expected to help in some chores and, of course, in the defense of the place."

"Please thank the council. Tell them that we are ready to help and we want to help."

"I'll do that." He expelled a sigh. "Nicole, the situation here is not too good. Our numbers dwindle and there will be no further expeditions to find help. We'll stand as we are." He paused. "With each attack our chances dwindle." His eyes studied Nicole's. "Let's walk a bit."

He led her to the fortification walls. "This place is a very solid structure. The walls are Ponderosa pine." They stood under the ramparts. Matthew rubbed one of the timbers. "They're pretty new. Put in place a couple of years before the asteroid. The people here are..."

Nicole yanked on his hand. "Asteroid? What are you talking about?"

"You don't know?" His eyes widened and he smiled. "I guess that's possible." He pulled her into a short hug.

Matthew explained what happened, that the climate change and the earthquakes were probably a result of the impact. He told her the radio stated that the object hit somewhere in the South Pacific. "The effects will continue for some time." They walked on and Matthew rubbed his nose with his thumb and index finger. "There hasn't been much on the radio...of late." Nicole gazed at the ground.

Matthew waited a few moments. "I guess it'll take you a little time to absorb that one."

Nicole didn't look up. "I thought things were getting better." She paused. "I'll let the kids find out on their own." Her head came up and she took a deep breath.

Matthew spoke again. "If you're assigned to the walls, you'll be given a precise position to defend." He nodded his head. "There'll be practice drills."

Nicole turned, her eyes flashed. "We've been tested. We'll be of help."

"Oh, I'm sure of that."

Matthew stopped and turned to Nicole. "Should the worst happen. There are shelters...the nuclear war type."

Nicole smiled. "I don't think we have to worry about a nuclear war."

Matthew resumed the walk. "They'll be used for hiding."

Nicole's smile dropped from her face. Matthew continued. "They're supplied with provisions for three or four days."

Nicole tugged on his arm. "When was the last time the crazies attacked?"

"It was a few months ago, but it could happen tomorrow."

The couple spent the rest of the day together and then the night.

Nicole's family gained more information on the state of the world and there wasn't much to be optimistic about. A haunting notion that the worst was still to come lingered in the shadows.

Yet the women were among survivors, people tested, where the weak of body or mind met their end. With great difficulties forecasted, Nicole and her family were grateful for their inclusion into the society of Ravens in the Sky.

Weeks expanded to months, and peace continued, to the comfort of the community. The crazies that wandered near were in small contingents and kept their distance. They appeared nervous and fearful and sought no contact. However, a new danger emerged. Packs of wild dogs appeared often and in growing numbers. Quickly diagnosed as dangerous, they were shot on sight, though some disagreed with the policy, arguing that the dogs kept the crazies at bay.

But overall, morale of the community rose with the continued peace. Some even speculated the world had finally taken a turn for the better. Others focused on Nicole and her daughters, suggesting that their luck in the wilderness had clung to them and was now part of Ravens in the Sky. The trio achieved a mild celebrity status. The notion of their uniqueness, as Matthew once stated, found support.

This new perspective, annoying to Nicole, found favor with Julia and Chimene, bringing them attention and popularity. People sought to be near the family, inviting them to activities, and on some occasions, the guests of honor. In sympathy to Matthew, the failed mission flickered in a better light.

Even the weather cooperated. Gardens bloomed and produced bountiful harvests. The occasional earth tremors of the past ceased all together. Good news followed good news.

The household of Nicole, Julia, Chimene, Awa, and her baby Cheveyo, harmonized. The babe, the pleasure of the household, had at least one female always enthusiastic to meet his needs.

Awa and Nicole had blendable personalities and were soon confidantes. Awa, a Zuni, confessed to Nicole that her people welcomed the crumbling of the white man's society and had aspirations of returning to the old ways. However when the end came, few were prepared, and her pueblo scattered in panic.

Awa's life at the pueblo centered around her grandmother, a tribal shaman, who tutored her in the healing arts. Awa's skills were highly respected at Ravens in the Sky. She often prescribed for the sick, and Nicole and Chimene often helped with the pharmaceutical preparations. Chimene, fascinated by the art, assisted whenever possible, including the plant gathering expeditions.

Julia's flute playing contributed tranquility to the household, and Awa, enchanted by the instrument, took instructions from the girl. She learned quickly and produced music that flowed with rich, haunting undertones of her Native American culture.

Young men often appeared at the cabin to see one of the girls. They were mostly brash young men, their shyness driven away by exposure to turmoil and death.

Chimene lingered under the weight of Joey's death. Her personality tinged with a somber aspect, her relationships were short and had the semblance of being entirely physical.

Nicole and Awa sat at the large kitchen table, piled high with green beans, and baskets sat on the floor. The women cut the tips off and sliced them into short lengths in preparation for drying in huge food processors.

Awa grabbed a handful of beans. "Are you going to the book reading tonight?"

Nicole smiled. "Sounds like fun. I hear they're doing a play. Do you know which one?"

"No. But, if you get there early, they'll give you a part."

The door opened, and Julia ran in. "Hi. Just got off lookout."

She sat down next to Nicole. "Met this cute guy."

Awa looked up. "What's his name?" Awa stood when Cheveyo started fussing on the nearby bed. She waved a bean at Julia. "Remember, this is no time for babies. Bad things. The devils want babies." Awa went to the baby and gave him the bean to play with.

Julia smiled. "I don't know his name." Her eyebrows rose. "And I don't plan on having his baby."

Nicole tossed a bean at her. "You said you met him. That would suggest you learned his name."

Julia caught the bean her mother threw. "I was on lookout on the west wall, concentrating with the binoculars to my eyes." She took a bite of the string bean. "And I hear this. 'Hi pretty. You're Julia? Right?'"

Nicole smirked. Julia continued. "He's got long, black hair and brown eyes. I've seen him before, but never met him." She paused. "So he leans against the logs and looks at me." She took another bite of the bean. "I was really kind of annoyed. I mean, 'Hi pretty'?" She took a deep breath and shook her head.

Awa returned to the table and sat down at her previous position.

Julia stiffened and her voice shifted to a higher tone. "He says, 'Didn't mean to scare you.'" Julia raised her eyebrows. "I looked him right in the face. 'You don't have what it takes to scare me. Shouldn't you be at your post?'"

Nicole, still cutting beans. "Good girl."

Julia smiled. "He says. 'That's right. That's right. I should be at my post.'" Then he casually walks away, bumping his hand on the log wall. Like some sort of big deal."

She put her hands on her hips. "Now get this. He turns back to me. 'See you around the campus.' And he tops it off with this really over-confident grin."

Julia looked at Awa. "Pretty cool. Huh!"

Awa smiled. "Yeah, he's cool all right." Her eyes squinted. "I bet it was Jeffery."

Julia continued. "About a half hour later, I couldn't contain myself and I turned around and searched for him with the binoculars." Julia sat down. "I find him on the east wall. I watched him for no more than a few seconds when suddenly he turns around and waves at me. I almost died."

Nicole and Awa chuckled. Julia toyed with a bean. "It wasn't funny."

Nicole smiled. "Give us a hand with these beans. Have you seen your sister?" "No." She turned to Awa. "What does Jeffery look like?"

Awa wrinkled her upper lip. "Kind of ugly." Julia threw a bean at her and they all laughed.

The relationship Nicole and Matthew developed during the trip continued. They saw each other almost every day and their greetings started with a hug and a peck of a kiss. Their relationship wasn't passionate. It had simple warmth and the human touch in these difficult times was a need in itself.

On a cool summer night, after making love, Nicole and Matthew lay still, relaxing, anticipating a sound sleep. Nicole rolled to face him. "I have a question. It's about you. It's about the hell we are in and your composure in the face of it."

Matthew lay on his back, his hands tucked behind his head. He stared at the ceiling. "I don't know why you say that. I lose composure all the time." His head rolled to face her and he smiled. "Take for instance, a few minutes ago."

Nicole moaned in a sensual tone. "Yes you did and so did I." She stared at his nose. "Before I forget. Are you still hoarding candy?"

"So that's why you came to my bed! You want more candy."

"That's the second reason."

Matthew extended his left arm under the bed and hauled out a canvas bag. "Don't take the green ones." He handed her the bag.

"What do I have to do to be worthy of the green ones?" She picked out two lemon drops and handed the bag back.

He picked out three green ones and popped them into his mouth. "I'll know when it happens."

Nicole spat a lemon drop at him, hitting him in the ear. Matthew retrieved it and put it in his mouth.

Nicole swallowed a bit of the sweet lemon juice. "Now back to my question." She used her tongue and moved the candies into her left cheek. "I have seen you in very intense moments." She hesitated. Memories flashed. "The killing of the crazies, for instance." Again she hesitated, waiting for a reaction, but none came.

She propped herself up on one elbow. "That's it...right there. Your composure. A horrendous happening and you don't even flinch at its remembrance."

He looked at her. "Wouldn't you say that's a good thing?"

She blinked. "A good thing?"

"Sure. I did what I had to. It's over. I resolved it."

The last statements induced silence.

Moments later Nicole rolled toward him again. "Do you know something special? Something, deeply special. Was there some moment of insight in your life?" She paused, and he lay quiet. "You don't speak with religious zeal, but what keeps you propped up?"

Matthew extended his arms away from his body. His fingers opened and closed in a gripping motion. "No, no. Nothing religious." He paused a moment. "Maybe it is religious. I don't know." He thought for another moment. "No. It's not like that. It's just a hunch, a quiet feeling. It comes from the gut." His arms came down, and he rose up on one elbow and looked directly at her. "I feel," he paused. "No, I sense that things are OK." He blinked a couple of times. "Even when I lose, I know it's somehow OK." He paused another moment and laid his head down. "I know you hate it when I talk of you and the girls as being special, but I truly believe that. It's another gut feeling." He smiled. "I'm simply here to help."

Nicole shifted. "I like the first part...that things are OK, past and future. I like that. Although it's hard to assimilate. All those horrid things that have happened." She paused. "It's the last part. How can I accept such a thing?" She smirked. "Zeus has sent you to me? I'm on a mission of the Gods?" She waited for a response and spoke when none came. "Matthew, all I'm trying to do is to keep myself and my children alive."

"Nicole, we're all on a mission. You'll see, you'll see." He reclined on his back. "I have a gut feeling that tomorrow will be a remarkable day. Get some sleep."

Nicole, though unsatisfied, pushed no further. She extended an arm across his stomach. Sleep came quickly to both.

The next day the sun shimmered in a radiant, blue sky, most fitting for auspicious news. A hunting party returned to the settlement early, only two hours after leaving. In their midst, three strangers, buckskin clad and weapon carrying men. The lookouts spotted their approach and the news spread quickly.

The populace congregated near the gate and buzzed with speculation.

Two men pushed the gate open. The people watched the contingent draw closer and separated when they entered the compound. One of the hunters shouted, "These guys are from a place in the south." The crowd pressed forward. He shouted again. "Easy does it. We're taking them to the council room."

The party strode to the meeting hall and disappeared inside. The people congregated and murmured with speculation, Nicole and Matthew among them. She looked into Matthew's eyes. "A special day, as you said." She poked him in the belly.

Matthew tapped the side of his nose with an index finger. "The nose, knows." Nicole laughed.

Matthew smiled. "Jimmy Durante. 1935...I think."

Twenty minutes later the head of the council confronted the waiting crowd. The brightness of his eyes indicated good news. Their buzzing grew loud. The chairman raised his arms, and silence swept across the throng. His message was short and to the point. Almost laughing, he proceeded.

"The travelers are from a large settlement to the south. A place with a population of approximately one thousand two hundred. It's located on the shore of a great, new inland sea. The purpose of their expedition is to make contact with other groups of civilized societies and extend an invitation to join them."

Pandemonium ensued. Men threw their heads back and howled. People jumped up and down, kissed and hugged. At last there was hope. Nicole flung her arms around Matthew's neck. "The nose knows. The nose knows." She gave him a hard kiss on his smiling lips. When she let go, she saw Chimene and Julia pushing their way toward her. "Mom, mom, did you hear?"

Nicole shouted back. "Yes, I did. Oh, yes I did." More hugging and more kissing followed.

The noise level rose higher when the three travelers emerged. They were swept away and escorted to the grandest house in the compound to be fed, bathed, and pampered. A spontaneous celebration commenced.

Women rushed to prepare food, and the men piled wood for large fires. Like magic, tables and chairs appeared in the central plaza. From all the homes, jugs of wine and beer, home-made and potent, quickly dotted the tables. Soon the food started to arrive. Slabs of meat were skewered and racked to roast. Musicians and instruments appeared, Julia and her flute among them. Soon music reverberated through the air, and the first communal celebration in a long, long time commenced.

As the sun set the festivities flowed in the harmony of the happy mood. The heroes of the day arrived, clean and refreshed. Their presence electrified the crowd, and the populace struggled to shake their hands and plant the occasional kiss.

From the houses more food arrived. The musicians organized themselves, and cheerful tunes filled the air. The few children about became the objects of the people's joy. They were picked up and passed around, danced with, stood on tables and cheered. The fires blazed high and meat held near, sizzled. The dancing became a frenzy of many styles as ethnic backgrounds burst forth. It was a night of ruby wine and laughter.

Nicole and Chimene, of course, indulged heavily in the dancing while Julia and occasionally Awa made the rounds from one group of musicians to another taking turns on the flute. A glorious night, all gave themselves in fun and celebration, satisfying long-denied appetites.

The following day had a late start, the managing council not returning to assembly until late afternoon.

The chairman, affectionately known as "Horse", an old timer and one of the founders of the settlement, opened the meeting with the bang of a rawhide hammer. He stood quietly as people found a place to sit. Shortly he spoke. "I'm sure all here are aware of the visitors from the south and their proposal. However, I'll summarize. They come from a settlement in the southeastern part of New Mexico on the shores of a new inland sea. Their society is well established, having existed prior to the bad times. They have large amounts of provisions and trained personnel: doctors, scientists, artists. There are others. But, no need to mention more of that. They have not been subject to attacks as we have. They say it's because of their location. It's an area of low population and the new inland sea is a barrier to the east. They have invited us to join their group." The people erupted into cheers and loud chatter.

Horse banged the hammer three times. "Hold on, hold on." The noise abated and he pointed the hammer at the travelers. "They will lead the way." His gaze moved back to the crowd. "As you all know, our situation here deteriorates with each attack. The personnel we have for defense has consistently dwindled. I personally believe that our future in this location will not be long lasting. We dwindle faster than the hordes attacking us." He leaned forward, the knuckles of each hand planted on the tabletop, the hammer still in his right hand. "This is a decision that we must make quickly. All the facts are in. Winter is not far off and the men of the south will not wait."

He paused a moment to allow the people to think. He then turned to the leader of the contingent from the south sitting next to him. "I present Mr. Parker Chignik. He speaks for the southern settlement." Horse paused as he looked down at the man and then back to the audience. "Please be indulgent with our new friends. Their trip has been long and dangerous. One of their comrades was killed. They have, and understandably so, indulged in our fine wine and continue to do so." The chairman smiled and the audience applauded as Mr. Chignik stood up with a slight wobble.

A tall, thin man, he paused for a long moment as his eyes scanned the audience, as if looking for someone. He then put his hands on his hips. His body stiffened and he wobbled again. "I bring greetings *from*...the south." He paused another long moment. "I mean, from the place I come from." He looked at the other two men with whom he had arrived. "Isn't that right?" They waved and nodded their heads. One of the men started to stand up and another pulled him down. Parker turned back to the audience. "I will make my statement..." He waved his hand in front of his face, as if swatting flies. Then he nodded as if pleased with what he had done. The audience sat quiet and patient. "I'm not going to say much." His head wobbled and he looked again at his companions. "Isn't that right guys?" There was more hand waving, and head nodding. Again, his companion tried to stand up, but again they pulled him back. Mr. Chignik turned and squinted at the council. *"All,"* he made an immense swipe with his left hand, "Of those guys over there," he turned to his comrades, "know what's going on." His head wobbled a bit more and he placed his hands on his hips again.

"Sooooo! You're all invited." He lowered his head as if praying, then with a sudden move he looked up. *"But,"* he leaned forward, his brow furrowed, *"our losses are due to natural causes."* Again he paused and pointed at the other members of his team. "This expedition is humanitarian." He looked down at the tabletop. "This is also the last time I will do this." His head slowly came up and he looked at the people in a studious way. "Things are far, far, *far* too dangerous." He became quiet and it seemed as if he tried to look into the eyes of everyone present. "Lastly, I say we have a better chance..." his left hand swept through the air again, *"together."* He then sat down, though it would be more accurate to say he flopped.

Horse stood up. "Thank you Mr. Chignik. Thank you for the invitation." Horse turned to the audience. He smiled broadly. "I'm sure you get the drift of his words." Much laughter followed. Mr. Chignik simply nodded in acceptance. Horse hammered the table. "I now make a motion that we take an hour for a free discussion on the subject...among ourselves." The motion was seconded and people moved in all directions, rumbling the wooden floor loudly.

At the end of the hour, Horse rose to his feet and struck the table twice with his hammer. When quiet, he spoke directly. "I think it is clear, that all here are in agreement, that a prompt relocation to the south is in the best interest of all."

The audience sat mute. "All in favor raise your hand." All hands went up. Horse banged the hammer. "We go!"

A rumbling noise again filled the chamber as all stampeded for the door.

Horse banged the hammer one last time. "Meeting adjourned."

The vote was greeted with great joy by the populace. The war-weary habitants commenced at once the work of preparing for the journey. The trip would be difficult and dangerous. Traveling on foot, they'd either carry their goods or haul them in small carts. However, to the south there was hope, here there was none.

Within eight days of the festivities the preparations for the trip were completed. The only chore remaining was to store the excess equipment and supplies in the underground shelters, seal the entrances, and hide their existence. They chanced that in the future it would be possible to return and retrieve them. The atmosphere of the settlement glowed with the hopes of hundreds of people anxious to get underway.

Julia climbed to the ramparts of the west wall, a couple of pieces of hard candy from her mother in her pocket. She looked to the north end of the rampart and saw Jeffery striding toward her. They were seeing a lot of each other lately and today they planned to share the candy. Jeffery waved and Julia awaited his arrival with a bright grin.

"Hi pretty. You got the candy."

Julia smiled. "No, I ate it." Slowly she reached into her pocket and pulled it out.

"Wow! You really did get it." She held two, large, red candy balls.

"Go ahead, take one." Jeffery popped one into his mouth. "Cinnamon."

Julia put the other in her mouth and turned to the west. "We'll be leaving this place soon." She looked to the south. "Are you anxious?"

"You bet." He made a sucking sound and swallowed. "I want to be in front. Maybe I could be a scout." He looked at Julia with a serious face. "I'm sure they could use me for something like that."

"I'll volunteer with you. I've spent most of the bad times...out there." She looked to the west and her posture straightened. "What's that?" She pointed to a dust cloud.

Jeffery put the field glasses to his eyes and studied the cloud. "It's some sort of vehicle and...probably more then one." Moments ticked. He spoke without putting the glasses down. "Ring the alarm. I'll keep watching."

Julia hesitated. "I bet I know who they are." She ran to the bell and rang it three times. The lookout from the north wall came running. He arrived at Jeffery's side and followed his pointing finger. The boy signaled Julia to sound the confirmation alarm.

Julia shivered as the clouds sparked a remembrance, a dreadful remembrance. She swallowed spicy liquid and muttered, "Bikers," and rang the bell another three times.

More clouds bloomed repeatedly out of the north until they reached a place due west of the fortification. The dust settled and all indications of activity ceased.

On the following day, hours before dawn, a heavily armed scouting party departed to investigate the previous day's sighting. They were not gone long and returned with dire news.

Large numbers of crazies were gathering at points all around the compound. This had been seen before. What was new were the motorcycle riders who wore uniform-like leathers and directed the horde.

With heavy hearts, the managing council canceled the planned departure and issued instructions to make ready for battle. The lookouts were doubled and a few scouts sent out to ascertain general information of the horde's activities.

In the past, the crazies always attacked in a mob-like fashion and always at night. Most casualties occurred at the start of the attack with sleepy and unaware lookouts. On one occasion, an enterprising group dug a hole under the gate. Several entered and in a frenzy ran free, killing a few people and starting a number of fires before being shot.

But, for the most part, it was a matter of crude spears flying through the air and occasionally finding a mark. The defenders fired back, aiming instinctively. For the attackers, it was a matter of insane futility. With no climbing equipment or ramming devices, they accomplished nothing. The darkness kept their casualties low and the battles never lasted for more than several days. Eventually, the crazies departed, for what appeared to be, loss of interest. The greatest losses from crazies came from the ambushing of hunting parties.

This time things were sure to be different. The horde had leadership. This meant an organized attack and a plan to breach the walls. The old wounds of Ravens in the Sky would bleed again. Trepidation settled over the besieged populace and the people moved sluggishly. With short tempers they challenged The Powers that Be, who had for a short time lifted their spirits to an enormous high, only to find themselves overlooking a steep precipice. Death loomed in massive numbers and whispered of doom to intuitive minds.

In the black of a moonless night the besieging forces made their first assault. The defenders watched as large fires ignited in the north, east, south and west. From the large fires small ones danced away in large numbers. Hundreds of little fires bobbed in the night, while the moan of the bedeviled pulsated across the open plane. The torch fires kept their distance, moving in a counter-clock circle. The sight was enchanting, even beautiful. The defenders cursed and cried. However, the dancing flames served as a diversion.

The attack, already underway, startled the defenders with the foreign sound of fragmenting glass. The defenders peered over the west wall and wrinkled their noses to the smell of oil. Matthew fired a flare, illuminating scores of crazies rushing from all sides with containers of oil. The defenders opened fire and downed many attackers, but they had only two flare guns. The walls were soon soaked to half their height. All knew what was coming next. With the sound of blaring horns, the torch-bearers rushed toward the oil-drenched walls as the defenders did their best to find targets.

The sound of the horns ceased and the torches flew in high arches, assembling in the dirt as a fiery wreath. With no targets, the command to 'Hold fire' was issued, the flames still far from the walls. Shortly, torches levitated and swirled, before again flying at the walls. The defenders opened fire, but to little avail. Soon, another fire wreath flickered, a wreath much closer. The next throw would reach the timbers.

It was a short wait. Torches hit the wall and dropped to the base. Defenders rushed to fling buckets of water as more torches flew. The fires sprang up the walls and smoke screened the attackers. It became difficult to even look over the walls and the ramparts were abandoned.

The defenders gathered at the center of the compound. Horse, the chairman, jumped up on a table. "We have to make the shelters ready." He took a deep breath. "We'll need volunteers to stay above ground and fight." He waved both arms. "Get to it now. The fire will burn through the timbers faster than you think. At best we have one day before the walls fall."

Matthew found Nicole and Julia at the water station. "Get Chimene and Awa and meet me here. I found a shelter you can use. Hurry!" He ran off and Nicole and Julia shouted Chimene's name.

With flames and smoke rising high above the settlement, people rushed about in near panic. Nicole and Julia found Chimene, Awa and the baby and they scrambled back to the water station.

Julia turned to her mother. "Matthew said he found a shelter we could use. Does that mean that he won't be with us?"

"I don't know what it means." Nicole studied Awa. She held the baby tightly to her chest. Her face contorted with fear. Nicole could see her trembling. "Awa, how are you doing?"

Awa's enlarged eyes, glanced from side to side. "The devils are coming." She leaned forward, whispering. "And they want my baby." She pulled back in a hunched manner, her eyes again darting from side to side.

Nicole reached out and touched her. "Awa, we'll be safe in the shelter." She squeezed her shoulder. "They don't want your baby."

Awa continued to tremble. "It's not their baby. I'm sure."

The number of people moving about dwindled quickly. Most shelters being beneath buildings, the people seemingly vanished. Long moments passed, the women huddled together while clouds of firelit smoke swirled pass them. Nicole looked up at the ramparts. Men still ran with buckets of water.

At last Matthew's form appeared out of the smoky haze. "Follow me." And he headed for the west wall.

The shelter Matthew acquired, not built beneath a house, sat below open space near the west wall. The buried chamber consisted of a single room with a closet-like latrine. It was shaped like a lean-to, timbers formed the overhead. Four feet of soil covered one end and two feet covered the entrance. It's supply of food needed no cooking. There was ample water.

At the entrance, the women scrutinized the square, black hole in the ground. A shovel lay nearby. Matthew walked over to it. "It did have an air pipe. I pulled it out and filled in the hole. No need to advertise."

Nicole remembered Matthew's clarification that the holes were for hiding. Matthew spoke in a loud voice. "There's enough air for at least forty-eight hours. Don't move around and don't light candles without good cause." He looked at each one of the women in turn. "We still have time. Go back to the cabin and get anything you think you'll need." The women stood there looking at him. Matthew broke their bewildered stare. "Let's go, let's go. Back to the cabin." When the women turned to leave, Matthew reached out and stopped Nicole. He stepped close to her. "I put a revolver in the shelter. I'll try to find more weapons."

He stepped even closer and hugged her with one arm. "You're going to make it. It'll be OK."

Nicole grabbed his arm. "You're not going to be with us. Are you?"

"No. I'll stay above ground." He gave her a kiss. "Perhaps they won't think of shelters."

Nicole eyes narrowed. "Matthew. Do you think it possible that the bikers somehow followed us, that this fight is about us? Has anybody mentioned it?"

Matthew paused a moment. "I never told anyone about the attack on the road. It seems remote that this is related to that." He studied her eyes. "They've made no demands. The subject's moot. The battle is on."

He released his grip on her. "I'll try to talk to the people from the south. I was told that they did a lot of wandering and weren't sure how long it would take you to get to the place." He paused, rubbed his nose, his red eyes blinked in the smokey air. "Head southeast till you get to a large body of water and then search the shore." He winked at her. "That'll get you there." He leaned forward and kissed her again. "Bring everybody back here quickly and I'll instruct everyone on the shelter." Nicole kept looking at him as he walked away. He turned and swirled an arm in the air indicating urgency and then faded into the smoke.

A half hour later the women and Matthew stood at the edge of the hole. He smiled. "OK, everybody in. There's lots of room. Nicole! You should be last. Find a spot near the entrance. I'll explain."

The women approached the opening. Awa held the baby in one arm. Chimene reached to help her. Awa screamed. "No!" Her eyes squinted defiantly and she backed away. Chimene turned to her mother. Nicole sighed. "It's OK. Let her be." Gripping Matthew's hand, Awa and the baby descended into the shelter.

Julia and Chimene were next and finally Nicole. Nicole sat near the entrance and Matthew hollered to her. "Light the candle and see where things are."

Nicole lit a candle and looked around. Julia and Chimene sat to her left and Awa and the baby opposite her. Shelves of food and water filled the wall behind Awa. Matthew shouted again, "Nicole, there's a latrine to the right, behind you." The women looked around to locate other objects and verbally confirmed things with each another. Matthew lowered his upper torso into the shelter, and pointed at a loaded revolver on a shelf behind Nicole. He whispered to her. "You don't want to be captured by the crazies." Nicole quivered.

Matthew got to his hands and knees. "You'll find more weapons after you get out of here." He reached down and pointed with his thumb. "In the overhead to your left is a hinged trap door. You unlatch it and swing it up. It's held up with those two short poles." He pointed to her right. "I'll shovel soil over the top to hide the entrance. When you want out, all you have to do is kick down the poles. The trap door and the dirt will fall in." He paused a moment. "Does everybody understand?"

Nicole repeated his words. "Does everybody understand?" They all nodded. Awa's eyes widened. "Devils can dig."

Nicole turned to Matthew. "We understand."

Matthew got to his feet and shouted. "OK, everybody out. Go back to the cabin, eat something and use the latrine."

When the women were again on the surface, Matthew motioned Nicole to stay. After the others left, he pulled her into his arms. "I'm going to miss you."

Nicole rested her head on his chest. "Oh Matthew, I'm so sad."

He pushed her back. "Go back to the cabin and gather supplies for traveling. Stuff for the long walk south. I'll try to get better directions." Again he pulled her close, his lips between her hair and ear. "Time is short. You can get backpacks at the council room. You can take food from the shelter." He released her and gave her a little push toward the cabin.

Nicole walked away, her head down. Matthew shouted after her. "I'll let you know when it's time." He watched her a moment before turning toward the water station.

When he got there, Horse was directing water bearers to the west wall. Matthew walked up to him. "How much time do you think we have?"

Horse spoke with a grim face. "They seem to be concentrating on the west wall." He wiped his brow with a dirty rag. "It all depends on how much oil they throw."

Matthew picked up a bucket. "Daytime is not far off. I'm sure they'll back off when that happens."

He walked toward the west wall and shouted over his shoulder. "I'll try to get a look at the damage." Horse shouted an acceptance. "As soon as you can."

The crazies departed before light. As the sun came up, the defenders continued to pour water on the fires and by noon the flames were out, but the timbers still smoldered. Matthew walked the entire rampart, leaning over here and there to inspect the walls. When finished, he went directly to Nicole's cabin. Nicole saw him coming through the open door.

He stepped in. "Hi."

"Good timing, the tea's hot."

"I can't. I have to report to Horse. Is everybody ready?"

A gray shadow fell across Nicole's face. "Yes."

Matthew spoke from a face haggard and dirty. "I don't think the walls will last another attack. Meet me at the shelter at sunset."

He leaned forward and kissed her on the cheek. Her hands rose quickly and she kissed him on the lips. She released him. "We'll be there. You get some rest."

Matthew turned and walked away.

At sunset Matthew arrived at the shelter. Nicole stood there with the others, a pile of droopy backpacks near the hole. He spoke directly to Nicole. "I couldn't get any better instructions to the other place. It's somewhere on a new sea that borders New Mexico." He shrugged his shoulders and tilted his head. "The men from the south attempted an escape late last night. I hope they made it."

Nicole whispered. "There's something going on with Awa. I'm afraid for the baby."

Matthew looked over her shoulder. Awa stood quietly holding the child. He saw no movement beneath its wrap. He spoke loudly. "Awa, how's the little one?"

Awa smiled. "The devils won't get him. He's in good hands."

Matthew looked back at Nicole. "Strange." He paused. "No sense making a fuss now."

He took a deep breath. "OK, time to get in the shelter."

Awa, hunched over the baby, ambled to the hole. Holding the baby with one arm, Awa gripped Matthew with her free hand and descended into the shelter. Julia and Chimene kissed Matthew and disappeared below.

Then it was Nicole's turn. Tears rolled down her face. She stepped close to Matthew and a short hug led to a lingering kiss. Without words she stepped away and descended into the shelter.

Matthew spoke as candlelight flickered across Nicole's face. "You're going to make it." Nicole smiled and she swung the trap door into place. Matthew listened to the poles being stood upright. A moment later, Nicole's muffled voice spoke to him. "Take care love...we're ready."

Matthew hollered, "Till another time."

He picked up the shovel and looked around. A breeze blew a cloud of smoke away, and another man on the other side of the settlement stomped soil near a building. "This place is becoming a living graveyard." Matthew pushed the shovel into a mound of dirt.

Below, the wooden cover thumped to the cadence of the shoveling, the noise dimming as if moving away. The candle was blown out. Someone sobbed; someone coughed. It was dark, quiet, and smelling of earth. A tomb.

Above, Matthew finished the task by scattering dust and walking over the spot until sure of its concealment. He tossed the shovel at the fortification walls. "They'll make it. No problem." He turned his attention to the ramparts above.

A few men watched him. Matthew waved and they waved back. When he turned, he saw his old friend Jacob, a man nearly his age, one with whom he had often hunted. Matthew picked up his rifle and trotted after him.

He patted Jacob on the back. "Hey buddy, where're you headed?" Jacob swiveled his head toward Matthew. "Matthew." He smiled. "To hell, probably."

Matthew chuckled. "What say we do this on the west wall? Together."

Jacob put an arm across Matthew's shoulders. "I always did like hunting with you." He smiled. "OK, the west wall it is."

They climbed to the ramparts and found a spot to sit and wait. The men chattered of the days gone by as the skies darkened and a distant moan swelled in volume. Matthew reached into his pocket and drew out a handful of candy. He picked out the green ones and handed the rest to Jacob.

"Jacob! Have some candy." He smiled. "Things are going to be just fine."

"I'm sure they will, Matthew, I'm sure they will."

Under the cover of night the invaders again doused the walls with oil. Matthew and Jacob listened to the periodic shattering of glass. They ate candy and watched a man drag bodies to different parts of the compound. Horse walked from place to place, pointing in one direction and then in another.

Jacob turned to Matthew. "I hear we're out of flares."

"Yeah. That's true."

Matthew got to his feet and looked over the wall. The dance of the fire twinkled. "Jacob, take a look. It's kind of pretty."

Jacob stood up. "Do you think we'll fool them with those bodies?"

Matthew sucked on his candy. "No, I'm sure they'll look for shelters." He turned to Jacob. "I'm sure five will make it."

"Five? Now how did'ya come up with that number?"

Matthew tapped his nose. "The nose knows." He looked to the west. "Life is great!"

"You're a strange one, Matthew."

The dance of the torches maneuvered slower this night, more methodical, almost ceremonial. Shots were fired and a few torches dropped, but they didn't lay there long. They lofted back into the air and bobbed away.

One and a half hours after the attack began, the walls were in full flame. The ramparts were again abandoned and the men grouped at the center of the compound, awaiting the collapse of some section of the wall.

Matthew and Jacob knelt on one knee facing the west wall. Behind them more men knelt, they faced the east wall.

Jacob coughed in the swirling smoke. "This sucks. They're going to be on top of us before we see them."

Matthew's eyes watered, but he held his gaze on a certain spot a few yards from the west wall.

"Hang tight friend." He nudged Jacob in the ribs. "Don't let them drag me off."

"You got it, pal." Jacob coughed again. "And do the same for me."

Outside, the attackers gathered at the west wall. Men in colored leathers grouped before a swarm of crazies. Two in yellow and ten in green. A stack of long, heavy poles lay close at hand. The timbers smoked, but the flames were subdued.

One of the men in yellow yelled to the men in green, "Get them fucking logs against the wall."

The men in green walked among the crazies, pointing and shoving them to the pile of poles. In a short time, many polls were braced against a section of the west wall.

The man in yellow shouted again, "Throw more oil on the sections either side of the poles." He turned to his other companion next to him. "The smoke will keep them from sniping at us." His craggy and scared face smiled. "Get Puller over here. I want him close."

Black smoke rose up the wall and folded over the top. A bunch of the crazies with axes ran beneath the poles and begun to chop at the timbers. The one in yellow shouted another command, "Get some pressure on those poles."

Standing alone and to the rear of the mob, a man in red leathers watched quietly.

Within the walls of Ravens in the Sky, Horse spoke to the company of volunteers. He had turned them all to face the west wall. "They're coming through this section." He pumped his right thumb over his shoulder. The chopping thudded rapidly. Horse took a deep breath and bellowed. "Fight like fucking hell. It'll make the dying easier." He turned and knelt before his men.

Within an hour that section of the west wall bulged inward. Loud cheers sounded from the chopping mob.

Matthew extended a few candies toward Jacob. "Take half."

Jacob smiled and reached for the candy. "Green. Getting generous on your last day?"

"Nah. It's all that I have left."

Matthew took a deep breath and eyed a specific place just in front of the bulge. He smiled. "Marvelous, simply marvelous."

Jacob looked at him. "What's so fucking marvelous?"

Matthew, still smiling, his eyes sparked. "Life, Jacob, life."
Jacob shook his head.

Outside the wall, over fifty crazies were assembled, with
more behind, to run up the inward bulge and trigger the final
collapse. With a blast of a horn, the charge commenced. The
bulge collapsed with a thundering noise and a horrendous
gust of dust, fire, and ash. The defenders were driven on to
their backs from the hurricane-like blast. Only a few shots were
fired as the insane stampeded through. Jacob died when a
spear pierced his neck. Matthew soon followed, his head
pounded to a pulp by a heavy club.

The crazies raged through the compound killing anything
that moved and mutilating that which didn't. It was a scene
from the horrors of hell with the animal noise, the dismem-
bered bodies, and the flickering fire and smoke.

At midnight a contingent of lean, non-crouching figures,
two in yellow leathers and ten in green, but not the one in red,
appeared out of the darkness and swaggered into the compound. One of those in green walked at the side of those in yellow.

The others in green proceeded to the standing wall. They
raised their torches high and took long strides as they examined each corpse. The ones in yellow strolled about at random,
using their feet to roll bodies over.

The rampaging crazies occasionally found a shelter and the
inhabitants, whether dead or alive, were dragged to the feet of
those in yellow and the one in green. The unwanted were
hauled away to die an unspeakable death in the hands of the
insane. This procedure continued through the night and into
the new day.

The rising sun mellowed the mood of the crazies and most
drifted off to rest. However, the ones in leather maintained
their vigil, anticipating the still hidden to come creeping from

their hiding places. They stationed themselves within the council building, resting and eating their meals, oblivious to the carnage at the doorstep. Their intentions were to stay for three more days.

Earlier, when the battle raged and fires and axes ate away at the walls of the settlement, a child and four women huddled in a dark hole. They weren't prepared when the timbers collapsed with a thundering crash that rumbled the shelter violently, showering the inhabitants with dirt. The poles supporting the trapdoor fell away. The door swung its full arc and latched itself to the ceiling. The loose soil cascaded in and the air filled with choking dust and the blare of the battle above. Now, only the fallen timbers concealed the hiding place of the five.

Nicole fumbled for the revolver and her mind flashed with its intended use. Frantically she gripped the gun and swung it toward the opening. As she scooted to her left, she whispered commands to herself. "No, no. The kids, Awa." She swung the gun to the right, froze, and waited.

Moments passed without an intruder. Nicole trembled to the staccato of tramping feet. The pile of soil beneath the entrance was topped with glowing cools, lighting the ash that fell to the rhythm of the stomping. The women huddled as mice in the ash chamber of a wood stove, while screaming and howling humans sought their capture.

Nicole whispered to the others, "The timbers must have collapsed. They're running over us."

The girls murmured something. Awa whispered, "The devils are here."

Nicole responded, "Be quiet, be very quiet."

Occasionally a voice shouted directly into the chamber and the mice flinched with a fear that had real pain.

Then suddenly it ended. The drumming stopped; the screaming gone. The air-borne dust settled silently. Nicole leaned to her left and peered up at the ruby red of smoldering timbers. She sighed and slumped, her back against the wall. In a shaky voice she whispered. "There's time…timbers cover the hole."

Nicole lowered the weapon to her lap and shivered at distant noise and unintelligible words. She looked at the soft ashen dust coating her arms and her tongue sampled its taste with a flick across her lips. She gathered the soiled saliva and pushed it through her pouted lips. Hot, glowing embers illuminated the shelter in a feverous red.

Nicole's eyes shifted to Julia and Chimene and a moment later to Awa and Cheveyo. Her lips formed silent words. "Five people, six cartridges...and the first?" Nicole balked and closed her eyes tightly. "Discipline, Nicole, push your emotions away," she thought.

Slowly she contrived a death plan. Julia will be first and then, as quickly as possible, Chimene. Two more shots in the direction of Awa and the baby. Nicole closed her eyes again. "My aim will be true." For herself, inserting the barrel of the gun into her mouth concluded the plan. Nicole took a deep breath, scanned the phantom-like shapes in the hellish light and rethought the plan.

She injected more detail. There would be commotion from above, yelling and screaming as the timbers were pried apart. Then feet would thump onto the chamber. Capture being assured, she'd raise the pistol toward Julia. Perhaps a voice. "What's down there." That's when she would pull the trigger. Julia would slump over as she quickly pointed at Chimene and fired. Two more quick shots, the first at the child, the second at the mother. And then, finally the gun to her mouth. Nicole hung her head and wondered if the barrel would be hot, and if her suicide would be easy.

She repeated the death scenario, reinforcing her intentions with vivid imaginings of her loved ones in the hands of the berserks. Her breathing slowed and a calm state enveloped her. She raised her knees and held the weapon in her right hand, between her legs. She ceased her visual concentration and tuned an ear to the noise from above.

Julia watched her mother. She watched the movement of her head, and saw the gun in her hand. Julia's right hand clutched at Chimene's trousers, and she whispered to her, "I hope I am first."

Chimene, mesmerized by the glow of the coals, whispered, "You will be. I'm sure."

She reached over to touch Julia's hand. "Look at the red coals. They're warm and cozy." She paused and then squeezed Julia's hand. "I've been shot before. It doesn't hurt."

Awa rocked back and forth, the bundle cradled to her bosom. There was no sound from either.

In the living tomb, time slowed to a stagnant pool, it slouched and never flowed. Their light was the red of the coals, while tramping feet echoed as muffled thunder. Horror oozed with periodic screams of men, women, and children, fading screams that compelled unwanted images.

The earth's rotation propelled the compound out of the shadow of night and into solar light. The sun's rays poured a shaft of light between fallen timbers revealing ghostly forms, ash dusted, seemingly bloodless.

Nicole put the gun aside. A tear rolled from the outer corner of her right eye exposing living color. The girls sat with their feet drawn up, their arms across their knees, giving support to their heads. Awa's legs were stretched out, and the babe held to her breast, still quiet, still unmoving.

Nicole studied the cooled embers to her left. The next night would be in total blackness. But light is a peril for mice. Mice were easy to spot in the light and Nicole dared not a look up the shaft for fear of eyes looking down.

Julia lifted her head, moaned softly and looked around. "Water." No one replied. She crawled to a jug on the other side of the shelter and dragged it back to where she was sitting. She took a long drink and moaned again. Awa extended an arm toward the water and Julia handed it to her. She put it to her mouth and swallowed twice before handing it back. Julia nudged Chimene and handed her the jug. The water was passed around twice and emptied by Chimene.

From above, the sounds came periodically. They were sometimes garbled shouts and sometimes the sound of feet crossing the timbers.

Nicole stretched her arms and rotated her head. She whispered to the others, "Use the latrine. Eat something. Take care of things now. The night will be very dark. Be very quiet."

Slowly, all this was done and everyone assumed a position of comfort. The once angled shaft of light advanced to the perpendicular, decreasing its illumination. The day proved uneventful and time ticked by until darkness swallowed the hovel. The night separated into periods of sleep and wakeful hallucinations. Dreams bloomed in color and eyes opened to blackness, generating confusion and fear.

Above ground, in the night, the crazies milled about, some with loads of booty. Others had females whom they dragged from the settlement. They uttered weak cries and their struggling was more a consequence of stumbling.

It was after midnight and the biker dressed in red leaned against the west wall of the council house smoking a cigarette. The overhang of the building shadowed his face from the light of flickering fires. He was tall and lanky. The fingers of his right hand nervously pattered the butt of a nine-millimeter pistol holstered on his hip. An hour ago he walked across the smoldering timbers with determined steps.

This, his second visit, the first, in daylight during the initial search for three women, ended in failure. In annoyance he shot a few of the crazies, stomped from the compound and spent the rest of the day indulging in drink and drugs.

A short, stocky man in green leathers carrying a torch trotted by, but stopped suddenly, turned, and raised his torch toward the building. "That you, Spade." The torch was not bright enough to light the man's face.

"Yeah, it's me." He flipped his cigarette into the air.

"You want some women?"

Spade straightened. "I don't want *women, shit head*. I want *the* women."

"Right, right. We're looking. Puller's checked all the ones we found."

Spade leaned back against the wall. His speech, nearly a growl. "No women for anyone till my brother's killers are dead."

The man in green stepped a little closer. "We found this guy and got him to talk. He said the women were here, but he didn't know where."

Spade's fingers tapped his pistol. "Bring him here."

The man in green backed away. "Well, I'll check." He trotted off and spoke over his shoulder. His words nervous. "But, I think he's dead."

Spade rapped the wall behind him with a balled up fist and muttered. "The fuckheads." He stepped into the low light of lingering fires.

He had a shaven head and an angular face with a pointed chin. Deep-set eyes hid in shadow and small ears accentuated his bony look. He lit another cigarette, stepped over a few bodies and onto the smoldering timbers. "They're here." He sniffed the air. "We'll get 'em, Bro."

At that moment, a pulse of light expanded from the north. Its intensity increased until Spade raised his right arm in defense and dropped to one knee, his head down. The blast of light penetrated the space between the logs, exposing a hole and what looked like a short pole. The light faded and Spade positioned his head as if listening, but quickly rose to his feet. He stumbled on the timbers, but found balance with extended arms. He made his way toward to the council house, looking like a man gone blind. He stopped, put his hands on his knees and tried to compose himself. "What the fuck was that?" He looked to the north momentarily and then turned sharply back to the timbers.

Shouting and bobbing torches caused a distraction and he straightened. His entire contingent, scrambled to a position in front of him, jabbering and fidgeting. The crazies ran past and out into the blackness. A second flash struck. This one came more from the west, and the night was lit like day. The entire group dropped to the ground, and Spade turned to face the wall. The flash projected heat and then subsided. Spade turned and shouted again, "What the fuck is that?"

His men rose to their feet, hunched in fear. A man in yellow approached him. "There's some kind of bad shit going down. We gotta get back to base."

Spade pulled his pistol, but did not point it. "We finish this shit first."

The one in yellow stepped back. "We got people and things back there. We got nothing here."

A dim glow of short duration flared to the north. The contingent, agitated started stepping backward. Again the one in yellow spoke. "It could be more asteroids," he shouted, "We got nothing here, Spade." The contingent turned as a group and trotted over the timbers.

Spade threw up his arms. "Stop, you shit heads." His command had no effect. In less than a minute he stood alone.

He holstered his pistol and walked to a dropped torch. Picking it up, he hurried to the timbers and crouched above the hole. Again a burst of light engulfed him, and he dropped to his knees and stared between the timbers. As the greenish light faded, he rose to his feet. For a moment he stood as he was and then tossed the torch aside. He muttered quietly as his head swung from side to side. "Sorry, Bro. Fucking sorry." He ran a few steps into the blackness, stopped, and looked back. "Fucking shit, I can smell'm." He bared his teeth, clenched his fist and bellowed into the sky. "Fuck youuu."

A smaller glow lit the night. This one much farther off. "They must be dropping fucking bombs or something." He hesitated no longer and ran to join his comrades.

Earlier, below in the hole, Nicole listened to the clump of solitary feet and a moment later a strange greenish light penetrated the chamber. The glare froze the ashen faces of the others into macabre masks. Nicole closed her eyes and stiffened. A cold wave passed through her body. Something from the past neared. She knew the touch. Its presence oozed down the opening and raised the hairs on her left arm. Nicole's eyes popped open in recognition. "Bikers." The strange light faded.

Julia murmured, "Oh mommy, a moon-storm!"

Nicole puckered her lips. "Shhhhhh."

Above, the solitary one moved away, and Nicole's urgency eased. Shortly, a commotion commenced with people yelling. Someone ran across the timbers and more followed and more followed. Another glow penetrated and faded, more commotion, and more people running.

For a few moments, things were quiet. Then slow moving steps stopped close to the shaft and a dim light intruded. The ugly presence was back. Nicole's stomach cramped and she held her breath. Another green glow accompanied a thump from above and Nicole flinched to her right. The glow faded, the presence diminished with the sound of steps, and a powerful scream touched her with revulsion. Nicole shivered when cold air dropped into the hole. Then, surprising calmness enveloped her and she drifted into sleep.

Hours later, Nicole sat peacefully, her eyes closed to the blackness as she mused about the absence of sound from above. "I feel no threat. I feel like I'm just sitting in a hole." With her eyes still closed, she scooted to the top of the dirt pile and got to her knees. Slowly she extended her torso up to the logs and touched them with her fingertips. She waited and listened for what must have been close to half an hour and then sat back on her legs, her thoughts meditative.

Another half hour passed. Nicole sucked a deep breath and finally opened her eyes. Still blind she crawled back to her place.

Chimene, roused, whispered, "What were you doing?"

"I was listening at the entrance."

"What did you hear?"

"Nothing, absolutely nothing."

The night moved slowly in the continued quiet.

When the rays of the returning sun entered the hole, all were awake. Awa placed her baby bundle on the ground and went to the latrine. Nicole watched the bundle for signs of movement. She looked at the girls, but they paid no attention. Awa returned to her place.

Nicole stationed herself under the timbers again. This time there were sounds, though different. She discerned flapping wings coupled with bird-like noises, a few barks, and a few snarls.

She returned to her place. "I think they may have gone." The others listened without expression. Nicole bit her lip and her eyes shifted. "Have we been here two days? Or has it been three days?"

Chimene's chest expanded with a labored breath. "Two days." Her eyes closed. "I'm sure. Two days."

Nicole slumped and her cheeks puffed. "One more night."

For the rest of the day the women spoke in short conversations and moved only to get food, drink or to use the latrine. Awa fussed with the baby, but the others never heard its voice. She hummed softly and held the baby to her exposed breast. Nicole watched with deep concern.

Another night fell, oppressive and distorting to the mind. Nicole again held the revolver between her legs. The ugly task delegated to her, strangely, lost much of its intensity.

The morning sun found Nicole awake, listening again to the animal noises seeping into the hole. Nicole watched Awa rock back and forth. She turned to the staring eyes of her daughters. "Perhaps it's over." Matthew's words crossed her mind. "I think we made it."

Julia stood up and went to the latrine without comment. Chimene looked at her mother, and Nicole spoke to her, "I don't think there's anybody up there."

Chimene closed her eyes and arched her back. "Must be careful." She relaxed and shook her head. "But another night would be dreadful."

Nicole's eyes brightened. "I think we made it." Her head nodded a few times. "I think they're gone. If they weren't, the animals wouldn't be here."

Julia crossed to the other side of the shelter for food and water. "How can we be sure? They could be sitting there waiting for us."

Chimene moved to the latrine. "We can never be sure."

Nicole looked at Awa. The young women remained quiet, still rocking Cheveyo. "Awa, what do you think?"

She didn't answer and she didn't look up. "Awa, Awa, do you hear me?" Awa begun to chant. It was an Indian chant; the tones were soft, repetitive, and very sad.

Nicole went to her and bent down trying to look into her eyes. "Are you OK?" The chanting continued without distraction. Nicole studied the bundle in her arms, but couldn't see the babe.

"Awa, is the baby OK?" Nicole put her hand under the baby's blanket and drew it back with a jerk and a shudder. Whatever she had wrapped in the blanket was hard, much too hard for a baby.

"Awa, let me see the baby." She reached for the child, but Awa paid no attention.

Nicole stepped back to her place.

Julia whispered. "Is she OK?"

Nicole's brow wrinkled. "We have to get out of here. Get the latrine shovel."

Chimene turned to Awa. "Awa, can I see the baby? Let me hold him."

Awa stopped rocking and chanting. "The poor little thing is fine, just fine." She paused. "I just fed him. The poor little thing is fine, just fine." She lowered her head and recommenced the chanting and rocking.

Chimene turned to her mother. "There's something wrong. Isn't there?"

Nicole looked at the overhead. "We have to get out of here." She looked back at Chimene. "That's the first thing." Her eyes brightened. "OK. You and Julia start digging. Follow the line of the timbers to the end. Don't break through. I'll do that."

Julia knelt at the opening and dug the spade into the dirt pile. Nicole tapped her on the shoulder. "Be as quiet as you can."

Chimene and Nicole picked through the things in the shelter and topped off the backpacks with foodstuff and other things. Chimene slid one of the packs close to the entrance. "Where are we going?"

Nicole hefted a backpack. "The settlement in the south." She put more things in the pack. "Matthew told me how to get there."

Nicole turned to Awa. "We're leaving this place. We're going up. Get ready."

Awa ceased chanting and stared with vacant eyes.

Nicole shook the girl's arm. "We're leaving. Do you understand?"

Awa delivered a slow nod and moved to get up. Nicole restrained her. "I'll let you know when."

Nicole and Awa sat silently and watched the girls dig. Awa studied the lengthening trench. "Are they covering the grave? Are we leaving the kiva?"

At first Nicole wrinkled her brow and then she smiled. "No Awa. There's no grave. We're getting out of here. I think we made it."

Nicole turned to the girls. "How's it going?"

Julia answered. "The soil is soft. It's going fast."

A few minutes later both girls exited from the trench. Chimene looked at her mother. "We're at the end."

Nicole stared down the trench. "OK. When I'm out, Julia's next. Then Awa and the baby. Chimene, you pass up the packs." She picked up the shovel and tucked the gun in her belt. "It'll be OK. It feels right." She headed down the trench. "Let's do this fast."

The path, lit by a line of light squeezing between the timbers, extended for about eight feet. The thin beam warmed a narrow strip on Nicole's back. She crawled to the timber's end and sat quietly, listening intently.

Nothing had changed, only birds and dogs. Nicole picked at the last bit of dirt leading to the surface. A large chunk fell in. Nicole stopped and her hand went to the gun. A dreadful smell drifted from above. Two minutes passed and nothing changed.

Nicole dug some more, expanding the hole to allow her to poke her head through. She put the shovel down and pulled the gun out of her belt. "I'm going to take a quick look."

A moment passed, she gathered her nerve and extended her head above ground. She checked the area in all directions, ducked back down, and hollered, "It looks OK. Only vultures and dogs. I'm going up." She poked the hole wider.

On the surface she found herself in the land of the dead and rotting. Many bodies and parts of bodies lay strewn across the land. A heavy stench stung her nostrils and imparted the taste of rancid oil and garlic in her mouth. Huge vultures hopped about, their heads and necks wrapped in red skin. Annoyed with Nicole's sudden intrusion, they flapped their wings and spat a snake-like hiss.

Nicole, hunched, scanned the area with a slow turn. Satisfied, she peered down into the trench. Julia was watching her. "Come on up." Julia was quickly out. She was startled at the sight of the vultures and dogs and grabbed her mother's arm. "The smell's awful." She covered her nose and mouth and gawked at the sight. "Oh my God."

To the east, a heap of bloated bodies shimmered in the heat. Nicole eyed a scattering of cigarette butts, nearly at her feet, strange and macabre under the circumstance. The casualness indicated was unthinkable.

Nicole instructed Julia. "Help Awa."

It didn't take long to get everyone above ground. They stood together, their packs at their feet.

The drone from millions of flies, large, black, and bulging from their gorging, sang a nauseating song of death; the greenish meat laying about quivered with the next generation of the insects. Unlike the vultures, the fearless flies swarmed about the women. In repugnance, they pulled their shirts up, covering their mouths and noses. All except Awa, who seemed oblivious to the horrid spectacle.

Dogs sulked in the shade of the still standing timbers. Shamefully, they held their heads low and their open mouths exposed red tongues that throbbed in the heat. Their shifting eyes indicated guilt for their appalling deeds. Some whimpered with tails between their legs. Others snarled at the witnesses and hunched their backs as they sashayed sideways. The place, a fester and these, the cleaners, indicated that the humans must depart.

A blazing sun stilled the air. Lazy corkscrews of smoke twined into the blue sky. A short distance away, Nicole sighted a spear, its point, a knife. She spoke without looking at the others. "Hold here while I get that spear."

The girls remained quiet, but Awa resumed her chant. The melancholy tones intertwined with the lazy smoke.

Nicole returned. "Get your packs on, and we'll get out of here."

Nicole hoisted her pack to her back, hauled Awa's in her left hand, and picked her way through the dead. The flies swarmed, and only the fear of stumbling and falling onto a gas-bloated carcass kept the women from breaking into a run.

Now and then a vulture threatened, spread its wings, awkwardly hopped in a pseudo-attack, hissing, and vomiting a green-slime. The dogs, more sinister, moved around the intruders in wide circles. Others ignored the humans and licked the gaping wounds of the dead.

This blight of the dead extended a full half-mile from the settlement. When the women cleared the area, they took deep gulps of the cleaner air. However, a residue clung to their clothing and skin.

Nicole turned south. She pointed at a green line of trees that stood above golden grass. "I hope there's water there."

Chimene's sack dangled from her right shoulder. "My body is twitching with the feel of that filth. I don't even want to lick my lips."

They pushed through the knee-high grass as the sun baked sweat from their bodies. Awa's song continued in a low volume.

Julia trotted to the front of the line. "Mom, I can smell water. I really can."

At the trees they thankfully found a small stream. Nicole and the girls wasted no time in dropping their burdens and heading to midstream, clothes and all. They submerged themselves in the slow, flowing water, permitting the current to wash away the real and imagined filth.

Nicole stood up in knee-deep water. Feeling cleaner, she lumbered to a shallower section where water gurgled over a gravel bar only inches deep. She sat on the small, smooth stones, her legs stretched out and her back to the current. She relaxed to the feel of the soft water and a sun now warm instead of hot. Nicole calmed as she studied the twinkling liquid and the multi-colored stones. "We're still alive, Matthew."

Her soothing preoccupation was shattered by a blast from the revolver and she spun toward the sound. Awa slumped to the ground, a small curl of smoke escaped from the barrel of the gun. At her feet lay the baby's unfurled blanket and upon it, a piece of firewood.

The only survivors of the settlement, a mother and her two daughters, tended the last victim of the disaster at Ravens in the Sky, covering the body with the pretty colored stones of the stream. When done, the weary women gathered their meager supplies and headed south in search of yet another settlement on the shores of a new inland sea.

The Vision,
Lights at Night
(Justin)

Justin, Michelle, and Paul moved through the hills east of Oregon's Willamette Valley while frequent, brutal storms pushed in from the west.

The supplies retrieved at the time of David's death diminished. The most pressing need was for vitamins, soap, and dried food. They possessed several ways to make fire, but their supply of matches, a luxury of speed and ease, dwindled. Their clothing was adequate. They still had the ax, the cable, and the shovel. Their needs were not drastic, but replacement seemed wise. A trip to the coast was planned.

The trek to the western side of the mountain range took two days. The family dropped their packs and rested on a high hill overlooking the Willamette Valley. To their surprise and dismay, the valley glittered with the waters of a huge lake stretching from mountain range to mountain range. Neither the southern nor the northern ends were discernible. The family stood before a body of water they estimated to be at least twenty miles wide and of undeterminable miles long.

Paul sat with his back to his pack. "We could build a boat." He paused. "Make that a raft."

Justin studied the sparkling sea. "I suppose we could put something together. A raft would work with some sort of sail."

Michelle scanned the area with binoculars. "We could spend a lot of time doing that." She lowered the glasses and handed them to her father. "I think I saw some smoke on the far bank."

Justin took the glasses, adjusted the focusing, and put them to his eyes. The far shore stretched as a green line broken with patches of black. Justin located the smoke. "It's coming out of the trees. It could be either smoke or mist."

He handed the glasses to Paul and sat cross-legged next to his pack and bow. "Could be someone there we don't want to meet."

Paul looked to the south. "It'll be a long walk to find either end."

Michelle followed her brother's gaze. "Well, it's not like we have appointments to meet. We could cover a lot of ground in the time it takes to build some sort of boat or raft."

Justin put his hands behind his head. "If we walk the lake's edge, the going should be simple. I think Michelle has the right notion. We're not equipped to build a boat or raft." He pointed with a move of his head. "And then the big question...who's on the other side watching us sail across?"

Michelle reclined with her hands behind her head. "So then. A walk to the south?"

Justin waited for a comment from Paul. When none came, he inquired, "What do you think, Paul?"

"Cutting logs with an ax is a lot of work, a lot of time, and a lot of noise."

Justin rolled his head toward the south. "That's a lot of negatives to the boat idea." He looked into the sky and closed his eyes and relaxed. "OK. A walk to the south it is."

On that day, moving at a leisurely pace, they commenced the journey. There were many hills to climb, and each valley had its stream, creek or river to cross. To the family's delight, after three days of travel, the lake's girth shrunk by half.

The adventure was thankfully mild and being near water, game was plentiful.

On the fifteenth day, Justin alone climbed to the top of a hill. The lake waters no more than a mile and a half wide, he wanted to scan for its end. He situated himself on a ledge above a steep, treeless slope and waved to Paul and Michelle who, with their packs off, reclined in the shade of a large pine. They waved back.

The hill's height awarded a cool breeze that dried the sweat on Justin's brow. He opened his shirt and flapped the halves to cool his chest and then sat cross-legged, his torso hunched. Behind, a tall pine supplied comfortable shade. "I smell like two weeks of albacore fishing."

Justin looked down at his children. Twenty yards behind them, in a small clearing, a group of deer nibbled on newly sprouted brush. That being the only activity, his attention returned to the lake and he relaxed in the momentary isolation. The black water of the lake sparkled with tiny diamonds of light. Large stones, half hidden by tall pines, sporadically dappling the lake's steep edge, appeared as boulders of jade with their blankets of vibrant green moss. A soft blue sky and a blazing sun framed the tranquil scene.

Justin recalled the last time he sat on the back deck of the house in Winchester Bay. He mused about building a home here. "Any kind of home would be nice." Negative thoughts began to pepper his mind. He sucked a weary breath and rubbed his temples. "Enough of that."

He squinted and shaded his eyes. Even without binoculars he saw the lake's end. Moments later, he pulled the binoculars from a pouch on his pant leg and unraveled its cord. He put the cord around his neck and let the binoculars hang. He flapped his shirt halves again and raised the glasses to scan the lakeshore from due west to far south. There he paused to make a meticulous inspection. Something caught his eye and he uncrossed his legs and maneuvered onto his stomach. His elbows rested on the ground and steadied the glasses.

"Ahh, yes. Definite spires of smoke." A few moments passed. "I wonder who?"

He took the glasses from his eyes and rolled to his back. The ground, cool in the shade, sucked more heat from his body through his damp shirt. Justin closed his eyes.

Moments later he sat up, a strategy devised. They'd get close enough to see who made the spirals, but he dismissed the idea of making contact. Then they'd circle to the east and slowly turn to the west.

Justin descended the hill and sat near his children in their shady place. He took a few moments to catch his breath and drink some water. "Well...the end of the lake is occupied. Smoke in the sky."

Michelle rose up on one elbow and looked at her father out of the corner of her eye. "Are we going to take a look and see who they are?"

Justin leaned over and pulled a piece of jerky out of her pack.

Paul sat up and threw a small stone at Michelle. "Why even get close? Our policy is to avoid everybody."

Justin spoke with the jerky sticking out of his mouth. "True, but I want to see who's there. We're not going to make contact."

Michelle picked up the stone Paul threw at her and threw it back. "Perhaps things will look good."

Justin ignored the implications. "We get close and see what we can and we do it at night."

He chomped on the jerky. "Best to know what's there. We may need to make a wide circle or perhaps a small circle would suffice." He swallowed the meat in his mouth and bit off another piece. "We could save a lot of time and effort if we could cut through." They rested for another hour before continuing the journey.

The next night, the trio moved to within binocular range of the southern encampment. Paul stood near his father who held the field glasses to his eyes. "I smell goons."

Justin put the glasses in his pocket. "You're right," Michelle muttered, "Shit, damn it, shit."

As planned, the family turned due east in a circular movement. With each succeeding day their course changed by approximately forty-five degrees to the south. On the fifth day, with a half circle completed, they'd be headed west to the coast and well into northern California.

At the end of the third day they were in dry open country. The area showed extreme destruction in all directions. To the south, heavy black and white smoke blotched the sky. Much of the surrounding area was blackened by brush fires. The ground appeared twisted. Mangled mounds of dirt and craggy fissures required detours. Small rumblings in the earth indicated a continuing process. All the creatures in the vicinity were extremely timid.

On the fourth day, Justin stood in the morning light adjusting his backpack. "Today we move due west. I don't think we need to go any farther south." He smiled. "Besides, our mother-sea awaits our arrival."

Paul took the lead. He turned around and walked a few steps backwards. "I want to walk a sandy beach, and splash my feet in the cold Pacific."

Michelle fell in line behind Justin. "Dad, do we get to go through Winchester Bay?"

Justin wasn't really sure. "You bet. Look at the old house. Check things out."

Michelle skipped a step. "All right, Dad!"

Justin proceeded with caution, stopping often to scan the area with the field glasses. During one of these stops, they spotted a low-flying helicopter. A military craft, a sure indication of a government installation.

Justin took the glasses from his eyes, remembering the warnings from radio broadcasts to stay clear of government encampments. "I know they don't want us around, but a little information on what might be in front of us would be a big help."

Paul, with his hands cupped over his eyes, watched the dot in the sky drift north and disappear. "I think it landed." His hands dropped to his side. "Yeah, time saved and trouble avoided."

Michelle, ever eager for contact, agreed. "If we approach openly and in a friendly way a few words with somebody should be no big deal." She turned to her father. "Let's do it."

Justin put his thumbs under the straps of his pack. "OK. We'll approach slowly. If they shoo us off, they shoo us off."

After a few more miles across flat land, they stopped and Justin again studied the area with the glasses. He spoke as he scanned. "There it is. Fenced...a steel fence and...I would think. Yes. Razor wire."

He put the glasses down. "OK, let's get a little closer." He strode forward. "If anyone comes toward us, raise your hands above your head."

Another mile farther, Justin stopped for another observation. "Two fences. The first fence is much higher, perhaps electrified."

The observations were irritating to Justin. He conjured an image of self-important politicians hiding from the people they swore to serve, and whose money provided the civil workers with their means of survival.

The installation consisted of four buildings with smoke issuing from a stack at the southern building.

"They have a power station."

A few vehicles moved about the facility. Farther to the west, cultivated fields of crops sat under the spray of an irrigation system. Even from a distance, it was obvious that the compound provided a very comfortable sanctuary.

Justin pointed to the north side fence. "We'll follow that fence." He looked at his children. "We'll stay well back and look for an entrance."

They traversed the fence from a distance of nearly three-quarters of a mile, heading west. Near one of the buildings, rising like some sort of huge insect, a helicopter jumped into the air. The noise of its engine and throbbing rotary blades were audible. Justin waved his arms.

"Maybe we can get the information now."

The low-flying chopper flew toward the eastern fence. Then, with abruptness, it rose higher and veered sharply toward the north and the family. Justin stopped waving. The craft bore down on the family. Justin watched suspiciously. "Spread out." They moved apart.

In a few moments, the flying machine dove toward them. From its belly flashers of light appeared. Small geysers of soil erupted from the ground forty yards in front of the trio. Then came the cracking sound of machine gun fire. The family turned and ran toward the north. Again and at their heels, another rippling sound of spraying bullets. Michelle, in a fit of anger, yelled. "You fucking jerks." She tripped over a stone and fell forward. Justin rushed to help her to her feet. Another spray of bullets peppered the ground just behind them. They broke into another run. Michelle turned to her father. "I don't understand. What are they afraid of?"

Justin gasped, "Shut the fuck up and keep running."

The chopper closed in, its rotor blades throbbing. The air about the three exploded with flying dirt and stones. The family dove to their bellies and covered their heads. The rotor blast beat them to the ground with punches of air. Stones and pebbles flew like buck shot.

The chopper passed over and lifted high into the air, made a sharp banking turn and plunged for another close pass. The blasting rotor-wind again sweeping over the family, peppering with stinging stones. Even with heads to the ground, the dirt rose into their face, choking every breath.

The helicopter flew on. Justin got up on all fours, spitting dirt, and blinking the dust from his eyes. He rose to his feet, his arms and legs pained from the many hits. Puffing in short breaths, he trotted to the north and the others followed. Fifteen paces ahead, they found shelter in a shallow ravine with a small stream running through it. They collapsed against its southern wall.

Justin spat some dirt. "Fuck, a hailstorm of stones."

Paul brushed his face. "I guess that was a 'no'." Paul turned to peer over the edge of the ravine. The helicopter shriveled as it flew to the east and then slanted to the south. He pounded the ground with his fist. "Somebody, give me a rocket."

Michelle leaned her head against the embankment. "Those stones really hurt." She rubbed her right buttocks. "A big one got me right in the ass." She looked at her father. "What are we? A bunch of coyotes?"

Paul glared. *"A gun. Just one big gun."*

Justin hung his head for a moment and then he looked up sharply. *"Damn assholes. Wasn't any need for that."*

After a short rest, the family regained their composure, anger subsiding into the blues. Justin knelt at the stream and splashed water on his hot face. "Evidently that was routine for them."

He got up. "Let's follow the stream for a while." Paul and Michelle muttered something to one another and in a single file followed their father.

The family stayed in the ravine and occasionally looked over the edge to check their proximity to the government installation. They were moving gradually away from the site and in general, westward.

Near dark and after rounding a bend in the ravine, they saw a man lying on his back thirty yards ahead on the opposite bank. Without a word the group dropped to a defensive crouch.

The man appeared unconscious or dead. He wore buckskin clothing and his only visible weapon, a sheathed knife, on his hip. A dark stain on his lower chest indicated a wound. Quietly the family moved to the man's side. Paul and Michelle watched as Justin made an inspection. He pried one of the man's eyelids open. The dark dot at its center contracted. "He's alive."

Justin turned his attention to the stain. A small hole at the center suggested a bullet wound. He pulled the man's knife from its sheath and cut a slit through the bloody circle. With his index fingers he spread the slit. Large blood clots clung to the lower end of the wound. "It's a bullet wound." Justin released the garment and sat back. "If it came from that chopper, it's high caliber." He lowered his head. "I don't even want to look at his back."

A moment later Justin took another look inside the flap. Blood flowed in a tiny trickle from thickly jelled clots. "He's been lying here a long time." Justin again sat back on his haunches. "He'll die soon."

He rubbed his chin, closed his eyes, and envisioned flashes of light at a chopper's underbelly. An unsuspecting traveler waving an arm in greeting. Warning shots are poorly aimed, and a piece of hot steel drives a man off his feet with great force.

Justin opened his eyes. "What keeps you alive?" He pondered the calm, dirty face and was swept with sadness. Justin's gut tightened with an inkling that he knew the man. "We'll stay until he's dead." He paused. "Get enough wood for a small fire."

Paul and Michelle dropped their packs and left without a word. Justin dropped his pack, went to the stream, and cupped water in his hands. Back at the man's side he washed the ashen face and dripped a few drops into a gaping mouth. As if fed a magic potion, the man's face contorted and both eyes opened, the right pupil opaque with death. The man's mouth moved and Justin leaned forward to catch the weak words. "Justin." Justin shuddered, but held his position.

"Justin...go southeast...good place people." Justin slowly settled back on his haunches and watched the living eye cloud. Justin again closed his eyes, and his mind lit with the dim glow of violet light. Rippling lines appeared and formed an image of the dead man's face. Beautifully, its deadness dissipated. The face smiled and receded slowly into the violet light. "Destiny Justin, destiny." Justin opened his eyes.

He smiled and repeated some of the dead man's words. "The southeast...a good place and people."

Justin raised his eyes to the sky and saw Paul and Michelle standing on the rim of the ravine, firewood in hand. Paul dropped his load close to his father. "Is he dead?"

"Yeah. Just a moment ago."

Michelle slid down the slope, cradling her wood. "You mentioned the southeast and people. What's that about?"

Justin looked at her blankly, his mind stumbling. He blinked and the words flowed as if compelled. "He called me Justin. He told me to go southeast. He said there's people there."

Justin got to his feet and smiled at his children. A compulsion burned in his mind. But the insight felt awkward and coated with fear.

He climbed out of the ravine and stood next to Paul. "Jump down and hand up the body. The shovel, too. I'll take care of this myself." He avoided his children's eyes and said nothing.

Paul jumped into the ravine. He knelt down, pulled the man's torso onto his shoulder and stood up. Justin grabbed the man's collar and pulled him over the ledge. Michelle handed him the shovel.

The siblings watched their father drag the man away. Michelle turned to Paul. "That was strange. He knew Dad's name?"

Paul kicked at the firewood. "I guess." He bit his lower lip. "I hope this doesn't change things."

Michelle's eyes squinted. "You don't think he's going to do what the man said?"

Paul's cheeks puffed as he exhaled a breath. "Let's move a little way from here and build a fire."

They moved to another location, built a small fire, ate a bit of food, and waited.

About an hour later, Justin jumped into the ravine. His sudden appearance startled both Paul and Michelle. He smiled and went directly to the stream to wash his hands. A few minutes later he crouched over the fire. "Let me have a piece of jerky, please."

Paul handed him a large chunk. It wasn't very hard, purposely made that way to allow for quick consumption. Justin bit off a piece and chewed with gusto.

Paul sat with his back to the ravine wall. "You look very bushy tailed for someone who has just buried someone."

Justin ignored the statement. "Tomorrow we reverse course and head southeast."

Paul scowled. "I knew it."

Michelle, wide-eyed. "You're kidding!"

Justin's words rang with confidence. "He said there's a place with people." He paused and bit his lip. "He knew my name." His eyebrows went up. "He told us to go there."

Paul spoke slowly. "How far?"

"He didn't say. But, if he can walk it, so can we."

Michelle huffed. "That's not the point. Our supplies are the other way."

Justin's tone signified little room for discussion. "Tomorrow we head to the southeast." He looked into Paul's eyes and then into Michelle's. "This is the right thing to do. Trust me."

Paul and Michelle glanced at each other. Paul lifted his eyebrows, shrugged his shoulders, and turned back to Justin. "We should stipulate just how far we go southeast before turning around."

Justin took another bite of jerky. "We'll take it one day at a time."

The next day, well before first light and without a meal, the trio backtracked through the ravine. They passed the place of the helicopter chase and continued until the government compound was out of sight. Only then did they leave the gully.

Paul walked behind his father. "I don't think this is a wise move, Dad. We shouldn't move away from our supplies." Justin didn't respond. Paul spoke again. "That man was dying, most likely incoherent." Justin remained quiet. "Perhaps he got it wrong."

Justin stopped, but didn't turn. "You have to trust me on this, Paul." He started walking again. "It's a gut feeling." He took a few more steps. "I can't explain it, but we're doing the right thing." He flapped his left arm. "Besides, getting to Winchester Bay wasn't a guarantee."

Michelle strode to Paul's side. "But we were heading toward something we knew was there."

Justin stopped and turned. "The place to the southeast is there. I touched a man from the place." He turned and walked on. The conversation was over.

For days, they traveled to the southeast and moved into the state of Nevada. The trip was uneventful and their pace was sluggish. Paul and Michelle were understandably nervous. The items they had on hand were being used up, and they pestered their father daily. Justin, hoping to find the place quickly, or at least a sign of it, was reluctant to offer an explanation.

The area they traveled was once populated and they found food and a few supplies. On one occasion, they found an abandoned vehicle, which they ran until exhausting its fuel.

From time to time they sighted other people. However, they too were timid and rushed away at first sight.

At the end of two weeks travel, they rested in a dilapidated house. Michelle went over to her father and sat down next to him. "Dad, isn't it time to turn around? Every step we take to the southeast will have to be repeated on the way back."

Justin studied her eyes. "I know what you're saying, but I am sure we're on the right path."

Michelle lowered her head and looked at her feet. "I don't really fear for my life, Dad." She lifted her head. "And I don't see any likelihood of getting any of the things I once wanted." She paused. "They simply don't exist anymore."

She looked directly at him. "But the way we die." Her eyes saddened. "I don't want it to be starvation or...what if we get separated." She pointed to the north. "Back in Oregon, we might have been able to find each other. Here we will be...just lost."

A few moments went by and Justin took a deep breath. He didn't look at her. "I have no answer to that."

Michelle rose to her feet. Her mouth twisted and her eyes glared. *"We can't just keep walking south. Who cares about a dead man?"*

Justin looked up at her. "Trust me, please trust me."

"Trust you, trust you. You're the one talking about logic. Where in the hell is the logic in taking advice from someone almost dead?"

Justin got to his feet. *"OK. OK."* He paused, walked a few steps away and turned back to her. "I had a vision." Michelle slapped her thighs with both hands. *"A vision."*

"Yes a vision. Just after he died." Justin walked to the wall and leaned his back against it while folding his arms. He lowered his head. "It was all very real."

Paul had been resting on the other side of the room and spoke from a sitting position. "And you still think it's the thing to do?"

Justin looked up. "Yeah." He pushed away from the wall. "One more month, I want one more month."

Michelle's eyes widened. *"A month, another month?"* She turned to Paul *"He wants to go for another month."*

Paul stood up and walked over to them. He looked at Michelle. "He's been right about all the important things, so far." He turned to his father. "Right from the start." He turned back to Michelle. "If he wants a month, that's OK with me."

Michelle took deep breaths and folded and unfolded her arms. Paul returned to his place across the room and spoke over his shoulder. "There could be a big payoff."

Michelle looked at Paul and then at Justin and nodded her head. *"OK. OK."* She sat down next to the wall, drew her knees up, and wrapped her arms around them. A few moments later she replied. "A month it is. A month it is."

Justin sat down, closed his eyes and checked his doubts.

The next day, as the family walked, Paul and Michelle strode behind Justin, who, silent for the first few hours, suddenly spoke as if someone had poked him with a stick.

"I'm not out of my head, you know." Both Paul and Michelle startled at Justin loud words.

Justin took a few more steps. "That was the first and only vision I ever had." He paused, turned and lowered his voice. "Perhaps that's why it affected me the way it did." He turned and headed on.

Paul turned to Michelle and smiled. Justin continued, "I can't get it out of my head." Paul turned to face Michelle and silently mouthed the words Justin said. He bobbed his head around and made a silly face. Michelle's eyes brightened and she bobbed her head in a like manner.

Justin's right hand flew up into the air. *"What am I supposed to do? Ignore it."* His hand came down.

Paul turned to Michelle again, imitating his father's hand action and waddling like a duck. Michelle moved close and gave him a shove. Paul almost stumbled into Justin and stopped to gag his laughter. Michelle put her hand to her mouth and bent down to avoid the silly look on Paul's face. Justin continued. "We should pay attention to those kind of things." He paused and slowly turned to face his children. "The dead man was a messenger. Somehow I know him."

Justin stood his ground and looked to his children for a sign of understanding. Paul and Michelle stood there with a half smile and raised eyebrows.

After a long silent moment, Paul turned to Michelle. He made a funny face and his hand went to his mouth. He muffled his laughter with faked coughing. Michelle strode up to him and knocked his hat off. Paul retrieved it and put it back on his head. He took a deep breath and turned to face his father. Justin stood quietly, his brow furrowed, his eyes squinting. The moments of silence piled up awkwardly. Justin did not move.

Suddenly the two siblings spoke in unison. *"Really!"* They shot a quick look at each and doubled in laughter.

Justin bellowed. "Hey, you two, I'm serious."

The statement only added to the levity. The two youngsters sat in the sandy soil, their energy draining with their foolishness. Michelle removed her pack.

With growing annoyance, Justin instructed them. "You had better stop, or I'll start getting mad."

That, too, was the wrong thing to say. Paul fell to his side rollicking, and made some sort of gesture with his right hand.

Justin took a few steps to his son's side and kicked some dirt at him. *"You ridiculous ass. It's a very important thing."*

Michelle rose to her feet and came to Paul's rescue by flinging her arms around Justin's neck. "Dad, you're priceless." She dragged him around in a circle, giggling as she did. "It's a very important thing! It's a very important thing!"

Paul slipped off his pack and waved his arm. "It's a very important thing! It's a very important thing!" He then fell to his side howling with laughter.

Justin struggled awkwardly to stay upright and serious, but Michelle held on. Justin persisted, *"I think the dead guy was a friend of mine. From a previous life or something."*

Paul had tears in his eyes. "The dead guy...or something."

Justin smiled and his previous words sounded silly even to him. He went round and round with Michelle, laughing harder and harder. Soon, all three were consumed in mild hysteria. Michelle let go and they both fell into the dust.

The family made camp at that very spot and turned the evening into a time of jubilation. Two rabbits, taken earlier, were roasted, and a pot of herb tea was brewed. The trio sat around a fire, indulging in good conversation and telling funny stories from the past or poking loving jabs at each other's shortcomings.

Only a sliver of the moon rose into the star-filled sky as the family's conversation softened. The tired group rose to their feet and after a three-way hug, found spots for the night's rest.

Justin stifled the smoldering fire and reclined into his sleeping shroud. He looked into the sky, feeling calm and somehow relieved. For the moment, his family was safe and his inner self assured him that they were on the right track.

Justin beamed at the Milky Way. "My home." He took a breath of the cool night air and closed his eyes. In contrast to the stillness of the campsite, the low muffled sound of Michelle's weeping came to his ears. Shortly, she cleared her throat, and the silence resumed.

Justin was sure she felt hopeless in their situation. Gone were her dreams of love, romance, and children. He rolled to his side. "Things are worse for her." Justin's rolled onto his back. "The joys of a fulfilled woman, but not for her. Sweet wine poured on outstretched hands." He could understand her anguish; he could feel it and she could only sense the wine's aroma. Justin rolled back to his side. "The sun will rise and stop the nightmare."

The day was joyful, and the night troubled.

The family would soon be living totally off the land, the umbilical cord to their supplies stretched beyond its limit. As they made a trek into Utah and then into Colorado, the additional vulnerability gave them all an inner twinge.

The unfamiliar land required a lot of time to snake around obstacles and to search for food. Michelle's knowledge of plants and mushrooms was life-saving, but carbohydrates were a constant problem. Proteins they hunted, the internal organs supplied vitamins. When nourishment presented itself, they indulged and gathered a quantity to take with them. Often the bonanzas came from farm crops growing wild.

However, on one occasion they traveled three days with minimal food before downing a deer. It was an anxious situation, causing Justin to question the wisdom of his decision.

There was the occasional encounter with roving bands of goons. Most of the time they simply avoided them, but not always.

In early morning the family stood at the edge of a small wood. The air was cool and a lace-like mist clung close to the ground. For two days the group had followed a goat, trying to get within bow range. Michelle stepped out into the field and crouched between knee-high plants. After a moment she stood up and turned to the others. She spoke no words, but simply held a carrot at arms length.

Justin looked at Paul and smiled. "What's up, Doc?"

They walked to Michelle and Paul took the carrot. "I was hoping for potatoes."

Michelle smiled. "Goat bait."

Justin hoisted another. "That, too."

Every few yards produced another plant. They cut the tops off and placed the roots in a mesh bag. In the middle of the field with the mist burned away, Paul turned to Justin. "Carrot soup?"

Justin saw the blur of something to his left, and Paul ducked. A spear brushed by Paul's face. He reached to his forehead and dropped to the ground. Justin spun to his left. Michelle shrieked and fell forward, a spear in her back. The weapon tipped over and fell out. Justin hunched low and brought his bow to bear.

"Can you get back to the woods?"

Paul rushed passed. "I'm on my way." Blood ran through his fingers. Michelle came next. "I can make it, Dad."

Justin readied an arrow and stood up, listening to his children's retreat. He waited as long silent moments passed. Finally, Paul's voice boomed, *"We're at the trees."*

Justin stepped backward as a goon jumped up and threw a spear. It was easy to avoid. The man stood his ground and screamed unintelligible words. Justin released his arrow and the shaft passed into the man's mouth. He fell backwards. Justin ran to the trees.

All three trotted deeper into the forest and hid behind a fallen tree. After a few moments of quiet, Justin inspected the wounds. He looked at Paul's first. "Put your hand back on it. You'll need stitches."

Michelle removed her pack. "I think my jacket prevented a deep cut." She took off her coat and Justin lifted her shirt. "Stitches as well. Stay put, I'll get the stuff."

Justin rummaged through Michelle's pack. "I got it."

Justin treated Michelle first. "Try to stay quiet and keep an ear for trouble."

He took a deep breath. "I think they were trying to protect the field. I don't think they'll follow."

With the medical chores completed, they headed away, again toward the southeast.

The degeneration of the goons continued. Their vacated camps indicated the continuance of cannibalism and at some locations, the use of fire was not evident. With intensified hatred, Justin's family lost all compassion when administering death to the wretched beings.

The wilderness produced a new horror, a new death. It came in the form of wild dogs. At first, the canines were shy and scattered. Later, instinct drew them into packs, which stimulated bold behavior.

The goons were the dogs' easy prey. Their simple weapons were of little use against a large pack. Justin and his family frequently came upon evidence of such encounters and it became standard practice to shoot any dog on sight. The canine situation always required consideration at camp time. They picked places easy to defend and on occasion lit more than one fire. The possibility of encounters at unfavorable times and places was a constant worry. This situation arose in a wooded area of Colorado.

A pack of dogs approached from the rear, their periodic barking served as a warning and convinced Justin that they were being hunted. "We need a place before dark. The damn dogs are getting close." Justin turned to the howl of a dog. "We need high ground, or something."

Paul stepped forward. "Let's not waste time." He trotted off at a fast pace; the others followed.

By late afternoon, the family arrived at a stream and commenced skirting its bank in an upstream direction. A half-mile later the waters of the stream split and then recombined forming an island. The small island, with a single conifer tree near its center, seemed defendable. On the upstream side, a fallen tree trapped a large amount of debris, and the downstream side closed to a point consisting of gravel.

Paul pointed to the island. "We can set up there. The dogs won't be able to surprise us." He pointed to the upstream end. "There's lots of firewood."

Justin waded out to mid-stream. The water rose a little above his knees. "It's deep enough. They'll have to swim."

Paul and Michelle followed Justin to the island.

Justin dropped his pack. "Let's get some firewood." He looked around. "Two fires. One at the water to light things up, and one here at the center." He paused a moment and looked at the pine tree. "Let's make some torches with pine branches. They won't last long, but long enough."

They quickly established their position. With weapons ready, they waited quietly at the center fire.

The pack arrived at dark. They came to the water's edge and pranced the shore, shadows with eyes flashing in the firelight. Paul took aim and let an arrow fly. A dog yelped and the pack disappeared into the brush. "I might have nicked him. It didn't sound like a solid hit."

The night passed slowly. The travelers slept little and kept their weapons at the ready. It wasn't difficult to stay awake, but always, one person stood to avoid unintentional sleep by all.

With the rising sun, the situation remained unchanged. The travelers dared not leave the island and the dogs let their presence be known with barks and snarls. At midday, under a hot sun, and the air still, the people waited and the dogs waited.

At day's end, clouds moved in. Justin gathered wood and piled it at the center of the island. "With these clouds there'll be no moon tonight, and we burned too much wood last night. The fires will have to be smaller."

Justin and Paul walked to the upstream side of the island. Paul voiced a worry. "If the dogs enter the stream, they'll be tiny targets."

Justin wrestled a small limb free of a wood entanglement. "And tonight there'll be less light." He looked at Paul. "Do you have something in mind?"

Paul, his arms loaded with wood, turned toward the center of the island. "Yeah. But let me get rid of this wood." He walked off.

Justin soon followed with his load. Michelle arrived from the other direction with more wood.

Justin sat in the sand and looked at Michelle. "Paul's worried about something."

Michelle sat. "What's up, Paul?"

Paul stayed standing. "In the water, the dogs will be small targets. Especially tonight with smaller fires." He looked at his father. "If they do try to swim across, I think you and I should wade out to meet them. We could use the ax and make some sort of club." He looked at Michelle. "You stay and use your bow to protect our rear." He smiled. "And I guess I do mean our rear." He maintained his smile.

Justin rubbed his chin. "Sounds right to me." He looked at Michelle.

"Yeah, I guess that's good. I can use a torch to light the water."

Paul sat down. "I hope we get this over with tonight."

Justin got up. "OK, I'll find a club."

Thus prepared, they waited in the darkening night.

A few hours hence, dogs moved around on the shrouded bank. Michelle stirred the fire. "Do you think they'll try to cross?"

Paul stood up and walked to the water's edge. "I'm sure they're hungry. I doubt they are willing to hang around another night."

Justin tapped his bludgeon on the ground. "They'll either make a run at us or leave." He stood up. "I hope they go for it. Get it done with." He slung the club to his shoulder. "They might find us later in a bad place."

A bush on shore rustled and a large, white dog ran a short distance down the bank and disappeared.

Michelle picked up her bow and prepared an arrow. "I think they're making a decision now."

An hour passed and then another. Justin rose to his feet. "Let's see if we can make this thing happen."

He did a slow turn. "Everybody find a place to hide." Justin and Michelle went behind the tree, while Paul reclined on the ground nearly at Justin's feet.

In no more than ten minutes, there were five dogs standing on the far bank sniffing the air. A large black dog was the first to the water's edge, the others followed. Justin whispered to Michelle, "Take a shot."

Paul got to his feet. Michelle stepped from behind the tree and fired at a dog belly deep in water. The arrow hit its mark and the animal splashed furiously as it floated down stream. Paul and Justin rushed into the water, only three yards apart. Michelle ran to the fire and touched a torch to the flame. She took it to the water's edge and stuck it in the soft sand. It blazed up brightly.

Paul struck first. The animal's head approached as a black lump pushing a v-shaped wave before its nose. The young man swung his weapon without hesitation. The sound of the cracking skull resounded off the waters. No sooner had Paul's ax flashed through the night when Justin delivered a blow. Three dead animals drifted away.

Michelle shouted, "Let me know what's happening." Immediately Paul replied, "We got two and you got one." He spotted another animal and stepped toward it. Shortly, the fourth dog drifted away. Justin got the fifth. Paul took two steps backwards. The twanging sound of Michelle's bow sounded, her arrow finding its mark.

With the suddenness of a clap of thunder, Justin's scream filled the night as canine teeth dug deep into the back of his thigh. Paul rushed to his father's aid. His ax whizzed through the air and chopped the dog's backbone in two. The dog released its bite. Its head pointed upward, as did its rump while the current pushed the animal's form up against Justin's leg. Michelle lit another torch.

Moaning in pain, Justin reached down with his left hand to push the dead dog away. The beast, not dead, removed the little finger and ring finger of Justin's left hand. Another tortured scream filled the night. The dog, in its broken posture, drifted into the dark, its bloody jaws, mechanically opening and closing. Justin saw his fingers fall from the dog's mouth and sink into the black water. The man dropped his club and limped ashore, blood gushing from his hand. Michelle watched the horrifying sight, but held her ground to the approaching danger of the dogs.

She spotted two yellow eyes. With steady hands she aimed and fired an arrow between the two glowing dots. The eighth dog was dead. Michelle grabbed another torch and waded to Paul's side. They spotted two more dogs. Paul stepped forward and killed them quickly.

The brother and sister stood in silence making sure no other animals were present. None seen or heard, they stepped slowly backward to the sound of their moaning father and the hoot of an owl.

Justin sat with his back to the tree holding the gaping wound with his right hand.

Paul took a deep breath and turned to Michelle. "We have to get him closer to the fire." He didn't wait for Michelle's help, but grabbed his father by the back of his collar and dragged him to the fire. Michelle retrieved the medical supplies.

Paul looked at the glowing red coals of the fire and pulled his knife from its sheath. He plunged the blade into the hot embers, knowing he had to stop the bleeding quickly. Justin clenched his teeth and pressured the wound, while Michelle sliced his trousers to inspect the bite on his thigh. There were numerous puncture wounds though the bleeding was slight. "Infection will be the problem here."

Paul's eyes remained on the fire, watching the steel of his knife glow to a deep red. Without informing Justin or Michelle he pulled the knife from the fire. Keeping it low, he waited a moment for the glow to fade to a dull black. He then gripped of Justin's left wrist tightly and pulled it across his chest. With a quick movement he placed the hot blade across the gaping wound; for the third time that night, the noise of fearsome pain filled the air. Justin dropped into merciful unconsciousness. Paul shuddered. His nostrils dilated at the stinging scent of burning flesh and boiling blood.

The family remained on the island long enough to allow Justin time to rest and regain his composure. Michelle tended to her father's wounds, cleaning them twice a day with boiled water and antiseptic powder. The hand wound showed clear signs of healing. The leg wounds reddened around the puncture marks and oozed green pus. During the next four days, the wounds required lancing.

On the fifth day the family left the island and again headed southeast. Justin limped under the weight of a lightened load and cradled his left hand in a sling close to his chest. Unknown to his children, his mind swirled with the fear of rabies.

Justin and his children moved slowly to the southeast as instructed with the last words of a dying man. It was a warm day, sluggish and dull, and the group had taken many breaks. Justin sat in the shade of a tall pine. His children sat across from him, under another tree. Justin studied them as they chattered in low voices. He took a deep breath and broke his silence with shocking words. "There's the possibility of another problem connected to the dog bites." He cleared his throat. "Rabies."

Paul squinted and studied his father. "Shit, I didn't even think of that."

Justin toyed with a stick. "We need a plan."

Paul and Michelle continued to stare and long moments ticked by.

Justin tossed the stick away. "Only thing I know about this, is what I once saw in an old movie. The man with the disease had to be tied to a tree."

Paul took off his pack. "How long was he tied to the tree?"

"After awhile, in mercy...they shot him." Paul looked at Michelle and turned back to Justin. "Hollywood bullshit."

Justin tilted his head. "No, no, it's not bullshit." He picked up another twig and chewed it. "The disease progresses to extreme agony, insanity, and then death. It gets into the brain."

Paul looked at Michelle. *"Did you read any thing about this? What do we do? Some kind of plants or herbs. What?"*

His stare was constant, demanding. Michelle shrugged her shoulders. "I don't know anything about it."

Paul looked back at his father, his lips twisted as if he were angry.

Justin adjusted his sling. "There's no cure, or rather we don't have it. All we can do is wait." He paused and then stared into Paul's eyes. "Remember what I said about the movie."

Justin rose to his feet. "I think the chances are slight. All those dogs looked healthy, and we were in the water."

Turning to the south, he hobbled along. A cicada buzzed in the dry air as Paul and Michelle followed.

The days passed slowly with the strain of another potential disaster looming in the background. Mindful of Justin's injuries, the family rested for long spells whenever they came to water. Justin, knowing one of the symptoms of rabies to be hydrophobia, always sat near the water. He studied it, he splashed it in his face and drank it.

Once, while Justin sat near a stream, Michelle went to Paul and crouched in front of him. "He expects you to do it."

Paul glared at her for a long moment. He extended his hand to her knee and pushed her hard over onto her bottom and rose to his feet. His glare continued. "Well it's for sure...*you* don't have the balls to do it."

Michelle jumped up. "I didn't mean it that way." As he tried to walk away, she grabbed his shoulder. "Can you do it?"

Paul spun completely around and spoke in a harsh whisper, "I don't know. Perhaps I'll practice on you." He turned from her and went to the little stream for a drink. She watched him walk away as a small tear ran down her cheek and she whispered to herself, "I'm such an ass."

At the stream, Paul crouched next to his father and cupped his hands preparing to drink. "You spend a lot of time fooling with water lately." Justin turned and looked at him with inquisitive eyes. He didn't think his children were aware of the hydrophobic symptoms. Paul continued. "You miss the sea don't you?"

Justin relaxed. "You're right about that." He smiled. "I'm sure you do as well."

Paul took his drink. "True, true." He turned to his father and knitted his brow. "Why is it that men love the sea and women care little about it?"

Justin stood up. "The sea's female, a woman." He paused and smiled. "The high mounding waves, a deep, blue abyss. She's the womb of life on earth."

Paul stood, his eyes relaxed, and he smiled. "You know . . ." He put a hand on his father's shoulder. "You know. That does give reason to my feelings." His smile grew broader and so did Justin's.

Michelle watched and more tears flowed down her face.

In the following days, Michelle, consumed by the dreaded deed, spent as much time as possible with her father. She doted over him, giving him extra vitamins, watching how much food he ate, and always trying to cut short the day's travel.

In ten days, it was assumed that the danger of rabies had passed. In addition, Justin discarded his sling and now carried his full load. With a type of normalcy returned, the group walked with a lighter step.

That night, after a skimpy meal, Michelle dug through her pack and found the little radio. She held it up to the others. "Maybe we can get a little music."

She fiddled with the tuner for some time before picking up a government station from somewhere in California, the reception weak. The family listened in silence to a news broadcast; the message long and involved.

At the end of the message, Paul's face twisted in confusion. "I don't think I'm understanding this guy. It sounds as if we are on the brink of war." Justin stared at the radio as if it were some sort of incredulous being. "That's got to be nonsense, some sort of joke." He looked at his children. "What the hell is there to fight over? And with whom?"

Michelle fumbled with the dial. "Shit, it's fading out." She put the speaker to her ear.

Justin pulled on the long growing hairs of his chin. "The way I heard it, it sounded like..." He stepped to the fire and turned to warm his bottom. "There are still operational missiles around." He shook his head. "What ass is wasting time taking care of crap like that?"

Michelle interrupted. "The threat's from North Africa...Arabia."

A moment later she spoke again. "Some Saudi got control of the Russian missile system and he's threatening everybody." Justin's head dropped in disbelief. "The Russian missile system." He raised his head. "Well, shit."

Paul threw a stick at the fire. "How the hell did he do that?" He looked at his father. "That's absurd, simply absurd."

Michelle shook her head. "I'm surprised there's still governments capable of stuff like this." She smirked. "It's some sort of colossal bluff." Justin walked away from the fire, rubbing his bottom. "They couldn't have very many." He sat down. "There can only be a few here and a few there. Those weapon systems are complicated and require a lot of maintenance." He shook his head. "If this thing happens, it won't be widespread."

Paul stood up and looked around. "This area can't be a target." He walked to the fire and turned to the others. "Everyone is running around and living in holes. Where the hell are the targets?"

Justin stared at the ground. "Michelle has to be right. It's got to be a bluff or a hoax. It's silly. Half the people in the world must already be dead."

Michelle pulled on her lower lip. "I would think more." She took a deep breath. "But evidently not the right ones."

Justin shook his head. "It's not going to happen. It takes too much organization. Lots of teamwork, know how."

The radio message was the subject of discussion for the rest of the evening. In a joint conclusion, they agreed that a missile war, or any war, for that matter, at this time, was impossible.

Sleep came slowly to Justin that night. Wise enough to know that fools still existed, he believed that people with great power were always tempted to use it before it disappeared. Justin whispered. "War to the end."

He rolled to his back and looked into the starry night. He located the constellation Sagittarius. "The galaxy's center should be right through there, I believe." He closed his eyes and conjured an image of a massive black hole and plunged into the perceived power. Shortly he drifted into sleep, an adventure for his slumbering mind established.

Justin and his family were near to or in the state of New Mexico. The land, broad and flat, afforded vision for miles in all directions. Being accustomed to the cover of brush and trees, the exposure seemed dangerous. Even a small fire at night could be detected by goons. Still, the family needed fire to keep the dogs at bay. As a solution, they placed their fires in holes, reducing long distance detection. In addition, one person stayed awake to tend the fire and keep watch. This was taxing procedure, but absolutely necessary.

Days after hearing the radio broadcast, the family huddled around a fire pit, their faces red with the light of hot embers.

Michelle flipped a piece of sage into the pit, and it burst into a small puff of pungent smoke.

Paul ducked and covered his face. "I hate that shit."

Michelle giggled. "I like it." With sweeps of her hands she smudged her body from head to toes.

Paul stepped back from the fire. "It smells like skunk."

Michelle swept smoke toward him. "It's been accepted with reverence since ancient times. It has spiritual significance."

Paul smirked. "OK! It smells like dead skunk."

Justin boomed a laugh, Paul joined in, and Michelle smiled.

A few moments later, Paul's laughter subsided and he turned to his father. "I assume we keep heading southeast?"

Justin took a deep breath. The uncomfortable topic surfaced again. "We're a lot closer to the gulf then we are to Oregon."

Paul questioned. "It's all the way to the coast then?" He paused a short moment. "As to the logic of your psychic notion."

Justin eyed his son. "Yes." He arched backward and listened to the bones crack. He straightened. "And I promise I won't start building a boat once we're there." A smile spread across his face.

Paul sighed. "A boat. A boat. I'd love to have a boat. I'm so tired of this walking stuff and this dry land."

Michelle knitted her fingers together across the top of her head. "A settlement near the sea would make sense. Fish, water. I do hope it's there."

Justin took a stick and stirred the hot cools. "I've run the last words of that dying man over and over in my head. They still flutter my gut." He jammed the stick hard into the fire. It stood on its own. "I know it's there, and it'll save us."

Michelle smiled. "We're with you, Dad." Her hands slipped down behind her neck. "This is a try...for deliverance. And if it doesn't work." She paused. "Well...it was worth the try."

Paul pulled Justin's stick from the fire. "We can get back if things don't work out." He paused and studied Michelle's fire-lit face. "There isn't a weak link here." He turned to his father. "What the hell, Dad. No guts, no blue chips."

Justin picked up his cup of tea. "It's there...it's there." He bowed his head and closed his eyes. Several minutes later

Michelle threw a piece of wood into the fire. "I got the first watch." She raised her eyebrows. "It's late."

Paul snarled. "You stirred up that sage again."

A short time later the men wrapped themselves in their sleeping fabric for a night's rest. Michelle sat quietly next to a small stack of wood. After the last piece was used, she would wake Paul for the next watch. For amusement, she toyed with the fire, again using Justin's stick.

Time dragged, the wood only half gone. Michelle stood up and stepped to the north end of camp. It was a moonless night with still air. She took a deep breath and stared into inky-blackness. The night cooled her fire-warmed face and she listened to tiny nibbling sounds in a nearby bush. Other than that intrusion, the night was silent. Michelle looked up into a star-filled sky. She turned slowly in a tight circle, her eyes always on the sky. After two revolutions she stopped. Vertigo forced a stumbling step, but she continued to stare upward.

She whispered, "Some day I will have a lover and we'll lie naked on soft fleece and study the stars. Naked, naked, naked."

The young girl's attention shifted to the horizon at her left. The half-circle of a luminary pulse glowed and faded away. "Wow. That was big."

Approximately twenty degrees to the right another pulse expanded and faded. "They're like little suns." Michelle shuddered and gripped her stomach. "Oh, no." Another bloomed with the perfect symmetry, smaller and apparently farther away.

Michelle walked calmly to where the men slept and gently woke them. She whispered, "You have to see this."

Another glow expanded like a giant balloon and shortly deflated. The men quickly rose to their feet. Justin raised his hands to his temples. Paul stared in bewilderment. "What the hell was that?"

Michelle spoke in a shaky voice, "It wasn't the first."

Justin gasped, his arms fell to his sides. "How many have there been?"

She nodded toward the west. "That was the fourth." She paused. "I think the biggest or maybe it was just closer."

Paul pointed. "Four, four of those." He turned to his father. "Explosions? A refinery? An old ammo dump?"

To the west the sky brightened, but no sphere of light showed. "No, Paul. They're throwing missiles around." He shook his head. "Fat boys."

Paul squinted. "Fat boys?"

Justin took a breath. "It's not important." He put his jacket on and stepped a few paces away from the fire. "They're doing it. The idiots are doing it. The Goddammed idiots." He shook his head.

Michelle, still clutching her stomach, turned to the north. "I wonder how far to the north they were." She spun around to Justin. "Do'ya think they hit Oregon?"

A dim light appeared and faded far to the north. Michelle had not seen it. "Perhaps." He paused "Oh hell, how would I know?" He walked back to his sleeping bag. "Is this really happening?" He sat down and studied the horizon with anticipation.

Michelle sat next to him. "What do we do?"

Paul stood near the fire. "Well, we don't go west or north."

Another mini sun rose in the east and evaporated. Justin thought out loud, "Government installations are probably the targets. We should be safe." He lowered his head. "Any place near a glow will be contaminated." He turned to the south. "I didn't see anything happen that way." He turned back to his children. "Did either of you see anything that way?"

Paul shook his head. "No. Nothing to the south."

Justin looked at Michelle. "No, not that way." She rose to her feet. "That's good. We can still go that way. Right?"

Paul put his back to the fire. "What about the stuff blowing in the wind?"

Justin stroked his beard. "The south will still be the safer place. Weather moves to the east, in general. At least it did."

An hour passed without further incident. Paul assumed the watch. Michelle and Justin sat at the fire. Sleep evaded all.

As the real sun rose, smoke rose in the north and west, but not much.

Justin got up and walked to where Paul stared into the north. He put a hand on his son's shoulder. "I guess it's over." He looked to the east. "I don't think we're in danger."

Michelle came to their side. "I couldn't sleep at all." She rubbed her eyes, her posture slumped. "Is there any tea?"

Paul turned a dreary face. "Yeah, the pot's full."

Michelle returned to the fire. Paul still stared into the north. "Well, Dad. One thing's for sure. Your dead friend sent us in the right direction."

Justin wasn't cheered. Suddenly uncomfortable with his idealism, he exhausted a deep breath. His head throbbed and he mused, "But, why. I forgot the why." Justin returned to the fire and the hot tea.

He poured himself tea and went to his sleeping bag with tortured thoughts. "I've forgotten something. Life must be more than the growing of meat."

He could feel the strength draining from him. He rolled to his back and spoke in a loud voice. "Leave me be. Don't talk to me unless it's important." He rolled back to his side, closed his eyes and was instantly consumed by a dream. *A small man raced through his mind in search for a certain something. He checked a place and no, it wasn't there. The little man's body shivered with a need and a panic that prevented clear thought. "Where the fuck is it?" The little man took tiny, fearful steps in a giant empty city. "What the fuck was the reason? What the fuck is the question?" The little man found a dark cranny heaped high with garbage. He crawled* beneath the pile. "*I'll* wait. *It will come to me. It will be given back.*" All went still, all went blank. Justin slept in his sleeping.

The group stayed where they were, their father tucked into a tight, fetal position in his wish to be alone and they sat at the fire and mused about the strange life they lived.

The sun descended below the horizon and the children prepared for the night. They divided the watch between themselves. It was a restless, uncomfortable night.

———

In the light of the second morning, Paul and Michelle sat at the fire, a cup of tea in hand. Justin stood to the east, a black shadow before the shimmering red sun. "We need to move on."

———

Within an hour, the small group recommenced their journey southward at a slow walk, Paul in the lead and his father at the middle. Justin periodically shut his eyes for short moments. Oregon was no longer a consideration; the dead man's settlement was now their only option.

———

At the hottest point of the day, Justin straightened with an unexpected remembrance. It soured his mood. It came from years back, a beating he had taken as a small boy from his drunken father. He recalled the deep-toned command and the gin-soaked breath. "Come closer."

He knew what the command really meant. It meant, "I can't reach you." He took that step, and he remembered the fear and the warm urine. He remembered the pain of the blow and the relief at its completion.

Justin raised his head to his son's back. He murmured to himself. "My father called me closer."

Justin took a deep breath and spun to face Michelle. "You know that things happen the way they are suppose to."

Michelle halted at mid-stride. Justin spoke in a loud voice. "I called the bomb throwers assholes. Well...somebody has to be the asshole." Justin blinked and dropped to one knee. His head swam in a surge of dizziness. His stomach cramped and his mouth oozed saliva.

Paul turned. "Are you all right, Dad?"

Justin ignored the question and spat into the dust. "I love my father. He gave me what I needed." Michelle looked at Paul, bewilderment written across her face.

Justin studied the round flattened glob of spit, now lightly coated with dust. He stood, stepped on it, and looked up into the sky. "Change needs to take place." He stepped around Paul. "And it's important as to how it occurs." He looked into the sky. *And who am I to fucking argue?* He turned once again toward his children. "I forgot about the need for the bad guys. And when all is done, they may well be considered heroes." He turned and walked on.

Paul shrugged his shoulders and moved after his father. Immediately, Michelle reached out and held him back. She shook her head, and Paul relaxed.

The day passed with little conversation; as they were together, so were they apart.

Little Pond (Nicole)

A world event of nuclear war occurred near midnight of the second day while Nicole and her family huddled in the shelter at Ravens in the Sky. Now the resurrected women trekked to the south seeking salvation at another settlement. They were sure of its existence, they had seen people from the place.

They carried a meager supply of food and some equipment for catching small game and fish. A magnifying glass and matches provided fire. Their weapons consisted of three knives, a spear and a pistol with five bullets.

Nicole stood before the girls. "The settlement is somewhere to the south. We'll go all the way to the gulf and move east." She eyed each of her daughters. "There's supposed to be some sort of new inland sea. Perhaps part of the gulf."

Chimene's eyes widened and she leaned forward. "All the way to the gulf?" She turned to her sister, her head bobbing. "All the way to the gulf."

Nicole picked up her pack. "If anybody has a better idea, please let me know." The sun blazed on the eastern horizon. "In the mornings we'll keep the sun to our left. At noon it will be overhead and then to our right as the day ends." She took her first step south. "The weather will be hot, so we'll rest through the midday."

Chimene shouldered her pack. "Like the man said, one step leads to a million."

Hot, dull days rolled by. Wild food presented itself from time to time, mostly berries and nuts. The occasional orchard or field growing artifacts from past farming days offered welcomed gifts. At other times they halted to trap animals, and on one occasion, killed a crippled deer with the last bullets in the revolver. What they couldn't eat, they cooked and carried.

The trail south settled into an uneventful physical struggle. Each day started with a small meal and a drink of water, after which Nicole hoisted her pack, looked at the sun and commenced the walking. The girls mindlessly followed with little conversation. Nicole always took the lead and spent most of her day alone.

Outwardly Nicole functioned efficiently; inwardly, deeply stressed, her mind sometimes swirled with mild hallucinations. The glaring light troubled her eyes, and the heat drained her energy.

Each day, at mid-day, when she saw her shadow as a small circle around her feet, she'd mindlessly wave her hand and all three stumbled to the nearest shade.

The midday resting periods nearly always ended the same way. Automatically, Nicole's eyes opened and she'd stand, pick up her pack, walk to the girls, and nudge them with her foot. Robot-like, the girls stood and resumed walking.

Naïvely, Chimene and Julia drew heavily from Nicole's inner strength, oblivious of her near exhaustion. Out of habit they delegated the responsibility for their existence to their mother. A well from which they had always drunk, they never considered its limitations. Now they followed her, pulled by phantom umbilical cords, their minds dulled, giving relief from the surrounding stress.

Eventually, Nicole saw the futility of her effort. At midmorn of a hot day she stopped and slowly turned to face her daughters. They approached with labored steps. Nicole spoke in a timid, weak voice. "You have to help." The girls trudged by, oblivious to her presence.

Nicole sucked a quick feeble breath and then angered, her voice suddenly sharpened, "I need your help."

The girls halted and turned. Nicole scrutinized their blank, sullen eyes, her breathing came in tiny breaths. She gazed down at her feet and two small stones, one pale red and the other pale blue. The clarity of the sight appeared to float the stones above the soil.

Julia stumbled from her standing position and kicked a billow of dust into Nicole's field of vision, obscuring the pretty stones. Nicole's head snapped to an upright position. Her blue eyes transfixed on Julia intently. Lazy eyes stared back from the girl's wobbling head and she whispered lethargically, "I do that?"

Nicole dropped her spear and pack, but never took her gaze off Julia. She stepped forward, her left hand grabbed the leather of the girl's shirt just below her right shoulder. Holding her in that position she called to Chimene, "Chimene! Come here."

Chimene shuffled to her sister's side. Nicole grabbed her clothing with her right hand just above the breasts. "Chimene, Chimene, wake up!"

She jerked Julia back and forth. "We're dying!" Julia's head nodded with the force, her eyes fluttered and her pack fell to the ground. Nicole turned back to Chimene and shook her with greater force. "We're dying! And you're letting it happen."

The girls lingered in numbness, their heads bobbing as if on rubbernecks. Nicole's anger escalated to fury. The mother released her grip and with unrestricted force she struck. She hit Chimene in the mouth with the palm of her hand. The same hand came back and struck Julia in the nose.

"You fools. Wake up! You have to wake up. Now!"

The girls staggered away from their mother. Their eyes cleared and they raised their hands in defense. Nicole persisted with the onslaught, pushing Chimene, causing her to stumbled backward. She shoved Julia and the girl tripped over her own pack and fell on her bottom, red liquid dribbling across her lips.

Nicole screamed. "Are you awake? Can you hear me?"

Jarred out of their stupor, the girls simultaneously lunged at their mother. Julia stubbed her toe on a rock and fell against Nicole's knees. Chimene grabbed Nicole's right arm as it touched Julia's back. Pulling to the right caused Nicole to fall sideways. Nicole's left arm swung around and seized Chimene's hair. All three went to the ground in a billow of dust.

Nicole released Chimene's hair, and the girl quickly rose to her knees and straddled her mother. She sucked a breath in order to shout, but gagged on the dust floating in the air. She held Nicole's right arm to the ground as she spat and sputtered.

Julia rolled away from the pile and wiped her mouth with the back of her hand. Dust mixed with blood smeared her face. She rose to her feet and stomped to her mother's side. *"What in hell are you doing?"*

Chimene released Nicole's arm and stood up. She looked down at her mother, but spoke to her sister. "I think she's gone mad."

Nicole sat up and hunched forward. Her right hand waved in front of her eyes, dispatching the dust. "I'm mad all right." She shooed them. "Move back so I can get up."

The girls obeyed, and Nicole stood. Her head shook. "I'm not insane. I'm pissed."

Nicole looked at the bloodied, blotched faces and her anger diminished.

"We are dying and you two drag along. I can't carry either of you."

Chimene spat more dust from her mouth. "I don't know what you're talking about."

Nicole ignored the statement and walked passed the girls seeking the canteen of water. She shouted over her shoulder. "You both think of little else other than yourselves. You're childish, unthinking parasites. You take and give nothing back."

Chimene and Julia looked at each other in bewilderment.

Nicole, with the water in hand, moved to the shade of a tree and sat down. "I will no longer carry the load myself. I'm drained." She looked directly at them. "We're dying."

A tear ran across Julia's dusty face. "I'm tired, too." She spat some blood. "This hell won't end."

Nicole ignored her. "From this moment on you will not only be expected to carry your share, you'll also be expected to seek out your share." She paused, and her tone mellowed. "You must grow up. You must be women. And it has to be now."

Chimene glared. "You slap us around without a word of warning and tell us to grow up." She stood up, her palms up and outstretched. "What's going on?" Her hands went to her side. "Did I miss something?"

Julia licked some blood off her lip. "You're being unfair. We're doing our best. There's no need for all this." Her eyes slowly closed halfway and she clenched her teeth. "I hate all of it."

Nicole followed the girl with her eyes. "Together we have the strength. Not as one and a group of two." She took a drink of water. "We can get through this."

Chimene sneered. "Get through this. To what? Tigers to fight."

Julia sat in the shade of another tree. "It reminds me of the song, 'The Bear Went Over the Mountain.'"

Chimene concurred. "Exactly."

Nicole's head nodded. "OK, OK. He saw another mountain. But, what do we do? Refuse to climb the mountain? Sit down and die." She took another drink of water. "I can't carry you over the mountain."

Long moments of silence ensued. Finally Nicole rose to her feet. "Right."

She took a deep breath. "Let's find that settlement. We know it exists, and we know just about where it is."

Nicole retrieved her pack and started to walk to the south. She felt better; she felt stronger.

She raised an arm into the sky. "Matthew was right. We are special. There is something for us to do. All this is not for nothing." Her head dropped and she whispered her own encouragement. "There has to be a reason for all this shit. There has to be."

The girls watched their mother walk away. Julia stood up. "She didn't have to slap us around. There was no need for that. I can carry my own load. And part of hers as well." She picked up her pack. Her eyes alert, she strode after her mother.

Chimene quickly stepped to her sister's side. "I still think she's gone a bit mad." She took a few more steps. "But it would be great to find that settlement. I was told that it was a lot better equipped than Ravens in the Sky, and full of educated people. Artists, scientists. I heard that they even have an orchestra."

"I heard that, too. But I don't believe it." Julia smirked. "Do you think we're special?"

Chimene smirked in return. "Sure we are. That's why we have all this good stuff. God really likes us." And she pushed her sister away.

In the following days, the trio moved with greater efficiency, their morale improved.

During these travails, Nicole kept an approximate estimate of the distance traveled. When sure they were in New Mexico, she decided to inform the girls at the evening meal.

Nicole tossed a rabbit bone over her shoulder and wiped her hands on her trousers. "Listen up." Sitting on a stone, she leaned forward, placing her elbows on her knees. "I've been keeping track of the distance we've covered. Of course it's only an estimate, but I'm sure we're in New Mexico." A confident smile brightened her face. She leaned back and clapped her hands. Her eyes shifted from one daughter to the other. "Good news, huh."

Chimene spoke with her mouth full. "Yeah, mom. In truth we've been doing the same thing, but I think we got into New Mexico a couple of days ago."

Nicole's smile slowly faded. "A couple of days ago. Why didn't you tell me?"

"We figured you knew."

"Oh, yeah. Yeah, I knew." The girls continued to eat rabbit. Nicole smiled. "Good! Good job." She got to her feet and nodded her head. "I'm proud of both of you."

Julia smiled. "What do you think? Six or seven hundred miles to the gulf."

"That sounds about right. Six or seven hundred miles." Nicole's head nodded with a weak smile. She added a few more compliments and drew a deep breath. "I'm going to bed down. Love you both."

In the late afternoon of the next day, the trio strode through a lightly wooded area beneath a blue sky. A fresh breeze cooled their faces. The women rounded a large shrub and froze in their tracks. Not more than forty yards ahead, two large dogs lay in the shade of a large oak.

Transfixed, Nicole, Chimene, and Julia watched. Slowly one of the dogs turned to face them in a passive, relaxed manner.

Nicole spoke softly, "When it turns away, move behind the bush."

Not spoken softly enough. The animal's ears tensed as it rose to its feet. A handsome face sat atop a massive body. Wolf-like, it had glossy chestnut fur and a majestic mane. The animal watched, Nicole whispered, "He doesn't have our scent."

The wolfish ears folded, its back hair bristled, and curled lips exposed white fangs. The other dog, lying on its side, faced away from the women. However, his companion's movements alerted him and his head rose to gaze across his body. Only in his black color did his appearance differ. A growl from the tawny dog brought him to his feet.

An oak tree stood near and behind the women. Nicole whispered again, "Start moving toward the tree behind us. Move slowly."

Without further discussion the girls took slow, deliberate strides backward. The dogs, with their heads down, growled while taking slow steps toward the women.

With the attack in progress, Nicole spoke in a loud voice, "Keep going." The girls proceeded. Nicole held her position and the dogs halted at the apparent challenge.

Nicole shouted, "Run for the trees." She scooped a handful of rocks and dirt and threw it at the animals. Startled, the dogs stepped sideways and backward to avoid the stones.

The girls bounded, as if on springs, onto a lower branch and situated themselves to assist their mother now running toward them.

The dogs quickly recovered their composure and made for Nicole at full speed. Nicole jumped at the tree, her right foot finding a grip on the bark as she reached for the extended hands of her daughters. However, Nicole's foot slipped from the tree and she dropped to the ground.

Her left ankle twisted on an exposed root and she groaned in pain. Nicole struggled as the girls pleaded frantically, "They're close. Hurry, hurry!"

Nicole stood on one leg and reached to her daughters. They gripped her hands tightly and Nicole rose into the tree as if freed from gravity. The girls pulled her high, and at the apex, Nicole twisted and sat on a stout limb next to Chimene's feet. The girls immediately climbed to the next limb higher.

The action was quick, though for Nicole things moved slowly. She sat in the tree, her left foot and ankle numb. Below, the tawny dog leaped at her dangling legs and fell back to earth. Nicole watched as he recoiled and used the momentum to push himself upward with even greater force.

Nicole awaited the rising beast with its open mouth and instinctively tried to pull her feet higher. Only her right leg complied.

All three women watched in horror as the tip of Nicole's shoe entered the animal's mouth. The dog's jaws snapped shut and it yanked its head viciously. Nicole's mind blurred with the agony. The dog lost its grip and fell back to earth.

Nicole screamed as she fought to keep herself on the limb. Below, the dogs, with less energy, leaped repeatedly. Unsuccessful, they growled in agitation.

Chimene's voice trembled with panic, "Reach up. We can get you higher."

Nicole extended one hand to Chimene and the other to Julia. The girls pulled and Nicole rose to the next limb. She leaned against the branch and extended her left leg toward the trunk. Chimene, leaning against the trunk, bent down to steady the injured ankle.

Nicole's face contorted in agony. "I think something broke," she moaned. "The pain is making me sick."

Her eyes fluttered. "Loosen the laces." Chimene straddled the limb and undid the ties.

For the rest of the day and all through the night, the dogs kept the women at bay. They prowled about the base of the tree and occasionally barked or growled. At night they fell silent.

A night of extreme discomfort followed. No position afforded relief on the narrow branches. Nicole fought spasms of nausea, and any movement caused pain. The night moved with irritating slowness.

Prior to dawn, the dogs again paced about the tree, noisy with hunger. It wasn't until mid-morning that they conceded. After a last bark and growl, they trotted off to the north.

Nicole lay slumped, exhausted from the pain in her ankle and her branch tortured back. Her head wobbled and she moaned with each breath.

Julia looked at Chimene. "How do we get her down?"

Chimene bit her lip. "First she has to sit up." She called to her mother. "Mom, mom. It's time to get out of the tree."

Nicole's eyes opened partially.

Chimene pleaded, "You have to sit up."

Nicole bent forward weakly. "Right…right."

Chimene helped Nicole lower her legs from the branch. The position change intensified her pain and she swooned.

Chimene instructed Julia, "The faster we do this the better. Get next to her and help her stay steady."

Julia climbed to Nicole's branch and straddled it. She reached out to Nicole's slumping form and held her steady. Chimene lowered herself to the limb below and looked up.

"Mother, mother. Come on now. We need your help."

Nicole looked around trying to comprehend. The girls waited in silence.

Nicole took a few deep breaths and raised her head. "OK, OK. What do you want me to do?"

Chimene extended a hand. "I'll guide your right foot to this branch. You have to lower yourself until you're standing on this branch." She paused. "Do you understand?"

A moment ticked by. "Mom! Did you hear what I said?"

"Yes, yes." Nicole paused another moment. "OK, I'm ready. Let's do it."

She leaned backward and rolled to her stomach as she slid down. Julia steadied her and Chimene guided her right foot to the lower branch. Nicole stood on one leg, her arms and chin resting on the vacated branch.

Julia lowered herself to her mother's side and looked at her sister. "Now what?"

Chimene didn't say anything. Nicole took a few more deep breaths. "I feel weak. Help me over to the trunk."

Holding on to the limb, her injured foot danged, and with the help of Julia, she took little hops to the trunk and leaned her back against it, one hand still on the upper limb.

Chimene dropped to the ground and looked up. "Mom, can you lower yourself to a sitting position?"

Nicole closed her eyes to surging pain. Her right leg quivered. She opened her eyes and looked down at Chimene. It was a good ten feet to the ground. She grasped the tree trunk behind her with both hands.

Julia watched apprehensively. "You can do it, Mom."

Nicole allowed her hands to slide down the rough bark of the trunk while lowering herself with only the strength of her right leg. Without warning, her right leg collapsed. Her bottom hit the lower branch with her right buttock. She slid off and struck the back of her head on the limb. All went black.

Chimene caught her as her feet hit the ground and both fell in a heap.

———————

The girls made a litter from small saplings. They cut up some of the fishing line to support Nicole's weight between the poles and used their backpacks as cushions. When placed on the litter, she lay quiet in total exhaustion.

The girls stood side by side and bent down, each grabbing a pole. Chimene looked at her sister. "South and some kind of shelter." Julia simply nodded.

They slowly dragged the litter for the rest of the day and then deep into the night. No place of refuge was found and the girls, at their limit of endurance, stopped for a rest. The rest became an all-night sleep.

———————

Chimene opened her eyes at first light lying next to Nicole's litter. She sat up and studied her mother's face and then turned her attention to Julia, who lay on the other side of the litter. "Julia, Julia, wake up."

Julia woke with a start. "Is everything OK?"

Chimene arched her back. "Mom seems OK. But, the left side of my back is killing me."

The girls got to their feet and took breaths of cool air, strong with the scent of water. Beneath their feet, lush, green grass cushioned their steps. Standing at the top of a small knoll, Chimene took a few strides toward the rising sun and scanned the area. At the base of the knoll, a small pond shimmered in soft light. Chimene beckoned Julia to come and look.

Julia walked to her side. "Oh! This is nice."

The pond sparkled increasingly in the rising sun and large willows graced the far shore, their droopy arms touching the water. Mallard ducks cruised at the near end while a small doe drank near the willows. The girls contemplated the beauty as the sun rose and warmed their chilled bodies.

A breeze skimmed the pond surface and slender water reeds swayed with a whispering hiss. Metallic dragonflies hovered and dashed about the waters and butterflies fluttered like bits of painted paper in the blossom sprinkled grass. Small birds darted in and out of the willows, their voices tiny chirps. The deer at the far end of the oblong pond finished its drink, raised its head and stared at the girls. Julia nudged her sister and nodded toward the deer.

The doe backed out of the pond, turned, and waved a fluffy white tale. Leisurely, with high prancing steps, it moved toward a nearby wooded area and stopped at the edge. It swung its head again to look at the women. The creature's motion, provocative, stepped into the forest shadows.

Chimene blinked with a sigh. "Let's get Mom to the water." She pointed. "Over there, where the deer was drinking." She turned back to the litter. Julia stepped backward with a continued stare. At the litter each hoisted a pole. Nicole stirred and opened her eyes. Her ankle throbbed when the litter moved. She couldn't see the pond, but she could smell its morning dampness. Her left hand fell to the side of the litter and brushed through the cool grass. Her mind calmed and mused a sensation of sanctuary.

Julia whispered, "The deer was a little girl. I think she spoke to me."

Chimene nodded. They dragged the litter down the slope and headed for the other end of the pond.

Chimene inhaled a deep breath. "This place is clean. A nice nature-clean." Her nostrils flared. "Freshness."

At the far side of the pond, they placed Nicole in the shade of the willows. Nicole still rested, her eyes closed. The girls strolled to the water's edge and removed their shoes. They entered the water until they were knee-deep, splashed their faces, and swallowed a cool drink. Chimene removed her shirt and soaked it in the pond. She smiled at Julia. "You go ahead and wash up. I'll start cleaning Mom up." She turned away without waiting for an answer.

Nicole awoke and raised herself on one elbow. She watched Chimene approach with the sodden garment.

Chimene knelt before her mother. Nicole smiled. "My head's fuzzy." She lay back and looked into Chimene's eyes. "You two must have been carrying me?"

Chimene patted her face with the wet cloth. "Yes, and we found a nice place to rest. It really feels nice." She moved to Nicole's injured foot and removed the shoe.

Later, after building a fire and boiling water, Julia ventured into the forest where the tiny deer had vanished. A small trail led through the thick brush. The very narrow trail required that she step with one foot precisely in front of the other. After a short distance, a little clearing opened up. Julia stepped into it and slowly turned a tight circle of inspection. Most conspicuous was a house size rock nearly fifty feet high and almost as wide. The stone's face had a hollowing in it, like a small amphitheater, but deeper and certainly ample enough to afford reasonable shelter. Julia rushed back to the others.

"I found some shelter. Just a little ways from here." She pointed toward the forest. "Just beyond the brush."

Chimene followed Julia to the place. The forest formed a thin canopy over the clearing, allowing a few pleasant rays of sun to filter in. The soil was sandy and sparsely spotted with tall grass.

Julia repeated her tight circle, her arms extended out. "This place is glorious, absolutely glorious." Chimene touched the rock. "Nice...this is very nice." She turned to Julia. "Let's get Mom over here. And then we'll set up a campsite."

The enclosure gave the women a much-appreciated feel of security. Chimene gathered leaves and grass for bedding. Julia went down to the pond, caught a grasshopper for bait and soon had a trout dangling on the end of a fishing line. She caught two more fish, which they roasted for dinner.

The idealism of the place became evident in the succeeding days. Berries grew in the sun, mushrooms in the shade, and a little deeper into the wood, wild asparagus stabbed at the sky. Another gift came in the form of honey oozing from a crack in a nearby tree. The hive was higher up inside a hollow, and there was never the problem of an annoyed bee.

As the days passed, Nicole's injured foot improved. The swelling went down, though the skin color remained purple. Nicole was soon hopping around on a staff. The location, accommodating in so many ways, took on an air of mystery.

Four weeks hence, after adequate rest and sufficient food, Nicole's injury healed, though it was still painful when applying her full weight. The healing extended to the entire family, refreshing them mentally and spiritually. They even gained a few pounds.

One evening after a dinner of rabbit, the family sat around the remains of their cooking fire. They took turns sipping tea out of their one tin cup. Nicole took a drink and passed it to Julia. "My foot's pretty well healed. It's just going to take a little more time and exercise." She reached down and rubbed the ankle with her right hand. "No telling what I did to it." She straightened and smiled. "I can walk."

Julia sipped the tea. "They're a lot of bones in an ankle, aren't there?"

Nicole again reached down to her foot. "Yes. A bunch. It's tender when I squeeze it near the instep." She sat up straight. "It may never be perfect, but it'll be OK."

Chimene threw a twig on the fire and changed the subject. "This place...I remember people talking about energy vortices, special places with special powers. Do you think this place may be something like that?" She looked at her mother.

"An energy vortex." Nicole's eyes squinted. "I know what you mean." She paused a moment in thought. "There is energy here." She paused again. "I can feel it at night when I settle down to sleep and then again in the morning, but never during the day."

Julia raised her eyebrows. "Sounds like Matthew," she smiled, "with his special people and places."

Nicole reached for the tea. "At any given moment I don't feel special, but when I look back at what we have been through," her voice cracked, "We keep surviving...how many behind us have died?" She put the cup of tea on the ground.

Julia stared into the fire. "Makes me think of religion." She turned to her mother. "You and Dad were never involved in any religion, were you?"

Chimene stood up. "Where did that come from?" She walked over to her sister. "But now that you bring it up," she turned to Nicole. "I always felt kind of funny about it. Everybody was something. Baptist, or something. I didn't know what to tell people."

Julia looked at her sister. "You know what I used to say?" She smiled and her head tilted to the right and then to the left. "Oh me! I'm a little this and a little that." Her eyebrows went up. "But, they always gave me a strange look."

Chimene chuckled, "A little this and a little that?"

Julia spoke with mild annoyance. "Well, what did you tell them?"

"I told them that I didn't belong to an organized religion."

Julia bantered, "So you belong to a disorganized religion?"

Chimene smiled. "Julia, you're beyond hope."

Nicole picked up the cup of tea. "We raised you to understand that a Higher Power existed, but we wanted you to have the freedom to choose a religion or not." She paused and took a sip of tea. "When you were old enough and hopefully wise enough."

Nicole looked at the girls' inquiring eyes and anticipated their next question. "I was raised a Catholic. Not in a very strict way. I lost interest when in college. Your father was raised Protestant and gave it up when your grandparents died." Nicole smiled.

Chimene reached over and took the cup of tea from Nicole. "So how does all of that fit into all of this?" She swept her right hand through the air. "Our situation. This pretty little speck in the middle of hell."

Nicole took a deep breath and smiled. "Ask me ten years from now."

Another month passed and the daylight hours grew longer. The women guessed the time of the year as near spring. Nicole's injury improved to a point. Pressure at the ball of her foot caused pain and she sometimes hopped on her heel.

On a clear moonlit night, the trio awakened to the dreaded sounds of howling dogs. Though terrifying for the girls, Nicole was calm. "It's time to leave this place." She smiled. "You remember, the settlement in the south."

Chimene squeezed her mother's hand and whispered, "Other people. Right. Time to leave."

Julia whispered, "How close do you think the dogs are?"

Nicole lay back on her bed. "We'll pack up and leave tomorrow. There's no protection here from dogs." Nicole rolled to her side and fell asleep. Chimene and Julia could scarcely believe their ears and eyes. They huddled near their mother quietly and slept intermittently.

At sunrise they ate a quick breakfast. Julia gathered a few things and stuffed them into her sack. "We can always come back, if we want."

Chimene hoisted her own pack. "No. We don't come back. We find the place."

Julia looked to her mother. Nicole sighed. "We find the place."

Once packed, they rounded the pond and climbed the same slope they descended on the day of their arrival.

On top, they turned for a last look. From the path that led to their campsite, a tiny deer emerged into the open. Julia delighted at the appearance. "It's the same deer. I'm sure, I'm sure."

It stomped and nodded and then bolted around the far end of the pond and disappeared into a thicket. Three mallard ducks took flight, made a tight circle around the waters, and flew over their heads. A strong wind swirled the middle of the pond and the water reeds hissed and hushed. Nicole turned and hobbled off. "How does that song go? On the road again, just can't wait to get on the road again. The life I love is making....on the road again."

Chimene leaned toward Julia and whispered, "Let's hope she doesn't start singing 'The Hills are Alive with the Sound of Music.'"

Julia muffled a laugh. "Remember when Dad made us watch that movie?" She took a breath and hefted her pack. "You know that settlement might be a lot closer than we think."

Chimene followed her sister. "Wouldn't that be nice? A few days and we could be eating omelets again."

Chimene went to her sister's side and nudged her with an elbow. "The new place may be big enough to have cheese and pizza."

Nicole spoke over her shoulder. "We've been dining on fresh trout, wild berries, and mushrooms. Do you know what a meal like that would cost in Seattle?"

Chimene smiled at Julia. "No, but I'm sure it's more money than we have."

Nicole chuckled and turned to the girls. "Keep your eyes, ears, and noses tuned to water." She took a few more steps and mumbled to herself. "I wish we could carry more."

Nicole touched the knife dangling at her side on a strip of dried rabbit hide. A spark of panic flickered through her mind.

"Weapons, our weak point. We have to find that place, and soon."

She added weight to her injured foot, testing for pain. Knowing that time was not on their side, she tried to move faster.

At the end of the day Nicole grimaced. Pain dimmed her spirit and she chewed a piece of dried fish while slumped against a tree, her weight on one foot.

Julia watched. "There's not much taste to that stuff. I wish we had some salt."

Chimene sat on a log and tinkered with a small stick. "How's the foot feel?"

"Not too bad. I'm going to try and make some sort of cushion for it." She looked at the foot. "I think I can move faster with a cane or something." She grimaced. "Should have taken the one at the pond."

Julia got up. "I can find you something." She pulled her knife and headed for the nearby brush. Nicole followed her with her eyes. "Stay close, in sight."

Nicole slid to a sitting position. She picked up a piece of bark and tested if for flexibility.

Chimene watched. "We're moving very slowly."

Nicole flipped the bark into the air. "I know and that's not very good." She shook her head. "Time is against us."

Chimene crossed her legs. "We lost a lot of time today, backtracking out of that little canyon. And again when moving around those rocks."

Nicole jerked her leg straight out. "Shit, I got a cramp."

Chimene uncrossed her legs. "Do you want me to rub it?

"No, no. It'll be OK."

"Mom, I've got an idea." She crossed her legs again. "Why not let me and Julia take turns going out ahead to find a good path? We could avoid doubling back."

"No, we stay together."

"Mom! Where's the greater danger? If we keep going this way, the trip will be twice as long or maybe even three times as long."

Julia joined the conversation. "She's right, Mom. Her idea could help a lot." She walked out of the brush with a stout, short branch. "I think this will work." She handed it to her mother.

Nicole got to her feet and walked around testing the cane. "That is better, much better." She sat back down and took a deep breath. "I'll think about it." Her eyes met the stares of her daughters. "I'll sleep on it."

For the first two days, the new strategy went well and their progress improved. On the third day, a storm brought their travels to a halt. They found shelter beneath the overhang of a cliff. It kept them dry, but little else. For two days they sat in the cold and dampness. After the last drop fell, they wasted no time moving on.

They endured much on their trek from the ranch in the north. Their bodies were muscled, their minds keen, and most importantly, their spirits accepting and confident. They would have scarcely recognized the delicate creatures they once were.

On the third day after the storm, the women got a late start. Julia knelt on one knee and kissed her mother on the cheek. "We get closer every day." She smiled. "We're going to make it. I can feel it."

Nicole hugged her with one arm. "Don't take any chances. We're just trying to save time."

Julia, with a sweet smile and a final wave, dashed into the bush.

Chimene hefted her pack. "I bet we're close."

"I think you're right." She looked up at her daughter. "Put your pack down. We have a few minutes more."

Chimene dropped her pack. "Yeah. I'm just anxious today. I wish it was my turn to lead."

A few minutes later, Nicole stretched out her legs and looked into the high blue of the sky. A vulture circled and flew to the south. Her eyes closed in a meditative moment and then popped open, a startled look on her face. She got to her feet and Chimene followed her lead. Nicole took a breath to say, "Let's go," but instead she let the air silently seep out of her mouth as she heard the sound of barking dogs. Nicole grabbed the knife at her side and turned to Chimene. "Restart the fire and start another. She's not far off. I'll bring her back." Nicole grabbed her cane and ran into the brush ignoring the pain in her foot.

Chimene stood transfixed, staring after her mother. She bit her lip and dropped her pack. Her hands shook as she gathered pieces of wood.

Five minutes from camp, Nicole feverishly zigzagged through the brush wondering whether to shout Julie's name. She halted and sucked a quick breath at the sight of blood in her path.

A short distance farther, she came upon a small knoll surrounded by a sun baked meadow. The horror in the meadow etched a picture into her soul and produced a pain that would never leave her. A pain that would find relief only in its future familiarity.

Rest
and Waiting
(Justin)

Justin and his children continued their trek southeast, moving through the high country of New Mexico. They trudged through a scrubby desert, sweltering at day and chilling at night. But, soon the upward path led into the mountains and tall ponderosa pine shadowed the travelers in the heat of day. The terrain permitted easy travel and security with less exposure. However, food gathering was tougher.

At midday the family sat beneath a very old, stout pine after a morning of good progress. However, tired in an overall way, their stops were more frequent and longer. Not having found any sign of the settlement, and haunted by the flight of the missiles, their enthusiasm diminished.

Michelle sipped water and the men ate pinion nuts roasted the day before. She tossed a pinecone at Paul. "How long have we been on the move?"

Paul grumbled. "Are you kidding? Forever. Maybe longer." He reached for her water. "You mean, since we left California?"

Michelle lay back on a small patch of dry grass, her head close to the tree trunk. She gazed up into the huge majestic branches. "Why don't we take a break? Set up a shelter. Rest a while. Eat a lot of hot food." Minutes went by with no responses.

Justin thought of objecting, but said nothing. Paul rested on one elbow. "I've seen a number of caves. Perhaps we could find a big one. Set up some nice beds."

Michelle encouraged, sat up. "Yeah, a supply of wood that would last a week. And a good supply of food as well."

Paul turned to his father. "With rest we could move faster, later." His head tilted. "We need the rest."

Justin still said nothing. Inwardly, his aged body pleaded for rest. He had pushed himself hard.

Michelle continued. "We could set up a base and scout into different areas. We can't be very far from the coast."

Paul faced his father. "She's right, Dad. And I'm ready for a rest as well. It feels right."

Justin smiled. "OK. Resting time is here. We do it."

A four-day search produced an adequate cave midway up the side of a canyon wall. The canyon, closed at one end, gave the family a sense of security. They settled in.

They made a rapid adaptation to their rocky shelter. Each picked a niche to personalize and reestablished simple comforts long denied. A warm and dry enclosure and solid separation from the dangers roving the land were accommodations absent since leaving Winchester Bay.

The days combined into weeks. The cave totally occupied the interest of the travelers. They produced soft beds and comfortable chairs that sat near a cozy fire that didn't require a person to be within burning distance of the flames. A large pile of wood sat against a stony wall and a store of food cooled in the deep end of the cave. Time was available to make use of hides for clothing and night covers.

By the time their stay had extended into months, the interior of the cave exhibited comfort, ingenuity, and dedication. They swelled with pride at the achievement and fantasized about other possibilities if tools were available.

A small fire crackled near the entrance of the cave. Paul dozed in the comfort of a lounge seat, constructed of tree limbs lashed together with strips of hide. Michelle sat on her bed and punched small holes in a piece of leather. Justin prepared strips of venison for drying. He looked at the fire. "I'm going to start cooking these strips." He bent toward Michelle and smiled. "I'm sure the smell will wake Paul."

Michelle smiled back. "He's been like a bear halfway into hibernation." She punched another hole. "I wish we had some pasta or a potato, a piece of bread. Good old carbohydrates."

Justin jammed skewers of meat into holes drilled into soft rock. "I could go for some good old fat. This meat is so lean."

He stood up. "Look at us." He rubbed his hand over his stomach. "Lean, mean machines. Fit and trim." He laughed. "I want some fat. A big wad of fat. Let it sizzle and save the grease."

Michelle punched another hole. "A goose, a big fat goose."

Paul opened his eyes. "A pig, a wild pig. There might be one of those about."

Justine looked at his son. "Give this meat a chance to cook." He smiled. "We might find pigs farther south."

Justin ambled to the cave entrance. He looked to his left and right. "Speaking of the south, it's time to do some scouting." He turned to look at his kids.

Paul stretched and leaned forward to study the cooking meat. "Yeah, it's time. I feel very refreshed. And now I have fat on my mind."

Justin moved to his lounge and sat down. "OK. Let's see." He thought a moment. "A week's trip to the southeast, moving fast."

Michelle dropped the hide and went to her chair. "The way I feel, I could do it on the run."

Justin adjusted his decision. "We'll do a two-day trip out and two days back."

There were no disagreements.

The trip resulted in an uneventful week. There were no signs of humans or the settlement. Before returning, they climbed a high peak for an aerial survey. The only thing of interest was a large body of water to the east. It's far sides weren't visible.

Justin handed the field glasses to Michelle. "That's a very large body of water, but it can't possibly be the Gulf of Mexico."

Paul used his hands to shade his eyes. "Why not? What else could it be?"

Justin thought a moment. "Nah. We couldn't have moved that fast."

Michelle handed the glasses to Paul. "If we are in New Mexico..." She pointed toward the water..."Then that's Texas."

Paul spoke with the glasses at his eyes. "Or was Texas!"

Justin rubbed his chin. "Shit." He paused. "Something must have changed."

Paul handed the glasses back to Justin. "Well...it doesn't mean the place doesn't exist."

"True, true. But I was hoping for some sort of indicator."

Michelle turned and started down the slope. "Let's go home."

Paul followed her. "Don't worry, Pop, we have the rest of our lives to find it."

Justin took up the rear and chuckled. "Well, I guess that's the right attitude."

As they retraced their steps, they planned another expedition. This one, directly to the south, and as Paul suggested, a two-week trip and possibly to the coast.

The cave bestowed a genuine calm upon the family. They talked lovingly of it and their returning steps were unconsciously faster. They felt a sensation that related to their other home, but then, the emotion was vague; now, the feeling was sharp, intense, and very apparent.

Back at the cave, the family's next endeavor was to replenish their stores. During a hunting venture into the low land desert, Michelle stepped on a cactus. It was avoidable, a matter of haste and thoughtlessness. She awakened in the middle of the night with the need to relieve herself. In a rush, she scampered into the surrounding brush bare-footed. A portion of the spines broke off beneath the skin and the hunt ended with Michelle hobbling back to the cave.

In short time, the embedded thorns produced festering sores that required periodic lancing. Justin canceled the scouting trip.

The injury persisted for over a week and the food supply dwindled to a very low level. They didn't want to leave her, but the food needed replenishing. So, the men planned a one or two day hunt. Michelle understood the need, but felt anxious at being left behind.

Paul and Justin entered the cave with a load of wood that they dropped near the entrance. Justin walked over to Michelle. "That should be enough wood for a few days, just in case we get hung up."

Michelle looked at him. "No getting hung up. *No...getting...hung...up.*" She paused. "Do you hear me? No getting hung up."

"We leave in the morning. With luck we'll be back soon, and I promise we won't get hung up."

Paul took a swig of water. "Our being here has chased the game a little farther away. I don't think we'll have to go far."

Michelle bit her lip. "I don't like this."

Late that night the weather changed and rain fell. By morning a robust wind canceled the hunt.

The family waited one day and then another. They spent the time relaxing, sipping tea and contemplating the crackling fire as storm breezes quavered its flame. Only the gusting wind and the occasional boom of thunder interrupted their conversations.

Justin tossed a twig into the fire. "Rain or not, tomorrow we head out." There was no comment from either Michelle or Paul. Justin continued. "There's plenty of jerky and nuts." He paused. "I think of that as our emergency supply."

Paul's eyes shifted to Michelle. "We could get lucky and find something fast. The rain will help."

Justin settled back in his chair. Paul's words reassured him, and he drifted into quiet thought, his eyes closed. The sound of the trickling rain at the cave entrance reminded him of his beloved Oregon. He put his hands behind his head and pondered. "All those people dead. I wonder how long Zoe lasted."

The cave lit white with a flash of lighting and thunder reverberated up the canyon. Justin drifted into a dream state where he watched the *Orca* as she crossed over the bar and motored toward the bay. *He could hear the heavy rumble of her husky diesel engine and felt the security it projected. "There's nothing like a diesel engine." He saw himself tie the boat to the dock and shut the engine down. Suddenly he was driving the old pickup home. How nice, how comfortable.*

Michelle got up. "This party is too much for me. I'm going to bed." She limped to the back of the cave. "I said, I'm going to bed!"

Justin's eyes blinked. "Good-night, Michelle."

Paul grumbled. "Yeah, yeah, me, too." He squirmed in his chair and fell back into sleep.

Justin resumed his fantasy. *The contentment of those days was like warm feet. Yes, like warm feet. I hate cold feet.* He snorted when the wind drove a bit of fire-smoke into the cave. *A warm fire, the kids gone, a shot of brandy.*

Thunder rolled by the cave like cascading boulders.

Justin ignored the rumbles. *Transition. A world in transformation and we get to see it...why I wonder, why?* The rain poured with increased intensity.

Justin slumbered into a deeper state. *He found himself at sea leaning over the side of the Orca, his head immersed in a turbulent sea on a black night. Unlike the surface, all below was quiet, calm and shimmered with strange clarity, somehow disconnected from his eyes. Far below something huge materialized. A wind of heat swirled through the sea and swept into his mind. A soft female voice whispered in his ear, "I love you." As the thing below rose, a strange heat warmed his mind further and the temperature increased as the thing neared. Again the female voice whispered, "Sweetness the true, we fly." The thing from below dimmed to invisibility and Justin pulled his head from the water. His chest swelled with a mighty breath and he expelled his physical self onto the sea where a small whirlpool sucked it down. Bodiless, his mind beheld the violent sea and a mountain of a wave rose before him. A female form burst through the crown of the giant swell. She hovered there, glowing in the night air. What was left of Justin slid up the surface of the swell and joined the female at the crest. She looked at Justin with a mischievous smile and extended her right hand, revealing a large gray-black pearl. "For you, my love." The woman looked into the night sky as did Justin and they spiraled upward in a trail of little sparkling things. The female voice spoke a last time, "It is done."*

The storm moved on during the night. Justin still slumbered in his chair. Michelle restarted the fire earlier and water bubbled with herbs in a small pot. She touched her father's leg. "Dad, Dad. It's time to get up." His eyes opened to a sunshine-lit cave. He smiled. "I feel so...so rested." He swung his legs to the ground and stood up. He looked at Paul's chair and then at his bed. His son hoisted his bow.

"Hi Pop, ready for the hunt?"

"Yeah, let's eat something quick and head out."

Michelle added a pinch of mint to the hot water. "Would you guys get me some more wood before you go?" She gave Paul a stern look. "I just want to be sure there's enough."

Paul left his bed and put down his bow. "No problem." He picked up the ax and headed out of the cave. As Justin followed, he turned to Michelle. "I guess breakfast will be jerky and nuts." He turned away and then turned back. "We'll take some with us."

———————————————

In less then an hour the men returned, sweating and breathing heavily. Only Paul carried wood, a small amount. He threw it in the corner, and picked up the water bag. Justin went directly to the fire. He scattered the coals and stomped the flames. Paul gulped some of the water and started sprinkling the fire. Michelle turned to her father. "What's up?"

Justin stepped back from the fire. "There's a bunch of goons near the mouth of the canyon."

Paul took another long gulp of water and put it down. "They probably won't be there long. We're going to have to stay put a bit longer."

Michelle sat in her chair. "I think I may be fit to walk in a day or so."

Justin went to the foodstuff at the back of the cave. "We can have a small fire tonight, but it has to be very small and here at the back of the cave." He paused. "Just to cook our last rabbit. No fire in the daytime."

He came back and sat in his chair. "And we should keep our voices down as well."

Paul went to his chair, sat down and grabbed a piece of rabbit jerky. "They'll be gone in a day. There's nothing here for them."

———————————————

The next day the goons still camped at the canyon mouth. A few of them passed close to the cave in the early morning. The family heard them coming and quickly gathered their weapons. Michelle stood near Justin, peering down into the canyon. "Filthy things," she uttered.

Justin nudged her with an elbow. "Quiet."

The goons turned about and headed away. The family retreated back into the cave, placing their weapons near their chairs as they sat down.

Michelle grumbled, "Why don't we go after them? We could hit them from three sides." She looked at her father. "They'll run for it."

Justin gave her a stern look. "Your plan would probably work, but we're not going to kill if we don't have to."

With a huff Michelle sat back in her chair. Justin's stare continued. "They're humans."

Paul sat up straight. "We could do what we did in Oregon." He paused, waiting for them to remember. "You know. Make a lot of noise, bark like dogs. Make them think there's a hundred of us."

Justin studied the cave ceiling. "We have time, we can wait a bit more. No need to look for trouble."

Near dark, they heard the first howls of the dogs. Justin rose out of his chair and went to the entrance of the cave. Another dog howled. He turned toward the sound. "They're after the goons." He came back into the cave. "I'm going to make a fire." He frowned as he walked to the woodpile. "Closer to the entrance. A small one."

He picked up a few branches. "Those poor suckers don't have fire and not much for weapons."

A surge of pity bowed Justin's head as he conjured an image of the pitiful creatures huddled together, unprotected, knowing that soon the dogs would come. He added a few larger branches to the stack cradled in his left arm and with his head still bowed he walked to the cave entrance in thought. "We could help them." He turned to his children, his mouth open as if to say something.

Paul waited, and then spoke, "What?"

Justin blinked. "Nothing." He dropped the wood. "It sounds like a large pack."

Periodic barks and howls continued. Justin whittled on wood. Paul cycled between fiddling with his weapons and playing with the fire. Michelle talked almost continuously, trying to extort conversation from the stoic men. Her words had little meaning and were ignored.

When the light of the moon glared, the dog's howling intensified making sleep impossible.

Justin studied the stick he had been whittling on. It portrayed nothing and he threw it into the fire. The man stood and walked to the cave entrance. He bowed his head. "Damn, this stuff." He raised his head. "I wish we could shut it out."

Paul and Michelle sat quietly in their chairs. Their father, his head bowed, sank to his knees and then to his bottom. He rested his back against the side of the hill. The clamoring of the dogs ceased.

Michelle went to the fire and knelt on one knee. The bottom of the small pit was covered with glowing coals and small bits of wood added little flames here and there. Calmly, with a short stick, she pushed the bits of wood into a small pile at the center. The flames intensified with the gathering.

"I prefer the dogs."

A short moment later a human scream sliced its way up the canyon and rushed into the cave. Michelle's back stiffened. She shuddered and the stick dropped from her hand. A brief moment of silence passed while Michelle stood up and took a deep breath. Paul covered his ears with his hands. Justin moved from the entrance and returned to his seat.

Michelle stared into the night and listened to a different sound. The sound of someone or something running up the canyon. A moment later a husky voice yelled. "Mo me...mo me." It was clear and near. A dog growled. A human screamed in pain. "No! No!...Mo, me. Mo me...mo me."

Justin tried cupping his ears. To no avail. All three heard the struggling of the human, his grunts telling of his efforts, his screams telling of his failures. After long minutes the man gurgled his last, "Moooo, me...mooooo."

Justin's face contorted as he stood up and rushed to the back of the cave. He stood there, confused, looking from place to place. He picked a corner and crumpled into it.

There would be similar sounds as the night dripped slowly by. The animals, unskilled in killing humans, their method were slow and sloppy.

Paul jumped to his feet. "I can't bear this." He ran to the cave entrance. *"Let that be the last."* And then whispered, "No more, no more."

Michelle scuffled to her father's side with tear-laden eyes. She huddled near him. Justin whispered. "This is a bad thing." He paused. "Don't get lost in this. Don't get lost."

Through the night, the ugly sounds continued and were duplicated by canyon echoes.

Michelle struggled to her feet and stepped to her brother. She swallowed and wiped her eyes. "We can make a psychic effort to end this horror." She straightened and took a deep breath. "Let them have death; let them be free of pain." She poked Paul with her right hand. "We can do this; we can help."

Paul never raised his head. "You do it for yourself."

Michelle ran to her bed and sobbed.

Paul spun toward her. *"This is what you wanted."*

Justin's hands went to his temples. *"Don't, don't. Say no more. You're making more pain for later."*

Michelle's sobbing ceased and only her occasional cough was heard. From time to time she shivered beneath her cover.

The night ended and so did the carnage. When the sun rose with warm brightness, Paul and Justin ventured out to determine the situation. They found a high perch with a clear view of the canyon entrance and the flat plain that extended down and away from it. At the entrance, only one dog sniffed about. With no other sign of life, Justin raised his field glasses and scanned the flat plain.

"There they are. They're moving to the west."

The bulk of the dog pack strolled behind the humans at a leisurely matched pace. A forsaken sight of predatory horror.

Justin handed the glasses to Paul. He put them to his eyes for a moment and handed them back to his father. "The dogs are following them."

Justin put the glasses in his pocket. "Their bellies are full." He took a deep breath. "For now."

Paul watched the lone dog as it trotted toward the rest of the pack. "Perhaps Michelle had the right idea." He turned to his father. "We could have killed them all. Killed them in a better way."

Justin bit his lip. "No. We did the right thing." He turned and spoke over his shoulder. "We can only do what we think is right." He sighed. "Even if it turns out to be wrong."

Paul spoke to his father's back. "I'm drained. This pathetic shit gets to me."

The family, weary from the lack of sleep and emotional strain, rested through the day. They gave Michelle a simple report that the danger had passed and that tomorrow they would go on a hunt. She sought no other information.

The next day the men made quick preparations for the hunt and stood by, ready to leave. The dangers, of most concern for Michelle, had come and gone. Nevertheless, the men stacked extra wood and some green brush. The brush would burn with a lot of smoke and act as a distress signal. Michelle deployed her weapons strategically and set the makings for additional fires at the entrance.

Justin turned to Michelle. "Well, we're off. You all set?"

"I guess, but I don't like this."

Paul put an arm around her. "We won't be long." He kissed her on the cheek and headed out of the cave. Michelle watched as the only two people in her life made their exit and disappeared around the corner of the cave. She put her hands on her hips and turned slowly while inspecting the empty cave. She ended the rotation at the cave opening and gawked at the bright light of the day.

After a long moment she stepped softly to her chair and flopped into it, her fingers running through her long hair. "Shit, I'm not going to wait more than two days...one and a half."

Her body gave a sudden, short shiver. She took a breath and fixed her attention on the strands of dried grass besides her chair, the makings for a basket, she didn't touch them.

A few moments later she looked at the pile of firewood.

"A small fire will do." She turned toward her weapons. "What good will they be in the dark?"

Long moments passed in cool, rock-hard silence. Michelle's gaze fixed on the entrance and her eyelids hung half closed. A short shudder passed up her left arm, across her shoulder, and dissipated with three short blinks of her eyes. Moments expanded into minutes. Michelle sucked a deep breath. "Like the night before." She jumped to her feet. "It's not going to happen to me."

She rechecked her weapons. The arrows were ready. The blowgun lay with a dart in its chamber and others placed for easy reach. She strapped on both knives, one to her right calf and one to her left calf. She took the vial of poison from her backpack and dipped all the darts. She pinned one dart just above her breast. "This will be my last escape."

Michelle spent the entire day in restless motion. She cleaned the cave twice and adjusted the weapons numerous times. Often her own voice broke the silence with curses directed at Paul and Justin. "Never again, never again."

In the end she returned to her chair, sat down, took a deep breath, and reached for the strands of grass at her feet.

Justin and Paul traveled north at a moderate, constant pace. They moved cautiously, zigzagging, covering a lot ground. Gone four hours, a direct trip back required only one hour.

The men emerged from a grove of trees and stood before a field of sunburned grass with a steep knoll at the center. Defensively crouched and hanging back in the shade, they examined the terrain before them.

Silently the pair moved out onto the grass. The sun streamed hot rays in contrast to the cool shade of the trees. All was quiet with the exception of a few buzzing insects.

Abruptly Paul stopped. He grabbed his father by the shoulder. Justin halted. Paul held one finger to his lips. Apprehensive moments passed. Paul held an upright palm to

Justin and took a few more steps up the knoll. Another moment passed and he signaled Justin to move next to him.

The first growling sounds were now audible to Justin as well. A yelp and then a high-pitched bark resounding from the top of the hill.

How many dogs were there and could they be eliminated? Justin reached over his shoulder and pulled the blowgun from his pack. He placed it in his left hand against the stock of his compound bow. Arrows were at the ready in their quiver. The men, thus prepared, headed for the top of the knoll.

Near the crest they halted to listen again. The sounds were louder and no longer muffled. The men, horizontal, their bellies to the earth, concentrated on the din flowing over the knoll. Flying insects buzzed. The sun-baked droplets of sweat from their skin. Paul raised four fingers. In truth, he guessed only three, but added one for safety. Justin concurred.

The dogs growled in low constant tones, indicating they were probably feeding, and more importantly, preoccupied. Justin touched his son and pointed to his own eyes. Paul nodded. The men crept through the dry grass to a position close to the top of the knoll. With weapons ready, the hunters rose in unison, but only as high as necessary to make an assessment of the situation.

There were three dogs, all feeding. The animal's meal was a young girl, in pieces and the grass was blotched crimson with her blood. A large yellow dog gripped the girl's ribs in its mouth and dragged the upper torso about, her long black hair and one remaining arm trailed behind. Her eyes, wide open, but dead, bulged from a face frozen in a look of disbelief. The lower half of her body occupied the attention of another beast feasting on internal organs. This dog, a female, swallowed large chunks in rapid succession. Near some brush, the third dog pulled a thigh muscle free from a lily-white bone.

Both men dropped from sight. Paul lay with his face close to the ground and uttered a short staccato of sound. "Ah, ah, ah."

Justin, his face close to Paul's, whispered. "We'll take the close dogs first. You take the one to your left and I'll take the one to my right. Do it fast and get back down." Justin allowed his son a moment. "Get ready."

Paul nodded. The men shifted their bows, put an arrow in place, and laid the weapons before them. They pulled the sheathed, broad, blade knives and stabbed them into the ground. Justin drew his blowgun and his fingers tapped the weapon as if it were a flute. Paul placed his pouch of spare darts near the knives and hoisted his blowgun. The blowguns were quickly loaded.

Justin, using silent finger movements, counted to three. The men, once again, rose in unison. They located the targets and the deadly missiles were sent on their way. The action was so quick that the men were concealed before the darts struck.

The two dogs targeted jumped and yelped at the sting of the needles. One beast contorted to reach the projectile and with snapping teeth it pulled the object from its flank, but the poison was in and the animal doomed. The dart that struck the other dog penetrated deeply, numbing the wound.

The action didn't escape the attention of the third dog. Even before the darts were fired, her sharp instincts signaled trouble. She swallowed the flesh in her mouth and her tongue licked her jowls. With eyes steadied she trotted toward the crest. After three strides the figures of two men appeared. She froze in place. Suddenly the vision in one eye vanished and the animal's brain exploded in pain. The beast leaped into the air and wildly pawed at its eye while another dart pushed deep into her neck tainting the blood rushing to her brain. Only moments of her life remained.

Justin and Paul understood the science of the poison, and stood their ground, observing and reloading their blowguns. Justin pointed to the last dog as it fell to its side twitching.

With a sudden movement the men crouched into a defensive posture. To their right, loud thrashing sounds emanated from the brush. Fear gripped their stomachs. How many dogs were coming? Had they guessed wrong? Each man felt his pouch containing the spare darts. They knew the count, but still they counted.

To their astonishment a woman broke free of the brush. She ran, or more precisely hobbled, toward the dying dogs, toting a large stick in a determined attack.

One dog lay dead. The other two, in a drugged stupor, stood on wobbling legs, watching the advancing woman.

Justin pushed to his full height and shouted. "Stay back, stay back." He tried to wave her off. But, the woman paid no heed and moved without distraction. Paul stood and added his voice to the warning. "Stay back, stay back."

The woman raised her club and continued her advance. Justin took a step to run down and physically restrain her when yet another commotion came from the right. From the same bush that the woman dashed, a large, muscular dog appeared. The beast, like the woman, moved with obvious intention.

Automatically, both men lifted their blowguns to their mouths, took aim, and fired. Both darts hit the dog, one in the chest and one in the rump. Undeterred from his one-minded pursuit, the dog continued the attack. Justin and Paul reached for their bows. Justin raised his first just as the black beast pounced.

The dog's large paws, studded with hook-like claws, grown sharp in soft soil, penetrated the softness of the woman's shoulders. The strike of the animal, also a push, drove her forward and off her feet. Lacerating claws tore her shirt, tore her skin, tore her muscles, and scored her bones. Blood of the daughter and blood of the mother, colored the grass.

The dog's paws gripped the small of the woman's back and his eyes widened with the anticipated kill. Strands of sparkling silver oozed from his jaws and the loose skin around his mouth curled, exposing large, brilliant, white incisors. To affect the kill, the beast thrust his head down, its upper fangs puncturing the woman's left cheek, dislodging one of her teeth and tearing her tongue. The animal's lower fangs dug into a soft spot at the base of her skull and to the right of the second vertebrae. Powerful jaw muscles contracted with the ability to crumble the vertebra and sever the delicate nerves within.

At that precise moment, a heavy arrow from Justin's bow struck. It smashed through the dog's skull destroying the small primitive brain. In a spasm of death, the beast jerked its head up, tearing the flesh of face and neck. The dog fell on top of the woman. The men rushed to her.

Skinning the Soul (Justin and Nicole)

Justin and Paul, in a coordinated pace, rushed across the rough terrain with the form of a dark-haired woman. Unconscious, twitching, she moaned, "Julia...Chimene."

The men's sweat mingled with blood as they strained with the dying burden. Half her face, ripped into ugliness and the other half, soft beauty. Blood and dirt spattered a firm, well-shaped body, heavy for its size. The men pushed hard and their chests heaved.

As they neared the cave, Justin took the woman's entire weight and instructed Paul. "Go." He took a deep breath. "Tell Michelle to prepare."

Paul ran ahead. Justin struggled with each step. A few minutes later, gasping for air, he stopped and leaned on a large, sun-warmed boulder. The woman's head hung back, her breathing gurgled with oozing blood.

Justin hunched forward and moved from the rock. He struggled another minute or two and found yet another stone to lean against. He thought of setting the woman down, but to his relief, he heard the noise of Paul's return.

Paul jumped from a stone and landed near Justin. "Michelle's getting things ready. Here's a drink." He set the water bag down, took the woman from his father, and walked toward the cave. Justin gulped water, allowing some to run over his chest. His hands dropped to his knees and he took a few deep breaths. A moment later he straightened and caught up to Paul. "Put her down and we'll each take an arm and a leg."

With the maneuver completed, Paul looked at Justin. "Do you think she's a goon?"

Justin hesitated and then shook his head. "She didn't behave like one."

Paul sucked in a deep breath. "I scared the shit out of Michelle." He groaned and stepped over a log. "The blood."

When the men entered the cave, Michelle directed them to Justin's bed. The exhausted men laid the woman down and backed away. Michelle whistled at the sight of the woman's wounds. She began to pour water across her back.

Justin spoke between gulps of water, giving Michelle an account of what happened. He placed the water bag near Michelle. "I think there's others. She called out names."

Michelle picked at pieces of grass and dirt. "Are they goons?"

"I don't think so." He paused. "I'm going to have to take Paul with me."

Michelle poured more water over Nicole's wounds. "OK. I'll see what I can do."

Justin lingered. "Do you need something before we go?"

Michelle held two fingers to Nicole's neck. "Her pulse feels strong. Perhaps she didn't lose that much blood." Her voice cracked. "No, but hurry back." She looked at her father. "I'll try to stop the bleeding. Justin backed away, turned, waved at Paul and exited the cave.

Michelle poured disinfectant into some water and sprinkled it over Nicole's back. "Tell me you're not a goon."

Nicole moaned. "Chimene...no, no."

Michelle studied the left side of Nicole's face. "There's gonna be scars." She reached for the suturing kit. "It's time for the needle work." She leaned close to Nicole's ear. "I'm going to start with your back. Try not to move and put the pain out of your mind."

She pulled separated tissue together and began suturing. It took close to an hour to completely close the lacerations. Michelle, kneeling before Nicole, sat back on her heels, "Your back wounds are closed." She washed Nicole's back again and sprinkled more disinfectant. "It looks OK."

She studied Nicole's torn face. Her cheek was split to the back of her jaw. Two dislodged teeth and the damaged tongue were visible. The bleeding was slight and mixed with saliva. Michelle poked at the broken teeth with a pair of tweezers. She looked up to the cave ceiling. "I can do this." She took a deep breath and returned to the task.

As Michelle nervously attended to Nicole's wounds, Justin and Paul stared at the bloody mess at the grassy knoll. Justin turned away and gulped a breath of air. "Retrieve your weapons. The darts if you can"

Paul, his face pale, made no reply.

Justin pointed to the north. "Let's see if we can follow her trail through that brush."

After about one hundred yards, Justin stopped and shouted, "Chimene...Julia." He turned to Paul. "Keep your bow at the ready."

Paul pulled an arrow from his quiver. "I don't think we should push it. We could be setting ourselves up for a bunch of goons. Or more dogs."

Justin bit his lip. "Maybe dogs...but I don't think goons. She acted different. A goon would've run off."

Justin wiped his brow. "But it's hard to be sure about dogs or goons." He paused. "OK, you move thirty yards to my left. Let me do the shouting. Make it look like I'm alone."

Paul took two steps to his left and turned back. "How long do we do this?"

He looked at his son. "Not very long."

Paul disappeared into the brush. Justin waited a few moments and then shouted, "Chimene...Julia."

Chimene stood with folded arms at the spot where her mother entered the brush. Behind her the fires crackled. She turned and walked to the center of the clearing, head down. In

a sudden move she straightened and turned. Her eyes squinted and she remained still for several moments.

Finally, she let out an exasperated breath and walked to
each fire and poked at them with a stick. Eventually she found
herself back at the same spot, staring in the direction her mother had gone.

A moment later, the sound of her name drifted ghostly
through the air. Her brow furrowed and she heard Julia's
name. She wrapped her arms around her stomach and quivered.

A voice repeated her name then Julia's. She stiffened. Her
hesitation lasted only a few seconds. She faced the sound and
cupped her hands at her mouth, "Over here! Over here!"

She waited and shouted louder, *"Over here, over here!"*

Justin turned his head. "Paul! Get over here." In a few
moments, Paul came crashing through the brush. Justin pointed. "There. Somewhere to our right. I'll go ahead. You stay out
of sight and back me up."

Paul nodded in agreement. "Sounds like a young girl."

Ten minutes later Justin stood before Chimene. She stood
back from him, a spear held by both hands. Justin spoke in a
low voice. "We can help. Are you Chimene?" She said nothing.
"Then you must be Julia." He turned to face the bush. "Paul,
come on in. It's OK."

Chimene relaxed a bit, stood more erect, and shifted the
spear to one hand. "Have you seen my mother...my sister?"

Justin hesitated and then replied somberly. "Your mother's
badly hurt, but she's with my daughter and being tended to."
His expression softened. "Your sister is dead."

Chimene crumbled to her knees. "Oh no, please God, no."

Justin surveyed the camp. "This is not a safe place." He
looked down at her. "We should go now." He reached to help
her to her feet. "Julia, it's best we leave now."

Chimene murmured, "I'm Chimene." Her eyes streamed tears.

"Do you have any things to take?"

She pointed to a bush. "Over there, three packs."

Paul came into the camp. He looked at the distressed girl, then at his father. Justin's face strained as he turned to Paul. "No need to linger here." He pointed to his left. "Get their stuff behind that bush."

Paul hesitated. Chimene stood next to Justin, her head down, and her face covered with both hands. Justin bit his lip. "The girl's her sister and the woman's her mother. She's Chimene."

After extinguishing the fires they headed back to the cave with Justin in front, Chimene in the middle and Paul behind.

They circumnavigated the carnage at the knoll. With concentrated effort and no conversation, they were soon standing at the cave entrance. Chimene spotted Nicole and rushed to her side. She sucked in a breath at the sight of her mother's wounds. She sank to her knees and implored, "Let me help. I know some medicine and there's supplies in our packs."

The hard look on Michelle's face relaxed and she sat back on her haunches. "You know her?"

"Oh yes, she's my mother."

Michelle straightened up. "You can wash the wounds on her back. That powder is a disinfectant. Sprinkle it around, mix it with water."

This process took time. Nicole lay still and her breathing rhythmic. In due course, all that could be done had been done.

Michelle stood, went to the cave entrance and faced a southerly breeze.

Chimene reclined near her mother. Her eyes closed and her right forearm rested across them.

The men, though tired, still had the difficult task of dealing with the remains of the young girl. Justin approached Michelle and whispered. "We have to take care of her sister's remains."

Michelle turned and sighed. "OK...but why are they here...it hasn't been our way."

Justin shrugged. "It just kind of happened."

Michelle bowed her head and her voice cracked, "Obviously they're not goons...are they?"

Justin put an arm around her. "No, no. They're not." He squeezed her with his right arm. "You did a great job on the woman. I'm proud of you." He kissed her on the forehead and released his grip.

Justin turned and signaled Paul, who walked to the entrance. "Nice work, Sis." He put his hand on her shoulder and gave it a little squeeze. Justin stepped out of the cave and Paul followed.

The men completed their burial chore with a small grave of piled stones. They left the site exhausted and without words. They hoisted their weapons and walked back to the cave, stopping once at a small stream to clean themselves. Paul splashed water in his face. "That was ugly."

Justin rubbed his closed eyes. "Beyond words." A vision of Nicole running at the killers of her daughter passed through his mind. He looked at Paul and murmured a silent plea. "Please not me, please."

The following days passed slowly. Nicole's condition intensified when infection set in. Her facial wounds swelled, making her incapable of speech. Mostly she drifted in a state of semi-consciousness. Chimene stayed close and used her knowledge of herbs to treat the infection.

Justin briefed Chimene on the events at the knoll, certain of the need for the information when her mother revived. Chimene wept the entire time. After the young girl absorbed the initial shock of the story, she returned to her mother's side.

Justin watched both of them for several minutes before walking over to Chimene. He squatted in front of her and spoke softly, "Where did you come from?"

The young girl looked at him with watery eyes. "We came from the north." She waved her hand as if annoyed. "A settlement of people, Ravens in the Sky." She sniffed. Her head slowly lowered as if pushed by a weight. "A bunch of crazy people killed everybody." She looked up again. "Except for us." She wiped her cheeks with the back of her hands. "We headed south. We're special people." The words mixed with sudden sobs and her body trembled.

Justin rose to a standing position. "Rest. This place is safe." He studied the girl for a moment and walked away.

A day later Nicole awakened with a moan, but didn't open her eyes. Pain burned through her body and a few muscles on her back quivered. Chimene, at her side, whispered in her ear. "It's me, Chimene. We're in a safe place."

To Nicole, the voice echoed as if spoken through a pipe. She could only open her right eye to blurry images and shapes of black and white.

Chimene spoke again. "Can you take some water?"

The words were incomprehensible to Nicole and she closed her eye to ugly images of bloody grass and a dog-faced girl that snarled and snapped inches from her face. She passed into blackness.

"Mother...mother." There was no response.

Days later, the somber mood of the cave dwellers continued. The sun hovered at its high point and the people rested after a noon meal. Paul and Justin reclined in their chairs. Nicole slept on Justin's bed. Chimene leaned against the cave entrance and Michelle sat across from her. A friendly relationship developed and they spent much time chatting. "Your mother's a lot better."

Chimene blinked slowly. "Oh...yeah. A lot of that bright redness around the wounds is gone." Her eyes closed.

Michelle scribbled with a twig in the dirt. "Sorry about your sister."

Chimene sighed and massaged her temples. "I miss her." She took another deep breath. "Our family is getting so small."

Michelle dropped the stick. "I lost a brother back in Oregon." She bit her lip. "His name was David. Some trees fell on him."

Long moments passed in silence until Nicole coughed. Chimene turned and watched. Nicole sat up and took a drink of water from an old tin can that Paul had found recently. She turned to Michelle as Nicole lay back on the bed. "I was sitting here the other day and I saw my sister." She pointed toward a group of trees in the canyon. "Right over there. She smiled, waved, and walked away."

Michelle turned toward the trees. "Have you told your mother?"

Chimene shrugged. "Later maybe." She looked at Michelle and smiled. "But it was nice." She put her face into the sun. "It's a good thing you found us. It probably would have been the end." She paused. "Perhaps that would've been better. I'm tired of all this."

Michelle rose to her feet. "My father says things happen the way they're suppose to."

Chimene looked up at her. "And what does that mean?"

Michelle eyed Chimene and smirked. "It means, all of life is good and there is no bad."

Chimene blinked. "No bad?"

Michelle smiled. "Yeah! You got it." Her head tilted to one side. "There's a lot more to it than that." She leaned toward Chimene, her eyebrows up. "Sometimes it even makes sense to me."

Chimene shook her head. "I'll never see the good of this stuff. It's a whole lot of pain and wasted time."

Michelle spoke as she walked away. "Guess what?" Before Chimene could reply Michelle responded. *"Rabbit for dinner."* Michelle twirled in a full turn. "Big surprise. Aha!"

The first light of the following morning streamed through a veil of smoke, issuing from a half-burned branch at the fire's edge. Nicole lay with her eyes open, intrigued by the slow, graceful movement of the smolder. She reclined on her side, her hands folded as if in prayer, tucked beneath her head. She yearned to pull her legs up, but hot pain ran down her back. A tear rolled across the bridge of her nose.

Her tongue investigated the extensive wounds within her mouth. She found a tender spot and pushed with her tongue. Her eyes closed to the pain and she moaned when she tasted blood.

A muscle in Nicole's back twitched. "You again." She pushed her legs as straight as she could and from her waist down she rolled to her back as her left hand slowly slid across her body and dropped behind her back. Positioned palm down, it held her back off the cot and allowed her hips to roll. The torment of the twitch contorted Nicole's face. Muscles pulled on unhealed wounds and warm blood trickled down her back. She took a breath and held it. The cramps relaxed almost instantly. The quick recovery, a shock in itself, made Nicole expel a long sigh and she moved her left hand back to her front. "Julia, forgive me."

Nicole closed her eyes, then she saw Michelle walk over to Paul. "Paul, we need more wood. We have to keep this place warmer."

Paul smirked. "Sure, we can do that." He turned to his father. "We have to start bringing in more wood...keep this place warmer." His eyebrows went up. "So says Michelle."

Justin grinned. "Well, let's go do it." He put a hand on his son's shoulder. "It's better than just sitting here watching her fuss with this and that."

The men walked to their weapons. Justin put his hand on Paul's shoulder. "This is a first for you, isn't it?"

"What do you mean, a first?"

"Well, functioning to supply the needs of the womenfolk." He picked up his bow. "It's an ancient thing. Prehistoric in fact." He stood up. "It's because we have bigger muscles."

Michelle listened to every word. The men walked toward the cave entrance and Justin turned to Michelle. "We're headed out to get some more wood. Keep this place warmer."

He looked at Paul. "I just accepted the responsibility to increase the wood flow."

Paul smiled. "I guess we're back to the prehistoric."

"Like they say, son, history repeats itself."

Michelle watched them, half smiling and half grimacing. Paul turned and spoke to Chimene. "Need any herbs or something?"

Michelle mimicked his words. "Need any herbs or something?"

Michelle stood between the two. Chimene answered Paul, "No, nothing, but thanks for asking." She smiled.

Paul lifted a finger in Michelle's direction.

A few days later, Justin sat near the cave entrance scraping a rabbit hide. Chimene walked past him on her way to meet Paul at the base of the canyon. They were out to set a few traps and gather some herbs for tea.

Michelle spun around to see her father gazing at the young woman as she walked away. "Pretty, isn't she. And so very young."

Justin turned and frowned, but a moment later laughed. Michelle ambled up close to him and spoke in a low tone, "You're leering."

Justin maintained his smile. "You're being absurd." His brow wrinkled. "Beauty is beauty. What's with the leering comment?"

Michelle's scowl suddenly softened and her shoulders slumped. "I don't know." She leaned against the cave wall. "Life has gotten so strange." She looked directly into his eyes. "What if we're here till we die?"

Justin melted as his little girl's eyes welled with tears. He put his arm around her. "That won't happen, but I know what you mean." He tugged on her shoulder. "I got a good feeling about the future. We'll find that place. Things won't be as they were, but I think they'll be just as good." He waited. Michelle wiped the tears from her cheeks, walked over to her chair, sat down, and gazed at the outside world. Justin exhausted a deep breath and he whispered to himself. "Never the chance to be a woman." His voice boomed, "We're close. I know it." Michelle's right arm rose in the air and waved a dreary acknowledgment.

Justin saw Nicole sitting up. He walked over to her. "You're doing pretty good. You look a lot better " Nicole's eyes twinkled from a face discolored by old bruises. Talking was painful and her speech difficult to understand, so she nodded stiffly.

Justin was caught up in her beauty, however marred, his mind flashed with his last look just before the dog pounced.

Nicole struggled with a few words. Justin took a moment to decipher them. Nicole watched him think.

He tilted his head. "Are you trying to thank me?" She blinked positively.

"You're welcome." He smiled. "Besides, your daughter has thanked us many times."

Justin glanced over her tortured body. "Can I get you something? Water, food."

She closed her eyes tightly and slowly rose to a very erect stance. Her breaths were short and shallow. A moment later she tried to bend forward. Justin took a step closer. "Can I help?"

She looked at him with soft eyes. Justin nodded his head. "You don't want help."

With two fingers of her right hand she gestured a walking motion. She had made the effort several times in the last few days.

Justin smiled. "I look forward to the day when we can have a conversation." She gave him a quick blink with her eyes. Justin walked away. He passed Michelle and strode from the cave into the light of the day.

Nicole watched him until he was out of sight. She sighed and took a tortured step.

Michelle also watched Justin leave. Her glum expression continued. After he was gone, she spoke in a low tone, "Unsubstantiated optimism. Really." Her arm dangled to the cave soil at the side of her chair and her fingers found a small stone. She picked it up and tossed it into the canyon. "Two for them and what's there for me?"

Michelle rose out of her chair and walked to the cave entrance. She saw Paul and Chimene kneeling near a bush. Justin moved toward them. More tears rolled from her eyes and she kicked the pebbles at her feet. "Things better get better." She spun around and walked to her chair.

A short time later, Paul, huffing, entered the cave. Michelle raised an eyebrow. "What's the matter? Is play time over?" She got up and marched to the water. "You want some water? What's the problem?"

Paul wiped his brow. "Me! What's my problem? I must have missed something."

Michelle shook a finger at him. "You know Paul, you're an ass." She took two deep breaths and straightened. "I'm going to help Dad. You seem too busy to help." She marched out of the cave.

Paul turned a confused look at Nicole. "What in hell was that?" Nicole moved the only part of her body that didn't cause pain, her eyebrows.

Paul glanced around. "Cave fever. That's it. She's flipping out." He went to where a smoke-dried rabbit hung from a stick rammed into a crack in the rock. He tore a leg off and gnawed on it. He stopped chewing and looked at Nicole again. He extended the rabbit leg toward her. "Want some?"

Nicole closed her eyes for a short moment. Paul swallowed. "I guess not."

Within a few moments he had the meat off the bone. He turned and flung the remains through the cave opening, just as Chimene came in. The bone whizzed by her head.

She smiled. "I'm glad you weren't eating a cow."

Paul chuckled, his face reddened, and his eyes sparkled.

Eleven days produced significant healing. Nicole now took her meals with the others around the fire. She conversed, but haltingly. Still in pain, she socialized for only short periods. For the others, conversations were light, and seldom dealt with the past.

A branch of green pine crackled in the heat of the fire. An owl hooted in the dark. The chatter among the five seemed spent and Chimene leaned back, her eyes focused on the ceiling of the cave. She spoke in a dreamy voice. "When we were headed this way, looking for that settlement, we came across this beautiful place. It was a little pond…"

Justin jumped to his feet and rushed to her side. "A settlement! Did you say you were looking for *a* settlement?"

Chimene looked up. Justin dropped to one knee and faced her. Chimene smiled. "Yes, a settlement, but I told you that."

"No you didn't. No you didn't." He actually jumped into the air and when he came down he ran to Michelle. He grabbed both of her hands and pulled her to her feet. "I told you, I told you. We're close, we're close."

Paul stood up. "Wait, wait. Let's make sure we're talking about the same thing." He sat next to Chimene, something he arranged. "Tell us about this settlement."

Justin let go of Michelle and went back to his seat. He sat down and focused on Chimene. "Tell us."

Without hesitation Chimene divulged the information in a short statement. "Some strangers came to Ravens in the Sky from the south, just before the big battle. They were going to lead us back there."

Nicole leaned forward. "We…were told…it to…the southeast." She swallowed. "On the bank…of a …sea."

Justin leaned his head back. "If I take a deep breath, I'll float into the air like a balloon."

He in turn recounted his family's tale of the dead man and their search to the southeast. The stories fit together perfectly and a wave of conviction flowed over the group.

Michelle's eyes widened. "Dad, the waters we saw from the hilltop. Remember, we were trying to figure how it could be the Gulf."

Paul shouted at the cave ceiling, "The new inland sea."

An awesome weight lifted from Justin's shoulders. "The settlement does exist."

Justin smiled. "Tomorrow we celebrate."

The next day Justin and Paul rose with the sun. In a lively mood they prepared for a hunt with hopeful expectations of providing something special for the festivities. In quick order their weapons were in hand as well as a supply of jerky. The women woke with their movement.

Michelle threw a small stick at Paul. "Be careful." The men departed.

Michelle turned to Chimene. "I guess we clean this place up and get ready for the celebration." They both jumped to their feet and walked to the cave entrance.

Michelle shouted, "Bring back a pizza." She smiled at Chimene.

Paul turned and walked a few steps backward. He waved and mumbled softly to himself, "Oh Chimene, you boil my blood." Turning away, he took a deep breath and exhaled with a low moan. With energetic steps he swiftly passed Justin.

Michelle headed back into the cave. Chimene continued to observe Paul and whispered to herself, "I know you've been watching me." Paul disappeared into the brush. Chimene glanced at her deformed arm and headed back into the cave, her eyes sparkling, her mouth grinning.

Paul and Justin made their way to the closed end of the canyon and studied the rim of the mesa at its top. In the hot, stagnant air their sweat flowed profusely and their shuffling feet sent up puffs of dust particles that stuck to their wet skin. Paul stepped forward. "I see a way."

With little difficulty they ascended the slope to the top where a fresh breeze of cooler air ruffled their long hair and dried the moisture on their skin. Justin scanned the vista. A fresh growth of grass, bright green, swayed at knee height. Thousands of lavender blossoms spread across the mesa scenting the air sweetly. Scattered clumps of short, sturdy pine, like misshapen umbrellas, stood in the swaying grass.

They rested on one knee, their heads rotating in slow scanning sweeps. They conversed with eye and hand movements only. Both anticipated staying downwind, which meant skirting the mesa from its north edge. Justin stood and took several strides along the rim. He turned to signal Paul, but Paul wasn't there. He retreated and found his son lying on his back, his arms and legs spread. Justin dropped to one knee and whispered, "What are you doing?"

Paul whispered back, "Dad, lie down with me. It's great. The grass is soft, the air cool, and the sky is so blue. It's like looking into the sea."

Justin smiled, and thought, "Hormones, hormones," and did as requested. "Oh yeah, look how deep the blue is over head."

Paul whispered, "I really miss music."

Time ticked by. They lay there, head to head, the sun low and shaded from their eyes. Justin's eyes narrowed to mere slits with sleepiness. He heard Paul sucking air through his mouth.

Justin alerted to the sound of a thump. He held his breath. Thump…thump, thump.

Justin smiled. A deer was near. Paul whispered to his father. "That sucker is close."

"He sure is." Thump, thump.

Paul whispered again, "What do we do?"

Justin, still smiling, answered, "We might as well get up before he steps on us."

Paul smiled. "On the count of three we sit up."

"One, two, three."

They both sat straight up and their heads spun to face the wind. Fifteen feet away a big buck jumped straight up into the air. When it came down, it headed at full speed to the north. The men got to their feet and watched it scamper to the mesa edge. Its rump rose up and a white tail flickered. The men's smiles transformed to laughter. The animal was soon out of sight and surely headed off the mesa.

Paul hefted his bow. "Think there's another up here?"

"Could be. Let's follow the rim."

They moved unhurriedly and with caution. Near the spot of the animal's disappearance, the men stopped. After a few moments Paul pointed down the near cliff-like slope of the mesa. Bounding away on the flat plain, at least one-hundred-and-fifty feet down, the deer, appearing small, vanished into a thicket. Justin turned to face his son. The new position lessened the noise of the wind, and the man caught a different sound. The unmistakable sound of bees whispered like music.

He made a quick survey. On a slope leading to the mesa edge stood the limbless carcass of a once tall pine. Near its top buzzed the bees. The hulk of wood appeared soft and rotted.

Justin pointed. "Sweet stuff!" The honey was even more welcomed than fresh meat. Rarely found, this was the first find since entering the southern land.

Paul's face lit up. "Oh happy day."

With the new quest, silence lost importance. They ambled over to the tree. The opening to the hive was about thirty feet up the tree and not having limbs to climb, the only way to procure the honey, required cutting the tree down.

Paul patted the hulk. "If we cut it down it's probably going to roll over the edge."

Justin dug a piece of wood from the tree with his fingers. "Rotten stuff...we'll need the ax and the cable and something to hold the honey."

Paul eyes brightened. "You wait here, Dad. I'll get the stuff. No need for both of us to go." Paul scanned the many blue flowers swaying in the cool breeze.

Justin, delighted, sat down. "OK, I'll wait here." The young man departed, and Justin scooted to a softer spot of grass. He reclined on his back and again dove into the blue gaseous sea above.

He lay listening to the clicking of grasshopper wings and watched two vultures circle high on a rising column of air. Justin's mind swam in the pleasant state of things. The settlement existed; tonight they would have honey for the celebration. His mind took a dreamy turn and silly, bizarre things floated.

Justin's eyes opened when a shadow crossed his face. Paul was back. He rose to a sitting position and looked at his son. He jumped to his feet, though much too quickly. His mind still hazy, he stumbled a trifle on the slope.

As his father stood up Paul sat down to catch his breath. "The women really flipped when I told them about the honey." He had a big smile on his face. "I picked some flowers for Chimene." He smiled. "She gave me a kiss."

Justin stared down at him. "Well, shiver me timbers." He smiled. "The power of honey never ceases to amaze me."

Justin took the cable that sat near the baskets and moved the short distance to the derelict tree. Paul kept up his chatter, but the words passed Justin in the wind.

Both ends of the cable had a spliced loop. Justin wrapped the cable around the tree and passed the length of the steel rope through one of the loops forming a cinch around the tree. He pushed the cinch up the tree and over a couple of lumps in the soft bark to hold the loop in place. As he backed away, he played out the cable. Paul rose and took the other end. He doubled a small section of the steel wire forming an open loop which he then passed through the spliced loop. Paul stuck his arm through the cinch to support the cable's weight.

"Things are going good." He looked at his father. "That place we're looking for. I'm sure it's near that water we saw." He paused. "You were right. At least I'm pretty sure you are."

Justin picked up the ax and ran his thumb over the edge. "Not very sharp. I might have to knock it down, instead of chopping." He shuffled back down to the tree.

Paul turned and trudged up the slope toward a short, broad stump over which he intended to pass the wire cinch.

Justin guessed the honey tree to be close to three feet in diameter at the base. "This shouldn't take long."

As Paul neared the stump, Justin picked a spot on the tree and took his first swing. To Justin's utter surprise the ax head buried itself in the soft wood. The tree shuddered and large amounts of debris cascaded down. Justin raised his left forearm to fend off the falling rot. Without looking up he pulled the ax free of the tree.

A loud cracking sound split the air, followed by a deep groan. At the same moment a strong breeze blew across the mesa. The hulk of wood started to topple amidst a storm of tiny particles. Justin raised his head to shout to Paul, but the flying debris entered his mouth and choked his words.

The falling tree quickly took the slack out of the cable. Snare-like, the cable bit into Paul's wrist. He screamed in pain as it yanked him off his feet and onto his back. The tree hit the ground, broke in two, both ends rolling toward the cliff's edge, dragging Paul who clawed at the ground with his free hand.

Justin struck a blow with the ax at the wire snake moving through the grass. The effect, nil. He dropped the ax and grabbed the snake, but its strength was beyond his. The tree continued to roll and slide toward the edge.

Justin retrieved the ax. His eyes flushed and sickness stirred in his stomach. His mind fought for control. He stood two feet from the steel snake, powerless to kill it. The tree would drop at great speed after it went over the edge. Paul slid toward him, a scant ten feet away.

Paul strained his head back and saw another horror. He saw the clear image of the man he loved against the bright blue sky, the man's eyes wide, his teeth bared, the ax high. And most dreadfully, his loud distinctive scream that pierced Paul's ears with its meaning.

"I must...I must...Jesus...I must."

When the moment to strike came, Justin bellowed from the depth's of his belly and the ax whizzed through the air, centrifugal force trying to pull it from his grip. But Justin persisted, and his ears refused to hear the pleadings of his son. Only a loud hum filled his head. The ax struck about four inches above Paul's wrist.

At the moment the tool made contact, the sun flashed off the blade's steel and blasted Justin's eyes. They closed. Fate spared the father the sight of separation, but the man felt the splash of warm blood on his face, and its moving force drove the red liquid through the spaces of his clenched teeth. He knew its taste.

In the canyon, within a cool cave, three women turned in unison toward an agonized wail.

Sadness permeated the cave for weeks. Depression oozed from tragedy after tragedy, saturating the environment with the oppressiveness of cold steam.

Nicole's shrunken and twisted muscles protested whenever manipulated, but she avoided any audible display of her discomfort. When standing erect, her head could turn only a few degrees in either direction, but she persisted.

More dreadful were her recurring reflections. These were sickening moments with images of killing dogs, the feel of fangs, and the flow of warm blood. This always led to fits of vomiting and retching that tormented her twisted muscles.

Eventually, exhaustion overcame her and she would lie upon her bed capable of nothing.

Her conscious moments achieved minimal comfort. The sight of Paul's short, heavily bandaged arm brought tears to her eyes. And then there was the boy's father. For the most part he was quiet and dullness shadowed his once sparkling eyes.

Chimene told her mother the story of what happened on the mesa. A story that required Justin three days to tell. A story that did not include the trepidation and the hysteria of the moments when he struggled to get his son back to the cave.

Justin often doubled in stomach pain, but still he went about his routine work. Rarely did his eyes make contact with Nicole's, an avoidance on both their parts. Their faces, mirrors too revealing; guilt dripping.

Michelle again functioned as the doctor on the day of her brother's injury. The wound, clean and neat, was all the more terrifying. The young girl performed the operation, but not without revulsion. Chimene stayed with her and together they managed. These shared terrors produced a bond that made them sisters as they picked up the pieces of the mind shattering events.

Paul made a quick recovery. Clear, conscious thought came in a matter of days, but his feverish stare lingered for weeks. He showed a disregard for the physical pain.

Chimene sat at Paul's side changing his bandages. She adopted Michelle's style of explaining the situation with each inspection. "The cut is clean and there's no sign of infection."

Paul stared with stern eyes. "I miss my hand. Half of what I can do is gone."

Chimene washed the stump with a solution of herbs and water. "You'll find ways to do things." She looked at him. "It's a matter of time."

Paul's eyes shadowed. "What good is an arm without a hand?"

Paul blinked and his face contorted. "I've seen people with missing limbs." His lips twisted. "Compensating or not. I found them revolting." She cringed and tears welled. "That's immature."

She tried to smile. "The wound doesn't bother me at all." Chimene bowed her head. "Your father is in a lot of pain."

Paul looked up at the cave ceiling. "As to my father," he paused, "I fight not to hate him. I've gone through the moments. Again and again." His voice cracked. "It was the only thing to do."

Chimene concluded Paul's treatment.

Justin watched Chimene tend to Paul. Neither saw his stare. Justin twinged with stomach pain and continued to linger in a hell of culpability and love.

Time heals. Gradually Nicole and Justin overcame their stress-induced shyness and spent more time together. This encounter had distinctiveness. Encased in suffering and extensive guilt, the cosmetic shrouds of superficial concerns were stormed away, stimulating moments of utter flexibility.

Nicole responded intuitively. She felt Justin's warmth, like the feel of an old friend. She lost count of the number of times she caught herself just before reaching out to kiss him at some casual moment. Whenever he turned his back and walked away, she knew the separation was temporary.

The involvement of the two adults did not go unnoticed by Paul, Michelle or Chimene. The apparent interest the elders showed for one another found a way into their conversations and was warmly received. The youngsters often found reason to leave them alone.

Nicole moved about the cave with increasing ease. Her efforts with self-therapy had good results, although she still limped. The wounds from the dog attack healed, but the stitching, the work of an amateur, resulted in deformities on her left side.

Paul softened to the events at the top of the mesa and eventually thanked his father for what he had done. He confronted the frustration of the missing hand with Michelle's help, who fashioned a deer antler into a two-prong tool that he tied to his stump.

Justin absorbed most of Paul's workloads. His wound would never heal and he silently adjusted to its closeness. He forced optimism in the presence of the others, but he felt exhausted. He found solace with Nicole, a pleasant distraction for his mind, and the thoughts of the settlement to the south always lifted his spirits.

Michelle bubbled with energy. She made no bones about the fact that she wanted to get under way. She kept close track of the recovery of the injured. She supplied the nursing and made sure they ate. She talked almost constantly about the trip and commenced the task of making preparations.

Chimene mourned her sister, assisted her mother and consoled Paul. Her demeanor was emphatically sad, but she delighted at her mother's interest in Justin.

A few weeks passed and all were ready to tackle the quest to reach the settlement on the coast. On a clear, warm day, they talked enthusiastically. Michelle stood at the entrance to the cave, her pack shouldered. The others stood in line behind her. Her eyes scanned the rock hollow. "It's been a good shelter, but I hope we don't have to come back." She smiled and turned the corner away from the cave.

The others, without comment, patted the wall at the entrance and followed Michelle into the open.

Nature's touch, of late, seemed peaceful, or so it appeared. The group moved at a slow, leisurely pace, following a river flowing east, sure it would lead them to the sea they sought.

Although they carried food, additional food was abundant. The absence of any signs of either dogs or goons added to their comfort, and for that matter, they encountered nothing at all of a life-threatening nature. The pleasantness of travel heightened their morale, and amplified their optimism.

One week into the trip, the travelers were resting and taking their noon meal. They sat on the southern slope of a low hill just above the river. They chatted light-heartedly as they passed bits of food.

Justin held the field glasses to his eyes and scrutinized the banks of the stream. The shallow river sparkled like broken glass.

Abruptly, Justin's sweeping movement stopped and he leaned as if to get closer to what he viewed. He straightened, lowered the glasses, and ran a hand across his sweaty brow. He took a shallow breath and put the glasses back to his eyes.

Without moving he spoke, "Paul, come over here. I want you to take a look at this."

Paul ambled over. "What's up?"

Justin handed him the glasses and pointed. "Over there. I want to be sure I'm not hallucinating."

Paul reclined across a rock and propped his right elbow to steady the binoculars. "What am I looking for?"

Justin made no comment. Suddenly Paul stiffened and leaned forward as his father had done. "No shit." He looked at his father. "Three men standing on the river bank?"

Justin smiled. "And they're not goons."

Paul put the glasses back to his face. "By their dress, they're not goons."

Justin slapped his thighs. "That's it, people." Paul stood up. "From the settlement?"

Justin eyes brightened. "How's the arm?"

Paul understood the inquiry. "It's uncomfortable, throbs when I move it, slows me down. Take Michelle."

Justin nodded. "After we're gone, explain to the others. Then follow at any pace." He turned. "Michelle, come with me. We have to check something out." He patted Paul on the shoulder and handed him the glasses. "Take these and check on us to make sure all is going well. They have to be the people we're looking for." He retrieved his pack and started down the slope.

Michelle ran after him, putting her pack on as she did. As she passed Paul, she questioned him. "What's up?" Paul smiled and said nothing.

She soon caught up to her father. "What's doing? What's going on?"

Justin moved at a fast pace. "We saw three men on the river bank. Less than a mile off."

"Three men…so we go to meet them?"

Justin slowed and then stopped. "We'd better stay out of sight." He looked at Michelle. "Get closer. Make sure it's safe."

Michelle smiled. "You think they're from the place by the sea?"

"We're close to the sea. If they're not from the place, they must know about it."

Justin started walking. He followed the river, staying close to the brush line, guided by a mental image of the river turns and the location of the three men. "One more bend and we'll be pretty close." At the bend, Justin turned to Michelle. "Let's get into the brush."

They snaked through mesquite bushes, half-crouched. The bush stifled the breeze flowing with the river. Michelle touched her father's shoulder and pointed. Between some branches they could see the three men, two standing and a third kneeling on one knee. He pointed a stick in one direction and his other hand pointed down at something in front of him.

Justin smiled. "They're not goons." He bit his lip. "I think we can take a chance. Paul's watching."

Michelle took another look. "Let's do it." She smiled broadly and started to walk toward them. Justin grabbed her shoulder. "Hold on, I'll make contact and you watch from here. If it's OK, you'll know."

Michelle nodded. "OK. I'll wait."

Justin moved into the open.

He cupped his hands around his mouth. *"Hello. Hello."* Then again, louder and slowly. *"Hallow! …Halloww!"*

When the three men turned, Justin walked toward them. They were young, without beards, and wore their hair long.

They appeared fit and well fed. Justin's appearance made little change in their manner and they simply waited for his arrival.

Justin extended a hand. "Hi, I'm Justin."

One of the men, tall, blond with blue eyes, reached for his hand. "Good day, I'm Jason, and this is Scotty." He pointed to the man on one knee. Scotty had rugged features, a jagged scar across his nose, his eyes, soft and doe-like. The third, looking the youngest and smallest, grinned broadly. He had dark skin and very black hair, a handsome face with African features. "Hi. The name's Abdul, everybody calls me Abby."

His eyes squinted. "Where in the hell did you come from?"

Justin grinned. "Oregon!"

Jason released Justin's hand. "That's a long walk."

Scotty stood and all three men looked beyond Justin. Justin turned, rightly guessing that Michelle approached. He grinned. "That's my daughter, Michelle." Abby poked Scotty in the ribs. Scotty knocked his hand away and smiled. "Any more like that?" Justin's eyes sparkled at the question.

Michelle rushed to Justin's side, she gripped his left arm tightly, her eyes widened with interest. Justin could hear her anxious breath. Her right hand jutted out to the closest male, and she almost shouted her name. "I'm Michelle." All the young men smiled and bumped among themselves to extend a hand in greeting.

The gravel bar projected out into the river and the shifting feet made grinding noises as the small stones rubbed against one another.

Paul, grimacing, emerged from the tree line and jogged toward the gathering. When he arrived, Justin had already informed the others of his name. They answered in near unison. "Hello Paul." A surge of chatter ensued.

Next, walking at the river edge Chimene and Nicole appeared from around the river bend. Nicole could not sustain a fast pace and Chimene gave her some support. Justin could see their smiles. He turned to Scotty. "We're in search of a settlement. We were told it's on the shore of a new inland sea." Justin bit his lip. Scotty nodded. "You've come the right way. It's where we're from."

Justin smiled. "Music to my ears. Oh yes. Music to my ears."

Scotty gave him an inquisitive look and tilted his head. "Heard about us, huh." His eyes shifted to his companions and back to Justin. "We'll talk about that later."

Justin announced the good news to his party. Chimene cried in Nicole's arms.

Another man came out of the south. He was a tall man with broad shoulders, black hair, and black penetrating eyes. A hunter, he walked with a light step. As he approached, he spoke to himself, "Shabby bunch. Must've been in the wild for a long time." He studied the man with a missing hand and soiled bandages and then his eyes shifted to the large man with brown hair and a beard touched with gray. "I bet they have a tale to tell."

A woman stood with her back to him. He focused on the shape of her bottom. "I hope the front is as nice as the back." He quickened his step and came up behind her, putting his hand on her shoulder.

Michelle jumped at the touch and spun around to see his manly and handsome face. Their eyes met and the man spoke his name softly. "I'm Griffin."

Michelle blinked. "Michelle...my name is Michelle." She reached for his hand, but he turned toward the others in another exchange of names and greetings.

The four men from the coast had scattered earlier in the day to locate game. They chose the gravel-bar as a place to assemble and discuss their findings. With the arrival of the strangers, the hunters lost interest in previous plans.

Frank extended an invitation. "We have lots of food at camp. No need to stand around in the gravel. Let's cook up a big meal."

He looked at Paul and Nicole. "You can get medical attention back at the cavern."

Paul turned to Nicole, a silly smile on his face. "Medical attention? They can give us medical attention?"

Frank smiled. "Oh yeah. We have a few doctors and a place for them to work, lots of medicine and some equipment."

Scotty questioned, "You'll be coming to the settlement? Right."

Justin smiled. "You bet, most definitely."

In a jovial mood, the group moved downstream. Griffin turned about, taking a few steps backward, eyeing Michelle once more. She gave him a subdued wave, but her eyes were telltale.

The group walked slowly in the late afternoon. The hunters were constantly probed for information about their home. They stated its location on the extended portion of Gulf of Mexico, which covered just about all of Texas. A long one day's march from their campsite would get them there.

In less than an hour, they arrived at the hunter's camp. A fire soon crackled and a meal was prepared. All were very hungry, and it wasn't until their bellies were full that conversation settled into a leisurely flow. With a little persuasion, Griffin gave a brief description and history of the settlement.

Griffin stood up and rubbed his eyes. "There's a lot to tell." His eyes shifted to each of his companions. "You guys give a hand with this if I screw up." He smiled and looked at the travelers. "It's been a long day. Try to save most of your questions till we get to the cavern." He took a deep breath. "The place, which we call New Atlantis has been in existence, that is to say, a habitation, since some years before the bad times." He raised one finger in the air. "Oh yeah, it's a cavern by the way. A big hole in a cliff side." He smiled at his companions, who chuckled in response. Griffin turned to face Justin. "The fella that found it was a geologist. A Mr. Noah Shoski. He worked for a mining company and found the cave when looking for any mineral of value. Because of its size and all the passages he spent a lot of time there."

Griffin sipped his tea and winked at Michelle over the cup's edge.

"His interest was scientific. However, the world was turning to shit and another notion came to mind: using the place as a shelter in case of some sort of disaster, or if society collapsed."

Scotty spoke in dramatic tone. "A secret society came into existence." His eyes squinted. "It was called 'Swan Song.'"

Frank added more information. "The founder and all but two of the original society are dead."

Griffin continued in a quick factual manner. "The idea turned into a project to make the cavern livable. They also decided that mere survival wasn't enough. They concocted a reconstruction plan. For when the bad times passed."

Paul interrupted. "We had a little plan like that."

Griffin looked at him. "Let's hope the time is close."

The group sighed in unison. Griffin drank more tea. "They gathered supplies and people as well. From all over the world. A very intelligent lot from a wide range of fields. They were given an open invitation to find shelter at the cavern whenever they wanted. In return, they were asked to contribute to the supplies and ideas. They were also asked not to make the issue public." Griffin sat down as close as he could to Michelle.

"Replies came from everywhere. The money rolled in, the supplies rolled in, as well as ideas. At the location of the cavern, only a small group existed and only a few of the minor projects were put together."

He smiled. "No doubt those contacted considered their investments as well-spent insurance."

He looked into Michelle's eyes in the same way he had when they first met. Michelle slid a short space away and spoke without emotion. "Please go on. It's very interesting."

Griffin's stare continued. "When the world actually began to fall apart, those contacted started to show up. Scientists, physicians, biologists, physicists, and so on. Equal numbers of people representing the arts arrived as well. Dancers, musicians, sculptors, painters, and others. Most came with their families and a few friends, but that was expected." He thought a moment. "Oh yeah, no pets allowed."

Griffin looked at the group in a general way. "Space was available for all. The final number was small in comparison to the number contacted, but this, too, was expected. In all, at the start of the bad years there were close to one thousand men, women, and children. Most of us, I mean the guys here, were the youngsters that came with the invited ones."

A full moon shined, and the fire burned high. Frank stood up and left the circle. Griffin watched him as he talked. "Of course there were many difficulties." He looked at Michelle. "And there still are." He turned away from her.

"But, there's order, an organization and things move smoothly." He smirked. "Most of the time."

Michelle got up and walked over to Chimene. Griffin raised his voice and spoke in her direction. "There were also periods of misunderstandings."

Michelle looked down at the seated Chimene. "Is he watching me?"

"I think he just committed the shape of your ass to memory." Michelle smiled approvingly and sat down near Nicole, who sat next to Justin.

Griffin continued, "During the earthquakes, the cavern was a dangerous place to live. People moved out, but stayed near. But lives were still lost with each quake. And then the low lands began to fill with sea water." He paused. "This used to be a very dry place."

Griffin stood up as Frank came back holding a small ceramic jug. He held it up. "Whiskey, of a sort."

He walked over to Justin. "You're the oldest. Please have the first."

Justin took the jug. "My, my, it's been a long time." He pulled the stopper and took a swig, paused and took another. "Thanks." And he handed it back. Frank passed the jug on and all took swigs.

Griffin sat down. He rested his forearms on his thighs and his hands massaged one another as he spoke. "After the climate change people came from everywhere." He paused. "There was a lot of fighting." He wrinkled his nose. "The place stunk with the smell of rotting vegetation and animals. The land got soft." He paused and looked at his feet. "Disease came, and a lot of people died. There were dead to bury almost every day." He took a breath and looked up. "But the population still remained close to one thousand." Griffin's discomfort with this part of the story was obvious. "Starvation was not an issue. We had lots of supplies." He ran his fingers through his hair. "And the dead always left more behind for the living."

He stopped again and thought for a moment. "Well...enough of that." And he waved his hand through the air. "Let me tell you some good things." He swallowed another swig from the jug and passed it. "Deep within the cave there are hot pools that produce a lot of steam. The engineers channeled it to where it was needed and then used the condensate for drinking water and bathing. The system is still in use. Recently the boiling has increased and allowed for an extension of the duct work."

Griffin rubbed his eyes, stood up, looked for the jug, found it, took another swig, and sat down. He scanned around the group and stopped at Frank. "I'm just going to tell them about the expeditions and leave it there."

Frank shrugged his shoulders. "Sure. That'll be good enough."

Griffin started again. "We had plenty of food and other stuff." He waved a hand through the air. "In the name of humanity and to add to our number, it was decided to send out scouts in all four directions."

The words clicked in Justin's head. He stood up and Griffin nodded an acknowledgment. "I met a man back in California just before he died. He wore buckskins like yours. He was the one who told us to come this way."

Frank questioned Justin. "Was he alone? Can you give me more information as to what he looked like?"

Justin did his best with a description and it was enough.

Frank took a deep breath. "You met Malcolm. He and five others had gone west, but never returned." He paused a short moment. "He was a good friend. I still had hopes." He bowed his head.

Jason said his first words to the group. "He was my uncle. Prior to the bad years he had a great career in biology. He published a few books. That whole thing about looking for other people was his idea. I remember how insistent he was about being the one to go west. Mom said he talked as if he had to meet someone."

Frank cleared his throat. "Malcolm worked hard to persuade the people of the value of the effort. Some thought that it would just bring more trouble. But, he said it was something we had to do." Frank rubbed his chin. "He told me that he knew the area to the west and was sure there were people in need."

Griffin tossed a stick into the fire. "In any case, he talked everybody into it and they went on their way. His group was one of the two parties that never returned. Only half of the group that went east returned, and they came back with ugly stories of subhuman people. Those that went south came back with similar stories and met people who chose to stay where they were. They also found out that the Americas are now separated by a sea of water. In the end these efforts were considered a failure, and no more trips were planned."

Nicole spoke up. "You made no mention of the group that went north."

Griffin looked up. "Oh yeah, they, as well, never came back."

Nicole lowered her head. "I believe they died at the place I came from." Nicole told the story about the siege and her escape. At the conclusion of her story she stood up, struggling to stand straight. "They died and we survived and I'm here now. I will always be deeply grateful for their efforts."

Justin stood up as she sat down. "Their efforts did produce results. We are five saved people and who is to say there'll be no more. The expeditions were not failures." He raised the jug of whiskey. "I toast the fallen." Everyone stood and the jug was passed.

At this point individuals talked among themselves and others drifted away in small groups. Justin, preoccupied with thoughts of Malcolm, wandered away from the noise and fire.

A potent sensation of predestination swirled in his contemplation.

Justin's chest rose and fell with slow deep breaths and he whispered into the cosmos, "Malcolm ! I'm here." He turned toward the moon. "But, why here?" Justin's mind clicked through the events of the past looking for clues. His head lowered and an image of Nicole formed. Then his heart twisted and he doubled over, gripping his stomach. "Paul...oh Paul...my heart bleeds." The surge of pain evaporated. He stood erect and he wiped a tear from his eye.

Justin looked back toward the camp. The fire blazed higher and revealed the silhouette of a person coming toward him. "Nicole."

She had watched him leave the campsite, feeling his presence move away. Now she moved toward him and thought, "Where are we going Justin?...What are we doing?" She could only see his shadow against the blue night sky and when she reached him, she wrapped her arms around him and placed her head on his chest. "Stay here with me, it's been a special day." And he did.

The preparations for the short trip back to the cavern took all of the next day. They packed the meat and hides, built litters, and stuffed backpacks, a lot of work to be sure.

Paul did his best to help and he took special interest in the equipment of the hunting party. Their weapons were bow and arrow although they carried pistols as side arms. Paul, curious, questioned Abby, "I see you have pistols, but I don't see rifles. Why not?"

Abby explained, "We do have rifles and at one time we did our hunting with them. But, the noise scared off much of the game and at the same time attracted attention." Abby finished tying a cord around a piece of rolled up deer hide, and looked up at Paul. "Back at the cavern we have more firearms and a large supply of ammunition that will last a long time." He stood up and put a hand on Paul's shoulder. "The present rule at the settlement is that firearms are to be used for defense only. Hunting is to be done by bow and arrow."

Abby pulled on Paul's shoulder. "Let's get a cup of tea." They walked to the camp fire and poured a cup.

When they sat down, Abby continued. "There used to be a lot of controversy on the subject of firearms. Some were singularly opposed to them. Considered them dangerous. You know, accidents, fights. That kind of stuff." Abby took a sip of the very hot tea.

Paul sat his cup down. "It's starting to sound like my father's reasoning." He looked at Abby. "Which was good. Guns and ammunition would have been a big hassle." Paul's head went down. "I can't use a bow anymore."

Abby smiled. "Hold on there. We have craftsmen and tools at the cave. I'm sure they can come up with something."

Paul's eyes lit up. "You think? Something to hold onto a bow with?"

"It doesn't sound like a big deal to me."

Paul looked at his stump, his brow wrinkled. Abby patted Paul on the knee. "They'll come up with something. Hang in there."

Paul smiled. "Finish what you were telling me about the fire arms."

Abby squinted. "Well, let's see…It was also thought that the weapons might bring people looking for them…if somehow the word got out." Abby paused. "On the other hand, they proved their value more than once, if you know what I mean." He knitted his fingers together. "Many lives had been saved because of them. They hand them out only when a group leaves the cave. Like this hunting trip." He drank more tea. "Most people are satisfied with the bows and arrows." Jason chuckled. "The survival of your group, two men and three women, alone in the wilderness for so long without firearms. That'll be a story by itself." Abby studied Paul for a moment. "I've got a lot of questions, but I'll wait."

Paul smiled. "And I for you. Do you guys fish in that new sea?"

A long conversation ensued and a friendship grew.

The next morning, while still dark, the campsite stirred into action. The trip would require most of the daylight hours if they traveled at a moderate speed.

After chomping down some left over meat and a cup or two of hot tea, the group headed out. All were accomplished travelers and they quickly fell into a rhythm of movement.

As the day progressed, the air temperature rose into the nineties and Nicole showed signs of fatigue. Frank went to her side. "Would you like to rest for a bit?"

Nicole smiled. "No, no. I've pushed hard for months. I can handle this."

The land about the river varied from plush to sparse, the result of an ecosystem in transformation. The once dry, scrubby desert, now moist, had a blend of plants not normally mixed. The cactus drooped with flesh gone soft and at times the sweetish smell of decaying plants drifted in the humid and still air.

Justin walked near Nicole. "The new sea must be adding to the humidity. I think this place will probably turn into a jungle."

Nicole turned her head toward Justin and grunted from a stab of pain. "I've been walking for a thousand years." She managed a small smile. "But, I don't know if it's forward or backward."

Justin reached behind himself and adjusted his backpack. "It's forward." He took a few more steps. "It's always forward."

Nicole, now accustomed to Justin's philosophical chatter, smiled. His beliefs were unique and interesting and something akin to Matthew's. "You don't believe in the devil, do you?"

Justin paused a moment in thought. "Well…if life is an illusion, than anything is possible." He took a few long steps and turned to face her.

"Except for free will." He smiled.

Nicole smirked. "No free will? That's outrageous."

Justin continued in his backward strides. "If you're part of an illusion, how can you have control?" He turned and walked at her side.

Nicole remained quiet for a few steps. "Well, I can truthfully say that the present situation was not my idea." They both laughed.

Justin adjusted his backpack again. "I know what you mean and after I'm dead there's a few questions I'm going to ask." He smiled broadly.

Nicole's eyes lit up. "Yeah! Me too. I think I'll start a list."

Justin nodded. "There's just some shit I see no reason for." He smiled again and hurried forward. "I want to ask Paul something. Be back in a bit."

Nicole watched him trot away. Her thoughts drifted to the past. The little pond and the near death situations, Adam's supplies, finding Justin, finding the hunters. "Lucky stuff…I guess." She looked at Justin's back. "I'm only going to think from step to step."

Nicole smiled as her mind unexpectedly conjured an image of a blue sea surging with huge waves and the singing of humpback whales.

The travelers made a few brief stops at newly opened fissures from which steam issued. Frank explained. "It's of interest to the scientists back at New Atlantis. We were asked to estimate if the activity has increased. Some think another disaster is in the making."

By early evening, the caravan arrived at the mouth of the river and the new inland sea. Although it was not truly an ocean, it was enough to lighten the heart of both Justin and Paul. At once, Justin fantasized about sailing or swimming. He questioned Frank. "How well established is the sea life?"

"I'm told that the marine life has made good progress. Lots of sea plants and sea birds and fish and crab." He looked seaward. "Most of the fish are migratory and at times there are few about. Still, the waters are our main source of protein. The hunting for land game is mostly for a change in diet and supplying leather."

Griffin moved up to them. He pointed toward the waters and smiled. "One day the reincarnated soul of Jacques Cousteau will dive below these waters and rise to the surface, gasping with unbelievable news. 'I've found Texas, it really did exist.'" Justin laughed.

Presently, the contingent turned inland and ascended a steep grade to a high plateau and snaked around huge, white boulders. The soil, sandy and white, had few plants. To their left, high sheer cliffs of white rock curved slowly to the west and then to the north before dropping sharply to the sea in the east. It was a half circle, a crescent moon laying on it's side.

The walls stood in the shadow of a day near over, but the mornings were sure to catch the first sun rays of the new days. Near the top and to the north on the west wall, gaped the opening of a huge cavern. Nicole stood at Justin's side. "That's stunning, absolutely awesome."

The mouth of the cave was carved into a perfect circle. It set on the inside base of an equilateral triangle, not touching the adjacent sides. The triangle protruded from the cliff, a pyramid emerging from the white stone. The spectacle was not without color. The space within the pyramid was painted sapphire blue giving the illusion of a black ball suspended in the sea. The frontal view of a humpback whale hovered above the ball, its pectoral fins extended to either side of the sphere. Painted shafts of light descended from the apex of the pyramid. The sculptural notion projected an intensity that ignored its location and soared into the southeast. Both Justin and Nicole turned as if to see the circumstance of the cavern's interest.

The hunters watched as the new arrivals took in the brilliant sight. Griffin stepped to them. "Stunning, isn't it?" He smiled. "The cliff stone is quite soft and easy to work, and as previously mentioned, there are many artists among us." He followed their stare to sea. "Do you see something out there?"

Nicole looked at Justin, but spoke to Griffin. "No, I just felt something."

Justin blinked. "It was like someone turned me. Made me look."

Griffin continued. "The outside work is not complete and there is more art inside."

Justin took a deep breath. "It's much more than I expected."

Michelle strolled over to Griffin. "Are you an artist?"

Griffin smiled. "You bet! I work with paint. I love colors."

The party moved directly toward the north wall. Carved into the cliff wall, a footpath, much like a three-sided tunnel, ascended to the cavern entrance. A small group of people waited at the base of the path and relieved the arriving party of their burdens.

The hunters were first in line, followed by Nicole, Justin, Chimene, Paul and Michelle. The trail was meticulously carved, although steep. Nearly five feet wide and smooth, it rose steeply with broad flat platforms every ten feet. To the left and east of the ascending party the vast new sea sprawled across the horizon.

Paul, Michelle, and Chimene laughed, chattered, and pointed fingers. Justin periodically whispered in Nicole's ear or kissed her on the cheek. She openly laughed, oblivious to the tears on her cheeks.

The opening to the cavern rose thirty feet in height and a smooth, raised path lead inward to a round central stage one hundred feet in diameter. The inner overhead ascended to over one hundred feet and the girth of the cave spread to over three hundred feet. A small, adobe village with some structures two stories high, lined both sides of the cavern. Huge murals of lavish colors added life to the walls. Most were duplications of prehistoric cave paintings from the ice age. The rest were interesting abstractions that blended with the cave art. Sculptures, two of great size, stood at the inner sides of the entrance, sensuous shapes that hinted at the female form. The blackened walls above them suggested that fire once blazed on their flattened tops. Small statues graced the areas about the adobes. Their styles were varied. A few whale forms were carved into the cave walls. They depicted graceful movement and had a definite metaphysical feel.

Justin, Nicole, Paul, Chimene, and Michelle stood at the entrance and at the start of a ivory white path that descended to a central stage. The stage was painted the same blue as the sea on the outer wall. Here most of the populace awaited their arrival, dressed in a mixture of buckskin and linen. Some of the women wore sleeveless robes in a variety of colors.

The men of the hunting party led the contingent to the center of the circle. Standing separate, a group of three men and three women waited. All the hunters, except Frank, drifted to the side of the circle and were greeted with handshakes and pats on the back. Frank walked up to the group of six and turned to Justin, waving him to his side. "Over here, Justin. Over here."

Justin complied with quick steps. Frank put his hand on Justin's shoulder and introduced him. "This is Justin, we found him and his group a day's walk from here." He smiled at Justin. "This, Justin, is our governmental group." He pointed to individuals. "Janette, our chairwoman, and her staff, Buciac, Aquilino, Lorna, Mikko, and Hamish." Justin shook hands with all and they welcomed him and his group.

The crowd of bystanders closed in with growing elation. Formalities began to dissolved with the excitement for the five from the wilderness. The crowd talked loudly, making normal conversation impossible. Frank pulled Justin closer and waved to the people. "Hold on, hold on." The noise continued.

As Justin stood at Frank's side, he pondered the forms of Nicole, Paul, Chimene, and Michelle. Against the background of these clean, well-groomed cave dwellers, he was astonished at the tattered and decrepit appearance of his tiny group. He had become used to their rags and the messy unkempt hair, but now, compared to these people, they were spots of grease on white linen.

Justin felt his scruffy beard with one hand and he fingered a tear in his trousers with the other. Frank spoke some words to the crowd and they fell quiet. Justin, nudged by Frank, heard his voice pronounce the names of Nicole and Paul, as he studied the sight of their dirty bandages. Then he looked at Michelle and Chimene. For him, during the entire journey, they were young female flowers. He had seen only their charm and beauty. Now, their appearance was almost humorous. He pointed to them and spoke their names. They simply stood there smiling, oblivious to their own shabbiness.

A lump rose in Justin's throat. The noise of the crowd burst into his ears. He straightened and his chest expanded with a deep breath. He looked at his group again and a broad smile crossed his face and tears watered his eyes.

Janette suddenly spoke in a voice, both clear, and strong. "We bid the new arrivals welcome and express admiration and amazement in regard to their survival." The populace broke into cheers. They surged forward to shout questions at the bewildered arrivals. At that point, a male committee member, Aquilino, with a booming voice came to their rescue and managed to quiet the crowd.

He turned to the new arrivals. "With your permission. Women over here." And he pointed to his left. "And men over here." And he pointed to his right.

Once separated he spoke again. "With your permission. Allow us to give you a short examination by our medical staff to be followed by a hot bath and a change of clothing."

Justin looked at the others. They all smiled with faces lit with wonder.

Janette came forward again. "After which," she smiled at the little group and turned to the populace. "These wanderers of the wilderness will be the guests of honor at a celebration." The crowd cheered. She waved for silence. The crowd quieted. "I now request the preparations be made." Again there was a great cheer and everyone moved off in different directions.

Nicole, Michelle, and Chimene were escorted in one direction and the two men in another.

The medical examination consisted of a quick look at sustained injuries, a bandage change, an inquiry into any other problems and lastly, an injection of vitamins.

Next came the hot bath. Justin and Paul were led by one of the male committee members, Buciac. He spoke with a Slavic accent and had an austere manner. Not quite forty, a physicist, he spent years working on a solar power project not far to the east. Sadly, he was the last member of his family. His wife and three children died in some tragedy at the cave.

A twisting trail, lit by oil lamps, led to the hot baths deep within the cave. Buciac explained, "At first there were only hot water streams running through the lower levels. We dug pools and channeled water to them. Each pool gets a continuous flow of hot water with the excess overflowing back to the main stream. The chambers around the pools were enlarged and other smaller rooms were dug into the rock producing a very nice bathing spa."

Buciac had actually understated the place. It was exotic to say the least. The chambers were large and oil lamps flickered red and yellow, their intensity mellowed by the passing steam clouds. Numerous stalactites, some were carved nudes in the style of ancients, adorned the passage way. Evolving stalactites dripped into tiny pools. In the places where steam condensed, the drip off stimulated musical chimes that sang softly. The tones were cooling to the warm place.

The hot streams were beyond sight, hidden in the darkness where the cave ceiling dropped to a narrow slit that required a man to stoop to enter. The floors of the baths were shaven smooth and wooden benches provided places to rest. Shallow stalls, carved into the rock, cascaded with continuous streams of condensate pouring off protruding stones, soft as rain itself.

Buciac explained, "Far upstream, duct work gathers the cool condensate." His smiled. "Most pleasant after a hot mineral soaking."

Paul nudged Justin. "Hot pools and cool showers. Can this be real?"

Buciac frowned. "There has been an increase in the water temperature and that's a concern. But, the baths are still very enjoyable."

Justin smiled. "Do you have racket ball?"

Buciac's expression became serious. "Yes, we do, but you have to be a member and you'll need ID for that." He suddenly laughed in a very deep and loud voice that ran through the chambers like thunder.

Justin looked at Paul with raised eyebrows.

A few moments later, at the bathing pools, Buciac pointed. "The women of your party are not very far downstream. Perhaps you wish to join them?"

Neither Paul nor Justin answered. They were already removing their clothing. When naked the men went to the pools and slowly immersed till only their heads bobbed. Neither spoke as heat penetrated deep into flesh and bone.

Buciac stood at the pool. "I'll leave you for now. Shortly a lady will be here with soap and other things...enjoy. I'll be back later."

Justin peered through droopy eyes. "Thank you Buciac. I am so pleased."

Paul added. "Oh yeah, this is great."

Their bodies tingled with increased sensitivity as the hardened outer layer of dead skin stripped away to expose the pink and tender below. Muscles warmed to incredible looseness and heat invaded the joints. For Paul's aching stump, the relief was immense.

Some minutes later a woman entered the chamber. She was beautiful, a redhead, and wore a white linen gown that clung to her voluptuous form. She flashed a bright grin and sauntered to the pool's edge. "My name is Oceania. I'm a barber and a masseuse."

Paul ogled. "Green eyes. I don't know if I've ever seen green eyes." Oceania smiled again. "I'll take that as a compliment."

She bent her knees in a crouch and sat two vials at the pool's edge, along with a couple of gourd body scrubbers. "The vials contain soap. It's peppermint, very refreshing. I highly recommend it." She winked at Paul. "I won't be far off. Just call my name if you need something." She turned and sashayed from the chamber.

Paul looked at Justin. "Wahoo!"

Justin blinked. "Lily white skin and amber red hair. My, my." He turned to the soap. "Peppermint." He looked at Paul. "Peppermint!"

Paul chuckled. "That's right Dad, peppermint."

Justin stood in the waist-deep water. "Oh, my." He smiled. "Peppermint."

He pulled himself from the pool and looked at Paul. "Peppermint."

Justin picked up a scrubbing sponge and soap. On weak legs he ambled to one of the showers. As he stepped in, he sucked a quick breath. "Cooler than I thought."

The soft water caressed his body with a smooth touch and he relaxed. He poured a liberal amount of soap on the scrubber and put it to his nose. "Paul," Paul turned, Justin extended the frothy sponge, "Peppermint."

He ran the pad across his chest and large gobs of frothy suds erupted. He studied the bubbles. Paul climbed out of the pool, strolled to a shower, and dipped under the cascading water. A few moments later he went to Justin and extended the sponge. "Some peppermint, please." Justin poured a copious amount and Paul returned to his shower.

Justin poured soap on his head and sighed. "Oh my. It's a summer breeze." He smiled broadly as Paul sudsed up.

Justin repeated the scrubbing of his body, and he stepped back into the shower, tingling with new tenderness. Water gurgled over his head and he thought of Nicole.

A couple of minutes later, he stepped from the shower and went to his son to assist him with some of the scrubbing.

Later, Justin re-entered the hot pool. His skin, with amplified sensitivity, induced chills as he sank to his neck. Paul joined him and they quietly allowed the time to tick away.

———————————

Oceania returned. "Excuse me." The men opened their eyes and looked up. "Sorry to disturb you." She hung two robes on pegs protruding from the wall and flashed another brilliant smile. "Is there anything you need? Or perhaps want?" The men shook their head, watching her every step.

She pointed toward a different passage way. "Through there is a resting room. You can lie down and there's refreshments as well. I can also cut your hair there and give you a shave, if you like." She smiled again and left.

Paul turned to Justin. "Are you going to cut your beard off?"

Justin didn't hesitate. "Absolutely."

"Me, too."

Reluctantly, they exited the hot waters. Tottering, they retrieved the robes and headed for the resting chamber. Oceania, waiting for them, stood up and handed each a large ceramic cup. "It's a mild fruit wine, raspberry." She directed them to a couple of cots. "Rest awhile. I'll be back shortly." The men drank a few gulps of the wine and laid back on the cots.

———————————

Fifteen minutes later Buciac joined them. "Are things proceeding well enough?"

The men, recovered, sat up on the cots. Paul responded, "I can't tell you how fine I feel. I have a new body, new skin." He drank more of the wine.

Buciac fetched a large clay pitcher in the corner and refilled their cups. "This would be a good time to explain how this community works."

Justin rotated on the cot to face Buciac. "Yes. I'd be very interested in that. The hunters, the ones that brought us here, gave us some of the history."

"Good, I'm pleased to hear that." He sat down on a bench near them. "This place is very liberal in nature with leadership composed of a committee of six." He emphasized the word liberal, with a bit of disdain. "These positions are filled on a rotating basis. In fact, if you stay long enough you'll eventually be asked to serve. The colony has gone through a lot of hard times and as such, we are composed of mature individuals who accept self-responsibility and understand the need for honest behavior. To date there has been little need for heavy-handed authority." He paused. "So far." Buciac stood up and poured himself a glass of wine. "Personally, I think a little authority is wise."

He looked at Justin. "Some call me a hard-nose or even insecure, but I see nothing wrong with a few rules and the threat of punishment to back them up." He thought a moment and looked up. "They tend to ignore me. They say I have little flexibility and fear in my heart." He turned back to the men. "They say it lowers my survival ratings." He drank some wine. "In these troubled times."

His mouth twisted and he paused in thought. "Oh well, enough...Supplies of food and medicine are plentiful. However, we are a bit low on hand tools, rope, equipment such as that. On the other hand, we have an abundance of musical instruments, painting and sculpting supplies." His eyebrows rose high on his forehead and he leaned toward the men, his voice again sarcastic. "I am sure there are enough violins and brass to supply the New York Philharmonic and enough canvas and paint to fill a few museums."

Paul extended his glass and Buciac filled it. "We were told that you have many scientists here."

"Yes. In fact, we are mostly scientists. Little laboratories are set up here and there with many ongoing experiments. Our major project, and one acknowledged most important, is the development of new energy sources, solar power being the prime interest. I lead that team."

At that moment Oceania entered the chamber. Paul sat up straight. Justin smiled. She gave Buciac a passing glance. "Hi, the barber's here." She went to a small table near a chair. With precision she laid out her tools, scissors, razors and combs. She turned to the men. "Who's first?"

Paul quickly got to his feet and moved to the chair near Oceania. "Me. I'm Paul."

Oceania gave him a big smile. "Shave, and a hair cut?" Her hips swayed as if to music.

Paul sat down. "You bet. All of the beard and you can do what you want with my head."

Oceania moved to a position behind him and swirled a cloth around his neck. "Let's start with the beard." And she picked up the scissors.

Buciac's eyes followed every movement Oceania made. "Well I doubt you two can concentrate with lovely Oceania around."

Oceania smirked. Buciac backed out of the chamber. "I'll return later. After Oceania has done her thing."

Oceania dropped the scissors to her side and frowned. She said nothing and watched Buciac leave. She raised the scissors again and clipped at Paul's beard. "He can be such a pain." She brushed a few loose hairs from Paul's beard. "But, he's been through a lot." Her hands went to her hips and she thought for a moment. "And haven't we all." She started to clip again.

Justin propped himself up on one arm to watch the shearing of his son. "I've forgotten the details of what you look like." Oceania's ample body swayed beneath her thin gown.

She cut handfuls of his beard close to the skin and Paul's barbaric appearance softened. When only stubble remained, she wiped soap into a froth and painted his lower face.

It took less than five minutes for Oceania to remove the rest of Paul's facial hair. The change was startling. Paul's uncovered youth glowed.

Due to the difficulties in the wild and the responsibilities placed upon Paul, plus the aging effect of his beard, Justin thought of his son as an older man. The shearing shattered that image. The boy no longer appeared as the tough and dependable man Justin relied upon and survived with. Only in Paul's eyes could one see he had carried heavy loads, both physical and mental.

Justin studied his son with pride and he opened his mouth to say something. He thought of Paul's hand.

Justin's stomach knotted. He laid back on the cot and stared at the solid rock above his head. He could hear the clip of the scissors and the idle chatter of the young man and the woman. But the sound, like the sound of a fast-moving train, vanished.

This craggy, exotic place, flickering in red and smeared with steam, unnerves me. A woman cuts the hair of a one-handed man. Moments pass and he hears what sounds like the hum of an electric motor. "I remember the taste of a boy's blood." He rolled to his side, his mouth filled with saliva. "I smell mad dogs and see a beautiful woman." Clammy bumps peppered his skin. "I miss David and hear Michelle's birth."

Justin forced a long, deep breath. The oxygen, infiltrating his blood, seeped into his brain. Like the rush of a narcotic, the element faded his bizarre thoughts. Justin sat up with a feeling that he had dropped from the sky. He turned to Paul.

A strip of rawhide bound Paul's shortened hair and hung between his shoulder blades. His lower face, pale after the shave, highlighted his plump lips and square jaw. Paul's angular nose seemed smaller and his smile broader. He glowed with youth, confidence, and genuine joy. When shown a mirror he rubbed his face over and over. Still smiling, Paul jumped from the chair and ran to his father.

"You're next. You're next." He pulled his father to his feet and over to Oceania's chair. Justin sat down. "The beard comes off. Take half the hair."

Paul stayed on his feet, constantly walking around his father, making faces with each clip of the scissors or stroke of the razor. More and more of Justin appeared. "Dad, I don't remember what you looked like." He looked into Justin's eyes. "Really, I don't remember."

Lean, rugged features materialized. A firm, square jaw, full lips, and a bit of a smile when relaxed. Paul delighted with the result and held the mirror to allow Justin's inspection. "What do you think of that?"

Justin smiled, almost embarrassed with the feel and look of his nakedness. For a few moments he studied the image. "It's recognizable, but older." He rubbed his face one more time. "I like it." A broad smile erupted into loud laughter.

Buciac returned with clothing for the men. Oceania strolled past him without a word. Paul yelled after her, "Thanks, Oceania." Justin shouted the same.

She turned directly in front of Buciac. "Oh, you're very welcome and I must say that you're both very beautiful men." She spun back and sort-of whirled around Buciac to get to the exit.

Buciac followed her with his eyes all the way out the door. He turned to the men. "I gather her work was satisfactory?"

Paul and Justin expelled compliments at the same time and at rapid speed.

Buciac put his hand up to stop the barrage. "Yes, yes, of course."

He gave them buckskin trousers, very light in weight and extremely comfortable. Then he handed them a pullover shirt of white linen, wide at the neck with puffy sleeves and a broad collar.

When the men were dressed, they looked most attractive.

Nicole, Chimene, and Michelle enjoyed a similar treatment, the difference, a massage with perfumed oils. They too wore buckskin trousers and the same type of pullover shirts, but with a choice of several pastel colors.

Nicole's long, blue-black hair, after shampooing, trimming, and brushing, shone with the luster of polished onyx. It hung to the small of her back, its fullness spreading across her shoulders to frame her tanned face. With gem like blue eyes and full lips, now reddened with fruit dye, her beauty swam in mysticism. Only the scars on the left side of her face distracted from her stunning appearance. She chose a pale blue blouse that draped over her trousers with a dark sash tied at the waist.

Michelle's once brown hair, now bleached to gold by the sun, fluffed in fullness with brushing and softened her narrow face. Young and strong, the grooming brought forth her womanly self. Her eyes sparkled and her cheeks blushed with the excitement of socializing ahead, she thinking of dance and a chance of romance. Her ruby lips bloomed in a constant, irresistible smile. A deep red blouse complimented the luster of her hair.

Chimene chose to twine her hair into a single braid. Its blackness shimmered in the light of the torches. The pulled back style emphasized her high cheek bones and dark eyes. With highlighted lips, her youthful beauty was in a movement away from innocence. She smirked at her deformed arm, but found confidence in the fullness of her breasts which strained against the confinement of her blouse. Her beauty was sharp, exotic, and cat-like. She wore a pale green blouse.

The men proceeded back through the passageways toward the main hall. They hushed to the first sounds of music. Deep tones reverberating through the corridors.

Justin hesitated a moment. "Music. It's been a long time."

The sounds were produced by true artists on finely tuned instruments. With each advancing step, higher notes took form and the fullness of the music blossomed. The men's hearts throbbed to the base, their skin tingled to the treble.

When near the great hall, the low light of the chambers ceased with one turn in the corridor. The brightness of a day near-end, heavy in blue, combined with cool air, sparked the energy of the men and their nostrils flared at the flowery scent of candles.

Eleven more steps and the trio entered the huge main chamber. There, close to twenty musicians, situated outside the central blue circle, played the classics as people completed the last preparations for the celebration. Others danced to a waltz.

Placed around the circle, at the four compass points, were tables of food and drink. There were varieties of fish prepared in different ways and platters of crab in cracked shells, fruit, vegetables, honey and venison. To the absolute delight of the men, there were assortments of carbohydrates: potatoes, bread and even pasta. Large clay pots brimmed with fruit wine and herb tea.

Buciac turned to the men. "Mingle freely and, of course, help yourselves to the food and drink. Later the committee members will again welcome you to our abode and request you stay on permanently."

Justin smiled. "Thanks for the escort Buciac. One other thing." He put a hand on Buciac shoulder. "Where are the women of our party?"

"Of course. Excuse me. Where's my head at?" He pointed at the far side of the circle. "They'll enter through that opening." With that, Buciac smiled and left them on their own.

Justin and Paul walked to one of the tables. "Paul, look at the food."

Paul swallowed. "Holy cow. I wasn't expecting this. That's spaghetti over there. And sausage."

Justin turned to the other end of the table. "Look at the seafood. Oh, I'm going to start there." He headed that way.

Paul walked with him. "I smell Mexican. This is incredible. I'm afraid to start."

Justin picked up an oyster on the half shell. "I wonder if they have liverwurst?"

"Dad, you and your liverwurst." He chomped down on fried fish and pointed again. "There's more tables over there."

The vast size of the cavern had allowed the stockpiling of many foods. With the smattering of ethic groups, celebrations at New Atlantis were gastronomical treats, considering the times.

Twenty minutes later, Paul swallowed half-chewed food and nudged Justin with his elbow. Justin's eyes darted across the circle.

Nicole, Chimene and Michelle stood radiantly in the light, their transformation, astonishing. Justin focused on Nicole. "Oh my." His face flushed. He patiently watched her scan the crowd.

Nicole recognized him only by his eyes. They reached across the hall with a force that seemed to have mass. She had felt it before, though now it touched with added intensity. Her blood warmed and she physically wanted him near.

Chimene clasped Nicole's little finger. "Would you look at them!"

Nicole's eyes twinkled. "They sure clean up nice."

Michelle giggled and stomped her foot. "What a difference." She stood on the other side of Nicole and leaned forward to speak to Chimene. "Do you see Griffin anywhere?"

Before she could answer Michelle spotted him as he waved from the other side of the hall. He immediately started walking toward her. Michelle spoke without taking her eyes off him. "Let's get over to Dad and Paul."

The newly cleaned travelers greeted each other in a manner one might expect from people long separated. They hugged, kissed, laughed, and carried on totally ignoring the people around them, who watched in amusement.

Griffin arrived on the scene quickly, though he hesitated and watched the joy of the new arrivals. His smile broadened to equal theirs.

Buciac pushed through the crowd and entered the small circle of people from the wilderness.

"Are you really so close that a short separation has such a dramatic effect?"

Nicole gave him a stunned look and smiled. "We have been running around in the middle of nowhere for so long, that we started looking like it." She grabbed Justin's arm. "We're so pleased, our blood's bubbling like champagne."

Justin touched her gripping hand and looked at Buciac. "There's a feel of safety here. We've been rescued."

Buciac angled his head to the left. "It would be more accurate to look at it as a semi-rescue."

Nicole's eyebrows levitated. "Rain on our parade?"

Justin smirked. "Half of a good thing is still a good thing." He turned back to Nicole. "Time for food and wine."

Buciac stood silently as they walked to the nearest table. Paul and Chimene followed. Michelle went to Griffin and they talked quietly for a few moments and then joined the others.

The celebration continued late into the night while the musicians played an assortment of dance music, mostly from the forties. Nicole, though aching, could not resist moving to the tune of a few slow numbers.

In the days that followed the new arrivals blended into the community. With an ample supply of apartments to choose from, they situated themselves as they wished. Most apartments were near the west wall. The location caught the morning sun with warm, windless rays. At night, with all artificial light extinguished, the stars and the moon glittered through the huge, circular entrance illuminating the space in blue-black and gray.

Paul and Chimene acquired a place of their own. The small three room apartment, situated on the second floor of an adobe, had adequate furnishings, a few manufactured things from the past, and the rest homemade. Justin, Nicole, and Michelle obtained a larger place in the same area with similar accommodations.

The community required four hours of their time for day-to-day chores. Free time could be filled by engaging in one of the many ongoing projects that functioned in the sciences or in the arts. To do this, they needed only to make themselves available to the appropriate people engaged in the project.

Nicole and Chimene spent their free time with the musicians and a small dance group. Justin, intrigued by the work of the sculptors, contributed to the production of a huge relief carving on the cavern wall and ended each afternoon covered with dust. Paul, forever the hunter and fishermen, found friendship with the hunters they had first met at the river. To his added delight, an engineer and a craftsman teamed up to produce a somewhat nimble and very useful device to replace his lost hand. Once again able to use a bow, the handicap of the missing limb lost much of its significance. Michelle, to the surprise of all, involved herself with the scientists. At first she wandered from one group to another functioning as a helper. Eventually she settled in with the biology group that studied the changing environment of the local area. It also gave her opportunities to make trips with Griffin when he went on a hunt. These were comfortable days, with adequate food, water, and genuine security, not to mention social life.

Justin and Nicole acted as spokespersons for their respective families and spent considerable time giving detailed accounts of their exploits.

Justin reported his buried supplies in Oregon and gave a description of the contents. Their recovery was classified as a worthwhile endeavor, if the situation presented itself.

And so it went. A seemingly new hold on pleasant living.

Fire
and Ice

As the cave dwellers made optimistic adjustments to their lives, nature composed another crushing assault. This time it was fire and ice. Its duration was short, though catastrophic in nature, and came close to total elimination of the more complex life forms on the planet.

The temperature's increase in the cavern's hot springs and the newly formed steam fissures were recognized by the community as harbingers of another calamity. Makeshift instruments recorded seismic rumblings emanating from deep within the earth. The falling rock and cascading dust within the cavern were both dangerous and annoying.

On a clear, sunny day, an observer seated atop the cavern cliff reported billowing smoke in the west that drifted to the north. An investigation quickly verified volcanic activity. The eruptions were small, numerous, and advancing to the east. This activity meant ash, and lots of it. With that in mind, the new Atlantians developed a plan for securing the cavern entrance.

The nearest wood stood thirty miles away at a higher altitude. In a Herculean effort, the needed timbers were stacked on wagons with crudely made wooden wheels and hauled by long lines of people. The approaching black cloud supplied the incentive for the laborious task.

They tightly sealed the entrance and the gaps were stuffed with hides and clay. A single, large door permitted entry. The cavern dwellers were already in the survival mode and the encasement was the only preparation that needed enactment.

The boiling clouds and orange flames advanced upon New Atlantis. Warm winds from the south slowed the assault and a gaseous cloud poised above the walls of New Atlantis allowed only the morning sun in the presence of the hovering blackness.

Then fifty miles to the south, the earth split and gushed volcanic ash. The last of the sun, the morning sun, was smudged away. The only worldly light came from the glow of lava, and the fires it started. The air swirled with particles of warm ash amid dying vegetation. Large and small creatures moved away.

As hot gases ascended, cooler air rushed in, exploding firestorms that swirled like blazing tornadoes. Rooted trees lost leaf and limb to the sucking heat. Insects, birds, and all animals without a grip, became momentary sparks in the whirling furnaces. Within the new sea, the water boiled and a mountain grew.

In the cavern, no flame entered. Only the sound of the screaming wind with a hellish shrill that caused pain to the ear invaded. With teeth of ash and sand, a monster gnawed at the cavern timbers.

The fury was great, but the duration was short. With a final howl, the monstrosity bowed to a silence identified with the snows of winter. A muffling fluff, grey and warm, draped the irregular and all appeared smooth. Hidden holes were instant graves to anything heavier than a fly. People ventured out only when disposing of the dead. The weeks languished. A lackluster sun dribbled photons.

The light-loving humans cringed in the darkness of the cave where only tiny candles flickered. It became a place of touch and sudden fright when unexpected hands reached out. Below, the hot pools boiled excessively, issuing clouds of steam that crept to every nook and cranny; condensing in a constant dripping that drummed in the hollow of rock. Tiny drops collected in puddles that spilled into shallow rivulets gurgling to the boiling below. With shaking hands the inhabitants plugged their ears to the crescendo. None of the apartments were built with the concern of rain, and shelters had to be built within shelters.

Without the cleansing light, a small scratch bloomed into a festering sore. Infections of the lungs lingered, incurable in the dampness. Coughing became the echoed music of the grotto.

Time slowed in these ugly months and the people strained for their sanity. When judgment was lost, physical bonding became the only solution. But, many of the witless individuals found the door and dashed into the world of ash. The fortunate of these fell over the precipice to a sudden death.

Beyond the cave the sea heaved beneath the weight of powder too dry to sink. Near the shore, nature's filters clogged. The deep sea, now the only refuge.

This volcanic episode occurred at many points around the world. The vented heat of the earth warmed the atmosphere under a blanket of ash. A year-round summer extended to the earth's poles, and much of the captured water melted into the bulk of the seas. The waters bulged upon the land or dissipated into the warm atmosphere. The sky, energized with turbulence, lit with the light of electric flashes and boomed countless thunders into a continuous throb. An airborne cauldron of chemicals cooked a substance gritty in texture, greenish in color, and acid in content. The sterilizing liquid fell to earth and stripped the land of the soft and dissolvable. Life had to be well hidden to escape its sting.

With the fury of volcanoes spent, the swelling of the earth's crust ceased. Newly opened vents produced a stability for pressure relief, and rains cleared the air of its particle content. The days of black skies transformed to pastel pink. For the living, it was not yet the light of life, but the light of hope. With the partial clearing of the sky, the inhabitants of the cave ventured from their sequestered place and found a barren land studded with the skeletons of plants. It was a place growing cold. Airborne particles still lingered and reflected much of the incoming warmth of the sun. The polar caps regrew quickly and sucked water from air, sea, and land. And as speculated by the scientist, a tiny ice age commenced.

The bitter cold was the final thinning of life. Many species vanished and others were pushed into small pockets of refuge. The pitiful goons succumbed with the fire and most of the dogs had their last howl in the frigid winds. The cavern dwellers, being prepared for the cold, endured the frigid temperatures in relative comfort.

Around the planet small pockets of life persisted, as was the plan. From this point on, life would reclaim its previous domain. Life is tenacious; death, its strengthening friend, returned as an occasional visitor.

Whispering Whale

The sun's brightness cloaks our days, blinding us to the universal vastness of spinning fire balls and multi-colored marbles. But for that which is about our feet, it's a vision of clarity. Only in darkness can we see the truly distant. It is the time we call night. In one of those nights the sailing craft *Cristine* gathers a warm breeze and prowled across low swells, two humans astride her back.

Nicole commanded the helm of the *Cristine*. Justin stood at the bow, having completed a topside inspection. All was well. He moved aft to Nicole's side in preparation to relieve her at the helm. He put his right hand on her shoulder, gripped the helm with his left and she stepped back.

The man's palms tingled as he comprehended the craft's vigor. Broad swells heaved and abated soothingly, rhythmically. Justin designated a course and found harmony with the forces of the moment and place.

Nicole sat on the cockpit bench. She rubbed her hands on her knees and smiled at Justin's silhouette glowing with a moon-spun aura. "I wish the helm could be a place for two."

Nicole rose and climbed atop the forward cabin. Barefooted, she made her way to the bow. The wind flowed steadfast from the east. The *Cristine* heeled to port. Nicole made a study of the trimming lines and sails, she was now their keeper. At the bow, the movement of the craft was exaggerated. Tiny splashes of sea water pattered her feet. She took a slow, deep breath and found the fragrance of land gone. She headed aft.

At the main mast, Nicole leaned with the lean of the craft, her back to the pillar of wood. She slid to a sitting position, her face to the wind and a moon that showered the sea with ivory rays. With everything right, her only comment, a shallow sigh.

Neither individual will sleep this night. The air was permeated with energy. An energy that made no demands. An energy that made itself available. In consumption of that energy all things in this part of the sea, whether seen or unseen, touched the force, which produced a balance perceptible to all.

One of the unseen swam not far astern of the *Cristine*. This leviathan of the deep, this old one, showed crusty patches of raspy barnacles, crooked battle scars, and tattered flukes that stung with unhealed splits.

Most serious was the weakness within the beast. His massive heart strained to push life-sustaining blood. Relentless in its effort, though its last beat was not far off. The whale was cognizant that a rip and a quiver would occur, the flow of blood would cease, and death would come in a rush. However, he had a task yet to be done.

He listened to the swirl of water at the *Cristine's* stern, the sound he had followed on the long voyage from the north, waiting for the proper moment. A moment that must certainly be close.

The whale calmly listened as the sound dwindled. The vessel moved away, its speed too swift for the old creature to sustain. His pace would be slower, constant, straight and over the long haul, he would keep up.

The minds of the humans were discernible to the whale. He perceived their moods, comprehending their fear or joy or hate or love. He perceived the lesser moods as well, discomfort, boredom, delight, to name a few. His occasional mind intrusions, always apparent to the humans, were soft and misconstrued as functions of their imagination.

This perceptibility was not exceptional to his species, it mirrored their highly evolved form of communication. Eons ago, when the ancestors of the whales made their re-entry into the sea, an extraordinary spark flashed through their intellect. A spark not unlike the one that engrossed the land-dwelling primates. The light grew to a great flame, though its use would be, by design, vastly different from that of the apes.

The primates descended from the trees with manipulating fingers and the all important grasping thumb to facilitate the investigation of their world. The animal's groping and stumbling eventually resulted in a technology that emphasized security of life and longevity. Their achievements were vast and even extended beyond the planet.

In the case of the whale, the door to technology was entirely shut. Without the grasping appendages, physical investigation and manipulation of their environment was impossible.

The water world, draped in shades of blue, had a sky that shimmered with changing geometric patterns and a blackness below that required audio perception. Without physical control, the whale's world became contemplative. Due to the creature's great size, physical survival was relatively uncomplicated and achieved without domination of its environment.

Man, at odds with his environment, sought heat for his body and found fire. The whale sought warmth of the soul and found music. The consequences of these discoveries were of equal importance to both species, stepping stones toward their destinies.

Thought transfer became the sea mammal's means of communication, where distance and physical objects were of no consequence. This capability allowed distribution of information instantaneously, if desired. This furnished the foundation of their society, transcendental in temperament and passionately adventurous. Whale intellect found expression through the powers of the mind. Only music and dance were demonstrated in a physical aspect.

Their metaphysical science required artistic sensitivity, as symmetry and harmony were required for its understanding. The accumulated knowledge matched any human endeavor.

However, transforming them into the concrete of the physical had no meaning in the whale society.

The old whale that followed the sailing craft, a metaphysicist, excelled in the discipline of innovative orientations. His efforts were in the area of cosmological essence, a science comparable to man's theoretical physics, but differed with its spiritual inclusions. Using contemplative maneuvers, a skill of the mind and not a science, the physical requirements of his body, such as moving, feeding and even the avoidance of danger, could be accomplished without the distraction to the intellect's escapade. The duration of the separation was a matter of talent, education, desire and of course the physical functioning of the body. For the highly skilled, investigations into the universal vastness, or the infinitesimal, was possible. This whale that followed the *Cristine*, a prodigy, found this type of advanced separation available to him.

As a youth, his spirited character found expression more in physical exuberance and a love for adventure. He lacked maturity and meaningful depth in his contemplations. Therefore, adhering to tradition and the wisdom of elders, his first ethereal excursion, as many to come would be, was chaperoned. He and an elder with synchronization spirited between the earth and moon. There, the blue globe framed by the vastness of incomprehensible depth, glowed in beauty. It was also a speck of water and dirt. Even smaller was the small of himself. From this justifiably humbling sight, the largest of the earthly creatures learned his fleshy place as an iota in the "All that IS."

The most descriptive way to define the science that preoccupied the old one, and to state it as a whale might, required only one word, "Why." It was the base science from which all their science sprung. Ancient in its genesis.

Logic was fundamental to their understanding of the "Why" and required consideration of all forms of information, encompassing the physical, the emotional, the intuitive, and the transcendental. With non- intrusive probing of the mind by employing contemplative maneuvering and all-inclusive logic, the trained intellect avoided physical disruptions that could alter observations. Microscopically, achievements progressed to the study of matter at a level of absolute singularity and to the macroscopic of universal wholeness. This was possible due to the above-mentioned technique that transmuted the power of the mind into the dimension of the nonphysical. Since the source of the physical was the nonphysical (an ethereal realm), observations from this perspective were all-inclusive.

These expeditions commenced with the ingestion of hallucinogenic, deep-water algae. This alga, discovered in ancient times in the vicinity of thermal vents and once a necessity for universal exploration, was now purely a shortcut. It isolated the mundane, prevented that intrusion, and triggered a rhythmic sensation of emotions that synchronized to the frequency of the force that bridged the two basic realms of the "All that IS." The mind trekked with requested orientation and sought the permissiveness of the "Powers That Be."

Our whale, by the time of mid-life, achieved attunement to perspectives of the origin of the physical and determined that the unfurling of an additional dimension, there being eleven in total, was possible without catastrophic effects. From indicators seen beyond the material edge, emphatic agreement for predestined evolution of the whale species signified achievability. "The Powers That Be" provided the whale with a means to take a conscious step into its next evolvement. A universe composed of five dimensions manifested astride our actuality and would be imperceptible in present reality. The result of all of this was a method that allowed the transference of any mind to a specific microscopic singularity with the use of contemplative maneuvers. When the minds of the evolving were present, the unfurling of the fifth dimension could be enacted. This comprised the essence of the breakthrough.

The age of the whale on earth was at its end. The species, through the power of its evolved mind, was capable of taking its next step in evolution, a conscious step. The procedure discovered possessed true validity and permitted the formulation of a plan that allowed the entire whale species to enter the new realm en mass. It would occur at mid-ocean in very deep waters suitable to receive the bodies of the transcending beings. The transfer would take days.

When the time came, it was under a new moon and billions of stars dominated the sky. Our whale's spirit hovered near, but his body was to the north in meditative repose. He would not go, he would be left alone, he had one more task. Here he would only be a witness.

Many of the elders had made the transition and now waited to receive the others. The procedure, well practiced and fine tuned, was transmitted to all the whales and their whale-like cousins. Thousands and thousands of the creatures moved toward the chosen place in the sea.

In preparation, all of their voices thundered a music that enraptured the water world. It was a song sung by all the leviathans of all the seas. The music drew them together. The music pushed to the bottom of the blue-black sea and echoed the happening to all the aquatic creatures. With that harmonic throbbing, the algae ascended.

The old one, bodiless, dove into the sea and positioned himself in a place he knew to be central in the unfolding episode. "I alone…the joy be later."

The algae, phosphorescent, spiraled in a massive column to the surface, opened like an umbrella and twirled. A living ring of slow-moving giants touched the outer edge in gathering numbers. Their music pulsated in a cadence with accumulating intensity. Colors flashed in blues, purples and golds. Soon the massive bodies begun to plummet into the deep like rain at an umbrella's fringe, swirling slowly, gathering momentum.

The old one trembled at the spectacle. He felt the joy, he felt the essence of those departing and he twirled with them and sang their song.

Thousands of whales added to the harmony and the vortex achieved great speed. The old whale stayed for just the night, his accumulating loneliness much too stressful. The indescribable joy too tempting. But, the beauty he would hold in his mind and take with him.

The transcending whales in the meditative repose of the magic algae were guided through a labyrinth of mental images to the very essence of their minds. Their physical forms dropped into the vortex and their minds streamed and proceeded with the guidance taught by the old one.

For days the procession continued and the air hazed with the final breaths of the whales. The event peaked after five days and dwindled for another six as the last of the creatures drifted in a slowing circle of the abating maelstrom. In the end, all the whales departed their earthly home, all, except one. He would impart a gift. A gift for all humans, as decreed by "The Powers That Be."

The *Cristine* cruised in the light of the morning sun with Nicole at the helm. The day promised to be hot and the sea, as if in anticipation of the heat, slowed its movement. The wind dwindled to a whisper, its bulk sought another place and only the diminishing chop of the sea was telltale of its bygone presence.

The pressure of the helm light, Nicole's knee held the course, the craft more drifting than cruising. The fast-moving night, consumed by a joyful cruise, remained sleepless. Nicole's shoulders sagged, her fatigued muscles twinged and her eyes swelled. She yawned deeply and her dulled conscious mind allowed her tireless subconscious to play a tune. It was a soft song, barely audible even to herself. Her lips and tongue formed each lyric, though her breath was not sufficient to give the melody true birth. Her head swayed to the noiseless beat, and her eyes succumbed to sluggish blinks.

The sun blazed to starboard and Nicole felt the heat penetrate her skin. It sucked at the last vestige of her energy and in defense she turned her face to port to cool in the shadow of her head. Her trance-like gaze lingered on the watery sail shadow.

The non-reflecting shade comforted her hot eyes. With this peace, mild hallucinations swirled.

The *Cristine's* slackened speed allowed the whale to catch up during the early morning and he lingered beneath her bulk in a pensive state, his body almost catatonic. Nicole's lethargic mind seeped into his and startled him into alertness. "The moment." However, the impulsive interpretation was wrong.

His body popped to the surface and shattered the sea exactly in line with Nicole's gaze. The whale's breathing valve opened emitting, an eruption of gas, moisture, and steam, and his bulk tossed a wave at the side of the *Cristine*. The craft heeled sharply to starboard. The movement flung Nicole's body across the cockpit and she bounced once on her rump. With bulging eyes she stared through the descending spray of whale breath and a rainbow framed the after deck.

Nicole heard the short, powerful sucking sound of the whale's sniff. The leviathan, realizing his mistake, descended quickly to depth. The craft rolled back to port and then to starboard with decreasing violence. The boom swung ungracefully with the lurching of the craft.

Below, the great whale, his heart pounding, quaked in pain. His colossal cry boomed and trembled the *Cristine*. More heart tissue tore, but the torture slowly abated, and the whale quelled his huge body. He hovered at middle depth. Equilibrium established, he mentally examined the failing pump. The massive muscles contracted in unison, but quivered between beats. He had little time left.

Nicole, shaken by the sudden appearance of the whale, sat where she landed, in the aft starboard corner of the cockpit. She made no effort to get up. Her mind reeled from some sort of mental punch; confused images unfurled and she heard something voice-like. The abstraction dissipated and she snatched at a fleeting insight. But, its flight was too fast.

The last of the breath spray settled and the rainbow vanished with the pulse of a mystical thought. Nicole rose to her feet and scrutinized the foamy sea to port, utterly bewildered.

Prior to the whale's arrival, Justin, below decks, occupied himself with the preparation of the morning meal. Within the cooking stove, a small blaze crackled. Justin sat at the galley table lethargically watching the flame through the open door. His head nodded to the drowsy haze of his mind, and he periodically succumbed to true sleep, only to momentarily awake with a start. He took a deep breath, determined to stay alert. He moved to the stove and studied its structure. A relic from a farm house back in Oregon, homemade, it had charm and craftsmanship good enough for the maker to sign his initials with a welding rod, the double letters of F and Z were durably scorched in the upper left-hand corner.

Justin decided to fetch another piece of wood. With a languid gait, he headed for the fuel stored to starboard. Even before he got there, he saw the stick he wanted. Precisely the right size, it lay loose at the base of the woodpile. He bent to retrieve it.

At that precise moment the whale surfaced to port. The craft lurched to starboard in the direction of Justin's momentum and launched his relaxed body into a forward flip. His vision whirled, and in an instant his weight shifted from pressure on his feet to pressure on his shoulders and upper neck. His legs and half his back came to rest against the woodpile. The rest of him lay flat on the deck. The *Cristine* lurched back to port. Justin gagged, his chin driven into his chest and the air squeezed from his lungs. He grimaced and pushed hard with his feet against the firewood in a calculated move to allow his feet to pass over his head, conduct a back roll, and leave him perched on his hands and knees. However, the boat shifted back to starboard and his position remained the same. He relaxed in defeat and a thunderous sound vibrated the deck beneath him.

Justin lay there in mild panic, waiting for the craft to find equilibrium. "Crap. I hope we didn't hit a reef." Again he tried to push off with his feet, but his hair stuck under his back, pulled when he tried to slide across the deck.

Nicole burst into the cabin. "Justin."

She spotted him lying on the deck and knelt behind his head, looking directly at him, water dripped from her hair into his face. "What are you doing?"

Justin grimaced. "My new meditative position. Is everything OK topside?"

Nicole smirked. "Doesn't look very comfortable. Yeah, everything is OK."

She put her hands on both sides of his head. "Did you bump your head? You won't believe what happened topside."

Justin brushed water from his face. "Please, Nicole, move out of the way so that I can get up."

Nicole obliged, and he pushed on the woodpile with his feet, did a back roll and stood. He looked at Nicole. "I bet you never saw your face upside down."

He ambled to the table rubbing the back of his neck and sat down. Nicole followed. "This whale popped up, right under my nose."

Justin's eyes widened. "Under your nose!"

Nicole poked him in the shoulder. "Listen." She crunched her eyebrows. "Something special happened. There was a rainbow and I heard something."

Justin looked at her. "I take it, that the whale rolled the boat?"

Nicole put her hands on her hips. "Well, what else? But, that's not important." She clasped her hands. "No, no. I mean the whale *is* important." She looked into Justin's eyes. A few silent moments went by. "It was special. There was something there. An insight...oh...you know what I mean." She looked at him questionably. "Don't you?"

Justin caught the urgency in her voice. "Perhaps a playful whale on a slow day?" He paused. "I heard what sounded like thunder, and the deck quivered."

"Yeah, I heard that too." She sat down at the table, talking in a whisper. "Something extraordinary happened up there. Dream-like. Eerie. Yes, that's it. Eerie." She paused. "No, that's not it either." She leaned back. "Maybe the whale hit the boat."

Justin put his elbow on the table and gripped his chin with his thumb and forefinger. "Why are you whispering?"

She looked into his eyes. A moment of the whale episode flashed at the question. "Whispering." Her eyes brightened. "That's what it was. I heard a whispering." She hesitated, her mouth still smiling. "But I don't remember what."

Justin waited a moment as she thought. Then he spoke, "I remember the first time I saw the *Cristine*. I knew it would be part of our lives. Was it like that?"

Nicole spoke in her normal voice. "No." She got to her feet. "No, not destiny." She ran the fingers of both her hands through her hair. She looked into Justin's eyes. She saw him striving to understand. "I'm sure it's a good thing, whatever it was."

She grabbed Justin's right hand and pulled him to his feet. "Go topside. I'll cook."

He gave her a kiss on the cheek and climbed the ladder. "I'll look for the whale."

"No…no…it withdrew."

Justin turned on the ladder to face her. "It *withdrew?*"

Nicole shook her head. "I don't know why I said that. Go catch a fish or something. I have to clear my head."

Justin mumbled and stepped topside. He looked about. With the wind totally abated, the *Cristine* sat quietly on a smooth sea. He turned a full circle scanning for the whale. There were no signs of the creature. None. The main sail hung as if exhausted, and Justin made the boom fast in a mid-ship position. He proceeded forward and hauled the main down. He did the same with the jibs and made a meticulous inspection as he returned to the cockpit.

From the small pipe protruding from the galley, smoke issued in a gathering cloud that seemed to cling to the main mast and climb its height. "Burning wood. It's out of place at sea."

He yelled down to Nicole. "The smell of fire belongs in the forest. We should eat our fish raw." There was no answer.

Justin looked to the west in the direction of the nearest land. It lay beyond the horizon. He stuck his head through the galley hatch. "We'll be able to sleep together. As calm as it is."

Below, Nicole proceeded to prepare a meal of poached fish, instant mashed potatoes, and fruit. The potatoes were part of the recovered supplies from Oregon.

The stove, nearly ready for cooking and the heat discomforting for Nicole, she removed her thin leather vest and draped it across the woodpile. The vest was her favorite garment and a gift from Chimene. Chimene made it for her prior to her departure for Oregon. Nicole moaned with homesickness, but smiled a moment later realizing that the trip was almost complete.

Her body glistened in the heat of the cabin. She leaned her butt against the edge of the table, her arms supporting her upper body. A pan of water heated. Nicole looked down at her naked torso. Her stomach hard, and flat, her breasts firm. Physically she was in excellent shape, a product of the rugged lifestyle and good food.

Justin ducked his head into the galley and saw Nicole's nakedness. He jokingly raised his eyebrows. Nicole smiled with the thought of chucking the meal overboard and finding rest in the arms of her lover. However, her empty stomach disagreed and she waved Justin topside.

"Later love, later."

Justin pulled his head up from the heat of the cabin. "A full meal will put me to sleep."

Nicole leisurely wiped a few globules of sweat from her stomach. Pregnancy had never been an issue. Justin had the proper operation years ago. Nicole recalled the young Indian girl Awa. "The last baby I've seen." She bowed her head. "Their bones surely dragged off, powder in the wind."

The water on the stove bubbled. The noise jogged her sleepy mind.

"Why did I volunteer for this?"

She took the battered aluminum pot from the stove, poured a bit of the hot liquid into a frying pan, and placed it on the stove. On the table lay some fish fillets that Justin prepared. She gently placed them in the pan, covered them, and turned to prepare the potatoes. From two packets she dumped white powder into the remaining hot water. With a wooden, homemade spoon she stirred the substance. A rivulet of sweat ran down her neck and across the mound of her jostling breast. Unnoticed, it proceeded to the nipple and cascaded into the potatoes. Nicole saw the droplets just as they hit the potatoes. She mumbled something about salt and continued the mixing.

Presently, satisfied with the consistency of the mixture, she put it aside. Next, finding two peach-like globes, she sliced them into wedges. On a metal plate, Nicole tried to arrange the slices into an attractive pattern. The wedges did not comply. "Bull shit," And she pushed them into a jumbled mound.

From the table she retrieved the potatoes and scooped large portions onto the two plates. When finished, she grabbed her vest, slipped it on and headed topside for a breath of cooler air.

Justin worked near the main mast. Nicole watched in silence. He wore only leather shorts. Strong muscles rippled beneath the brown skin of his back. Bleached body hair gave him a golden hue. His long hair tied in a simple knot at his shoulders, descended to the middle of his back.

Nicole laced the front of her vest with a piece of rawhide as she eyed Justin's back. It was often the object of her foreplay and the remembrance titillated her mood. Nicole mused. "He's so right for me."

She loved to lean on his powerful character and fathomless endurance or bathe in his tenderness. Interestingly, he had many moods. His humor had spontaneity and often caught her unprepared, and much of it was humorous to him alone.

Then there were other times, those special times, times of imaginative temperament. Nicole could always see them coming. They were her favorite moods. Like a kitten finding the warm sun and awaiting a gentle stroke, she would comply to his touch, pleasantly aware of the mutual joy.

Justin's large blue eyes would soften and a mellow thought would flow from between his lips. And then another and another. Nicole, ever confident of his sincerity, utterly relaxed in the romance. Erotic whimsy gushed through her mind with expectations of sensations. Justin eyes would twinkle, and Nicole willingly sank with him into the sensual adventure.

Nicole and Justin were perfect companions and their enjoyment with each other totally genuine. At these special times of lovemaking, Nicole's initial passiveness proceeded to womanly aggressiveness; taking the lead with a power and an energy precocious to her gender. Their souls and bodies thus intertwined produce moments that later neither of them spoke of; always they emerged from these salacious pools graced with mutual insight.

Nicole finished tying her vest and Justin completed his chore. He turned. Upon seeing Nicole, he spontaneously launched into a true account as to what happened to him below decks when the whale surfaced. Nicole was soon laughing hysterically. Justin continued to explain about the episode as he jumped into the cockpit. Nicole, still laughing, went below to fetch the meal. In a twinkle she returned with two plates of food and handed one to Justin.

Justin dipped his fingers into a bucket of sea water and sprinkled his fish. They were hungry and neither spoke during the meal.

Justin, the first to finish, leaned back on the bench. "A full stomach is an effective tranquilizer."

Promptly he sank into drowsiness and was nearly asleep when Nicole adjusted her sitting position, disrupting the stability of the boat. The movement awakened him.

He spoke with a drowsy mind. "What I want now is our soft bunk, your back against my chest and empty blackness." A tiny strand of hair on the man's head stirred with a feeble whisper of wind that produced Lilliputian ripples on the oil smooth sea.

Nicole finished the last morsel of her meal. With tired eyes she scanned the sea for signs of the whale. There were none.

She turned to Justin and extended her hand toward his plate. "The whale is near. I now know the touch."

Lethargically, Justin stared and after a movement he handed her the plate. Nicole put one plate on top of the other and with the flick of her wrist, flung them through the open galley hatch. The rattle of the plates, clamorous in the silence of the becalmed sea, caused the couple to gawk at the galley, mesmerized.

Finally, Justin rose, breaking the spell. "Come, my sweet, to oblivion bliss."

Nicole pulled the cord of her vest. "I will sail that cabin sea with thee."

As they slept, the *Cristine* moved not across the water, but through the air in the grip of a river that snaked the sea, a river of vastness equal to any that flowed on land. About the hull, small bits of flotsam bobbed. Some clung to the craft with strange magnetism. Beneath the still waters and the floating debris, near the bottom of the river, a whale hovered.

The old whale, in deep meditation, his bodily functions slowed, his heart moved more with a rumble than a beat. Moving, yet not moving the massive creature, the sailing craft, the humans and the tiny bits of debris made use of the river in the sea. The exhausted humans lulled in the comfort of dreams, dreams joyful like fairies and children and awesome with their truth.

The day progressed to early evening and a gentle breeze puffed the sea to ripples. The ripples grew to chop and the sailing craft wobbled on her round bottom. The gentle sway jostled Justin to consciousness. His eyes opened and gathered the light of the blue-gray sky. He rolled to face Nicole, asleep on her back. Justin closed his eyes and oozed his presence around her, contemplating her name more as a song. Nicole moistened her lips and shifted her bottom seductively. Justin felt her movement and smiled. He never told Nicole of this fun, and he wondered why.

He planted a short sucking kiss on her shoulder. Justin spun away and rose to a sitting position at the edge of the bunk. Nicole opened her sleepy eyes and blinked. She reached for Justin's hair, but he leaned forward and her hand slid down his back as he rose to his feet. Her hand dropped and dangled over the edge of the bunk.

Justin spoke abruptly, "I'm going topside to hoist the sail and get underway."

Nicole's eyes followed Justin and she smiled. The smile became a sneer. "Justin, you are a terrible shit, and I hate every molecule of your body."

Justin spun around. "I've known that for quite sometime. It's not love, it's my money you're after."

"I spit on you." She mocked the gesture. "And it is your money, and I will have it. Your addiction to my body and the way I move in bed makes you my slave and lackey." She spat. "I hate lackeys."

Almost immediately she added. "Justin, I'm not really in the mood for this. Please."

Justin smiled broadly. "How am I going to make it in show business without practice?"

He pulled on his shorts and headed topside, but abruptly turned back to her. "Spit on me, will you. There will be no sex for you until further notice. You can check the bulletin board for any change in this policy."

Nicole forced a reply. "Please, not that."

Topside the wind blew at a growing sea. The *Cristine* lurched in and out of small troughs catching the breeze to starboard. Justin took a deep breath, stretched a time or two, and moved to the bow. He was a seaman, but not a trained or accomplished sailor, most of what he did on the *Cristine* was improvised.

He hoisted the jib and returned to the cockpit. There he pulled the jib line taut and the craft gained headway. He turned her into the wind and the jib luffed in the breeze now coming over the bow. Justin quickly moved forward and hoisted the main sail. In short order the *Cristine* moved along smartly.

Nicole felt the lean of the craft and she came topside to compliment him on his efficiency.

"Not bad, lover, not bad."

Justin smiled. "The success of this maneuver has put me in a good mood. I have decided to allow you sex this day…a sort of amnesty."

Nicole eyes widened. "Oh. goody." And she disappeared into the galley.

Justin tied off the helm and moved to the lee of the boat. His left hand found a main stay for balance and the low safety rail supplied a brace for his knees. With his right hand he untied the cinch about his waist and prepared to urinate. Justin stared at the sea moving past and scrutinized the yellow spattering the blue.

Nicole took two steps up the ladder and spotted Justin's bare bottom and awkward position. Quietly she climbed topside, stepped close to his back, and gave his right shoulder a sharp thump.

Justin's urine stopped flowing and his left hand rotated on the cable. His knees pained from the pressure to hold his position and his right arm reached back to find a grip on something. With nothing there he hollered, "Nicole!"

Nicole grabbed his flailing arm and pulled him back. Justin, wide eyed, shook his left hand to dissipate the burning sensation and his shorts slipped below his exceedingly red knees. Nicole backed away, her face dominated by a smile of satisfaction. "Remember the telephone?"

Justin's grimace popped to a smile and then to laughter. He hoisted his shorts and returned to the helm. "You can have all my money."

Nicole moved behind him, strapped her arms around his chest and whispered in his ear.

"How much farther do we have to go?"

"Well, we've moved past that foot-like projection of Mexico, which puts us into the gulf. From here it will soon be no more then a sail across Texas. I'd say, something like two weeks."

Nicole again spoke into his ear, "We've been gone so long, I wonder about the kids and what they are doing."

"Probably making babies."

A moment of silence followed.

"Justin, I've forgotten what it's like to hold a baby. What it feels like, what it sounds like."

Their minds drifted into the past, the birth of their children, another man, another woman, another genuine love.

Justin pointed to the horizon. "If we could see over that mound of water, the settlement would be just about there."

Nicole gave him a short squeeze. "I bet there's more than just the cave. I bet some of the families moved out. I bet there are little houses here and there with gardens of vegetables."

Justin moved the helm to starboard and caught a bigger chunk of the wind. Nicole released her grip.

For the next two days, they held the craft hard to the wind, driving the *Cristine* on tirelessly, seeking every measure of speed. They took turns at the helm while the other, when needed, tended the sails. They slept at will, but never together. The food, kept simple was mostly cold, but neither complained.

At the start of the third day, the wind shifted to blow from the stern, and the speed of the *Cristine* slowed. The craft settled and the helm steadied with little of the wind's force felt by the humans.

Nicole, at the helm, hollered, "Topside please."

Justin stuck his head through the hatch of their berthing compartment. "You called."

She looked to the west. "Let's head for land. Our food supply is getting low and soft." She turned to him. "I need a rest and a bath."

Justin nodded. "Sounds good to me. Perhaps we can find some *meat*."

Nicole eased the helm to port. Justin came topside and trimmed the sails on the established starboard tack.

By day's end they dropped anchor in a small protected bay. Ashore, low rolling hills with bushy vegetation and the jungle absent, indicated their movement northward.

Justin sniffed the wind. "This looks like good hunting."

Nicole climbed atop the forward cabin. "I don't see any sign of fresh water."

Justin rubbed his hands together. "We got plenty of water. A bird or a rabbit is what we need." He scanned the shore. "There's not going to be much in the line of fruit."

After a short discussion, they brought the *Cristine* closer to land, and deployed two anchors. At the completion of the chore, the couple went below decks for a full night's sleep, the hunt being scheduled for morning.

Out to sea the whale, lagging, lumbered on. He reached out to the humans. "They rest in shallow. Minding them 'til morrow."

He hadn't eaten for a very long time, indeed he knew he'd never feed again. The whale closed his eyes and contemplated the sea water streaming past his massive head. "Soon no more the soft, cleansing." The old one mused in a melancholy mood. "Please, to retain memories, liquid love."

As a youth, and with other youth, in a spirit of adventure, he sought the heaviest storms and thrashed through mountainous seas or rolled on the steep watery slopes. The danger real; the storms long; exhaustion a threat.

"What of pretty loves. No heated blood. Gone will be and replaced I'll hear."

The whale recounted the communal bliss of the new life episodes and the many females that had chosen him, and wondered if the new existence would have something comparable. "Pity if not."

His thoughts shifted to the approaching event of his body's death and the end of physical pain. He had experienced the new dimension, heard its music, saw its images, and understood that the lesser of the old dimension would dissipate. Its greater would be the lesser in the new realm. More importantly was the elevated understanding of the "Why," the proximity of perfection, and the augmentation of love.

He envisioned an intensive quest toward the new love, with minds conjuring ideas to explain it and portray it in the new arts and sciences. Most would be wrong, but a few close. More importantly, the venture toward the higher truth would persist and eons will pass with designed reflections and balance. And then, if the "Powers" aspire, another evolvement.

A song boomed from the old one, a song not sung alone. The spirit-mind of the departed whale beings were with him.

They conjured the music and provided energy for his physical form.

To the west, aboard the *Cristine*, Nicole and Justin awoke. Energized by the pleasant night sleep, they chattered continuously while tending to chores. They talked of home, its nearness, and the anticipated joy at arrival. They longed for the comfort of home and the touch of their people of blood and shared events. People longing for them as well.

When the *Cristine* sailed from Oregon, the overland contingent departed for New Atlantis and would have reached it before the *Cristine*. Therefore, Justin anticipated a beacon fire by night and a column of smoke by day as a final guidance to their destination.

Justin, in the cabin aft, checked the weapons in preparation for the hunt. He held his bow with a tender touch. His companion for years, it served him well. His hand slid over the weapon. "Your arrows know how to find their mark." Justin placed the bow on the bunk.

He turned to his knife. He strapped the blade, sheathed in leather, to his right shin. A flap covered the handle. The steel and bone were Paul's parting gift to his father. The unique blade made the object more of a tool than a weapon. The knife was originally a bayonet, but Paul spent many hours with file and grinding stone reshaping the blade. Its tip had an exaggerated up-sweep with a cutting edge on both sides. With a touch of flexibility, it trimmed close to the bone of fish or mammal.

Paul gave a knife to Nicole as well. It was shorter and stout, strictly a weapon with a straight blade and a deep blood grove. The slender handle fit snugly in Nicole's hand. Paul knew

Nicole would always be at his father's side and the gift supplied a measure of protection for herself and his father.

When Paul presented the knives, Justin saw disappointment in his eyes. Paul wanted to make the trip. Though the reason remained unspoken, all knew his missing hand was the concern. Paul, with discomfort, accepted the wisdom of the decision.

Justin banged his fist into the bulkhead. "I let him down." Secretly he yearned for his son's presence throughout the trip.

The flight of the ax flashed in Justin's mind and he wiped his forearm across his mouth. He stood and studied the scars around the two missing fingers of his left hand.

Justin heard Nicole moving around topside. He blinked and cleared his throat. He didn't want Nicole to find him this way. With a deep breath he regained composure, but the sadness would remain until the events of the day shook them loose.

He called to Nicole, "At the hatch, weapons." After handing them up, he pulled himself topside.

Nicole had launched the dinghy and packed a few supplies. The plan was to hunt, cook a meal ashore, and spend the night on the beach. She looked forward to the small adventure, anticipating a tasty meal, the glow of a fire, and a sleep on a surface not moving.

Justin made a final check of the anchors and the boat in general. With the preparations complete he joined Nicole in the dinghy.

Nicole volunteered to row. Justin, not protesting, sat at the bow looking at Nicole's back, pleased she couldn't see his face. Nicole pulled on the oars.

Shortly, the dinghy encountered the sand of the beach with a loud hiss. Justin jumped from the boat and pulled it up on the wet sand. In a short moment, he and Nicole dragged the craft onto the dry sand and unloaded the equipment.

With weapons in hand they studied the area. Nicole turned to Justin. "There's not much vegetation."

Justin shrugged. "Game should be easy to spot."

Nicole sniffed the air. "It's been raining."

The hunt moved inland at a brisk pace. The cool breeze of the beach gone, the inland heat quickly baked their bodies to a glossy sweat.

From the top of a low hill, they spotted a group of small goat-like animals on the other side of a shallow valley and moved toward them. When they arrived at the spot, the animals were gone. However, their activity was evident. Low laying brushes with blue, plump berries dotted the area. Nicole and Justin spent a relaxed hour eating and their fingers stained deep red from the sweet fruit.

Nicole pointed to her left and down a slope. "Let's try this little valley." At the bottom of the slope the land flattened to a broad plain of sandy soil and clumps of brush.

Justin popped a few more berries into his mouth. "I hope these things grow near the cavern." He looked to where she pointed. "OK, maybe we can flush something out."

They both pulled an arrow from their quivers and descended into the valley. The lower they got, the more intense the heat. Justin flushed a rabbit, but its speed was quicker than his aim and the arrow half-buried its self in the soft soil. The hunt continued in silence as the two wove their way through the vegetation, eyes and ears alert.

Abruptly and in unison, they halted to the sound of rustling in a nearby bush. Nicole, closest, dropped to one knee and prepared for the first shot. Justin positioned himself to back her up. Attentively, they waited. The bush rustled again and a low growl, unmistakably that of a dog or a dog like-creature, issued from the scrub. Justin whispered, "Let's back away slowly." He took one slow step, stopped, and watched as Nicole's back slowly expanded and contracted with a heavy breath. She didn't move. Justin, concerned, whispered again, "Back away…back away." Nicole made no indication that she heard.

Then, from behind the bush, no more then ten yards away, a large, black dog emerged. With its head low, it stepped slowly forward with teeth displayed. Nicole raised her bow and her upper body twisted slightly to the right, angling her left shoulder toward the dog. The arrow pointed squarely at the dog's head, precisely the small section of bone between the eyes. Nicole fixated, beads of sweat ran off her brow and into her eye, but she did not blink. Gently her fingers released the bow string. Her eyes sparkled and her face beamed when the arrow struck. This was no simple kill.

The huntress, more precisely, the killer, was efficient. The shaft shattered the bone. The small brain pulped from the impact and with instant death the creature's legs collapsed. The body flopped, the head extending between the front legs. Nicole lowered the bow and studied her deed. The heavy arrow protruded from the animal's head, one eye rotated in and showed only white. The other globe slowly revolved back into the socket and then fell out of the head, dangling from a long blue tendril. From the animal's snout thick red blood oozed to the soil, a bulging puddle too viscous for absorption. Nicole took a deep breath, her tense muscles relaxed. She was pleased.

Justin maintained readiness, anticipating another dog. Nicole, consumed with the kill, her bow dangled at her side.

"Stand ready Nicole. There could be more."

Nicole walked to the corpse with casual, long strides and kicked the creature hard in the chest.

"Damn it Nicole, reload."

Nicole kicked the dog again, her hands trembling. Justin moved to her side and gripped her arm. Slowly he stepped backward, pulling her with him. She trembled and coughed. Terrible visions crawled through her mind.

Justin's bearing remained defensive. He glanced at the dead dog and considered Nicole. His head circled ninety degrees to the left and then ninety to the right. The dead animal was the first dog they had seen since the dawn of the age of fire and ice.

Justin pulled at Nicole. "This is a bad place. We must leave now."

Justin froze in his tracks, and Nicole crouched as more rustling issued from the same bush. Nicole's eyes blazed. Again the killer, she readied her bow.

From beneath the low-laying branches of the shrub, a small black ball of fur waddled into the clearing. With a lumpy trot, the pup moved to its dead mother. Sniffing and whimpering it moved around the corpse nudging it with its nose. In a useless effort, it tried to push beneath her belly, seeking a nipple.

The pup took a few steps backward and small black eyes searched in confusion. Presently, they settled on the two tall creatures not far away. With the innocence of the newly born it resumed his lumpy trot heading this time toward Nicole. Her bow lowered to her side.

Nicole, quiet, studied the lump. Justin stood guard and ignored the pup, his eyes darting to locate true danger.

Nicole whispered, "Kill it."

Justin, without hesitation replied, "No." His eyes darting. "The pup's no threat." He glanced over his shoulder and turned to Nicole. With the pup nearly at her feet, Nicole stiffened, anticipating its touch.

Justin whispered. "Use your knife."

Nicole dropped to one knee and tossed the bow into the dust. From the sheath tied to her right leg she drew the dagger. The pup ambled near and Nicole's left hand flashed out to the loose skin at the nape of its neck. With a quick jerk and a twist she secured the creature, stomach exposed. The animal, paralyzed by the grip, bared tiny teeth in a forced grin. Nicole looked at the exposed, plump, pink belly. Her head throbbed. Justin quietly maintained his alertness.

Her jaw muscles tightened as her blade slowly lowered toward the pup's abdomen, its sharp tip piercing the taut belly skin. The cut one half-inch to the side of the tiny penis bubbled a drop of blood. Nicole dragged the knife toward her and sliced the length of the hairless skin to the foreleg. The wound, though not deep, spilled blood. Nicole prepared for another stab. This one, the final one. She raised the knife high.

Poised to kill, Nicole hesitated and began to tremble. She released the pup. The creature, its motor functions restored, screamed in pain and waddled back to its mother. A trail of blood colored its path. Nicole lowered her knife and bowed her head.

She threw the knife into the dirt and stammered in a weak voice. "No, no." She chased the pup down, the recapture quick, she frantically tried to stem the flow of blood with her fingers. Justin saw her plight. "Use some soil."

Nicole, befuddled, grabbed a handful of dirt and pressed it to the wound. Justin took a step closer. "We must leave this place. There are sure to be other dogs around."

Holding the pup in a tight grip, Nicole looked at Justin with fearful eyes, but said nothing and turned toward the slope they had descended. Justin annoyed, cursed under his breath as he retrieved her abandoned weapons.

Nicole quickly climbed the slope and headed for the beach. Justin ran to catch up and with the additional equipment to carry he jogged awkwardly behind her. Nicole trotted with her usual slight limp. Justin watched her hair bounce in rhythm to her gait that periodically exposed the scars on the left side of her neck.

The trot back to the beach took close to an hour and Nicole led the entire way. They arrived, dripping in sweat, and still had one hundred yards of soft sand to cross. Nicole didn't hesitate and trudged to the dinghy, breathing heavily. She deposited the pup into the bilge of the craft, ran to the bow, and gripped it with shaking hands. As she leaned her weight into the effort, she gazed at the tiny dog. The movement sloshed the bilge water, producing swirls of red around the pup.

Justin arrived. He said nothing as he placed all the weapons in the boat. He then straightened and took a few, deep breaths, while the dinghy moved slowly by. He wiped his brow and positioned himself behind the boat. Laying his palms upon the stern, he leaned back into the launching effort. His arms ached from lugging the heavy bows, and his help was minimal.

Struggling, the couple boarded the craft as it bobbed in the low surf. Nicole retrieved the pup. Justin pulled hard on the oars.

With the *Cristine* anchored close to the shore, few strokes were needed. They secured the dinghy to the starboard side by its bow line. Once aboard the larger vessel, the couple hurried to the galley. Nicole placed the pup on the table. It lay still while she retrieved the medical supplies. Justin filled a container with fresh water and brought it to the table. The pup moved and Justin grabbed it by the nape of the neck, its eyes bulging white.

Nicole dipped gauze into the water and dabbed at the dirt spattered wound. She wiped the sweat from her brow with the back of her hand. "Shit. This is too slow."

She tossed the gauze aside. "Hand me the pot of water." Justin did.

She poured the water in abundance across the cut and it cascaded off the table, pink and gritty. Again Nicole dabbed with a piece of cotton. "The damage is to the skin only. I can see a portion of the intestine." She sighed and wiped away the last few bits of debris.

She stepped back and stared, perplexed. Justin's brow knotted. "Sprinkle the cut with antiseptic and stitch it up."

Nicole grimaced. "Where did you get the idea to use dirt to stop bleeding?

"It was just a notion at the moment." Nicole glanced at him and turned back to the animal.

She shook her head from side to side and stepped farther back. "Please, please." She turned and moved toward the ladder leading topside.

With his free hand Justin grabbed her by the arm. "I can't do this by myself. You have a choice, hold or stitch."

Nicole allowed herself to be pulled back and took an exhausted breath. "I'll stitch."

From the medical box she hoisted the antiseptic powder and liberally sprinkled it over the wound. The stitching and bandaging took place in total silence. When finished, Justin released his grip on the pup and dripped water into its mouth using his fingers. Nicole wandered topside.

Justin carried the creature to their berthing cabin and found a comfortable place for it to rest. Recovery seemed assured.

The evening dragged on. Nicole found solitude at the base of the main mast. Justin sat at the stern, a fishing line in hand. Their meal would not be meat after all.

A fish took the bait and Justin pulled a small grouper aboard, adequate for two. He filleted the fish and returned the carcass to sea.

"Nicole! Come on, we'll cook it on shore."

Nicole, without comment, got to her feet and went to the dinghy. Listlessly, they rowed ashore, gathered wood, cooked their meal, and with little enthusiasm, consumed part.

The moon was a thin crescent. Justin and Nicole sat close together leaning against the beached dinghy. The fire crackled amidst the splash of small waves that washed the beach. The *Cristine* buoyed white and still on the black sea.

Justin tossed a chuck of uneaten fish into the fire where red coals blackened and shriveled the flesh. He turned his head skyward to avoid the sight.

Nicole watched the tops of the flames and scooped handfuls of sand that trickled between her fingers. The melancholy was the consequence of puppy blood.

Nicole turned to Justin. "Please, I would like to return to the boat."

They left the fire burning.

Earlier that day, the old one arrived at the landfall and reached out to the humans. He felt their distress, but was unconcerned. "Soon to pass, importance the coming time. Close, ever close."

In the darkness the whale heard the dip of the oars and the thump on the side of the *Cristine*. He wallowed at the surface with an occasional quiet puff. His monitoring of the humans continued even as he perceived their slumber. "Pain the past, pain the present. Harsh beauty, all sensitivity."

The old one conjured an image, a translation from the ethereal, of the soulful essences of the sleeping pair in the form of truthful hallucinations positioned low in the eastern sky. The entrancing sight fluttered colorfully in shapes not unlike the jelly creatures of the deep sea. The old one chanted to the sound of soft music, deep in texture and mystical in implication. With exhilaration he ascertained his part to the special heat, a heat to beautify the trembling things to lofty splendor, to cosmic adventure.

The whale, contented, his energy renewed, swirled the sea with his great flukes, and turned north, now sensing the pulse resonating to compose a symmetry of place and time.

By circumstance the humans will be guided and he'll be there waiting.

With the sun at mid-morn, Nicole awakened. She immediately rolled out of bed and stood up. The transition too quick, she paused to rub her temples. "Why did I do that?" She took a deep breath and sighed deeply .

She turned to where Justin had placed the pup. A pool of urine and a spot of blood glistened, but the animal was missing. Nicole searched, and shortly found it huddled in another corner. His dark eyes stared. Nicole watched for a moment without expression, turned, and departed the cabin.

She came back with a tin of water and a piece of old canvas. She wiped up the yellow and red puddles and again she left the cabin.

As she crossed the cockpit, she tossed the soiled cloth into the sea. Abruptly she stopped, turned and looked at the rag. "I shouldn't have done that." Cloth was hard to come by. She ducked into the galley.

Justin, awakened by Nicole's movement, sat up in bed. "Damn it's late." He scowled. "It's going to be a hot and sticky day." Naked, he went topside. His face somber, he looked toward land and decided to refresh his spirit in the sea. One long step got him to the side of the boat where he dove into the sea and swam toward shore.

Nicole felt the roll of the boat and the sound of Justin's splash. She stood at the sink, rinsing her mouth with water from the boat's tank. It had a metallic taste. She spat the liquid at the stove and stomped topside wondering what to do next.

The pup came to mind. "The cockpit's a better place. Simple clean up." She sighed again. The gloom of the prior day still clung to her.

She climbed to the cockpit, headed for the aft cabin, and turned to see the splash of Justin's swimming.

"That's an idea."

In the aft cabin she found the pup and took it and its water to the cockpit. She carried the pup by the nape of the neck, her face expressionless. She put the creature down and placed the water in front of it. The pup sniffed at the liquid, unsure what to do with it. A slight roll of the *Cristine* sloshed water into its face. Startled, it sneezed. Nicole stepped to the side of the boat, poised for the dive. Behind her was the sound of the puppy slurping the water.

She looked straight ahead and rose up on her toes as tears welled in her eyes. With blurred vision, she dove toward the sea, but forgot to suck in a breath. Once submerged, panic struck and she thrashed to the surface, gasping as air going down met a sob coming up. Feeling foolish, she twirled to find Justin, but his whereabouts eluded her and she turned back to the boat. Not far from her face, the urine, blood-stained rag, bobbed.

"Shit! Shit! Shit!"

From the corner of her eye, she spotted Justin's splash and the smooth, shiny lump that was his back. She kicked and clawed her body to the horizontal. Putting her face into the water, she frantically propelled herself in the direction of her lover.

Justin stroked energetically. He took a deep breath and pushed harder. Swimming close to shore, he made a wide turn back to sea. With head down he concentrated, ignoring the pain of the all-out effort. Below, only dark blotches on a sandy bottom were distinguishable.

Shortly his lungs rebelled and a breath burst from his mouth. He stopped his swim and jerked his head free of water; his anxiety subsiding with large gulps of air.

As he rested, he eyed the *Cristine* and spotted Nicole's head bobbing toward him. Although his muscles still throbbed, after a moment, he resumed his swim, this time using a breast stroke. He fixed his eyes on Nicole and spat water with each forward beat.

Shortly he discerned the features of her face framed by a cape of shiny black hair. Something splashed to her left, but quickly disappeared.

Nicole ceased swimming and watched Justin. No longer swimming, he thrashed as if trying to rise higher in the water. His eyes looked past her. Suddenly, his face went down into the water, his arms extending with speedy and powerful strokes.

Justin stopped at her side breathing heavily. He spoke one word, distorted by the water running down his face and across his mouth. "Shark."

Nicole spun to see the telltale fin cutting through the water, ever so evil when viewed at the horizontal. The path of the dorsal trailed from the bow of the *Cristine* to her stern. Nicole knew the fin was midway on the creatures back and that the large orifice lined with razor teeth was somewhere forward of the moving dorsal; she could see its form rippling beneath the water.

Justin looked to shore. It was too far. He looked back at the fin. Fear burned in his chest. They had no defense, none at all. He couldn't even punch the creature or grab it by the throat. They couldn't climb a tree or hide in a hole. He had no weapon. A terrifying vision of their legs dangling beneath, tempting one of nature's best-designed eating machines, was a distraction to the pressing need to think clearly.

The fin moved past them. It moved with power and cursed confidence. At the stern of the *Cristine*, the thing turned and headed for the far side of the craft. It's primitive, simple mind, seemingly preoccupied with the larger object. Perhaps it looked for a piece of dangling flesh from the large corpse-like craft.

Justin shouted, "Swim to the dinghy. Watch to the left. I'll watch to the right."

They propelled themselves with quiet, quick breast strokes, needing to cover forty yards. Nicole shuddered. "It's worse when you can't see it."

Justin's face paled. He would rush the creature, give Nicole time, but he doubted his courage.

The fin reappeared at the bow. Justin clenched his teeth. The timing had been wrong, absolutely wrong. The shark, too close, the boat too far. Both swimmers ceased movement and watched the approaching animal.

Justin's heart pounded, he did not want to die this way. Sharp teeth, cutting and crushing, the sea red with blood, a sudden jerk with a portion of his body torn loose and swallowed. And the wait for yet another strike and yet another piece. Any other death would be better, a fall from a cliff, the club of a goon, but not this. Justin's stomach cramped; the taste of bile oozed into his mouth. The shark approached, the time for commitment, now. After a swirl of water behind the shark, Justin, his face wide-eyed and ashen, lunged at the gray death.

Nicole screamed with a voice of a child and reached for Justin's feet, but fast moving and slippery, she only fingered them as they moved away. Her mouth opened and shut noiselessly.

From the deck of the *Cristine*, something black fell into the water. The sounds of tiny splashes fluttered across the sea. The grey fin altered its course and streamed toward the little black ball. Justin and Nicole watched. The fin submerged and an instant later a grey snout broke the surface. The red of its gaping mouth was startling in contrast with the subdued color of its skin. It was a terrorizing display.

Abruptly, it vanished with the little black ball. Nicole and Justin rushed to the side of the *Cristine* and Nicole rolled into the dinghy. Justin rocketed out of the water and up the side of the sailing craft, panic persisting until his feet cleared the sea. Nicole, trembling violently, managed to climb aboard the

Cristine. Once there, she stared down at the violence of her trembling body.

Justin, on his hands and knees, convulsed with dry heaves. Tears blurred his vision, and like a dead horse, he fell on his side. The terror was humbling, ever so humbling. Justin limply crawled to the side of the *Cristine* and convulsed, sour-green bile splattered thick on the sea. His stomach muscles burned in pain. With head down, he mouthed a noiseless cry for Nicole.

———————

The day was beautiful, bright, clear; the temperature was mild. A passing frigate bird soared in graceful flight while a short way to sea, a gull squawked in delight and dove for a piece of floating flesh. There was no evidence of past trauma, no blood, no carnage. The struggling pup lay hidden in the belly of the beast.

———————

The couple withdrew to the cabin aft, reclining on their sanctuary bunk. They held their tongues hoping to warm their minds and soothe their bodies while the hours of the day dripped by. Sometimes they sought each other and sometimes they were separate. At night their sleep was coma-like, and thankfully, void of dreams.

———————

WHEN I DIE
MY BODY, PLEASE
FROM A PLANK OF POLISHED OAK
SLIDE MY FORM
TO THE FOAMING WAVES OF THE SEA
AND I WILL GIVE
MY FLESH AND BONE
TO THE CREATURES THAT BE
FOR I AM SURE TO RETURN
AND BE, AGAIN
ONE OF THE CREATURES THAT NEED

Justin lay on his back. The hot sun poured through the open hatch irritating his skin, making it feel tight and hard. He raised his hands to shade his eyes and studied the area of his missing fingers before dropping his arms to his side.

He turned from the sun to Nicole's reclining form. She didn't look attractive to him, and he turned away. A strange notion of guilt swirled in his mind, and his mouth moved to his thoughts. "I made a mistake...again." He sat up on the side of the bunk.

"Again and again."

He looked down at his feet. "My toenails are too long."

His shortened his sight to his stomach, and detected its sagging skin. "Age."

He contorted his tongue in the pasty taste of his mouth, and whiffed his own body odor lofting to his nostrils. Laboriously, he lifted his form to a standing position. His bladder needed draining. As he climbed the ladder topside, he mumbled softly. "Again and again."

On deck he ambled into the cockpit and stepped on the overturned water bowl. He looked at the white fiberglass deck and a yellow blotch. "Dry urine. The pup, my savior."

Justin proceeded to the bow. He didn't want Nicole to hear the dribble of his urine. Holding on to the jib stay, he aimed his penis seaward, and a yellow stream arched. Slightly to his left his shadow lay upon the blue water. He redirected his penis and urine splashed the silhouette.

Later, Nicole sat topside after completing her morning functions and heard Justin rummaging around in the galley. She stared into the orifice leading below. Her shoulders slumped and she exhausted a tired breath. She had not spoken to Justin, nor seen him.

Nicole stood, her eyes lazily scanned the area. She noted the tiny dinghy bobbing alongside, the oars dangling precariously in their locks. Nicole stepped to the side rail and the *Cristine* rolled slightly.

"Don't." Justin's voice boomed from the galley. Nicole, startled, fought to steady herself. Justin rushed into the cockpit.

"God damn it Justin, you scared the shit out of me. What's wrong?"

Justin answered apologetically. "I was thinking about the shark. When I felt the boat sway, I thought you were going for a swim."

Nicole, annoyed, "No, no, I'm just going to get the oars out of the dinghy."

Justin turned and stepped down toward the galley. "Sorry." At the same moment he bumped his head on the cross member with a solid thud, but continued on down.

Nicole climbed into the dinghy, mumbling about the distastefulness of the anchorage. "The sooner we're out of here, the better."

She sat at the center of the boat with her elbows on her knees and her fingers massaging her temples. The rose-colored bilge water was mesmerizing and the steel of her knife blinked below the surface.

Reaching through the water, she retrieved the knife and tossed it on deck of the *Cristine*. Then she released each oar from its lock and pushed them over the rail into the cockpit. Each oar thumped loudly as it settled.

Nicole took a deep breath, "That didn't take long enough."

She turned to the gap between the two vessels and studied the dancing patterns of light on the side of the *Cristine*. "That's irritating." She then turned to the cool blue of the little bay.

Mechanically she scanned the surface for the bent triangle of a dorsal fin. She mused, "Perhaps he cruises below."

Her gaze rose to the ivory and green of the shore; she wondered if death pranced there as well. She lowered her head in fear of the waters and in fear of the shore.

She mused, "A wolf-dog prowled in search of its pup and the killer of its mate...safely in this little boat. Away from tooth and claw. Away from justifiable revenge."

Nicole squinted toward shore, but perceived nothing relevant. However, her ears discerned something. "Perhaps the wind, perhaps a howl."

Nicole straightened and gripped the sides of the dinghy. With her arms propping up her torso her head hung above the pink puddle in the bilge. Apparitions materialized. *A wolf on the hunt carried success between his teeth and made haste back to his den, back to his mate, his pup. He hesitated. The smell of death stung his nostrils and he dropped his kill. He found his mate and sniffed the air for the pup.*

A small movement of the dinghy momentarily rippled the hallucination, but it quickly settled. *A wolfish creature stood on shore. It was the end of the trail and he signified his loss with a long, lonely song of despair.* "Or was it the wind."

Nicole bowed deeply, envisioning herself a sulking hyena, sulking after some ghastly deed in the night. Her heart pained for the small pup and its short, ugly life. A witness to its mother's destruction, its belly ripped and death in the acid darkness of a monster's gut.

"But my love and I live." She closed her eyes. "Not even a pat for the little pathetic...ball of fur."

In despair, Nicole climbed back aboard the *Cristine*. She must find Justin. She must confess.

Nicole stepped sluggishly into the galley. Saying nothing, she sat away from Justin. He watched in silence. After a moment he began surveying different parts of the cabin, and periodically, Nicole's downcast head.

His eyes moved to the hatchway of the forward stateroom. The compartment, nearly filled with retrieved trunks from Oregon, was difficult to enter. A small trunk near the opening caught his attention, a trunk meant for the time of rebuilding.

There were mostly books, some CDs, DVDs, pictures, things of information on the arts and sciences. However, more delightfully, the nooks and crannies were stuffed with a hodge-podge to take up empty space. Both he and his children made the choices with total freedom. It was the enjoyable part of the packing. All the items were memorabilia of luxury, fun or beauty.

Justin squirmed. Every little trunk contained a flask of his favorite brandy. He walked to the hatchway. Nicole watched.

He untied a few securing lines and heaved on the chest until it slid free. Justin dragged the chest to the galley table and turned to the wood stove where his indispensable, adjustable wrench hung from a nail. He retrieved the tool.

He loosened and removed the securing nuts. But, the lid still held tight. Nicole, now inquisitive, rose to help. Together they pried, hammered, and strained at the lid.

Justin took a breath, "I put a sealant around the edge. To keep things dry."

Nicole ran her hand across the top. "What's in it?"

"You'll see."

Both got at one end and Justin held the box down by the handle as Nicole pried up. The top came loose with a loud ripping noise.

A cloth of pale blue covered the contents. Justin handed it to Nicole. The material lay upside down, and when turned over it revealed the rich beauty of deep purple velvet. Nicole sighed and spread the fabric across the galley table. Succumbing to its invitation, she stroked the cloth. "Ohh, gimme goose bumps."

Justin's mood twinkled with the opening of the treasure. "Artifacts. Never thought they would be artifacts."

From a niche he jerked on a string and a leather pouch jumped into the air. He snatched it in flight. He untied the puckering blue bow and dumped a diamond into his palm. It was only glass, but precisely cut and clear. He hoisted it by its gold chain and moved it into a beam of sun rays. Splotches of miniature rainbows pulsated about the tiny compartment.

Justin smiled at Nicole. "A bit of wizardry, my lovely."

Nicole's face glowed, she twirled with the rainbow and reached for the gem. Justin released it, and she danced again. "Somewhere...over the...rainbow blue birds fly."

Justin returned to the treasure chest. From another corner he found a piece of lace and unfolded it upon the velvet. The deep purple showed through the intricate design. Nicole placed the glass gem at the center and turned her attention back to the chest.

She reached in and smiled. "May I?"

"But of course, my dear. But of course."

She found a small box that contained a long, gold chain. Justin took the chain, doubled a loop and put it over her head and around her neck. It was stunning on her darkened skin. "You should have precious things. You give them life."

Nicole smiled. "That was well put." She planted a kiss on his lips.

The fun of discovery continued. Near the center of things, Justin spotted the shining chrome top of the brandy flask. With a cheer he pulled it free. "The king will celebrate the queen."

Nicole beamed. "And the queen shall," she paused and smiled, "Give the king anything he wants."

"Can I have that in writing?" Justin unscrewed the cap, sat out two shot glasses, and poured. "Brandy, and of fine quality. We toast the glory that was." He poured the brandy and passed the open flask beneath his nose. "Ah, the aroma is strong and sweet." Saliva oozed and his speech slurred.

Nicole hoisted her cup. "To life, to love, to the kids, to us and to what was."

Justin clicked his cup to hers. "To this moment."

The bronze liquid went down smoothly and warmly. The two delighted in the long forgotten flavor and warmth. They completed the toast with a long sensuous kiss.

Exhilarated, they turned back to their fun. From a cranny, he hoisted a small porcelain bird. So true an image, it lacked only the movement of life. Nicole placed it on the velvet. Another leather pouch had Paul's name burned into it. A handful of multi-colored marbles poured out. A brass whale, more pieces of fine lace, and a few candles appeared. From beneath the spot where the marbles had been, Justin extracted a small plastic container, a small pipe, and a book of paper matches.

Justin bobbed his eyebrows. "Guess what this is?"

"My! A little bit of everything," she paused, "I'm going to have a few questions for you later."

Justin popped open the lid. "Oregon's finest. From the Roseburg area, if my memory serves."

The contents, covered with sugar, remained dry, and happily, mold free. Justin pinched off a small portion and pushed it into the pipe. He held the pipe between his teeth as he swiped the match across the striker and held the igniting match over the bowl. Justin inhaled. The yellow and blue fire tucked into the pipe. Both Justin and Nicole watched the red glow of the burning substance. He pulled the match away. The ember in the pipe shriveled to nothing. Nicole watched curiously.

Justin held the smoke down. It was harsh and perfumed in taste. He nipped another piece of the weed and stuffed it into the pipe. He handed it to Nicole and a burst of smoke whooshed from his mouth.

Nicole struck a match. "With all that smoke, I only have to breathe."

Justin coughed and gagged, but mostly laughed.

Nicole puffed on the pipe. Justin settled in his seat, his back resting against the bulkhead. The beautiful velvet and treasures to his left, and the chest in front of him. The drugs he consumed mellowed his mood, as expected.

He looked across the table to Nicole. "Why do women puff so much? Just take a toke."

Nicole ignored him.

A large, brown manila envelope protruded above some books, its top bent over. Justin rolled forward grabbing the envelope and then rolled back to his resting position. Words were scribbled across the bag. "Confidential stuff. And things to remember." Justin smiled at the phrase.

Nicole finished smoking and fiddled with the book of matches.

"Would you like to be truck driving? It's V.A. approved."

Justin tore the envelope open. "Sounds good," he paused. "Nah, I don't think I can handle all that moving around."

He reached into the envelope and extracted a paper. "Shit. It's a bank statement, I'm over drawn." There were other business looking papers inside. "Aha!" He tossed the envelope aside.

Next he retrieved a greeting card. Within, a pressed rose, a poem, and the signature of his dead wife. "A thousand years ago." He looked at Nicole. "From my wife." He handed her the card.

Nicole read the poem. "Nice."

Next he extracted two report cards. One was Michelle's and the other Paul's. They were from grammar school and the marks good.

Nicole fiddled with the greeting card. She bit her lip. "I have no mementoes."

Justin's face calmed and he leaned back. Nicole smiled and pointed. "Oh, well. What's in your hand?"

Justin extended a slip of yellow paper. "A coupon from Wendy's. A hamburger for half price." He pulled it back. "Instead of cooking tonight hun, let's do the fast food thing."

Nicole giggled. "Yeah, oh yeah. Make mine a whopper. No make it a double whopper with fries and a chocolate shake."

"They didn't make whoppers, that's somebody else."

Nicole screamed, "Pizza!"

Justin jumped at her outburst and Nicole added, "With Canadian bacon and pineapple."

Justin retaliated with a shout in her face, "Hot pastrami on rye with mustard and a cold beer."

He lowered his head to the table. "Oh Lord, the best things are silly."

Nicole tapped him on the head. "Peanut butter and bananas."

Justin's body relaxed and his arms dangled beneath the table. He raised his head and pleaded to Nicole, "Liverwurst, liverwurst."

Nicole cringed. "Liverwurst? Yuck! How can you think of liverwurst?"

"I grew up on liverwurst." He dropped his head to the table, but this time a bit too heavily, and there was a loud thump. "Oh shit, that's twice today. And in the same spot." He rubbed his forehead vigorously, and they both laughed.

Justin produced a lustful grin. "Give me a sheepherder sandwich."

"What's that?"

Justin's eyes narrow and he leered. "Two slices of bread and a piece of you."

Nicole's expression didn't change. "The bread I don't have."

Justin reached across the table to touch Nicole's breast, and she slapped his hand away.

Justin pleaded. "You must help me, you must help me get my mind off food. You must distract me with lewd sex."

"I have a headache."

"Is that a no?"

"Resuscitate yourself. Where did you put the brandy?"

Justin scratched the side of his chin. "Are you going to watch?"

"I wouldn't miss it for the world. The brandy."

Justin reached back into the chest, pulled the flask out, and handed it to her. "Pour me one, too." Then in a tone more serious, he added, "You know Nicole, it might be a good idea to open a hamburger joint when we get back to New Atlantis."

Nicole laughed, making it difficult for her to pour the brandy. Justin continued.

"Seriously, look at the money we could make. Enough to send the kids to college and maybe, with luck, enough for a chicken ranch in our retirement."

"Buzz off. What I'm looking for is a lawyer or a doctor with a bad heart."

Justin sat up straight. "Good thinking. You'll also need a lover on the side."

"I'll accept applications at any time."

"Right. I've got lots of good references."

Nicole made a fist. "Shit head." There was a long span of laughter and again Justin reached out for Nicole's breast. She again slapped it away. "I'm going to light a candle."

With the candle lit, Nicole leaned across the table and smiled at Justin. "Let's take the pot and brandy topside. You know, fresh air, the sunset and all that shit."

Justin's eyes widened. "Good idea, I'll pack a picnic and we'll drive out to the country. We'll get away from all this."

Nicole grabbed the intoxicants and headed topside. Justin loaded his arms with fruit and followed behind.

They climbed into a warm night and rested on the seats of the cockpit. Later, they sang a few songs and even danced. They hugged, they kissed, they danced some more, and for a time they were quiet. They ate most of the fruit, drank a little more of the brandy, but no pot.

A crescent moon rose above the horizon, Justin and Nicole sat in the dim glow of candlelight emanating from the cabin. Justin sat in the starboard corner of the bench. Nicole leaned against him, her legs extended to port.

The fingers of Justin's left hand tapped Nicole's stomach. "To bed soon. A good rest before another hard push."

Nicole sat up. "One more little toast." Her voice cracked and she swallowed. She stood and faced the rising moon. Justin poured a small amount of brandy into each steel cup and handed one to her. "Justin, come stand with me."

He moved to her left side and put his right arm around her waist. Nicole lifted the cup toward the moon. "Here's to a little furry guy. I took your mother..." Tears began to flow.

Justin's arm rose to her shoulder.

"I stabbed him with a knife..." She trembled.

Justin whispered in her ear, "I love you Nicole."

"I stitched his wound only to soften my guilt. In return he saved our lives." She drank the brandy and turned her head into Justin's chest and cried.

In the dim light of early morning, the couple awoke from a complete sleep. A fish caught in the night, found tethered to the fishing line, became their first meal of the day.

Thus refreshed, they hauled the anchors and in a light, steady breeze, they set the sail and achieved a course. The bow of the craft pointed at the huge, red star of the day, and split the waves of the blue and crimson sea. The *Cristine's* wake gurgled. From the hills of the departed land, the howl of a beast projected toward the craft. The howl went unheard.

The northern breeze grew to a wind, and the sailing craft hastened with foamy crescents on either side of her bow. This would be a day of tacking and the activity was welcomed. It eased their eagerness, and they sailed through the day and through the night.

Away to the northeast in deep waters that were crystal in clarity and cooler, the leviathan waited. Often he rolled at the surface and gazed to the south, watching for billowed sails. As he waited, he sung in vibrant low tones, conducive to his meditative state. The sounds carried on into the night, and faded when the moon was high.

Aboard the *Cristine*, all had gone well through the night. As the sun rose, Justin was at the helm maintaining a starboard tack. The wind faded with the night, and the sea flattened. The craft no longer heeled. Its passage slowed until its headway was lost.

Justin scanned the horizon for signs of weather and spoke to himself. "It's all blue sky, blue water." He turned to starboard and the quietly vanishing plume of a whale and smiled when giant flukes rose with exuberance and thumped the surface.

Justin waved. "Good to see you this fine morning."

At that very moment, Nicole, laying in bed, awakened. "The boat's level." She heard an agitated ruffle of the main sail, followed by a sharp snap as it filled with the last gust of the day. "He's back."

Nicole sat up and then stood, her head protruding through the open hatch. Already dressed, she was ready to go topside. The morning air felt good on her face and lit her mind with instant clarity. For a moment she watched Justin's back as he stood at the helm and almost sang her greeting to him. "Good morning."

Justin spun around, a smile on his face. "Good morning, I was just saying hello to what looked like a very happy whale."

"He is happy. I can feel it. It's the same whale." She smiled. "You remember. The choreographer of your forward flip. I know his touch." Nicole bounced twice on the bunk and hoisted herself up through the hatch.

She looked seaward. "I wish we still had the wind." She twisted around with energy and bounded into the cockpit. Only inches from Justin's face, she pleaded, "I want to be home."

Justin's eyes sagged a bit. "I'll turn the wind on after breakfast."

Nicole smiled. "Good." She bent over and took hold of a line attached to a bucket. "Leftovers for breakfast." She threw the bucket over the side and watched it sink. When full, she hoisted it aboard and set it down on the deck. Justin watched as she splashed her face.

"You know it's the same whale?" He inquired.

She looked up at him as water dripped off her face. "Yes I do." She turned her head seaward. "I think he woke me up." She dumped the bucket over the side and turned to Justin. "Intuition of some sort," she paused, "There's a notion from the past as well."

Justin sat down on the bench and she followed suit. In his tired state he spoke softly, "And today's notion came from the whale. Did you feel something?" He rubbed his eyes as he listened to her answer.

"Yes, I did." She paused, her eyes faraway. "It's like...like the feeling I get when I hear music that's right for me." She smiled. "Parade music does it. It's like when I was a child and went to a big parade, and a marching band went by. I almost couldn't stand it. It's something like that." She put her hand on Justin's knee. "And you. How does it come to you?"

Justin yawned and put his hand on her hand on his knee. "It's not that I feel something. It's more like...I know." He hesitated. "It's as if something is put into my head and then suddenly it plays out. It's like remembering something long forgotten."

Silence.

Justin spoke a few moments later. "I wish I could feel the way you do. You know when it's there. I'm more like, after the fact. It's not as much fun."

The movement of air stalled utterly. Justin stood and made the main boom fast.

Nicole rose to her feet. "I don't think there's a molecule of air moving." She stepped down into the galley and spoke from within. "Aha! We still have warm tea." Some minutes later she returned topside with food and drink. They consumed the meal without conversation.

Justin took a drink from his second cup of tea, sweetened with sugar. He set the cup down, crawled to the after deck, and with a low moan, laid his body down. The skin of the *Cristine*, pleasantly warm, dismissed the last bit of chill that lingered from the night sail. His backbone warmed, Justin slept.

Nicole stared at a mirror-like sea as the hairs of her body responded to an unknown force. The sails hung heavy with gravity, while an extraordinary silence encased the *Cristine*.

Nicole turned to a distant splash. Sound moved slowly in the warm, still air and the event concluded before she spied its disturbed waters. She sensed the whale's mysterious essence.

She set her cup down and stepped to the starboard side. The shift rolled the craft slightly beneath her feet and an inch-high wave hastened toward the horizon, causing a wrinkle in the perfection of the slick sea. Embarrassed, Nicole relaxed, her breath shallow.

Nicole whispered, "Oceanic magic. I can feel him."

A hot sun streamed photons that buried themselves in the sea. The energy, when sufficient, agitated the liquid to vapor, lofting skyward, wetting and fuming the air.

Nicole inhaled. "Delicious, sensuous." The sea, ignited with sparks of reflected light, contracted her pupils. Her head slowly bowed to the cool blue at her feet. A mystical seduction beckoned Nicole down into the deep waters. "Blue, blue abyss." Long moments passed in calm expectation.

She whispered softly, "Oceanic magic."

With the immersion, she spied movement. Nicole withdrew delicately while sniffing sea vapor. "Enchantment." She looked again. "He's there. I only need to wait."

Tiny, irregular patches of white brightened and swelled. "Perhaps I fall toward him."

Around the patches, a darker shape formed. Nicole smiled. "There he is." The whale rose, moving neither fluke nor flipper, its bulk expanding beyond her field of vision.

After a leisurely rise, the animal hovered tranquilly, only inches below the glossy surface.

Then, the waters above the leviathan bulged and spilled from its back, gurgling and swirling around a mound of flesh twice the length of the *Cristine* and many times its bulk. Nicole looked up at rivulets of sea water cascading off its mass.

The whale slowly rolled away from the *Cristine*. One huge eye confronted Nicole and she stood enraptured by the gargantuan presence and the stare of the purple eye, an abyss unto itself.

Nicole sucked a deep breath. Astonished, yet calm, she fearlessly ventured into the depth of the purple eye. There, a night's sky twinkled with a cosmos of its own. Nicole pulled back, overwhelmed by the force, vacillating between confusion and insight. The sound of trickling water ceased, and a sudden thought of Justin vanished.

A seductive beckoning imparted fascination and she was casual to a tiny tugging at her belly. After a moment, the tug intensified. It was pleasurable, intriguing. Nicole did not resist. She smiled at the point of the pull while soothing melodies bubbled through her mind and her eyes fluttered to enchanting images.

Her essence receded from her physical being and levitated between craft and whale. Nicole faced her body. "My body, Justin, the boat." Her words had no physical aspect. "I know that touch...the whale." Sublime warmth enveloped her.

Nicole's essence turned. "The whale's gone and the sky's different...it's color...there's no sun, there's no sea."

She whirled back to the *Cristine* and faced her body again. "I'm hallucinating. I can't feel my breathing." She paused. "Justin. Justin...Justin." He didn't respond.

The whale's touch intensified. Her thoughts swirled with brilliant images, lavender in color and throbbing with beguiling sounds. Her fear drained.

To one side, the *Cristine* sat motionless looking as if it were embedded in blue glass. To the other side, the color was blue green, without shape, without texture. Suddenly, a small fish darted through the plainness. "It's not the sky, it's the sea, the sea from below."

Nicole somehow entered the whale's being. She saw what the leviathan saw: the *Cristine* through the right eye, and the sea through the left eye.

What started as a murmur unfurled into a soothing, musical whisper. Nicole, fascinated, followed.

The whale rolled to an even keel, his bulk settling into the sea. "This be the time; this be the place."

From below, the sun's rays pierced a glassy canopy and lanced into the deep. The barnacle clad hull of the *Cristine* hovered in a water sky, ugly and obnoxiously out of place. A small fish darted around the hulk in constant inspection.

Nicole, detecting the whale's movement, brimmed with excitement. The whale circled the *Cristine* twice and turned away while sinking deeper. Nicole scanned the silver-blue above, whitish-blue ahead, and the blue-black below. Light diminished and vision faded, only to sharpen again, but now it was almost transparent with only a hint of color.

Something large materialized before them and the whale accelerated. The vast form of one fragmented into a dazzling, silver school of tuna that whizzed like bullets.

Sing-song sounds dissipated the oceanic scene and a dream story materialized within Nicole. It appeared as reality.

A young child, a little girl, naked, stood in the night before a frozen sea and under a purple sky dense with sparking stars. Nicole swooped to give her warmth and their embodiment became one and only one. Nicole extended her arms, her little girl arms, palms toward a throng of stars that she knew composed the galaxy of earth's genesis. She had been here before. Stimulated, her palms discerned the galactic focal. Her thumbs pointed inward, their tips touching as were her forefingers. The central stars thereby framed within the composed triangle, commenced to rotate with gathering velocity about a dark hole.

Faster and faster they spun until they melted into a homogeneous mass of swirling fire. The black hole expanded and consumed the whirling fire. From its center, a golden light streaked toward the girl and divided into two. One red, the other violet. The red struck her left palm and the violet her right. Her arms pulsated with the intensity of the focused forces. Her finger tendons glowed through her skin and the energies traveled up her arms, alloyed in her chest, and dropped to boil in her belly.

The child grew to the stature of a young woman. The streaking forces of the black hole blinked and were gone. The young woman lowered her arms and she sang a whale song. A song of farewell. In the purple sky, stars traced the form of a whale that swam deep into the cosmos. The young woman smiled, lowered her head, and eyed the flame at the center of her left palm.

The dream ended. Its notion vanished. Realization, for another time.

The whale banked to his left and arched downward into the deep blackness. When far below, he stopped and reversed direction, swimming toward the surface with accumulating speed. Ahead, the sapphire sea pulsated with flowers of jelly. A small fish, conspicuous in the watery vastness, darted from the path of the onrushing animal. Near the surface, the whale accelerated and Nicole, beyond thought, simply absorbed the sight.

Pushing upward, the force quavered the surface until it shattered like a slab of glass. With an explosive sound and a burst of blinding light, the whale ascended into the water-free atmosphere to half its length. At the apex of the jump, Nicole noiselessly gasped in the pause before descent. From the high perch, the *Cristine* appeared as a toy on a flat and vast sea.

The whale's bulk gathered downward speed and he acrobatically made a half twist, shifting the impact to his back. Nicole watched the horizon twirl and groaned with the awareness of falling backward. The sky dropped away, and they struck the water with a sound like the boom of a cannon. However, the sea enveloped them with tenderness. Submerged once again and the sun gone, the world of blue brightened with millions of tiny bubbles making their escape back to the world of gas.

Nicole whispered, "Magnificent." Music was the reply.

The whale mused, "Been time since leaping."

Massive flukes propelled the whale forward with great power. "Pity be, little thing, not a whale."

His pleasure was cut short by a familiar sharp pain. His heart muscle tore a bit more and he ceased movement. After a few quiet moments he regained his composure and rejoined his guest. He found her apprehensive and perplexed.

Nicole inquired, "Is there a problem? Were you hurt?"

The whale, purred another song that eased her once again.

Though in pain, the old one felt jubilant, sure his mission neared realization. The gift was bestowed to the female; only the involvement of the male remained.

With subdued maneuvers and gliding motion the whale returned to the sailing craft and surfaced at the same place next to the *Cristine*. The old one rolled as before, exposing his eye. Nicole studied her body a moment before turning her attention to Justin. Nothing had changed.

A push moved her across the water and reunited her body and mind. She again gazed at the whale's bulk and his purple eye.

Nicole, motionless, her mind muddled by the experience, struggled to affirm her situation. "The whale is before me." She shifted her body. "I'm back."

She rubbed her hands together. "It happened." She analyzed no more and smiled.

Nicole turned to Justin, and at once his eyes opened and he sat up. He jumped to his feet and eyed Nicole and then the whale and back to Nicole. "Nicole, move away." The whale was absolutely still. "Is it dead?" He spoke louder. "Nicole, you're too close."

Nicole smiled. Justin smiled weakly, shut his eyes tightly for a moment and opened them again. Nicole, still smiling, extended her right hand. He took a step forward and stopped. "Is that a pearl?" He looked into her eyes. "Where did you get a black pearl?"

Nicole ignored him. Justin stepped forward and reached for the jewel. His fingers were only inches away when Nicole's hand twisted. The pearl dropped to the deck and bounced over the side.

Justin stared at the plummeting gem. Nicole grabbed his hand and gently pulled him to her side. He looked at her and then into the purple eye. Without pause, and together, they fell into its depth.

Nicole delighted as she and her lover departed their bodies and breezed across the waters. "Justin, just go with the magic." Justin called. "Nicole." Her answer was simple. "I'm here."

"Am I still sleeping?" He hesitated. "That's it. I'm still sleeping."

Justin heard Nicole laugh. "You laugh like you're here." She laughed again. Justin scrutinized the *Cristine* and his and Nicole's forms standing on deck. "If you're here, wave your hand." Nicole didn't move, only laughed.

Justin whispered, "The whale should be behind me...not that me, this me."

Again Nicole laughed. Justine questioned, "Am I in your dream?"

Nicole sighed. "Justin, you and I are now somehow one with the whale. It's not a dream."

"If we're in the whale...How do you know what's going on?"

Nicole whispered, "My love, this is my second venture of the day. The first was while you slept. Now hush and enjoy."

"Hush and enjoy? I've gone crazy. Nicole, I'm crazy."

The whale had waited patiently for the male's adjustment, but time was short. He hesitated no longer and rapidly submerged. "She prepared. Understands." He felt Justin's surge of fear and rumbled a sound that was his laughter.

The sea closed in and the underside of the *Cristine* appeared. Nicole sought to reassure Justin. "It's all true love. You, me, and the whale now swim below the sea. You're not crazy."

"Drop your guard. Feel the whale, hear his song." Her voice, clear, without blemish, resonated in stereo. "Believe all of this. You're not dreaming."

Justin muttered, "Clever dream. Inside a whale. You got to love it."

"Justin, infinite probabilities, anything's possible." She paused a long moment. "How or why, I don't know, but I do know that we're here."

"Some kind of 'Pinocchio' thing. Is that what you're saying?" Nicole laughed. The whale rumbled.

Justin sighed, "OK, love. I hear your sincerity. Your choice is my choice. As you believe, so I believe."

The old one's laughter induced a song of joy, melodious, tranquil, and enchanting.

Justin whispered, "As you do, love, so do I." And a dream for Justin materialized.

A young Indian boy ran down a stone-covered beach. He gasped for breath, sucking in cold air, seeking greater speed. But, the boy's body was clad in animal skins that slowed his rush.

Justin felt himself whoosh up behind the youngster, fear struck his heart as he immersed into the fleeing form and instantly knew the reason for panic. Behind, a huge northern grizzly pursued. The boy had been told not to run.

The boy, many, many miles from help, strained toward a small kayak that bobbed on tiny waves near the shore. He had been told to pull it high on the beach.

The hood of his coat fell to his back, and he heard the sound of the bear's giant paws stomping into the gravel and the deep huff of its rhythmic breath. The boy knew his life would shortly end.

He ceased his run and turned to challenge his fate with a short spear. The bear came to a stone scattering stop. It was only yards away. Its jowls dripped with saliva, and even though the animal stood on four feet, the boy must look up to see its eyes. Its eyes were large, purple and sparkled like the sun on the sea.

With a deep huff, the grizzly blew its breath into the boy's face and rose to its full stature. The animal stood to a height equal to the length of the boy's kayak. Shuddering, the boy rushed the bear and stabbed toward its belly. His eyes widened as the spear evaporated and his hand buried itself in the bear's body. His fingers groped a huge, hot liver.

The boy shut his eyes to a surge of energy that shot up his arm, passed into his chest and dropped to his belly, where it boiled. The bear showed no pain and simply took a step backward. The move extracted the boy's bloody hand. A mighty paw swung through the air and struck the boy on the side of his left chest, lifting him high into the air.

When the Indian boy's feet touched the ground, he was no longer a boy. He was young man. He stood naked, and his body steamed in the frigid air. Without fear he watched the bear run into the sea, dive into the water and with the mighty spout of a whale's breath it disappeared. The young man raised his left hand and looked at the bloody palm where tiny sparks ignited into a tiny flame.

The dream ended, the notion vanished. Realization for another time.

The chore done, the horizontal movement of the whale ceased and he turned downward toward the blue-black of the deep. There was time for a bit of fun and the whale knew the way.

Presently, the song of the whale became a continuous drone, low in pitch and precise in frequency. The darkness of the deep brightened to gray, and animals materialized in shadowy shades of red.

"Nicole, its vision by sound."

"I think I saw the inside of that last big fish."

"This guy is taking us deep, very deep." Briefly, before them, a small, roundish object pulsated with a telltale silhouette that indicated a nautilus. They were close to the bottom and sporadic activity flashed in phosphorescence.

The dive leveled off. Moments extended into many minutes. The sights were numerous and confusing for the creatures of the land. Phantoms moved in strange ways and light flashed in exotic patterns.

Presently, something enormous rose from the bottom. Something of a shudder pulsed through Justin and Nicole and the whale instantly changed course and sped away.

A giant squid streamed through the abyss, tentacles trailing. The whale pursued, the squid maneuvered, the chase was dazzling to the humans and ended when the whale arched upward. Nicole's voice resonated with glee. "Jump, jump!"

The old one understood, his joy beyond theirs. "This for last, this for eternity." The pressure acting on his tapered body squeezed it upward with phenomenal speed, even to the old one. Exuberant, he ignored the apprehension of the humans.

The upward path produced a color change, the glowing gray flashed to a bright blue. The whale's swiftness generated tunnel vision with an aura of color changes at the periphery. The surface appeared as glass and upon impact, a booming-thunder was followed by an incredibly loud hiss. Water clung to the colossus and coiled into a breaking circular wave in the seemingly endless rise. Behind, the hole in the sea slammed shut with the sound of a cannon.

At the apex of the jump, the whale was free of the sea. Awed, the old one felt it a fitting gesture denoting the departure of his species. With a twist, the sun and sea whirled. The *Cristine* was the only other witness of the spectacular event.

The whale's downward flight commenced, and the sea boiled at the point of penetration. The titanic animal gained freight-train momentum as it slid back into its domain. After submergence, another cannon shot sounded and a geyser of great height and beautiful symmetry composed the final salute.

Below, the whale arched, sliding to the horizontal. Exhausted, he made no effort to move and his bulk slowly rose to the surface. His breath was rapid and weak and his eyes closed with the expectation of the final pain.

With his body trembling, he labored toward the *Cristine* and made no effort to submerge. Justin and Nicole were acutely aware of the creature's plight.

At the side of the *Cristine*, the two humans were pushed and skimmed across the waters, quickly merging into their bodies. The old one languished, but found strength enough to sing a song that broke with surges of pain. He expelled his last breath and with buoyancy lost, commenced his final submergence.

Justin and Nicole watched the whale evaporating into the blue, his crippled song lamenting and fading. Their joys diluted.

Nicole whispered. "The whale's dead."

Justin whispered, "Yeah." His left hand rubbed his forehead. "But I...feel no real sadness." They both stepped back and sat on the cockpit bench, back to back, their knees drawn up, Nicole looking to port, and Justin to starboard.

Justin bit his lip. "It really happened." His eyebrows went up. "Didn't it?"

Nicole looked across the sea. "Oh, yeah. That wasn't a hallucination. Of that I'm sure."

A long time of silence passed.

Justin stood up and put his back to helm. "My mind has never been this clear or calm." He frowned. "But, I forgot something. I just know I forgot something."

Nicole looked beyond Justin. "I can still see his purple eye, and the sparkle...like stars."

"Then you sensed him to be a male."

"Oh, yeah. That's for sure."

Justin flexed, and stretched his body, and made an examination. "My body seems different. Feels different."

Nicole stood. "Mine, too. Not the slightest tick of discomfort. But...I've lost some apprehension...concern. No, those aren't the right words."

Justin stepped closer to her and stared intensely into her eyes. "Why?"

"Why what?"

"Why did it happen?" Justin sat down.

Nicole thought. "Only the whale could tell us that." She sat next to him.

Justin supported his head in his hands, his elbows on his knees. "It really did happen."

Nicole jabbed him with her elbow. "Importance. It doesn't have the importance it had."

Justin snorted. "What's not important?"

"My body. I like it, but it's not me. It's not me at all."

Justin stood. "After leaving it." He patted his chest and clapped his hands. "Meat and bone." He smiled. "I know what you mean."

Nicole jumped to her feet. *"I feel strong, even powerful."*

Justin held his arms out. "Exuberance. *Untroubled.*" He leaned toward Nicole. "Passionate."

She smiled. "Oh, I do love you Justin." They embraced in a very deep kiss. Nicole smiled, their eyes locked together. "Wow. That was only a kiss of a different color."

Justin blinked. "I moved into you...or you moved into me." They separated and sat on the bench. Nicole touched his knee. "I don't think I'm going to dissect it any further."

Justin wrinkled his brow. *"What?"*

She extended her arms forward with palms down. "I'm just going to let it lie there and assimilate."

Nicole stood and turned to view the sea. "It's not absurd, nor is it impossible." She took a deep breath. "It's needed."

Justin turned, his eyes wide. "I didn't say absurd and impossible, I only thought it."

Long moments of silence went by. Nicole turned and smiled. "You only thought it?"

She faced forward, excitement and panic rumbling through her being. "It's ongoing Justin, there'll be more."

Justin put an arm around her and planted a kiss on her neck. "What's your opinion on the pearl?"

"What pearl?"

"The pearl you had in your hand when I woke up...the black one."

Nicole shook her head. "No...no. There wasn't any pearl. Where would I get a pearl?"

Justin released her. "I don't know, but you had one and it fell over the side."

Nicole shrugged again. "I guess that part's for you."

Justin envisioned the short episode. "And you made two trips?"

"Yes." Justin went forward and lowered the sails.

As the sun lowered to the western horizon, Justin and Nicole sat in quiet contemplation. The *Cristine*, still becalmed on a glassy sea, waited in the fire red of the day's end for a wind to carry it home.

Nicole rose, took Justin by the hand, and led him to the cabin aft. Together they undressed, climbed upon their bunk, and slumped into its softness. Nicole pushed her back against Justin's chest, sleep came quickly. Justin found rest only after an hour of deep thought.

With the dawn, the new day, and the new era, the physical world about the sailing craft *Cristine* had changed little. The sea lingered flat and glossy; the air still, warm, and humid with ocean evaporation. Nicole and Justin rose with ravishing hungers, having eaten only one meal in the past twenty-four hours.

Nicole rushed to the galley for a bite of fruit and to start a cooking fire. Justin went aft to prepare the fishing line.

Nicole heard the sound of Justin's line and bait hit the water. She popped her head topside. "I remember seeing lots of tuna yesterday."

Justin didn't reply. A fish struck the bait and he laughed as the line whizzed through his hand, forcing him to juggle to prevent any friction burns. He hauled the catch aboard and shouted to Nicole, "Tuna for breakfast."

The fish lay on deck vibrating at high speed. The noise on the fiberglass deck rolled like the beat of a drum. Justin whacked the creature with the club kept on hand for just such occasions. With his sharp blade, two slabs of boneless flesh were sliced from the fish's body, the remainder cast into the sea. He cleaned the meat and washed the deck with a bucket of sea water.

Nicole, while building a fire, rethought her statement relating to the tuna. She said it in a nonchalant manner. Now, she studied the statement.

Topside, Justin lumbered through his chore. He picked up the slabs of fish and stared at the sea aft of the *Cristine*. "The pearl, the damn pearl."

He looked westward. "Where the hell is the wind?"

He faced the galley hatch. *"Come topside. No wind today. No need to rush."*

Nicole frowned. *"Coming that way. Want a piece of fruit? It's kind of soft."*

"Yeah!"

The couple talked without reference to the previous day's adventure. They munched their fruit and waited for the stove to heat up. Ten minutes later, Nicole, with fillets in hand, went back below to do the cooking.

She returned with two plates of food and they gorged in silence.

Justin tossed his plate into the galley and quietly walked to the bow and sat down. Nicole stayed in the cockpit, sitting on the bench. She studied Justin and toyed with a piece of some very old rope that they used to lash the helm. Her mind caught flashes of his thinking.

She pulled her thoughts away. "Christ, how am I going to handle this?" Time drifted by and occasionally Nicole looked to her love hoping for a smile. But, it never occurred.

She grumbled, "He gets lost in that abstract thinking." She twirled the rope and watched Justin stare at the sea. "I wonder if we can leave our bodies again." Recalling the sensation, she smiled. "That was fun. Can't hardly wait to tell the kids."

She stopped twirling the rope. "Shit, they're not going to believe us. Hallucinations, hot day on a placid sea."

Nicole stretched out on the bench and again twirled the rope, this time above her chest, whirling it like the blades of a helicopter and stared into the blur. "The whale rose. That purple eye." She increased the whirl of the rope. "I remember the mesmerism. Close to deep meditation."

Nicole let go the rope. It slapped the bulkhead near the galley hatch and flopped to the deck. A wondrous thought sat her up straight. "I'll meditate and contemplate release."

She rushed to the cabin aft for a few pillows. Homemade and stuffed with bird feathers, they were very soft. Nicole glowed with the excitement of the adventure. The pillows were strategically placed, and she took a final look at Justin.

Nicole reclined on the pillows and settled into a meditative state that was both deep and active. Her mind groped for guidance. Remembering, she focused on her belly and immediately felt a movement. Colors in the violets, reds and golds, flashed and then gave way to a crisp black. A touch of vertigo quivered her mind. The black was a void and she hovered within. Nicole dismissed her fear and this provoked the notion that separation was imminent.

Partial separation occurred, but the force abated and Nicole fell back.

"Relax, no fear." She took a deep breath. "Do I really want to do this?"

The quick answer was 'yes'.

Nicole zoomed away from the *Cristine*, the sea a blur beneath her. "No!"

Instantly she stilled and hovered a few feet above the waters. Nicole looked around and giggled. "I did it." Nothing was dream-like. The *Cristine*, sat as a speck on the horizon. "Oh! Justin, you're going to love this."

She bobbed upward and downward and slowly twirled in a tight circle. "What now."

The sea was flat and only a few clouds dotted the far eastern horizon. "This is a very lonely place." Fear was again creeping in on her. "The boat's a long way off...miles."

Nicole sort of reached for the boat and moved with gathering speed. "Easy now, easy." Her speed slowed. "That's better." She moved to her right and to the left and then back toward the boat. "What fun."

She saw without her body. "I'm here and I'm not here."

Her field of vision turned in the direction from which she came. "Oh, I like this." She looked up. "OK. Up we go." She rose upward at great speed, but soon made an instant stop. She looked down. "Wow. I must be a thousand feet up." She sought to go higher, but nothing happened, so she dove at the sea. The drop was as fast as the rise and again the stop was instant. Only an inch above the sea surface, her vision was clear. "It's like looking through glass." She looked to the horizon, still only an inch above the surface. "I've got to do this in a storm."

Her thoughts sprang to Justin and the *Cristine* and in a flash, she floated about them. Justin, still at the bow, still in heavy thought, Nicole flew to him. She whirled about him, laughing, trying to catch his attention and moved to a point next to his ear. *"Yo, big boy."* Nothing happened. "Huh."

Nicole looked at her body lying on the bench. "I have to go back."

She hesitated. "I don't want to. This is too much fun." Like a child who just learned to ride a bicycle, she deplored the idea of putting it away, even for a moment. She hovered above her body, deliberating.

"Oh shit. How do I get back?"

She stared at herself. "*My God,* what if I can't get back?"

A few moments passed. "Calm yourself. Relax, you have to think."

The answer, simple desire. Instantaneously her forms merged. Her eyes popped open and she sat straight up. "Hah! She rubbed different parts of her body, feeling very rested, physically strong and energy charged. "Well body, you must have enjoyed my departure."

She jumped to her feet. "Justin's going to love this."

She called loudly, "Justin, Justin." She waved her hands and shouted again, "I've done it, I've flown again."

Justin frowned. He got to his feet and moved aft. "What are you bouncing up and down about?"

"I've just left my body and flew out over the ocean and back again. I flew around you, but you couldn't hear me. So I came back to tell you. It's easy, it's great, I'll show you. Come on over here and lie down. You'll love it. I mean you're going to love it." Like a rubber ball, she moved to the pillows and rearranged them. One for him and one for her.

"Here, lie down. Oh, Justin, it's wonderful." She used body movement to explain. "You can move this way and that way. You can go up and down and all around. But not too high. And your body feels great when you get back."

She patted the pillows. "Come on. Lie down, let's go."

"Nicole, wait a minute. What the hell, are you talking about."

Nicole saw his confusion. She took a deep breath and started pacing back and forth in the cockpit. A steady stream of words at high speed poured from her mouth. She turned about frequently in the tiny space. Justin stood four feet above her on top of the forward cabin. Nicole's moving weight rocked the *Cristine* with increased momentum. Justin's additional height above the water intensified the movement. He bent his knees slightly and extended his arms outward.

"Nicole, Nicole, please sit."

She stopped amid-ship. "Sorry." She sat for only a moment. Sitting still, her words continued to flow rapidly. Justin jumped into the cockpit, sat, and listened attentively. Nicole related her adventure again.

In silence she examined Justin's eyes, her own sparkling, a smile on her face and her posture suggested she may be poised for a leap upward.

Justin looked at her. "Please, one more time."

"Bullshit. That was the third time." She went to the pillows. "Let me show you."

"I know what you said." His eyes darted about. "It's all so sudden."

He looked up into the sky, took a few deep breaths, looked at Nicole, grabbed her by the shoulders, and shook her. *"You did it, you really did it, you shit, you did it?"*

Nicole's voice sputtered with the jostling.

"Let's...do...it again...Justin...you're...giving...me...a... head...ache."

"You did it, you did it?" He pushed her into the cockpit seat and hovered over her. *"Do it!"*

Nicole flexed her shoulders, Justin's suddenness catching her a bit off guard. His body seemed to balloon with anticipation. "Right. Like I said, you simply meditate with the thought of separation." Nicole reclined on one of the pillow, her head to port.

She motioned Justin to do the same. Quick to respond, he lay with his head to starboard, their legs intertwined. Nicole looked into the sky. "Just get into a meditative mood and think about a separation of the type you did with the whale."

Nicole sank rapidly and soon released. She hovered near her form. "How am I going to know when he's free?" She recalled her rapid flight across the sea. "I forgot to mention that."

"I'll stay put and see what happens." Moments proceeded into minutes. Nicole waited.

She felt a breeze, though not really a breeze. Nicole laughed. "That's him. I bet he went halfway to China."

More minutes passed. Again she felt the breeze. "That's him again. Shit, I sit here while he fools around."

Another breeze passed her. "Justin, damn it."

Nicole couldn't see him, but his presence was strong, similar to having someone standing next to you, you feel them without seeing them. The same as with the whale.

"Hello, love."

With a little bit of anger, Nicole replied. "I've been waiting."

As they had done with the whale, they united, and cruised away from the *Cristine.*

They spent the day engaged in play. If separated, reunion was merely a matter of desire, their spirits finding one another as if magnets. The range to which they could travel had the shape of a dome. They couldn't penetrate the sea and limits were perceived as an inability to move farther.

The hours passed and with the day near end, Nicole and Justin returned to the *Cristine.* The time spent in the escapade was actually too long. Nicole's body lay awkwardly upon the bench. Her right arm and leg dangled above the deck.

"Good grief. I'm sure every joint in my body is going to be stiff."

Justin hovered near. "Damn. What a mess."

Nicole erupted into hysterical laughter. His crotch was drenched with urine

Nicole giggled. "Next time, wear a diaper."

She gave Justin instructions on rejoining his form, though concentration for her required she control her giggling. Still, she achieved the transference before he did. As predicted, Nicole experienced pain and soreness. Her mouth was cotton-dry, and her bladder was ready to burst.

She stood, or rather stooped, and shuffled to the side of the *Cristine* with the grace of a ninety-year-old arthritic. Nicole chuckled between cries of pain. From a post in the cockpit she undid a battered life jacket and allowed herself to fall over the side.

She pattered around listening for sounds of Justin. In short order she heard his curse and the craft rolled with his movement. He splashed into the sea on the side away from Nicole and swam around the stern, a broad smile on his face. "Hi, Grace."

Nicole smiled. "Did you check the back side of your trousers, hot shot."

"No problem, I just swam over here to see if you were drowning."

"Buzz off, Peepee Pants."

"Peepee Pants? It's been a long time since anybody called me that."

"They used to call you that?"

"Just my sister."

They spent considerable time in the water, the exercise pleasant to their overly rested bodies. At sundown they climbed back aboard the *Cristine*.

That night, in celebration, they concocted a meal as lavish as possible. They bedecked themselves with the jewels from the treasure chest. The velvet hung on the bulkhead. The little things of beauty sat on the table, lit by candles. All things around them seemed new and glowed with greater beauty, all colors intensified. Justin turned to Nicole. "I can almost see into things. Just a little beyond their edges."

Nicole smiled. "Yes. And things that move ooze something like music. It's delicious." She took a deep breath and almost swooned. "I want to get into the sea, oh I want to get into the sea."

Justin stepped to Nicole and wrapped her in a tight embrace. "The sensation of these hugs. I love moving into you."

"Justin, how can we stand all of this? Every sense I have is heightened. Yet, so smooth and flowing, my energy is there."

Justin released his grip and stepped back. "I can still feel you in me. I think it's going to stay there."

That night the moon was full and bright and Nicole and Justin, their appetites sated, left the galley, their minds on love. They paused on deck and Justin dangled the large crystal in the light of the moon. A rainbow of the night beamed, and bubbled, and even cooled as if a rivulet from ice. Justin and Nicole absorbed the spectacle for many moments. Then Justin gathered the jewel and chain into his palm and with a whip of his arm he flung it into the sea. *"A tribute to our whale friend. To mark this place."* Nicole beamed. *"I know your touch. I've known it a long time."*

Nicole whispered, "Justin. It's a blue moon night."

That night their love was as never before. Their bodily intertwining tumbled into astral mingling. The rapture of the whale allowed the exchange of forms and they delighted with the knowing of the other's climactic joy. Their bodies drained, they left them behind and their essences soared into the night.

In slow flight, harmonized by the echo of the night's love, they passed just above the sea and arched into the sky. Their concentration, not on the stars or the moon, but the blackness between them. And such was the night.

The next rising of the sun found the *Cristine* bobbing in moderate sea swells. The wind was fresh and from the south. Justin and Nicole had risen together and set the sails quickly. The large boom swung perpendicular to the hull and the jibs filled like tiny spinnakers. The craft was light-of-foot and moved with ease to the north. The wind driven waves swept from the south, catching the sailing craft from the stern and the *Cristine* surfed smoothly with their passing.

The man and the woman aboard found a new freedom and a truer understanding of their body and soul. Their physical selves were less, their souls were more and better tuned to the music of "The All That Is."

The gift received from the last leviathan on the blue planet would pass on to all others in much the same manner that it had been received, being meant for all.

The sailing craft moved away from the place of magic where a whale whispered. The last whale. A being now enchanted by its own new promise.

"Justin, when we're near. We could fly off."

THE END

Frag's Ass
by Jeff Conine

Category: Mystery/Thriller   **Publisher: KMEditions**
Type: Fiction   **ISBN: 1589090365**
Copyright: 8/13/2001

Black comedy/thriller taking place in a halfway house in Reagan America with a cast of Sixties rejects.

The year, 1982, San Diego. A decade before a medical scandal involving Vietnam vets almost erupted at nearby Balboa Naval Hospital during Reagan's tenure as governor, these initiated by a shadowy high ranking now ex-military man who now has a stake in Reagan's presidency. Three of the novel's characters, who played different roles at Balboa, live at the Juniper Manor near the park—a halfway house for a colorful gaggle of loonies, Nam burnouts and alkie/druggies—presided over by Chancey, a tyrant with the most to hide from Balboa days. The book opens with another Balboa grad flipping out and disappearing to the VA Hospital psych ward. Enter John, a man with a dark past. He meets Tom, another angry cynic. When two of their friends are committed, they begin a series of pranks against the psychiatric community. John uses these to cover his agenda—one he's been hired for by a mystery man who figures highly in the events years ago. Mark, the third Balboa alumni—(as psych tech, patient, thwarted whistle-blower)—colludes with John early to get the CO at Balboa. Mark, too, has an agenda. Enter Carol, a disillusioned married Yuppie shrink, with whom John falls in love. Meanwhile Senate Confirmation hearings are airing on TV for a new Reagan appointee. Black humor, total irreverence, gritty dialogue, good action, some insight. A well-placed pall over the flowers and love of the Sixties. Dark, but cosmically humorous.

Last Autumn $10.00 US
Frag's Ass $12.00 US

Add $2.00 shipping & handling per book

For US and Canadian orders: Email Orders

kmeditions@tah-usa.net

OR: Order on Amazon.com